"An exciting, fast-paced piece of historical fiction—a narrative that grips and won't let go."
—Liz Williams, author of *Darkland*

Strange Bedfellows

The tent was small, and there was only one saddle blanket to cover them both on the single pallet. Lindsay looked at it and then at Alex. Her expression told him what he'd already figured, that he was to keep his hands off her. With a sigh, he lay down on the parachute and pulled the blanket over him. Lindsay followed suit and lay with her back to him. Alex began to drift off quickly, accustomed to sleeping in a tiny, steel room with three guys who all snored and had reading lights, and with jets landing on the deck directly overhead. But in the twilight of consciousness he caught sounds of weeping that pierced his awareness and brought him back around. Silently in the darkness, he turned his head to listen. Lindsay, who had kept a flawlessly brave front all day, was breaking down for a long, quiet cry.

The weeping tore Alex in a place he'd kept diligently hidden; he knew exactly how she felt and was at an utter loss to comprehend the extent of his grief over the damage done to his life today. He'd carefully tucked away his own pain, but he couldn't ignore hers. He rolled over to put an arm around her, and she let him. Lying close, he held her until she stopped sniffling. Then the fourteenth-century day finally swarmed in on him for good and he dropped off to sleep.

Knight Tenebrae

JULIANNE LEE

ACE BOOKS, NEW YORK

THE BERKLEY PUBLISHING GROUP
Published by the Penguin Group
Penguin Group (USA) Inc.
375 Hudson Street, New York, New York 10014, USA
Penguin Group (Canada), 90 Eglinton Avenue East, Suite 700, Toronto, Ontario M4P 2Y3, Canada
(a division of Pearson Penguin Canada Inc.)
Penguin Books Ltd., 80 Strand, London WC2R 0RL, England
Penguin Group Ireland, 25 St. Stephen's Green, Dublin 2, Ireland (a division of Penguin Books Ltd.)
Penguin Group (Australia), 250 Camberwell Road, Camberwell, Victoria 3124, Australia
(a division of Pearson Australia Group Pty. Ltd.)
Penguin Books India Pvt. Ltd., 11 Community Centre, Panchsheel Park, New Delhi—110 017, India
Penguin Group (NZ), Cnr. Airborne and Rosedale Roads, Albany, Auckland 1310, New Zealand
(a division of Pearson New Zealand Ltd.)
Penguin Books (South Africa) (Pty.) Ltd., 24 Sturdee Avenue, Rosebank, Johannesburg 2196, South
Africa

Penguin Books Ltd., Registered Offices: 80 Strand, London WC2R 0RL, England

This is a work of fiction. Names, characters, places, and incidents either are the product of the author's imagination or are used fictitiously, and any resemblance to actual persons, living or dead, business establishments, events, or locales is entirely coincidental. The publisher does not have any control over and does not assume any responsibility for author or third-party websites or their content.

KNIGHT TENEBRAE

An Ace Book / published by arrangement with the author

PRINTING HISTORY
Ace mass-market edition / September 2006

Copyright © 2006 by Julianne Lee.
Cover art by Judy York. Cover design by Annette Fiore.
Interior text design by Stacy Irwin.

"Brilliant Disguise" by Bruce Springsteen. Copyright © 1987 Bruce Springsteen. All rights reserved. Reprinted by permission.

ISBN: 0-441-01439-9

ACE
Ace Books are published by The Berkley Publishing Group,
a division of Penguin Group (USA) Inc.,
375 Hudson Street, New York, New York 10014.
ACE and the "A" design are trademarks belonging to Penguin Group (USA) Inc.

PRINTED IN THE UNITED STATES OF AMERICA

10   9   8   7   6   5   4   3   2   1

For
Ginjer Buchanan

ACKNOWLEDGMENTS

In writing historically accurate fiction, the importance of information sources and other support cannot be underestimated. I am most grateful for the gracious help of the following folks:

LCDR Alan R. Bedford, Sr., USNR (Ret.); Annie at Blockbuster video, Hendersonville, Tennessee; Teri McLaren; Laura Anne Gilman; Judy Goldsmith; Ward and Terry Weems; James A. Hartley; Trisha Mundy; Diana Diaz; Joyce Coomer; Maggie Craig; Susanne Dhomhnallach; the kind staff of Sabhal Mór Ostaig Colaiste Ghàidhling na h-Alba, Sleat, Scotland; braw and knowledgeable Robert of the Bannockburn Memorial, Stirling, Scotland; and the Cathedral Museum, Dunblane, Scotland.

For information, visit the author's website at http://www.julianneardianlee.com.

God have mercy on the man
Who doubts what he's sure of.

BRUCE SPRINGSTEEN

PROLOGUE

One last dive, just to make certain. The dig was finished,
the equipment returned to the ship along with the find and
he figured there wouldn't be anything more, but needed one
more dive just to make sure. The expedition had been so fruit-
ful, and so many intact objects found in the silt at the bottom of
the firth, he couldn't pack up and leave without taking a last
look around for a missed filleting knife or clothing buckle. So
while his crew began preparations to return to port he slipped
over the side and angled gently down into the dimness of the
water.

The Firth of Clyde was a wonderfully complex place, wide
and fed by many rivers. It connected with the Sound of Bute,
off the Kilbrannan Sound, and was guarded by islands all about,
leaving it clear in some places and impossible in others. That
the boat had been found at all had been a miracle. And thank
God they had been the ones to locate it. He smiled to himself as
he thought of the many trinkets and artifacts his crew had recovered from the fishing boat sunk here centuries ago, not to
mention the intact hull of the boat itself. Silt from the river had
covered and preserved the hull from complete destruction.
Much study would be made of the boat structure and everyday
items found here by the river mouth. It had been an incredible

find, and his career could be made by it. *Would* be made. The bright future before him now was nearly blinding, and a smile formed around his mouthpiece.

At the bottom of the shifting water not far from shore, shallow enough to see without artificial light, he began sifting through the loose bottom at the spot where the boat had been. Carefully and slowly, to minimize the inevitable clouding, he felt his way here and there among the rocks and mud already disturbed by the raising of the ancient boat. His regulator blowing bubbles in steady rhythm, and his heart keeping time with the breathing, he went methodically, left to right, then backward, right to left, his hands obscured beneath the swirling mud.

Then he frowned. There was something under here. Not rock, for it was too smooth and even. Unnatural. And there shouldn't be rock here in any case; there should be only more silt. He moved a hand slowly over it, and found the thing to be curved. Not curved like a river rock, nor like a stream bed with dips and channels worn away by running water, but perfect. A perfect long, smooth, *convex* curve. Another boat hull? Excitement surged through him. Another, *older* boat? It wasn't unheard of. A spot risky to navigate was likely to claim more than one craft. One hand dug, dislodging hardened silt to widen the exposure of the surface beneath, and amid the clouding he caught a glimpse of writing.

Writing? A dark-on-dark character came into sight for an instant, then was gone. Like a capital *L*. But it was once again beneath the silt, and he wasn't certain it had not been his imagination.

He pulled his hand back and looked, but the cloudiness obscured. As he waited for it all to settle and be carried off with the current, he listened to his own breathing and tried to keep from gulping his air while a queer, panicky feeling rose. He backed off, flippers waving lazily and hands spread for balance, and he hovered in the dim, rippled light from the surface. The hole he'd made in the silt cleared, and the *L* was still there, accompanied by a lowercase *t. Lt.* Slowly the topography of the area before him came into view. He backed off some more, and what he saw made his heart pound in his ears. A line this way, a curve over there, and the thing popped into his vision like an item in a "What's wrong with this picture?" puzzle. His mind raced, unable to completely grasp what his eyes told him he must be seeing. It was huge. And impossible.

For the shape he saw under the silt here in the Firth of Clyde, directly beneath the spot where a Scottish fishing boat had lain undisturbed and mostly intact for more than five centuries, was, unless he missed his guess, that of a modern military fighter jet, and he was hovering over the cockpit.

CHAPTER 1

"Good morning, ma'am. I'm Lieutenant Alexander Mac-Neil. I'm told you wish to speak to me." Alex stood nearly at attention, conscious of the appraising look from the young woman before him. She stood from the wardroom table to greet him with a gentle smile and an outstretched hand.

"Lieutenant. Thank you for seeing me." Her voice was low, but soft, lurking beneath the tinny sounds of silverware and crockery about the room. She shook his hand, and they sat opposite each other at the Formica-covered table. She was English, and pronounced his rank "leftenant," a habit he found less than enchanting. She was a newspaper reporter, and he was there to give an interview that already was making him uncomfortable, for she was staring at his eyes. He shut them against the intrusion. Women thought his green eyes "mesmerizing," and they always stared. When he opened them again, she was busy with her notebook as if she hadn't been staring at all.

Another reason he wasn't sanguine about this conversation was that saying the wrong thing in print would backlash in ways he couldn't possibly predict. The guys who had encountered her about the ship during her stay on board said she was a pretty weird chick, and Alex didn't figure he wanted to field any weirdness from her while he was speaking on the record.

However, on sight of her he began to think perhaps the risk might be worthwhile, for she was pretty in a tall, dark, angular sort of way. Extremely easy on the eyes, and soft in all the right places. He guessed he could stand to talk to her for a few minutes, particularly since he was under orders to do so.

She took a deep breath and began. "My name is Lindsay Pawlowski. I imagine your captain told you why I'm here."

"My information is you're writing a fluff piece and want to talk to a pilot about what it's like to fly a fighter jet." She'd been on the ship since it left port in Virginia, and they were now just past the Azores on their way to the Mediterranean.

A bemused smile touched her lips and irritation slipped into her voice. "Well, actually, we have our own jet fighters in the Royal Navy, not to mention the RAF, and so we don't really need to annoy you Americans with that sort of thing. Also, it's hardly a fluff piece. Unless, of course, you in the American navy consider yourselves exceptionally fluffy compared to the RAF."

A frown tightened his brow and he pressed his fingers to his face to get rid of it. If she kept that up, eventually he wouldn't give a damn how attractive she was. He stood. "Would you care for some coffee, ma'am?"

"Might there be tea?"

He nodded. "Certainly, ma'am." Tea. Of course. He excused himself and went to get it. At the other end of the wardroom a few other aviators, who had just awakened and were there for breakfast, sat at a table before bowls of cereal. Jake was there, hunched over his breakfast and struggling to look like he wasn't listening in, and Alex looked back at the reporter to decide whether she was out of earshot.

Nope, too close. So he maintained silence. Jake was Alex's Naval Flight Officer—"Guy In Back"—and caught Alex's eye with a roll of his eyes at the reporter. Alex discreetly shrugged one shoulder in reply to Jake's unasked query, and proceeded on his mission. On the way back from the counter with the coffee and tea, he swallowed as much of his coffee as he could get down without burning himself.

Bolstered and well caffeinated by shipboard road tar, he delivered the tea, sat back in the rickety, aluminum tube chair opposite the reporter, and continued the conversation. "With all due respect, ma'am, though it's no bother and I'm happy to talk with you, if this isn't for a fluff piece and you'd rather be talking to a British pilot, why are you here?"

"You've not heard about the recent find in Scotland?" She sipped her tea and didn't grimace at it. A point in her favor.

Alex shook his head and took another careful sip of his coffee as he watched her over the rim of his cup.

"A few months ago there was found an F-18 under some silt at the bottom of the Firth of Clyde and nobody knows how it got there."

He grunted and leaned forward with his elbows on the table. "So . . . you're here to find out if we've misplaced a plane?"

Now she smiled, and it was a broad one. Her mouth was wide and her lips full, and her teeth were very white. Suddenly she looked too young to be a reporter. "No, actually, I'm here for background on the American navy. I've discussed it with your captain, and some others of your senior officers, and they told me I could talk to you as a typical F-18 pilot. Although, I expect the fact that you have the best flying record on the ship makes you rather atypical." A note of cynicism had crept into her voice, but she smiled brightly again and the impression went away. "Also, I'm told you're quite the spit-and-polish sort of fellow."

Alex turned out the toe of one brown shoe for a look, and decided it was a good job, but still nothing remarkable. "I polish my shoes, ma'am, for the same reason you brush your hair. Because it looks bad if I don't. My father is an admiral; I was raised to be this way."

"I didn't mean it as a criticism."

He took a long sip of coffee, then set the cup on the table and gazed blandly at her.

Finally, she said, "Very well, your father is an admiral." She made a note in a small spiral book on the table before her. "If I know my American accents, I'd say you sound like a Southerner. From Texas, perhaps?"

All the Brits Alex ever met thought he was from Texas. "Nope. Born in California, and raised everywhere *except* Texas. My mother is from Kentucky. When I was a kid I wanted to be a cowboy. Maybe that's why I sound the way I do."

"Ah." She made another note, and consulted something else she'd jotted on another page. "Graduated from the United States Naval Academy."

"Affirmative."

"Honors?"

"No." One corner of his mouth lifted in a grin. "Does that mean you don't want to talk to me now?"

That brought another smile from her, and he liked that. *Note to self: keep her laughing.*

"Why did you want to join the military?"

"I told you. It's what I was raised for. It's who I am."

"You never considered anything else?"

"Well, there was that cowboy thing." Her smile made him smile, too.

"Political ambition?"

He shrugged. "My father is the one in the family with political sensibilities. For me, it's a job. The pay is good, I see the world, I get shot at every once in a while. Keeps me on my toes."

"You've flown in combat?"

He nodded, but didn't speak.

"Where?"

"Kosovo."

"What did you do there?"

"Most notably, I made a SAM site go away." In response to her puzzled frown he added, "Surface to Air Missile launch site."

"You made it 'go away'?"

"That's what things do when you hit them with a missile." He stared into his cup and waited for the next question. He knew what was coming; he could smell it.

"How did that feel?" There it was.

Alex sighed and looked at her. "It felt like my job."

"To kill people?"

"To follow lawful orders. It's what I do."

"Who you are."

Now he looked at her closely. Her dark blue, nearly almond-shaped eyes had softened. Widened. They had lost the look of challenge, and that had never happened before, no matter who was asking that question. It was almost as if she might be able to grasp the truth of what it was like to kill someone, and that suddenly made him uncomfortable. So he shrugged and said, "It's what we FAGs are paid to do, ma'am."

That made her blink, and she stuttered for a moment while her cheeks blossomed red. Finally she said, "Perhaps my understanding of American slang is faulty . . ."

"Fighter Attack Guy. I'm a Hornet driver."

"Oh." She sighed and laughed, and now looked at him with new eyes. That gave him a grin, and he took another sip of coffee to hide it. She said, "Nothing lacking in you for self-confidence, is there?"

"No." If there were, he sure wouldn't admit it to her.

A moment passed as she seemed to gawk at her notes while her blush calmed, then another moment. Finally, he said, "What's the deal with that plane they found? Somebody steal it?"

Her voice brightened, relieved to have the interview back on track. "Don't know. Surprisingly, it was an archaeologist who found it. They think it's very old. As in centuries." One vague hand waved in a gesture of approximation.

Alex sat back and blinked. "You're kidding."

"No. As I believe you Americans say, I shit you not. By the levels of corrosion and deterioration of materials, and by the fact that it was found beneath a sunken fishing boat that had lain undisturbed for a very long time, its discoverers are estimating it to be six or seven hundred years old."

A short bark of a surprised laugh escaped him. "Well, then, it's probably not one of ours. Must be one of those medieval F-18s, you know, the really early models."

A snicker burbled from the reporter's nose, and another smile tugged at the corner of his mouth.

"No, seriously, what do they think it is?"

She shrugged. "I really have not the faintest. They insist it's an American F-18. The name of the pilot, painted on the side, has been obscured but they know he was a lieutenant. They haven't found any of the identification plaques from it. Apparently part of it was burned, including one engine, and the other engine is missing entirely."

A realization made Alex's heart sink. "Wait a minute. You're not from one of those tabloid rag-type papers, are you?" His tone was unintentionally harsh, so he blinked and added, "Ma'am."

She sat up and said rather stiffly, "Not unless you consider the *London Times* a 'rag.' "

He shrugged and shook his head, puzzled. "Well, that's just nuts. Thinking a jet fighter could be that old. Must be in really bad shape, that's all."

"Perhaps."

"I mean, that's just nuts."

There was another long pause. "Well, then." Miss Pawlowski took a deep breath, glanced at her notes, and said brightly, "In any case, so you've been piloting fighter jets for how many years?"

The interview continued.

Alex felt relieved when it was finished, and he figured he hadn't said anything that would wreck his career. The mystery fighter slipped his mind easily, for the idea was . . . just nuts. He forgot about it as he changed into shorts and T-shirt in his stateroom and went to work out. Maybe throw off some of the tension of that interview. Exercise always made him feel better.

Tucked into a corner of one of the hangar decks was a slab of carpet on which stood a couple of weight machines and a stationary bike. Alex began by stretching, then warmed up on the bike.

Half an hour later, he was well loosened and had broken a good sweat when he moved to the weights. Sweat was trickling down the middle of his back and had made cooling lines from his hairline past his ears by the time he finished up his arm curls and let the weights down to shake out his arms. Then he bent over to stretch and loosen his back muscles and spotted small, sneakered feet standing on the carpet behind him.

He looked around, and caught that Pawlowski woman staring at his ass. Busted, she quickly flicked her eyes to his face as he stood and turned, but it was too late. She at least had the good grace for her ears to turn red, and that made him nearly burst out laughing. But he swallowed the smart remark that came to mind and said nothing more than "Hello" as he continued with his workout.

The reporter cleared her throat, leaned into the other weight machine to adjust the pin, took a deep breath, and lay back on the bench press. Alex paused to watch, curious to see what she would do. A mechanic nearby called to a couple of his buddies, and immediately there was a cluster of guys in dungarees on the hangar deck, staring, their speculative chatter an echoing murmur in the hangar. Alex thought idly of ordering them back to work, but found himself staring also, as Lindsay struggled with the bench press.

Though she'd adjusted the pin, she could still barely lift the weight. Her elbows shook. Tendons stood out on her arms and neck. Her face turned red. It seemed to take forever for her to extend fully, pause, then let the weights down properly. Alex found himself tensing to help her, shook his head, and wondered what this woman hoped to achieve with this. The crazy lady was going to hurt herself, and had no business using the equipment if it was that difficult for her.

But then Miss Pawlowski got up from the bench after only one rep, and walked over to the cluster of crewmen with an air of arrogance that puzzled Alex. The first mechanic had a disgusted look on his face and was nodding, shrugging. The woman reached out a hand and he relinquished a wad of bills, which she counted as she sauntered away with a self-satisfied look on her face and a grin for Alex as she passed.

Alex watched her go. *What the hell?* Then he stepped over to the other machine to check the pin. Two hundred pounds.

Whoa.

He looked around the corner of the bulkhead to continue watching her go, then glanced back at the machine. *Whoa.*

So it was with curiosity the next day he approached his flight assignment in the morning, for he was to ferry this very strange woman back to Great Britain. She awaited him just outside the ship's island, on the flight deck, wearing a zoombag and mae west, helmet under one arm, eyes bright and looking like she wanted to fly the bird herself. He eyed her, then said loudly over the sea wind and the roar of taxiing jets, "Good morning, ma'am. You're my GIB today?" She gave him a puzzled frown, and he elaborated. "Guy In Back."

Her expression cleared, and she nodded.

"Ever flown in one of these before?"

She shook her head, then tossed back her hair when the wind blew it into her face. "But I'm looking forward to it, very much. I enjoyed the training they required to grant my request and allow me to ride." Quickly she pulled a hair tie from her wrist— one of those poofy cloth ones, white with red stripes—and set her helmet between her knees. Inexplicably, the sight of her knees gripping that headgear caught his attention and held it. She took a moment to tie back her hair, then restored her helmet to the crook of her arm.

Alex's gaze returned to her face. "Enjoyed?" He found he had to clear his throat to get the word out.

"Very much, indeed."

Was this chick for real? He knew how strenuous that training was, just for the sake of riding in one of these planes. A smile tried to curl the corner of his mouth, and without saying anything further he gestured for her to follow, turned, and headed across the deck toward the gray fighter jet that awaited them on the forward catapult. Miss Pawlowski ran a few steps to catch up to him, her dark brown, wavy ponytail tossed in the Atlantic wind.

"What sort of plane is that, exactly?" Her voice was nearly snatched away by the wind and the various deck noises of taxiing and catapulting jets, but she was loud enough to be understood.

"It's an F/A-18D Hornet." A note of pride crept into his voice though he tried to control it, and he couldn't help adding, "My girl."

"Don't you ever wash your girl?"

"No, ma'am." His was not a new aircraft, and it bore stains here and there on its skin from fuel, oil, and residue from firing the nose gun. "She's clean where she needs to be."

"There don't seem to be any missiles on it."

He threw her a bemused look. "You hot to blow something up?"

Her smile was an embarrassed one, and she shook her head no.

"Well, if it'll make it more exciting for you, some jets of questionable character have been sighted in the area, so the nose gun is loaded. 20 mm slugs. Six thousand rounds per minute. Take just a few seconds to cut an enemy plane into little, bitty pieces. I know, 'cause I've done it." He'd meant to amuse her, but when he turned to see the effect of his jibe, her lips were pressed together. His grin left and he fell silent.

He didn't speak while he began the preflight check, and when she attempted to engage him in conversation he held up a silencing finger. No chatter allowed during this. When he was done with his external walk-around and ready to board, he found her staring up at the fuselage, just under where his name

and rank were painted in black just below the canopy. The other
writing was in flowing, blue script.

"Brat?" she said.

"My call sign."

She turned to peer at him. "*Brat*? Are you one, really?"

"My father is an admiral. I grew up in the Navy. I know you
know that, because I saw you write it down in your little book."

The light went on, and she nodded. "Ah. Military brat."

"Yup."

"I shouldn't think having a father in the Navy would especially distinguish you among your peers."

Alex gave a wry smile and held up four fingers. "Fourth generation." Then he ticked off each previous generation one by
one with his thumb. "Dad flew Intruders over Vietnam. Granddaddy MacNeil manned a battleship in the North Atlantic during World War II. *Great* granddaddy MacNeil—"

"Swabbed a wooden deck, I'm sure."

He laughed. "No, but pretty near. I've also got two younger
brothers in the Navy. Pete is stationed in San Diego, and Carl is
a midshipman first class at the Academy."

"Impressive."

"Yeah, the whole family is like that. We've got enough Mac-
Neil cousins in various branches of the service to start our own
war. We get together for a wedding, and it looks like a Memorial Day celebration."

Miss Pawlowski laughed at that, and Alex again admired her
pretty smile.

The plane captain was waiting patiently to sign off on the
walk-around inspection, so Alex gestured to the boarding ladder then helped Miss Pawlowski up. Once again his attention
was grabbed as he watched her ascend above him, and in his
imagination the baggy flight suit was gone, replaced by . . . well,
nothing. He snapped back to himself only when she began letting herself down into the back seat of the cockpit. He shook his
head to clear it and said to the guy at his elbow, speaking just
under the deck noises, "How pathetic is it when a limey in a
zoombag can fire a man's afterburners?"

The plane captain chuckled. "To each his own, sir."

Alex laughed, then climbed up and let himself down into the
front seat to begin the cockpit checks. The plane captain

climbed up behind him to secure Miss Pawlowski in the seat and help her with her helmet.

Finally Alex snapped on his face mask and said over the com, "All right, back there. Can you hear me?"

Her voice came immediately. "Yes." The plane captain finished with her and retreated down the ladder; there were thuds as it was folded up and stowed under the wing's leading edge extension. Alex warned her to rig her fingers in, flipped the switch to lower the canopy, and heard the woman continue. "Nice view from up here. I can't see you, though."

"Lucky you. Are you comfortable? We're about fifteen hundred miles out; we'll be in the air more than an hour." He began punching the instrument panel keypad, entering navigation data. "Hope you brought a book to read."

"Fifteen hundred miles an hour? Your girl is fast."

That brought a smile. "Well, closer to about a thousand. Maybe less on this trip if we dawdle. Hour and a half in the air, probably, give or take."

"Okay. I'm comfortable. More or less."

"Good."

"They certainly didn't overdo the seat cushion back here."

"No wasted space. See that thing sticking up between your thighs? Don't touch it."

"Will I go blind, then?"

Alex hee-heed into his mask. "That's the ejector seat pull ring. You're not supposed to be able to eject us, but fooling with it is a bad idea on principle. And especially, see all those fun-looking buttons and knobs back there?"

"Yes."

"Don't touch any of them."

"Right.

"Not even if something frightens you and you think you want to control something."

"Did I mention I rather enjoyed the training they made me take for this trip?"

"Right."

Alex fired up the engines, and his pulse picked up with that mild surge of adrenaline that always came before a catapult shot. Taking off from a carrier was the Navy's E-ride, and no matter how many times he did it, there was a charge difficult to describe. Maybe because he knew, no matter how many times he accomplished it, there was always the chance of SNAFU and him ending up dead. The vibration of the plane trembling to take off shook his bones. "Okay, ma'am, get ready to pucker." He signaled his readiness to the shooter.

"I beg your—"

The aircraft took a slight dip that felt like a lunge, and Alex's body pressed into his seat at more than three G's as the catapult hauled the twelve-ton aircraft down the length of the flight deck. Zero to 150 miles per hour in under three seconds, and suddenly there was no ship beneath them. Wings caught the air, and another dip then rising, the Atlantic Ocean zooming past beneath them even as it fell away. Throttles forward, stick eased back, and the jet climbing, Alex chuckled to hear Miss Pawlowski behind him exclaim to herself, "Good God!"

Then, on command of the controller, he took his heading toward Lossiemouth and sang off-key, ". . . and I'll be in Scotland afore ye!"

The next hour was boring, not just by comparison but by any standard. In between silences, Miss Pawlowski occasionally asked questions about the instrumentation before her.

"May I ask what that thing is in front of you, that looks like a hologram?"

Forgetting she couldn't see him, Alex nodded at the HUD and replied, "Heads Up Display. It tells me stuff I need to know without making me scan the instrument panel."

"It looks like something Luke Skywalker would have. What sort of information does it give you?"

"I could tell you, ma'am, but then I'd have to kill you." She chuckled, and he wished he could see her.

For most of the trip she was quiet. Alex sometimes forgot she was back there as he carried out the routine tasks of the flight, and at other times he suspected she'd fallen asleep. After about an hour and a quarter in the air, they came to the western coast of England and their course veered slightly as they began to slow and descend through a clear sky. In only a few minutes they were over Scotland, and they approached a cluster of civilization Alex knew was Glasgow, on their way to Lossiemouth Air Base on the northeast coast. The mountains below were green, looking like crumpled florist paper dotted with brown peaks and blue lakes glistening in the sunshine. To the left the ocean shone like silver, and islands in the distance lay in it like a herd of enormous whales breaking surface.

Alex began to think about getting something to eat once they were on the ground and squared away with the authorities on the subject of armament, and idly wondered whether Miss Pawlowski might consider joining him for some lunch. He opened his mouth to inquire.

But then he shut it as all the electronic displays on his instrument panel went blank. The master caution light blinked on instead.

He grunted. "Crap." He pushed the resets, but nothing happened. Quickly he checked his backup systems, and they were still functioning. He'd have to fly the plane by analog. Yet another pain in the ass thing to take care of on the ground. He glanced at his airspeed indicator as an odd shudder passed through the airframe.

"What's that?" Miss Pawlowski's voice was tinged with alarm.

Alex looked forward, through the blank HUD, and what he saw made his blood freeze. It looked like a hole in the sky, lined with fire. For a second he thought they were flying into the ball of a mushroom cloud, and against all reason it seemed the thing was looking at them with flaming, red eyes as deep as the abyss. Then they were in it. A hard thud shook the plane, and he figured an engine was gone. Still alive, they blew out the other side into a gray cloud, with the artificial horizon wobbling hard. That stabilized, but the compass was still going nuts. Flat spin. Warning lights flashed all over the instrument panel as systems went south. Both engines were dead, and to starboard he saw a reflection of fire from the clouds through which they were spinning. He punched the fire extinguishers, but they did nothing.

"Fffffuck." His heart thudded wildly in his ears. He knew he had bare seconds to decide what to do, and the presence of a passenger shaved those seconds even shorter. The ailerons weren't moving, the stick frozen in his hand. The rudder pedals were stiff, also unmoving. His plane was going down, and his only choice was to punch out. One more heartbeat, and he called to his passenger, "Eject! Eject! Eject!" He yanked the ejection pull ring between his thighs, and the canopy blew off.

Chill wind engulfed him, battered and slammed him about. The rear seat went with a hard thud, then his own. The cold, Scottish wind whipped into every exposed part of him, and he was free-falling, spinning, tumbling end over end, spinning through cold clouds.

Clouds?

Attention was required elsewhere as he flew through mist. For one alarmed, disoriented moment he feared his parachute had malfunctioned or that this was a fog bank and he was about to smack into a mountain. But once the chute had deployed, his cockpit seat fallen away, and he knew he would probably live, he looked around in hopes of seeing far enough to control where he would land. He prepared to cut his shroud lines in case of plopping into a lake or the ocean, and hoped Miss Pawlowski was as prepared. Still all he could see were clouds, but after a moment he descended through to clear air. It was overcast, solid as far as he could see, and cold as a witch's tit. Odd, for only a moment ago the day had been utterly clear. Now he looked for his passenger and spotted her chute not far, just below. She'd made it out okay, and he could see she was conscious and looking around.

Only then did he let the anger come, and he loosed a string of oaths and vulgarisms at full voice. His plane was gone, a trail of black smoke making a line from the cloud ceiling toward a big bay the other side of a range of hills. His heart sank to his boots as he thought of his father and the ragging he was going to take for the rest of his life. Dad was never going to let him live this down. The admiral had never lost a plane, let alone on a routine flight like this. Not that the old man would ever have admitted to taking any routine flights.

What the hell had happened? There was no fire in the sky now. No mushroom cloud and no evidence of one below. Alex had a brief, panicky moment as he wondered whether it had been an hallucination and he'd just trashed a very expensive piece of government hardware for nothing.

But, no. The engine had flamed. The trail of smoke in the air above was dissipating, but it was there. Something had happened to the plane; it was junk before he'd hung up the "For Sale" sign.

He looked down. They'd descended too far to see Glasgow any more, and the landscape below was remarkably empty of anything but green mountains and blue water. Trees. Lots and lots of trees. He looked for signs of habitation, but saw nothing. No roads. No houses. Just his luck not only to lose his plane but also to have to walk all day to a town after bailing. *Crap.*

The rest of the way down he kept track of Miss Pawlowski's chute. God knew how much control she had over the thing, but Alex noted she was headed for a pasture so he encouraged his own chute in that direction. They landed seconds apart, and he hurried to release himself from the harness so he could check to see if she was all right.

Her canopy wanted to take off and drag her away, and he ran to help her release it so she could regain her feet. She took his hand and he helped her up.

"Are you all right, ma'am?"

She removed her helmet and mae west and nodded, but he could see she was pale and shaken. Her hair tie was gone, and her dark hair flew every which way as she struggled to bring it under control. Alex pressed his mouth shut as he freed her from the parachute harness, and he could feel his ears turning red.

He said, "I don't know what happened."

"It was a gigantic fire."

"You saw it, too?"

She nodded again, and looked up. "But it's gone now."

Alex now turned, looking for a hint of which way to walk, and removing his helmet. "Did you see any buildings or roads on the way down?" He reached into a pocket of his flight suit for the two-way survival radio and set his helmet on the ground at his feet.

"No. I thought we were just short of Glasgow; where are we really? There's nothing here."

He turned to peer at her. "We are just short of Glasgow."

"Not possible. We must have passed it and gone into the Highlands." She looked around, and grimaced. "Except that these hills aren't high enough for us to have gone that far. This makes no sense."

Alex turned a complete circle. "I don't see any sign of habitation. They do have roads in Scotland, don't they?"

"Last time I was here they did." A smile came and she shrugged. "You never can tell with the Scots, though. Maybe they're staging another rising and they've dismantled all the roads." A wobbly chuckle, then she added, "And everything else as well."

That made him chuckle. "You live here, don't you?"

She looked around and sighed. "No, I live in London; I'm only here for the assignment. But I've been here a number of times. While we were in the air I thought I could tell where we were. We came in over the West March and crossed Galloway I think. I thought we were flying over the Garnock River. That would be it over there." She pointed down the slope toward a narrow river. "But if that's the Garnock, then there should be a road beside it. And train tracks as well. And houses, and shopping centers, and schools. So that can't be the Garnock. We must have come much farther than we thought."

Alex turned on the radio and keyed it to inform anyone listening that he was in need of assistance. But in return he received only static. Rather lazy, weak static. He hoped the battery wasn't about to crap out on him. Another try, and still nothing. He tried another channel. Nada. Now he wished Miss Pawlowski had been issued a survival vest so there would be another radio. He stared at the piece of junk again, frustration rising, and tried it all once more. Nothing.

"Nuts." He looked around some more, then discerned a thin line of gray smoke coming from the depths of forest not far away. Smoke could mean anything, but there was a good chance it might be somebody burning something and that meant the presence of someone who might have a clue where they were. He returned the radio to his pocket. "Come on." Leaving the parachutes and helmets where they lay, he led the way, and she followed across the heavily tufted pasture.

Alex found a dim track into the woods, and began to smell the wood smoke. Easy enough to locate, for the track led straight to it. No road, not even stepping stones, but there was a clear enough dirt trail.

They came upon a small thatched house, and Alex had a weird frisson up his back as he flashed on Hansel and Gretel coming upon the witch's cottage. Bare-branched vines grew up all over it, and the thatching was dark with mold in spots. Miss Pawlowski stopped in her tracks, and Alex held up to find out what was the matter.

"That's got to be the worst hovel I've ever laid eyes on."

He nodded. "Roger that."

She peered at him. "You can't possibly know what that means in English."

Alex frowned, then replied, "That's okay, so long as you know what it means in American." He pondered the house a moment, and said, "It looks like it's made of dirt."

"Peat. I saw a house like this once, but it was a museum and had a car park and walkways outside. This place is uninhabitable, but looks lived in nevertheless."

It did. A wood pile lay tumbled in the yard, and a goat grazed nearby. Chickens pecked at the dirt or roosted here and there, according to their mood. As he and Miss Pawlowski approached, the tiny wooden door of the house opened and a ragged man ducked out through the low frame. When he saw them he stopped cold, unmoving for a long moment. He seemed half-dressed, hairy legs bare beneath a tunic sort of garment belted at the waist. There were no shoes on his feet. The mouse-brown hair was shaggy, and his face bore a two-day growth of beard.

Alex raised his hand in greeting and said, "Hi. You all wouldn't have a phone here, would you?" He could have answered his own question, for there were no wires to the house and no poles anywhere that he could see.

The Scottish man's jaw fell open, and he uttered something completely incomprehensible to Alex, who then looked to Miss Pawlowski to interpret for her countryman.

But a puzzled frown creased her forehead, and her head tilted. "Pardon?"

The short speech was repeated, and she replied, "I'm sorry, I don't speak Gaelic."

Then the man said something else, and Alex thought he heard the word "welcome" in there somewhere, an impression strengthened by the gesture toward the door of the hovel. His was the most heavily accented English Alex had ever heard. Normally he could glean meaning from just about any dialect, but this was gibberish to him. He murmured to Miss Pawlowski, "Is this one of those places where they get people to actually live like they did in the past? There's one in upstate New York like that, where they've got sheep and stuff."

Miss Pawlowski said something to the Scot in that same odd

accent, and Alex couldn't make heads or tails from it. Then she smiled and said, "He's speaking Middle English." By her voice he could tell she was impressed by it.

"Seriously?"

She nodded.

"How do you know?"

"I'm a journalist; words are my life. My course of study at university was the English language, and I had a full year of medieval literature. I've read Chaucer in the original and had to memorize and recite parts of *The Canterbury Tales* out loud. It's not that far off from modern English; the variant vocabulary can be picked up like slang, and once you get past the appallingly archaic accent it becomes perfectly understandable."

"Well, you know, engineering major though I was, I've studied literature, too, and can't make out what he's saying."

"We were required to hear it spoken, and were taught something of how to converse in it ourselves. It's different from simply reading it."

"Ah."

She turned to the ragged man, and said something that included the word "telephone." But that only brought a puzzled squint even though she made a handset gesture to her ear when she said it. Then she said, "You do speak modern English, don't you?"

The man said something like, "Ye beent me rrayt welcome herteleh." He gestured to the house again. "Ah leck rrayt nowt fa soper." He nodded toward the door, where Alex now noticed a woman looking out. Three small children crowded at her feet to see the strangers, all of them dirty and ragged.

Alex said, half to himself, "You know, that's serious verité."

Miss Pawlowski said to the man, "This is a fascinating thing you're doing. Is it an anthropological experiment?"

The man repeated his gesture, this time with a measure of frustration.

She said to Alex, "I think he's inviting us to eat with him." Then she repeated her request for a phone, and still got only a puzzled face. The man came to herd them into the house. They went, not knowing what else to do.

Inside, the house was as authentic as it was outside. Not a sign of modernity. The hearth was a flat, gray stone at one end of the room, the fire vented through a hole in the ceiling, and over it was spitted a piece of meat that looked like a leg of something. It was still pink, but was beginning to smell pretty good, the greasy, smoky aroma permeating the room. Alex's stomach rumbled and reminded him it was time for lunch.

For furniture there were only a table and a few stools, and off in a dark corner Alex could see a stack of rough-hewn wooden bunk beds. Wooden boxes stood along the walls, heaped with belongings. The floor was dirt, scattered with dead grass and ferns that had been trampled to mush underfoot. He and Miss Pawlowski were offered two of the stools, and they sat at the table. Perched, really, for the stool Alex sat on was nearly too rickety to hold his weight. With care, he balanced so to avoid a collapse. Miss Pawlowski continued talking to the man, and Alex watched his passenger's face as she chattered but was only able to snag a word here and there. He smelled the meat on the spit and the grease that dripped from it and flared in the fire. But what should have been a homey scene only disturbed him. There was something wrong. The very realness of this family gave him the creeps.

Miss Pawlowski continued trying to communicate with the family, particularly the man, who didn't seem to understand much of what she said. He frowned and repeated himself often, and his barely contained patience with Lindsay's lack of fluency with the language showed in his voice. Her hands were all over the place, gesturing in attempts to supplement her vocabulary.

At one point she muttered to Alex, "He keeps calling me 'boy.' It's beginning to annoy me."

Alex sure couldn't see how she could be mistaken for a boy, but nodded to the woman in the long, ragged dress and said, "Maybe he's a religious nut and thinks anyone wearing pants must be male."

"Oh, he's an odd one, all right. He's saying all sorts of strange things." Then she addressed the man again.

Alex could see communication was happening nevertheless. Every so often a light would go on in the man's eyes as under-standing came. Then he would frown again when she asked an-other question. As Alex watched Miss Pawlowski talk to the family, he noticed her begin to grow pale.

"Now he's telling me his first wife was killed by the English ten years ago. She was raped and then cut open with daggers, stem to stern, and left to die. She was then burnt, along with their house. He was made to watch, then they let him go. He says for a long time he would rather have died with his wife, but now he lives to see the English all killed."

Alex peered at the guy, who appeared to be sincerely grieving for a murdered wife, sagging, old eyes glistening with unshed tears. "The English? I thought you all were one big country."

"I suppose he blames all English for the actions of one criminal. But daggers, though . . ." Her eyes darted around the room, and rested often on the children who were now playing and talking among themselves on the dirt floor. At one point she addressed them. "Hello," she said with a bright smile, "what are your names?" They only stared blankly at her, eyes wide and mouths open, until she repeated herself in the archaic English. Then they each replied with their names: William, Catharine, and James.

Alex was even more unsettled now. The children spoke Middle English, but not modern English? That was way more than verité. There was something very warped about that, even more warped than telling stories about English murderers with daggers.

Meanwhile, Miss Pawlowski grew more walleyed and apprehensive. As she spoke to the man again, her tone became more pointed and soon her voice was wobbly. She was plainly shaken.

"What's wrong?" Alex asked.

She raised a finger for him to wait a moment, asked one more question of the Scottish man, and on his reply she stood. "Alex, come."

"What?" He would rather have stayed for lunch. Or dinner, depending on when that meat would be ready.

"Just come with me." Her voice was trembling, and she was now as pale as anyone he'd ever seen. Rather than argue in front of these people, he followed her from the house and trotted to catch up with her as she plunged into the forest down the trail.

"What's going on?"

"Something has happened."

"Yeah. Our plane went down for no apparent reason, and we can't find a phone."

"We can't find a phone because there aren't any."

"Well, no, we're going to have to walk some more—"

"No, there *aren't any*. Anywhere."

"No phones in—"

"Anywhere. Something has happened. I don't know what." They came out on the pasture again, and she stopped to look around. The surrounding mountains were still and green, and the pasture sloped gently to the forest opposite. Other than some birds in the distance, nothing moved. "Listen."

Alex listened, but heard nothing and shrugged. "Listen to what? I don't hear anything."

"Exactly. You hear nothing whatsoever. No engines, nothing. No planes in the sky. When was the last time you looked up in the sky and didn't see a plane somewhere overhead?"

"I'm a pilot, ma'am."

"All right, if you were the average person, would you have ever not seen a plane overhead?"

He thought about it, then shuddered. "September 11, 2001."

"Right. One single day. An empty sky is strange and unnatural, because we're accustomed to seeing planes every day. Do you see any here? Have you seen any since we got here?"

He looked up, and felt that same uneasiness he'd felt four years ago when all commercial air traffic had been grounded for several days. An uneasiness akin to the realization he'd made of the children in that weird house.

Miss Pawlowski continued. "Smell the air. Take a deep breath and tell me if you don't think it smells different. Did you happen to see any roads while we were parachuting down? I didn't."

Alex shook his head. No roads.

"There should have been roads. That over there is Garnock River. I asked, and that man confirmed it. But there is no road near it. There's no indication there ever was a road. And there are no houses. We're supposed to be near Glasgow. There should be houses here. People. Lots of people. Right along in here there should be condominiums on that hill there." She pointed. "I remember them."

"What are you getting at?"

"You saw the plane go down. You saw where it was headed."

"A small bay."

"The Firth of Clyde." She paused a moment to let that sink in, but it only puzzled him.

"Yeah. So?"

"Remember the medieval F-18?"

A charge skittered up his spine as he remembered, but he said nothing.

She continued, "That man in there just told me the year is 1306. That plane they found, more than five centuries old, was piloted by a lieutenant. It was painted on the side." She reached out and poked his chest with an insistent finger, punctuating each word as she spoke. "I'm betting it originally said *Lieutenant Alexander MacNeil*. It was your name and rank painted on the side of that plane."

"But that doesn't mean—"

"They found the plane before it was crashed. Explain that."

Of course, he couldn't. Except . . . "It's not my plane."

"So the United States Navy loses a lot of aircraft in Scottish waters? I suppose, though, that over the centuries the numbers can add up."

"But that's just—"

"Nuts. I know. It's madness. It's . . ." Her voice trailed off as something behind Alex caught her eye and she looked away from him. He turned to see, and was astonished to find men on horseback coming from the trees at the other side of the pasture. At this distance they weren't particularly identifiable, but even so Alex could see they weren't ordinary riders. For one thing, they were all men. Alex had never in his life seen a group of pleasure riders with no women along. For another, the horses were fitted with faceplates, and the men wore dark chain mail. They carried painted shields that shone brightly in spite of the overcast day. And when they spotted him and Miss Pawlowski, instead of minding their own business as most pleasure riders would have done, they veered toward the two on foot and kicked into a gallop.

Alex said, "Let's get out of here."

CHAPTER 2

Alex pulled Miss Pawlowski by her arm toward the trees nearby, and they plunged along a path into the thick forest. He reached for his sidearm and quickly pulled the slide to chamber a round as they ran.

But the woman grabbed his arm and dug in her heels to hold him back. "Wait! Do you have any bandages in those pockets?"

He turned to her. "Are you hurt?"

"No. But I need bandages. Gauze or elastic, it doesn't matter."

Puzzled and impatient, he thought quickly. "I've got a first aid kit; I think it's got an elastic one." The thud of hooves approached in the distance.

"Give it to me."

"Why?"

"Just give it to me." Her outstretched hand waved and urged him to hurry.

He sighed and reached into his left shin pocket for the kit, and opened it one-handed. She snatched the bandage from it, and unzipped her flight suit. "What are you doing?" he asked. The hoofbeats came closer, and he raised his gun in that direction while hoping the riders would pass them by in the dense forest.

She didn't reply, but doffed her black T-shirt and bra. The

bra she tossed into a mass of ferns, and suddenly Alex was presented with her two luscious breasts. "Help me." She unwound the bandage and laid the end across her nipples. "Help me bind these."

"Why?" He looked away and busied himself restoring the kit to his shin pocket, lest his brain turn to mush. Now was not the time.

"Nobody with a choice would want to be a woman right now. You heard what that man said about his wife. I'm not wearing a dress; I've got to make them think I'm a man or I'll be a target."

He looked back at the approaching riders. "I think they'll be less likely to hurt you if they know you're a woman."

She waved a hand to catch his attention, then drew it to her and leaned in to emphasize her words. "*I'm not wearing a dress.* If those guys are as medieval as I think they are, they'll hurt me just for that. I've got to pass for a boy, at least until I can figure out what to do."

"How are you going to convince them of that?" Just then he couldn't imagine it.

"I won't if you don't help me bind these flat. Hurry!"

He reholstered his pistol and stepped behind her to help wind the bandage around her chest. He secured it with its two flimsy metal clasps, then helped her restore her T-shirt and flight suit. The instant she was somewhat pulled together, he grabbed her hand and hauled her along, deeper into the forest. She zipped her flight suit as she ran. "Knife. Give me your knife." He handed over his survival knife, and she started whacking off her hair to shoulder length.

Alex turned his attention to the approaching riders who had now reached the edge of the forest. "They're coming." There was crashing through the underbrush, and he could hear the heavy, snorting breaths of the horses. He stopped, reached for his sidearm once more, and prepared to hold them off.

But at that moment a shout came from within the forest ahead, and more riders bore down on them from the other direction. Alex retrieved his knife, pocketed it, then pulled Miss Pawlowski off the path and into a grassy clearing. Behind them, the two groups of horsemen clashed, horses bellowing, weapons and shields ringing. Swords whirled and clanged. Alex caught a glimpse of a mace wielded with deadly force. Wounded horses screamed and men shouted angrily as they tried to kill each other.

Alex guided his charge away from the fighting, but a member of the first group broke away from the fray and spurred his horse to follow them. "Go," he ordered, and shoved her into a thicket. Then he turned, leveled the muzzle of his pistol, and shouted, "Stop!"

The rider in chain mail kept coming at a gallop, and hauled back his sword to strike.

Alex dodged, and dove to the ground. The sword whacked a fern behind him. Leaves blew every which way. He uttered a vulgarism as he rolled away from the horse and scrambled to his feet in a thicket of the large, curling ferns. Behind him the rider wheeled and his horse reared. He shouted something, and when Alex turned to face him the visage inside the helmet was twisted and snarling, red-faced and ugly. The horse pulled up, and the attacker dismounted as casually as if he weren't wearing a shirt of mail over a tunic and under his flowing surcoat. He circled his broadsword like a windmill and stepped toward Alex.

"Stop, I said!" Alex lifted the muzzle of the gun and squeezed off a warning shot, but though the attacker flinched at the noise and his glance flitted for a moment, he didn't stop coming. Alex didn't want to shoot the guy, but it was beginning to look like there was no other way to teach him what a gun was. His mouth a hard line, he lowered his aim and fired at a leg.

Blood sprayed. The man in mail bellowed and spun, but didn't fall. He straightened and came on, the shot having done nothing but give him a limp and anger him more.

"Whoa!" Alex backed away a few steps, his gun still aimed. "Don't make me kill you, man!"

In response to Alex's retreat the attacker whirled his broadsword again, shouting what must have been curses on Alex and possibly several centuries of his ancestry, and limped toward Alex. Then he hauled back with the sword and assaulted at a run. There was no longer any choice. Alex took aim and fired straight into his face at close range.

The helmet, hit from the inside, flew off like a champagne cork and the attacker's head exploded in a rain of gore and brain and skull. He collapsed to the ground in a heap. Alex lowered his pistol and groaned as he stared at the corpse, transfixed.

It was ugly. Blood ran in rivulets from the ruined skull and soaked into the ground. Alex had killed people before, or at least assumed he had, but had always attacked from too much distance to see who'd been in the way of his missiles and nose gun. He'd had friends, uncles, and cousins who had died in crashes or were shot down or blown up, but had never seen death this close.

Now, as he stared at this body on the ground, a coldness came over him. Anger rose at the stupid sonofabitch who hadn't respected the gun. Hadn't even known what it was. The sword was just as dangerous, for dead was dead and the guy surely had intended to kill him with it; there had been no choice but to shoot. Alex ejected the clip, then emptied the chamber to put the round back into the clip, the clip back into the pistol, and slipped the weapon into a pocket of his flight suit. He jettisoned the holster, knowing now he could never use the pistol as a deterrent. In fact, the thing had made him appear unarmed and had actually invited the assault. It put him at a palpable disadvantage in a world where the sword was state of the art weaponry. In the future he could only draw it if he was already committed to kill. There were ten rounds left in the clip, and Alex hoped he would never fire them.

Miss Pawlowski came from the thicket, pale, gawking at the faceless corpse, and Alex looked up to see the skirmish was over. The survivors of the first group had run off, and the new arrivals that had come from the forest were now dismounted and approaching Alex and his passenger. Mail and plate clanked and rattled as three men stepped toward him over the ruined underbrush, ferns, and deadfall of the forest. Younger men holding the horses stood back.

Alex snatched his attacker's sword from the ground and turned on the approaching group, as threatening as he could manage with these odds. He held the weapon in both hands in an approximation of en garde, and hoped he was more convincing than he'd been with the pistol. Defending himself with an edged weapon was an alien concept to him, but he was having what was arguably the crappiest day of his life, was fed to the teeth, and was determined to whack the hell out of anyone who gave him any more guff. His face darkened into as fierce a glower as he had at his command, trying to appear as pissed off as he felt.

But the men wore calming smiles. All fairly large guys, one was about Alex's age, one a bit older, and the third was only a tall, lanky teenager. They came at him with cheerful hail-fellow voices, but with wary eyes, acknowledging his sword by keeping clear of it.

"What language is *that*?" Alex muttered.

Miss Pawlowski came up behind him to speak in a murmur. "I think it's French. Sort of. Its medieval equivalent, anyway."

"How many different languages do they speak in this place?"

"Well, when a land has been invaded as many times as Britain, it gets complicated. Be glad they're not Saxons."

Then the one who appeared thirtyish switched to what Alex now recognized as Middle English and addressed him. Though an irregularity of his lower teeth gave his speech a barely discernible sibilance, he sounded like he might be the one in charge. Miss Pawlowski said, "I'm fairly certain he's thanking you."

Cautiously Alex straightened his stance and lowered his sword, nodded, and said, "Okay." He heard gratitude in the man's voice, and believed her.

The other two men leaned over the corpse to examine the bloodied head blown to pieces. The three conferred with each other in soft, awed voices, and glanced frequently at Alex as if unsure what he might do next. The one who seemed in charge then turned and spoke to Alex again. The man had an aristocratic look about him, a square jaw and fine features quite different from the lumpen appearance of the half-naked family in the peat house. Also, he seemed extremely well dressed, even relative to the other men in his entourage who were also well turned-out in rich colors and smooth fabrics. The man's bearing was of command, his tone demanded respect, and everything about him seemed to assume it would be given. The others deferred to him in obvious ways, and he was plainly their spokesman.

Struggling to make himself understood by gestures, repetitions, and speaking slowly, his voice and demeanor remained patient as Miss Pawlowski continued to translate. "He's wondering . . . very curious as to how you killed that man, using no sword."

Alex bent and picked up a rock about the size of his hand, and the man's eyes went wide as he appeared to resist the urge to take a step back. Though it was impossible to have done what Alex did with just a thrown rock, in the absence of a more rational explanation they all seemed willing to accept an irrational one. Each, aside from the leader, stepped back a pace and Alex responded by dropping the rock. Their leader smiled and spoke again, still with wary eyes.

Miss Pawlowski translated. "Apparently you've killed an English nobleman who held lands nearby, whose loyalties lay with King Edward. First or second Edward, I can't recall and either they're assuming I know or else I'm missing something. By his tone, I'm thinking this man here on the ground was well despised by these other fellows. He seems glad you killed him."

Alex glanced sideways at Lindsay and murmured, "Ding, dong, the witch is dead."

She pressed her lips together hard to contain a laugh, then continued. "The man had come to avenge the recent demise of someone named Comyn, and it would appear you've done this group a huge favor."

Alex nodded again.

The leader pointed to Alex, then Miss Pawlowski said, "They want to know who you are."

He placed a hand over his chest and addressed the armored men before him. "My name is Alexander MacNeil."

That brought raised eyebrows and a flurry of inquiry, to which Miss Pawlowski nodded and replied, "Aye."

"What did he ask?"

"He said something about MacNeils on Barra."

"And you told them yes? Why'd you do that?"

Impatience tinged her voice. "I think he wanted to know who you're related to. I said yes to Barra so we wouldn't have to explain further. Columbus won't stumble over the New World for another hundred and eighty-six years, so confessing you're an American could make things quite dodgy and very quickly."

"Oh. Yeah." The back of his brain was still insisting these

guys were actors and this was all a put-on. It was going to take a while for anything to make sense.

The men were querying further, and Miss Pawlowski fielded their questions with more gestures and repetitions. Alex asked, "What are they saying now?"

She ignored him until there was a pause in the halting conversation, then turned to him and said softly and quickly with her head down where the others couldn't listen in, "I've explained to them—I *think* I've explained to them—that you aren't familiar with any of your MacNeil relatives because you've been fostered on the Continent from an early age and your father has never sent for you. You've lived your life far away in the eastern mountains, which is why you don't speak English as well as they do, and you don't speak Gaelic or French at all."

"Eastern mountains?"

"Hungary, actually. You fostered with my father's family, the Pawlowskis, which makes you my older foster brother. So perhaps you should stop calling me ma'am."

"Pawlowski sounds Polish."

Impatience grew in her voice, though she held her temper and gave him a tight smile for the benefit of onlookers. "It is. However, Hungary happens to be the only country I'm certain existed during this time that's far enough away from here to make me comfortable we won't be running into people with relatives there. I'd look it up, but I seem to have left my medieval atlas at home. So start calling me Lindsay in public, if you please."

Alex shifted his weight and looked around, puzzled. "Lindsay? I thought you wanted them to think you're a guy."

"Yes, I'm your younger and smaller foster brother, Lindsay Pawlowski, and I'm fifteen years old. Quite beardless, you see, and perhaps a bit clumsy in my youth, but tall for my age."

The armored man who seemed to be in charge asked Alex a question. Lindsay turned to him and shook her head no, then the man drew his sword and said something else. Alex pulled in his chin, resisted the urge to take a step back, and looked to Lindsay for help. Her expression was one of surprise at the man.

"What?" asked Alex. This didn't look good.

"Looks like he wants to knight you."

Alex's jaw dropped and he stepped back from the sword as if it had suddenly sprouted fangs. "Huh?"

The man kept talking, his tone firm, as if the issue were already settled and he was instructing Alex in what to do. There was an edge of command to his voice as he pointed at the ground before him. Alex wanted to laugh, but didn't dare, for the guy sounded dead serious.

Lindsay, still listening to the man with the sword, said, "He does want to knight you. He says they need fighters, and you . . ." She asked for a repetition, then said, "Oh."

"Oh, what?"

". . . and you being the bastard of—"

"What did you tell them?" Alex rounded on Lindsay, irritated and on his way to anger.

She talked fast now. "I didn't tell them that. But they've assumed you're the bastard of the MacNeil laird. And since that makes you of noble blood, he wants to knight you so you can join the fight." The guy with the sword waited patiently for them to finish arguing, watching them both carefully.

"What fight?"

"Damned if I know. Just tell him yes."

"I want to know what fight I'm getting myself into."

"It doesn't matter. Look at him—how he's holding his sword so he can swing it if he needs to. This isn't a request. It's a test. If you don't join him, he'll kill you. And even if he didn't kill you, do you have any better ideas of what to do at this juncture? I don't know about you, but I'm hungry. I think it would be nice to make friends with someone who might be inclined to give us something to eat."

She had a point. Alex looked at the dark-haired leader of this pack, his sword held lightly and slightly cocked, and sighed. Then he nodded and said, "Aye."

That brought smiles, as well as an air of relief, and Alex knew Lindsay had been right about the danger of not accepting knighthood. The men in armor seemed pleased they wouldn't need to kill him now. Lindsay said, "Kneel."

Alex knelt, and the leader lifted his sword. The man intoned some quick words, whacked Alex on the back of the neck with the flat of the blade, then scabbarded it. Alex understood the command to rise, and realized he was starting to catch on to this Middle English thing. Then the guy asked a question, laid his hand on his own chest, and peered into Alex's face. The voice was formal, and Alex could hear the tension in it.

Lindsay said, "Nod."

"Why?"

"He said allegiance and pointed to himself. He wants you to pledge yourself to him."

Without further hesitation, for he knew his credibility was on the line, Alex nodded. "Aye. I will."

His new companions slapped him on the back and welcomed him to their number, then turned to their horses to mount. Lindsay began to gather the fallen attacker's weapons and armor.

"I'll get those."

"No. I must do it. You need a squire now. I might as well be it."

"But—"

"No. You must let me do this."

Alex acquiesced reluctantly, then stood back, not knowing what to do. So he swung the sword in his hands to learn the feel of it. The thing was lighter than he'd expected, the blade thinner. It was a cross-hilt broadsword with a delicately carved hilt, and the knob at the end was of silver. Pretty fancy. The scabbard the guy wore was tooled leather.

Lindsay continued with the work, stripping the thigh-length chain mail shirt from the corpse. She handed it to Alex, who removed his bulky survival vest then proceeded to don the mail over his flight suit. It was surprisingly smooth, for each tiny iron link was flat. The sleeves were long and covered his wrists well, and the round neck was tied by a leather thong run through the top links. The stuff was heavy but not unwieldy; it shifted oddly when he moved, but not impossibly. It shouldn't take much to get used to this. He poked at the bloody hole in the tail of the shirt over his thigh, and decided it would be all right for now. He then accepted the dead man's spurs, scabbard, belts, and dagger, then finally the helmet. He declined to try it on just yet, preferring to wait until he could wash out the blood and gray matter.

The others were waiting for him to accompany them.

While Lindsay captured the Englishman's horse, Alex on a hunch leaned over to check the body again and found a lump in the top of what he could only think of as the guy's long johns. There, held in place by a narrow belt, was a small, leather draw-string bag. Alex hefted it and it clinked, and inside he found what must have been a couple of pounds of silver coins, some cut in half. And among them were several fairly large jewel stones of blue and green, and a couple of extremely large pearls. "Dang," he said under his breath. At least they wouldn't starve.

Lindsay had the horse by its bridle and brought it over. "Have you ever ridden one of these?"

"Yeah. During my cowboy phase as a kid I wanted to ride horses more than I wanted to fly planes. Used to do rodeo stuff out in California. I can ride nearly anything on four legs." A smile lifted the corner of his mouth. "And a few on two."

She blinked a little and mild amusement flickered on her face, but otherwise she ignored the jest and pulled the riderless horse around for him. "Good. Here, get on this. I'll help you up."

"Miss . . . I mean, Lindsay . . ."

"Do it. I'm your squire. I'll sit behind you."

Alex mounted the English steed, noting the horse was larger than the ones ridden by his new companions. Not a destrier like the enormous tournament horses in the movies, but large nevertheless. The saddle was a nightmarish torture device of high cantle and pommel, the stirrups straight down so his knees didn't bend, and he almost couldn't get his wide, thick-soled, blunt-toed leather boots into the stirrups. Lindsay had to help him shove them in. The high, narrow seat felt like perching on a rail fence. Built for ramming a lance down someone's throat, not for riding comfort.

For the past several minutes the guy in charge had been speaking to his men in a low voice. Alex reached down to help Lindsay up behind him, but she only stood there, staring at that man and listening to what was being said. Her face had gone slack, surprised. "Earl of Carrick?" She seemed to be saying it to herself.

"What's wrong?"

"Oh, God," she murmured, still staring at the cluster of knights.

"What?" Alarm fluttered in his gut, and he sat up to look around.

"You're not going to believe this."

"What?"

"That man over there is the king. Or he will be. Soon."

Alex looked. "What king?"

"Of Scotland." Her voice wavered with deep astonishment. "Alex, you've just been knighted by Robert the Bruce."

That stunned him speechless, and he stared at the man. He knew who Robert the Bruce was, from movies. And any king was a big deal to a guy like him who didn't know much about royalty. As he stared at the square-faced Robert, a smile came. "How about that? This is going to make a great story when we get home." He gave a dry chuckle. "Or not, if I want to stay out of the laughing academy." Then he reached down to help Lindsay up behind him and kicked his mount to fall in behind the others of his fellow knights.

Robert led the way, and they rode from the forest to the pasture. As they rode, Alex tried to think ahead. What had they gotten themselves into? How were they going to live? He half-turned in the saddle and said in a low voice, "Who are those other guys?"

She shrugged. "All I know is what I've overheard and pieced together. The older one is named Roger, and the kid's name is James." The teenager had shaggy, black hair to his shoulders, ruddy cheeks, and a don't-mess-with-me look about him. Angry youth. He rode in the lead with Bruce. The older guy, Roger, rode immediately behind. He was burly and strong, and had the thousand-yard stare of a combat veteran who'd been once too often in the thick of things. "I've no clue about the rest of them. I think those are all squires, and only these three are knights. Well, and you of course."

Alex said, "I don't feel much like a knight."

"You don't look much like one, either. Baggy jumpsuit—"

"Flight suit."

"Baggy pants and leather work boots don't exactly set off the ensemble."

He chuckled. "You know, I would think I'd feel all, you know, chivalrous. Or something. Like I should be charging off to slay dragons and rescue fair maidens."

"I think all they want you to slay is Englishmen."

"You mean, more Englishmen."

That gave her pause, and she coughed. "Yes. More."

"You figure we'll run into William Wallace?"

Lindsay thought for a moment, then said, "My memory is spotty, but I think if Bruce is killing Englishmen, then Wallace must be dead by now. If we encounter him at all it won't be more than a rotting piece of torso."

Alex grunted, mildly disappointed.

There was a pause while he worked up the nerve to approach the question that had been bothering him since Lindsay had bound her breasts. "What're you going to do when they notice you've got no . . . you know . . . package?"

"Package?"

"In your drawers."

"Ah. Excellent question, and I'll have to cross that bridge when I get there. And, speaking of that, are you circumcised?"

"Huh?"

"Of course, you're circumcised. All American men are."

"I beg your pardon?" He was, but that was beside the point.

"Don't ever let anyone here see your willie. Under any conditions. They'll think you're a Jew."

"And that would be bad because . . .?"

"A few years ago all Jews were expelled from Britain. Something about outlawing usury. Anyone gets a glimpse of your circumcised penis, you'll be deported. That's if they let you live, which they might not. Men of this century are horribly ignorant of other cultures, particularly cultures that have been kicked out of the country, and afraid of anything they don't understand."

"Oh." Wonderful. Yet another layer on this insanity.

"Wait." Lindsay slipped a hand into Alex's pocket for his knife, threw her leg over the back and slid from the horse, then took off running toward the mound of nylon they'd left in the middle of this pasture. Alex continued to follow Robert and his retinue at a walk.

As he went, a frisson skittered up his spine and he looked around. It was a feeling of being watched. But the riders ahead paid him no attention and the landscape was otherwise empty. Alex peered at the forest edge, trying to discern anything lurking among the trees, but found nobody. Nevertheless, the feeling persisted. Finally he returned his attention to Lindsay and tried to shrug off the creepy feeling.

When she finished cutting the shroud lines and bundled up the fabric, she was able to run back and hand it all up to him, along with their helmets.

"What's this for?" He snapped the helmets together by their face masks, and draped them over the horse's withers.

"It's cloth. It's lightweight, and it's not far off from silk in texture. Even if we don't use it, we can sell it.

Alex grunted and held the bundle under one arm while helping her up onto the horse with his other. They proceeded onward.

Shortly after nightfall they came to an encampment lit by torches and bonfires and surrounded by wagons on which hung many round, wooden shields faced outward as on a battlement. Except for the amazing array of colors and symbols on the shields, it struck Alex as having the appearance of a wagon train circled for an Indian attack. No doubt the shields served the same defensive purpose against arrows.

He and Lindsay had eaten nothing since before catapulting from the ship that morning, and his stomach was now a tight knot. This place was a long way from his world where fast food restaurants stood every mile or so, and even with the purse filled with silver in a pocket of his flight suit there'd been no food to be had on the trail. Smells of roasting meat wafted through the air here, making his mouth water and his stomach churn.

Once inside the camp perimeter the older knight went his own way, followed by most of the squires. Only the one young knight and a couple of squires continued on with Robert toward the tent in the center of the gathering. Alex took that as an invitation to buzz off for the time being, so he began to look around for a place to park.

The camp wasn't large, but had the atmosphere of a circus town. Tents were pitched in clusters between which were streets paved with trampled pasture, and entrepreneurial camp followers had set up shop in temporary shelters here and there. Blacksmith, baker, poulterer sold their wares to the scattering of men and boys who appeared to be Bruce's army of knights. There were women, but very few, and they all seemed to be maintaining camp for the men or hawking wares to them. A troupe of entertainers at a crossing of the "streets" attracted a crowd and amused onlookers in exchange for coins thrown. "This place looks like a Renaissance faire."

Lindsay replied in a low, tired voice, "Except the Renaissance won't happen for a while yet. We're still in the dark ages. These people don't bathe often, they think vegetables are bad for you, and they think any woman without a male relative is a candidate for rape." She considered her words for a moment, then said, "Of course, all those things were true during the Renaissance as well."

"Yup, makes ya wonder, don't it?" Alex wondered for a moment, then said, "You sure know a lot about this period."

"I'm English. Unlike you Americans, we take our history seriously."

That stung. "You think we don't take our history seriously?"

"How can you? You haven't any."

Alex had no desire to play that game with her, and so fell silent. There was a clear spot under a tall oak tree. He decided this would do, pulled up his horse and dismounted, then helped Lindsay down. "Here," he told her, "why don't you take these coins and buy us something to eat." Then he took his survival vest from her and pulled out the two condoms he carried there. "Here, wait." He handed over one of the foil packets.

"I beg your pardon?" She twiddled it between her fingers, looking like she wanted to hand it back.

"Relax, it's not a come-on. Just take this and fill it with water if you can find some clean. And see if you can get some wood for a fire."

"Do you know how to start a fire without matches?"

"Even better. I've got matches in my survival vest." He hefted the garment loaded with gear.

"You know you'll need to learn how if we don't find a way home soon."

He didn't want to think about that. Much better to look for a way home. But rather than argue, he said, "Yeah, but for tonight I'm tired, I'm starving, my legs are killing me, and my crotch feels like someone smacked me in the nuts with a log. That saddle was not meant for humans to ride." He reached for the horse's reins, but Lindsay stopped him.

"No. Allow me."

"I'll get it."

"No. You can't be seen attending to your horse. You're nobility and a knight. It would be a disgrace. I'll do it."

He considered that for a moment, then sucked air between his front teeth with an irritated hiss. "All right. I figure you're sure to know more about this class system than I do. Take the horse. Get him some feed. Do what you need to."

She hobbled the horse with ropes she found in a small saddle bag, removed the saddle, and put it on the ground nearby. She unbuckled the faceplate, removed the bridle and the long piece of chain mail draped over the horse's neck, and set them atop the saddle. Lastly, she hauled the enormous, quilted skirt from the animal's back. It was a struggle to organize and fold the heavy piece of fabric, but when Alex stepped close to help she warned him away with a look. Finally she hurried off on the errands, and Alex watched her go. Then he glanced around their chosen spot and wondered what to do next. Were he back on his ship, he would have eaten and crawled into his bunk by now, lulled to sleep by the clacking of Eddie's laptop or kept awake by Ron's raucous and irregular snoring. It seemed his body could tell it had traversed far more than just distance today, and he ached to lie down and be still. But there were things to do before he could rest. He bent to pick at the shroud lines binding the bundle of parachutes.

A knight in silk surcoat, and more than his share of plate armor while the man who was soon to be king wore very little of it, approached, and began talking to Alex in a voice thick with belligerence. With Lindsay not there to translate, all Alex could do was shrug and shake his head, hold his palms up, and explain in modern English that he didn't understand. The guy tried to crowd him, but Alex held his ground and repeated that he didn't speak the language. The fancy-dressed knight didn't seem to have a particular beef with him; his voice carried a sort of generalized challenge. Alex wanted to avoid it at all costs, and shook his head. A frown darkened the man's face, and he stepped in to crowd Alex again, and this time raised a gauntleted fist to strike.

CHAPTER 3

"Wait a minute. I don't want any trouble." Alex backed off a step, then another. But the fancy-armored knight crowded some more, growling at him in that weird French. "Hey, cut it out, or I'm gonna have to hurt you, man." Still the stranger crowded, spitting his words as he came. Finally Alex shoved him.

The knight hauled off, and Alex ducked the punch. As he circled, he raised his fists and noted his opponent's leather gauntlets were riveted with knuckle plates. "Listen, I don't know what your problem is, man, but if you don't get the hell away from here I'm going to have to take you out." The warning did nothing. Finally Alex broke for the gear and pulled his sword from the scabbard.

That made the knight go silent, for he had only his dagger with him, scabbarded at his belt. When he spoke again, his tone was far more reasonable. Alex wasn't in the mood for guessing what the guy wanted, so he pointed to the knight's chest, then flicked his fingers away in a brush-off gesture that indicated he should leave. For a long moment the knight frowned at him, then up at the tree under which Alex and Lindsay had staked their territory. Then with a single word that Alex took as an expletive of some sort, the knight backed away and left. Alex watched him go, his sword at en garde until his attacker was out of sight.

Nearby stood a man, looking like a monk with his face in the shadow of a deep hood. Alex stared, wondering what the guy had found so fascinating, then answered his own question with a glance at his dark green flight suit and heavy leather boots. His military haircut was attracting glances as well, and he noticed he was the only man in sight whose hair didn't at least cover his ears. He returned his sword to its scabbard, then looked back at the hooded man, but he was gone. Alex looked around, but there was no trace of him. Not the entire length of the camp.

He shrugged off the creepy feeling and turned to the tasks at hand.

Unwilling to just sit around like a lump for the sake of appearing noble, Alex unbundled the parachutes and shook them out. One he tied with a piece of shroud line at the middle of its leading edge to an overhead branch, then he went around the outside, spreading it into a tent, weighting the edges with rocks and leaving a gap at the front. As tents went it wasn't huge, not compared to the one into which Bruce and that young knight had disappeared, but it would keep the dew off himself and Lindsay in the morning. The other parachute he folded and laid on the ground inside for a sleeping pallet. Not the height of comfort, but better than bare ground.

His mail shirt fit tightly enough to be a problem. He couldn't just pull it over his head like a T-shirt, and it wasn't wide enough for him to slip his arms inside and push up. At first he bent over, trying to get it to slide off onto the ground, but it was too long and heavy to slip over his flight suit. He nearly got stuck with it halfway off. Then he thought a moment, and approached the job in parts. He hiked the bottom edge of the chain over his hips, then bent. Moving almost like an inchworm, he heaved the mass of chain up over his back and encouraged it to slide off onto the ground inside the tent. Lindsay returned as it fell into a sloppy, metal heap with a hissing, chinking noise.

"I could have helped you with that. Should have; it's my job."

He shrugged and picked up the shirt to shake it out. She had with her a roast bird of some kind wrapped in a piece of linen cloth, a loaf of bread, an entire cheese the size of Alex's spread fingers, a water skin that turned out to be filled with wine, the water-filled condom that looked like a balloon with a nipple at one end, a bundle of sticks, and some fodder for the horse. She handed back the purse.

"I only needed a few of those silver coins. Apparently those are pence. We've got a little over two pounds of silver in there."

"You weighed it?"

"I counted it. Two hundred and forty pence actually weighs a pound. That's where the word comes from. Anyway, there are also five sapphires of varying size, three emeralds, and two pearls. The smallest stone is apparently worth more than you would want to lug around in silver. There don't seem to be any pound coins around here anywhere. Some foreign gold, but no English cash larger than these pence."

Alex hefted the jingling leather sack, then tucked it into a pocket of his flight suit.

He built a fire, and beside it he and Lindsay proceeded to demolish most of the food and all of the wine. The roast bird was large like a turkey, but dark and greasy.

"What is this, a goose?"

"Swan."

Alex did a take. "Really? They eat swans here?"

"I imagine they eat pretty much anything they can catch and cook. And swans are plentiful."

Folks walking past stopped to admire the brightly colored parachute tent, and often reached over to feel the texture of the cloth. One man made an offer to buy it, but Alex preferred to hang onto his shelter, since he didn't appear to need the cash just then and had no way of knowing what might be a good deal.

Lindsay took a big swig from the wine skin to finish it, made a face, and said in a choked voice, "I can't believe they call that wine. It's more like grape juice gone off."

"I don't know, I kinda like it. Sweet."

She gave him a look that told him he was too pedestrian for words. "You have an American sweet tooth."

He opened his mouth for a crack about the wine being as English as she was, but changed his mind and kept it to himself. Instead he shrugged and said, "Okay, I'm not a big wine drinker. So shoot me."

She grinned.

With a nod, he indicated the people around in the camp. "How come you can tell what those folks are saying? Whenever I think I recognize a word, it turns out they're saying something else."

"Right word, different meaning."

Alex gazed at her and waited for her to elaborate on that obscure comment.

"You've got to think in terms of word roots. And concentrate on the basics. Nouns and verbs. And consonants. Vowels are a nightmare, which explains a lot of weird spelling conventions in modern English. Like this . . ." she looked up for a moment, plundering her memory, then again at him and recited, 'A kneegt ther was, and that a worthy man.' "

Alex hadn't a clue. "A *kneegt*?"

"Knight."

"No kidding?"

She nodded. "Think of how it's spelled, and pronounce every letter. The *i*'s will tend to sound like long *e*'s, that sort of thing. Lots of words will sound funny because they'll have an extra syllable here and there. The good news is that the basic grammar is more or less intact. Sort of. It's been said that Middle English is really German spoken with a French accent."

"That would be good if I knew French or German."

"If you can decipher Shakespeare on your own, you'll have a good shot at this."

Alex pondered that for a moment. "But, soft . . ."

Lindsay smiled. "Means, 'Wait, be quiet.' "

"Go on. Tell me more about that *kneegt*."

She obliged readily, and recited while they finished eating, translating each sentence as she went.

Later, gnawing on a leg bone and feeling better, but still hungry enough to consider breaking the bone and sucking out the marrow, Alex asked, "So, what's going to happen next?"

"How would I know?"

He sucked some grease from his lower lip and said, "You're History Girl, aren't you?"

"Well, it's not as if I have Robert's diary memorized, is it? Not that there was one."

"Okay, then how long do we have until Bannockburn?"

"You know about that?"

"Everyone knows about that. Besides, I studied the battle in school. Well, okay, it was mentioned in school. One of the first battles in which foot soldiers clobbered knights. Battle tactics. I was a wiz."

"Don't forget, you're now one of those knights."

He grunted. "I'm a pilot. A Hornet driver."

"I daresay that matters little here."

Alex had no reply to that, and only gazed blandly at her for a moment. Then he said, "So, how long do we have till Bannockburn?"

She thought, then replied, "1314. Eight years from now, if our host this morning was telling the truth. I think." She glanced up at the sky, then around at the trees and brush. "I think this is spring . . . —ish. Maybe. The battle was in summer, so eight years."

Once again Alex was disappointed, and he realized he'd hoped to see some action while he was here. But he expected to be long gone by 1314, so he probably wouldn't be doing any more fighting.

Supper finished, he began to feel fairly mellow and inebriated around the edges as he lounged against the pile of gear and horse tack while Lindsay used the linen cloth to wipe down the animal. Wine put a rosy glow on things, and now he minded less that he was not where he wanted to be. He wished Lindsay would finish what she was doing and come hang out by the fire. More than wanting to see her face, he longed for some company.

A man in chain mail approached the fire. His right hand raised, he reminded Alex of an Indian wanting to powwow. He was dressed well, all things considered, and looked like he may have washed his face this evening. His hands, though, still bore a film of grease from dinner. Alex peered up at him and called for his squire. "Lindsay?"

She shook out the cloth, folded it, and came to the fire.

"Lindsay, do me a favor and ask him what he wants."

She did, and Alex thought he understood some of the words. They were terribly archaic, but, by following Lindsay's advice and drawing on his knowledge of root meanings, he found himself picking out more and more words.

She reported, "His name is John Kirkpatrick. I think he's asking about Hungary. Wants to know what it's like."

Alex gestured for the visitor to sit, and chuckled. "Well, you don't need me for this conversation. You just tell him whatever story you've made up."

Lindsay spoke to the man, who then sat cross-legged by the fire. Alex noted the other knight appeared unarmed, and took that as good faith he'd come in peace and expected to be well treated. He listened to Lindsay describe in Middle English mountains she'd never seen, and concentrated on figuring out exactly what she was telling their visitor.

John spoke again, and Lindsay said to Alex, "He wants to know what moved you to come here."

"What did move me to come here?"

"I think you came to Scotland to make your fortune among your father's people, for there's no place for you in Hungary."

"Sounds good. Tell him."

Lindsay did so.

John replied, and Lindsay translated. "Apparently, your father, MacNeil of Barra, died last year."

Alex thought that over for a moment, and decided that was probably not a bad thing. It meant he'd never run into the guy he was spreading lies about. But he told Lindsay to say, "I'm sorry I'll never meet him."

John nodded at that, and allowed it must be a terrible thing to never know one's father.

Relaxing by the fire, Alex and Lindsay learned from John that he was a knight in the company of his cousin, Roger Kirkpatrick, the same Roger who had ridden with Robert that day. John held a small amount of land, and was eager for hostilities to begin in order to increase his fortune by plunder and glory. Alex was brought to mind of a hot-shot pilot just out of flight training, who could hardly wait to get into combat. Except that John appeared much older than Alex. His lined face, even in an era where people aged quickly and died young, showed a maturity that didn't match his words. Alex found it disquieting.

Then John related a tale of their leader, Robert Bruce, Earl of Carrick. Bare weeks ago, one of the other claimants to the empty Scottish throne had been murdered at the altar of Greyfri-

ars Church to the south. People were saying it was Bruce who
did the killing, but John assured them it wasn't the case. Robert
had only struck the first blow, and Comyn had still been alive
when Bruce hurried from the church. John knew this, because it
had been his commander and cousin, Roger Kirkpatrick, who
had gone in to finish the deed.

John related all this as if he were chatting about a football
game, and even seemed to be bragging a little about his cousin.
Alex had no reply, and John segued into other stories. They
talked for hours, until the camp quieted and the fire burned low.

Eventually, John bade Alex good night then left for his own
tent, and Alex and Lindsay retired to their parachute tent.

It was small, and there was only one saddle blanket to cover
them both on the single pallet. Lindsay looked at it, then at Alex.
Her expression told him what he'd already figured, that he was
to keep his hands off her. With a sigh, he lay down on the parachute and pulled the blanket over him. Lindsay followed suit,
and lay with her back to him. Alex began to drift off quickly, accustomed to sleeping in a tiny, steel room with three guys who
all snored and had reading lights, and with jets landing on the
deck directly overhead. But in the twilight of consciousness he
caught sounds of weeping that pierced his awareness and brought
him back around. Silently in the darkness, he turned his head to
listen. Lindsay, who had kept a flawlessly brave front all day,
was breaking down for a long, quiet cry.

The weeping tore Alex in a place he'd kept carefully hidden;
he knew exactly how she felt, and was at an utter loss to comprehend the extent of his grief over the damage done to his life
today. He'd carefully tucked away his own pain, but he couldn't
stand to ignore hers. He rolled over to put an arm around her,
and she let him. Lying close, he held her until she stopped sniffling. Then the fourteenth-century day finally swarmed in on
him for good and he dropped off to sleep.

WELL before dawn the camp awoke, breakfasted, and began
the process of dismantling and packing for travel now that
Robert had returned from wherever it was he'd briefly been.
Boys hurried back and forth, and voices seemed inappropri-
ately loud in the early morning dimness and cold. For Alex and

Lindsay there was only to bundle up the tent and saddle the horse, so Alex revived the fire to warm themselves and they lingered over their cold breakfast of bread, cheese, and water from the bloated condom. Lindsay was still shivering, while Alex was feeling nearly human again. He looked around for some more deadwood, and threw small branches on the fire for her.

She appeared less upset today than she had the night before, and he was relieved to see she was holding up. Her face was set, determined, but her eyes were clear and focused on what was before her. Alex watched her saddle the horse, impressed by her alacrity. By way of doing his share of the work without appearing too common, he untied the parachute from the branch overhead and began folding it into a small bundle.

Lindsay paused in her work, staring at the saddle before her, and said, "Alex, about last night . . ."

"It was cold." He wasn't up for this discussion, so he headed it off. His attention focused on the parachute in his hands.

She looked over at him, relieved. "Yes. It was cold." She continued with her work and they both maintained silence.

Once the camp was struck and they were ready, Alex mounted his horse with Lindsay behind and they went to join the other knights in a line forming along the trampled midway of last night's circus town. About fifty knights presented themselves, and the rest of the support folk clustered loosely behind them. A second line of younger men at arms also stood to the rear, probably all squires. Standing abreast the knights waited, and Alex figured he knew why.

"Inspection," he muttered. Bruce, gold-trimmed black surcoat lifted by the breeze and motion of his horse, came down the line with his personal retinue to review the troops, nodding to some and assessing others. When the earl reached Alex, he stopped before his newest knight and smiled.

"Sir Alasdair!"

Alex glanced to his right, but Lindsay quickly whispered, "That's you." Caught flat-footed, he responded by reflex, raised his chin, and lifted his hand in salute. Bruce then touched his gauntleted hand to his helmet in return, and didn't seem to think it strange.

The Earl of Carrick said, a bit loudly for a personal conversation, "Ye trewe kneegt, ye fowgt and slough manly as a kneegt."

Alex recognized 'kneegt,' guessed at 'fowgt,' and thought he knew what was being said. Lindsay confirmed it. "He's telling everyone in earshot that you fought well yesterday."

There was no reply to that except a nod, and that brought a wider smile from Robert. "Alasdair MacNeil, the noble conquerour," he said, as if a gentle jest. There was a chuckle from the retinue, then Robert moved on, having alerted the larger company of knights to the status of their newest member.

Alex turned to Lindsay and whispered, "Alasdair?"

"Gaelic form of Alexander. He was honoring your Celtic heritage as a MacNeil."

"Ah. Bastard though I am."

She chuckled. "I'm certain he doesn't care the least which side of the blanket you were born on. So long as you fight 'manly as a knight' and stay loyal to him and his cause."

Having reached the end of the line, Bruce continued on and the line turned to follow. The company of knights with their squires, scant baggage, and camp followers began to move out.

"Why does Robert give a damn about honoring Celts? Aren't all the ruling class guys Normans? I thought they all looked down on anyone who wasn't Norman."

She made a humming sound as she sifted through her memory for the answer, then she said, "To the best of my recollection, most of Bruce's early supporters were Highlanders. Also, his mother was a Gael, and his wife was . . . *is* Irish."

Alex watched Bruce at the front of the line. "Huh. I bet that hasn't done him any good getting along in England."

"Oh, no, he was very close to Edward I. Almost like a son. He did all right, I think."

"If he had done all right in England he wouldn't be here, trying to boot the English out of Scotland. Something must have gone FUBAR for him at one point or another."

Lindsay said only "Hmm," and left it at that.

The column moved on, headed north, according to the small compass in Alex's survival vest.

For several days they proceeded over rolling countryside covered with woodland interspersed with wide pastures. Each night they encamped to eat and sleep, then each morning

Lindsay rolled the parachutes into a tight wad and tied them inside the survival vest. She then slung the bundle over her shoulder by remnant shroud lines, and the helmets were draped across the horse's withers as before. Thus with all their worldly goods packed, they hit the trail again. There were no more weeping outbursts from Lindsay, and she seemed to come to terms with what had happened. Over the days as the shock wore off, they were able to speak of their situation on the long trail north, carefully, poking around for sore emotional spots.

The day was waning, and they sat by the fire after having eaten. Alex picked up a bit of kindling wood and shaved a sliver from it to use for a toothpick as he'd seen others in the camp do. He found it worked pretty well if he chewed the end first to make it more like a brush. Then he shaved off another and offered it to Lindsay.

"What do you figure did this?" asked Alex.

She took the toothpick and shrugged. "Act of God . . . magnetic atmospheric disturbance . . . secret scientific experiment gone horribly wrong . . . are you certain that plane of yours was an ordinary jet?"

"It's never taken me back to the past before."

There was no chuckle. "I've not the slightest notion what could have done this." She sighed and turned to look back the way they'd come. "Unfortunately, I think we might be losing our best chance at getting home again by leaving the area where it happened. Whatever that thing was we saw, it was back there. We're not going to find out anything elsewhere."

Alex looked behind them, and that strange, creepy feeling of being watched stole over him again. It made him not want to look to the rear, like when he was a little kid and had averted his eyes from the closet at night in the darkness so he wouldn't see the monster living there. He faced forward and said, "You're probably right. But we can't go back just yet."

"We can't?"

"What do you figure would happen if I turned this horse around and took off?"

Lindsay's sigh was desolate, and Alex could feel the chill of it brush across his soul. "Robert would send men after us and they would kill us for traitors."

"And they would be right. I pledged my allegiance to this guy, and I've got to keep my word. At least until the army stops moving and I have a chance to get my bearings. Then once I've lived up to my obligation—"

"You don't even know exactly what that obligation is."

"Do you?"

"No. Not really. I think there might be a certain time frame involved, but I don't know how long it would be."

"Then I'll just have to either serve or make an arrangement to get out of it."

Alex sighed as unwanted realization crept in. "Besides, there's a good chance we'll never learn what happened. If we're stuck here for the rest of whatever, we'll be better off with Bruce and his army on our side than to be wandering the countryside by ourselves."

"Point well taken." Even without being able to see her face, he could hear the resignation in her voice.

The next several days were hard travel while the ground seemed to rise before them, and mountains reared up on the horizons. The company camped in a wide valley and Alex noted there were people still joining them. The company had grown by at least five, maybe ten, knights and their retinue. Some of them had made themselves known to the new MacNeil knight, boasting of their past exploits and fighting prowess, and all seemed excited about the coming conflict with England.

Sitting before the cook fire, watching a piece of mutton drip grease into it, Alex said to Lindsay, "You know, we've been hanging out together almost constantly for over a week, and I know almost nothing about you."

She looked over at him, but said nothing.

He shifted his seat to lean toward her and pressed. "You know all about me because you grilled me the day before we got here."

Her face revealed nothing, and she gazed at him with bland eyes. "I only know the things you wanted printed in the paper. Which, even assuming they were all true, still told me very little."

"Well, I suppose. But you at least know where I went to school."

With a shrug, she replied, "University of Liverpool."

That made him smile and he leaned back against the

blanket-covered saddle again. "That's a start. How about your name? If Pawlowski is Polish, how did you end up so very British? Grandfather fleeing the Nazis?"

Her shoulders tightened in a shrug, and didn't entirely release as she poked at the fire with a stick. "Great-grandfather fleeing the Bolsheviks. He was from a family of ethnic Poles living in Moscow, and far too well-off and not nearly Russian enough to expect to survive the revolution. So he came to London. Apparently he saw himself as not the least bit Russian, and was some generations removed from Poland, so not much that is Russian or Polish has come down in the family."

"You don't look very Polish."

Now she smiled, carefully and without looking at him. "I look like my maternal grandmother, who was a granddaughter of a duke." A slight change in the timbre of her voice clued him as to how proud she was of this fact. But she didn't elaborate on it, and he assumed she thought it would bore him. And she was right, so he didn't ask which duke, information that would have meant nothing to him if she'd told him.

"So, you're practically royalty."

She chuckled and colored, finally glancing up at him. "Hardly. Any more, it's a struggle to even stay employed. I'm petrified we'll get home and find my job is gone."

Sore spot. The more time Alex spent not flying, the harder it would be to requalify once he returned. As terrified as she was of losing her job, he headed the subject back in a more acceptable direction.

"Did you always want to be a journalist when you grew up?"

Another hint of a smile played at her mouth, and he hoped it would grow. "No. When I was very small I wanted to be a high fashion model."

"No kidding?" The way she said it suggested the idea was embarrassing, but he was pleased to learn this about her. Even more, it pleased him to see she would confide to him something that sensitive. "I bet you could have made it. How come you didn't?" He could imagine her posing. Particularly for a lingerie catalogue, and the image warmed him.

She shrugged and shook her head. "I was a child when I thought that. And not nearly well enough connected socially for modeling. Never built for it, really, even when I grew older."

"Are you kidding? You're built like a brick . . . outhouse."

Her smile came in full, and she laughed. "Outhouse? Indeed? That's lovely to hear. And probably more accurate than you think, for I'm very strong. I'm simply not thin enough for modeling. Not frail enough."

Alex waved away the thought. "Eh. Who wants a girl who's skin and bones?" He hefted a hand as if weighing something. "I like a little . . ." His voice failed him as he realized what he was saying and who he was saying it to, and quickly he rigged in his hand and stuffed it into a pocket. "So," he said, and cleared his throat, "knowing you couldn't get by on your looks, you decided to use your brains and write."

"Yes, and I'm good at it."

"I'm sure you are."

Her eyes flashed warning, glittering in the firelight. "Don't patronize me."

He held up his palms. "I'm not. Sheesh. Try to compliment someone." He took his dagger to poke at the meat, hoping it might be done so they could eat, but it still bled red. Too red, even for him.

She went quiet, and talk stopped for some minutes, until Alex broke the silence. "Hey, how come we haven't seen any kilts or whiskey?" He looked around the camp as if hoping to see some.

"Not invented yet."

That truly surprised him. "No whiskey? Dang. That's seriously disappointing." As it sunk in, the disappointment grew. *No whiskey?*

"No ale yet, either."

Alex made a noise of disgust. "What do they drink around here, then? Just water and wine? I guess it's a good thing I like the wine, then."

"There's mead, I suppose. Honey wine. You'll like that—it's sweet. Whiskey won't be along for a few more centuries, and even then they won't start aging it until sometime in the nineteenth century."

"Huh. No whiskey, no kilts, no ale, and the bagpipes sound like clarinets. These guys aren't all that Scottish, if you ask me."

She shrugged. "Things change. Just because a tradition

only goes back a couple hundred years doesn't mean it's not a tradition."

A sly smile curled his mouth. "You mean, like the American Constitution?"

Her mouth opened for a quick response, but then she closed it and made a sheepish smile. "Touché."

He grinned and glanced around. "Do you know where we are today?"

She sighed and looked around as well, particularly at the mountains to the south. "Hard to say. What with avoiding towns and such, I haven't been able to catch any place names along the way. We're at least approaching the Highland line, though I can't be certain whether we've gone that far north yet."

Sir John Kirkpatrick passed near, and Alex called out to him in his best approximation of the archaic English he was slowly piecing together. "You! John! What place is this?" It was far easier to understand people speaking than to pull off a sentence of speech on his own, and he hoped John understood.

Kirkpatrick changed course and wandered over, apparently not in a hurry to get where he was going if there was fellowship to be had here with Alex and his squire. When he spoke, Alex understood about half of it, but picked up, "Tomorrow we circle Perth."

Alex chuckled. "A wide berth to Perth, eh?"

John gave him only a blank look, and continued, something about a place called "Moot Hill." Lindsay's Middle English was improving by leaps as she brushed up on what she'd learned in school, so she translated that they were going to a place in Scone called that. John grinned, a teasing look on his face, and Lindsay also translated the rest. "Surely, Alasdair, you knew that. All Scottish kings are crowned at Scone. If only the stone hadn't been stolen by Longshanks; wouldn't that be something to see then?"

Alex nodded as if he gave a damn whether the king sat on a rock during his coronation, and as if he'd known about the planned event. "Aye. A shame."

John sat with them, lounging by the fire as comfortably as in someone's home. Alex had come to know him somewhat during their trip, for he was outgoing and talkative, always ready to gossip. Alex knew enough about the world to keep his own counsel, but welcomed whatever friendship might be offered as well as whatever information might be had about the other knights. And any chance to learn the language was a big bonus, for even though he and Lindsay spoke to each other in Middle English for practice, they both learned when speaking to one of the locals.

Through John, and then Lindsay, Alex had learned that the young knight, James, who seemed always in Robert's company, was James Douglas, whose father had died in the Tower of London and who had been disinherited of his father's property by King Edward. Those Scottish lands were now in the possession of a man named Clifford, who was loyal to the English king. The consensus among the lesser knights was that James was the one man in Scotland Bruce could trust above all others, for the young man had no possible fortune with Edward.

As for Robert Bruce himself, the man appeared to be a strong enough leader. Alex found himself drawn to follow, and even found himself admiring the man's decisiveness and personal charisma. It made him think the army Bruce was gathering would hold together firmly, and Alex knew there was a certain safety in a cohesive unit where the men had faith in their commander. The more he learned about their leader, the better he felt about having pledged himself.

He gestured to the wine skin hung on the tree behind John, who gladly accepted the offer and took a long draught from it. Then he announced, and Lindsay's attention perked as she translated. "I may have a horse for your squire."

"How much for it?" Alex wanted Lindsay to have her own horse, but not enough to go broke for it. He had no idea when or if he would receive anything more for his service in this venture than the silver and jewels he'd lifted from the dead guy. Having fled Edward's court, Bruce and his followers were on the run from the English king, and Robert's toehold in Scotland was tiny, new, and untried. There was no telling what the immediate future held for any of them.

"Naught. I'll give him to you for nothing."

Alex shook his head and reached into his decidedly gamy flight suit to scratch a maddening itch inside his even more disgusting skivvies. He said to John, "No. I'll pay. I have a sapphire for it."

Lindsay frowned, but Alex insisted she tell John.

John's eyes narrowed. "Unwilling to be in my debt?"

"Unwilling to be beholden to any man, save my liege." He stood. "Show him to me. If he's worth having, the stone is yours for a fair trade. If not, I'll as soon not have to feed him."

The other knight rose, and led Alex to his own camp where John's squires maintained several horses for battle and burden, and the knight's weapons as well as his shelter. The beast in question was a type of horse the locals called a "rounsey," smaller than the courser Alex rode. The wealthier knights had one of these for everyday riding, to save the larger, trained horse for battle. But Alex's lack of land made it unlikely he'd have more than one horse for himself and one for Lindsay, for they were expensive to maintain as well as costly to buy.

"As you can see," said John, "he's a fine animal." Even had Alex not understood the words, the meaning came through in John's salesman's voice.

Alex didn't reply, but lifted the upper lip and found the horse tolerably young. Then he went to each leg and lifted the hoof for a look inside. He was no vet, but there didn't seem to be anything obviously amiss here.

"Are you sure you won't take him gratis?"

Alex pulled his purse from its pocket, fished his smallest sapphire from among the silver, and handed it over. "I'm sure."

"Very well. And your squire shall have the peytral as well." Lindsay pointed to the huge, quilted drape as she translated.

Alex's eyes narrowed at the generosity and he was inclined to reject the offer, but the quilted skirt would have been another hit to his purse and was important protection for his investment if there should be a battle. He grunted acceptance.

John held the blue stone to the sky for examination, then slipped it into his own purse. "You're a strange man, Alasdair MacNeil."

More strange than you could ever imagine. Alex smiled and took the horse's reins to lead it back to his own tent. That itch in his crotch was back, and he poked at his flight suit to relieve it. He muttered to Lindsay, "Dang, I wish they had showers here."

Or even a lake that wasn't frosty around the edges. But it was March, and bathing wasn't a good idea in this cold. Washing his clothes wouldn't happen until it was warm enough for them to not freeze before they dried, and the best he could do was hang his shorts out to air for a while every couple of days.

Halfway back to the tent an angry argument rose behind them, and they turned to see what was going on. John was being accosted by his cousin Roger, who shouted at him without regard to who might be listening. The shouting was about a woman John had bedded the night before, who Alex gathered was an injudicious choice for the lower-ranking knight, for she'd been Roger's mistress.

John spoke calmly, attempting to smooth his cousin's ire, but was slapped in the face for it. Anger flared, and John raised his fists, but still didn't swing at his higher-ranking cousin. He backed off, and Roger followed, shouting his intention to kill any man who would dare to encroach on his woman. Never mind that the elder Kirkpatrick was married to someone else, the mistress was also his territory. That amused Alex, and he found rising in himself a perverse urge to test the mistress himself just to mess with Roger, who seemed entirely too arrogant about her. But he shrugged off the idea as a pointless risk, and watched the fight progress.

Except it wasn't much of a fight as Alex would call it. Roger slapped John a few more times while the younger knight continued to reel away with conciliatory raised palms, bleeding from his nose now. Roger came on, then called to a young man standing nearby to toss him a mace. The weapon was handed over, and Roger went after John with it.

With a short cry, John raised his arm to defend himself. Alex heard the bone crack under the iron head of the mace, and John hunched over his injured arm as he backed in a circle. He talked fast now, begging to be let alone. Roger came on, mace raised and threatening to kill his cousin. Appalled, Alex watched Roger land another blow on John's shoulder.

"Do something, Alex."

"I can't."

"Roger is going to kill him."

"No, he won't." Nobody else came to John's aid, either, and Alex knew why he himself was powerless to intervene. Roger was John's cousin and his superior. This was between them, and anyone butting in would be subject to merciless retaliation from not only Roger, but anyone loyal to him. That much Alex had learned in school yards in his childhood. Many different school yards. He could only watch and hope Roger really didn't intend to kill his cousin.

Relief washed over him as the elder Kirkpatrick finally threw down the mace and walked away, stiff with rage. John sank to the ground and knelt there, dabbing blood from his nose as he watched his commander withdraw, and moved only when he was certain the action wouldn't draw another attack.

Before John could look around to see who had been watching, Alex and Lindsay moved along with their new horse.

The next day the company of Bruce's men, still no more than sixty knights, followed by the lesser folk, approached the abbey at Seone. As nearly everything Robert did, the event went smoothly, exactly according to his intent. Alex and Lindsay watched from their horses as the brown-robed abbots came from their crumbling abbey and the entire contingent trooped to the top of a nearby hill. It wasn't more than a flat-topped mound, covered in grasses and low, spongy heather of dark green, nearly black, and Alex wondered why this spot was such a big deal. But as he watched, several of the men attending to the Earl of Carrick drew small pouches from their clothing and scattered the contents on the ground. It was done with great solemnity, and it was plain this was a long-held tradition, whatever it was.

Then, barely having time to find a spot to hobble their horses, Alex and Lindsay hurried to the rear of the onlookers to see. He took Lindsay's hand in his in order to not lose her in the milling crowd at the foot of the little hill, and she held his tight in return. Her face was flushed with excitement, and he began to feel it himself.

A bagpipe among the brown robes played a single note, quiet but growing, a sustained sound that seemed to reach out to the crowd and bring it together. Then a low chant rose from the monks, voices riding the single note like an acrobat on a wire, soaring above it then swinging below it, and the pipes ever present and never changing that single note. The gathered Scots listened in silence, tension gathering for what was to come.

Despite his ambivalence about the Scottish throne—or any

throne—Alex knew the event was important history and its
gravity not lost on him. Over the past week he'd learned the
kingdom had been up for grabs, more or less, for decades.
Lindsay had informed him that even though it would take
Robert the rest of his life to reclaim the entire country from the
various Edwards of England, this ceremony today was to bring
a measure of stability to the Scottish succession that would last
for centuries. Alex found that impressive, and had to admit to
himself that Lindsay had a point about the long history of her
country.

Now came Robert Bruce from the abbey, dressed in a dark
red robe beautifully trimmed in white fur and embroidered in
gold thread. Even wearing the vestment of coronation, the Earl
of Carrick had not taken the time to remove his chain mail, and
the jingling beneath the robe as he walked to the center of the
mound was a dark, dull reminder that Robert was beginning the
fight of his life. The music swelled, voices raised to the sky, and
the crowd tensed as he made his way toward the men who waited
to bestow his crown. With no coronation stone on which to sit,
he knelt before them. With great solemnity, they placed on his
head a circlet of gold with points of fleur-de-lis. Then, with the
fanfare of a single trumpet, a banner of scarlet lion rampant on
a background of gold-yellow was planted behind the new king.

Alex expected the crowd to burst forth in applause, but there
was only a collective sigh and murmur. For himself, something
shifted inside his chest, and his gut tightened for a moment. The
feeling took him by surprise. He'd never thought much about
his Scottish heritage; his identity had always been American
and his loyalty pledged to a red, white, and blue flag. But today
there was a stirring in his core that baffled him. The sight of this
man taking on the job of freeing Scots from English interfer-
ence moved him in an odd, primal way. He had to look away for
a moment.

He turned straight into the face of a man wearing a hooded
cloak, the one he'd spotted a week ago, close enough to smell his
breath. Deep within the shadow of that hood, two eyes glowed.
Not reflection of light, but they actually glowed on their own.
Like two red coals that lit the inside of the hood.

It was the face Alex had seen in the vortex just before coming to this time.

CHAPTER 4

"Hey!"

The figure ducked into the crowd. Alex tugged on Lindsay's hand. "Come." They went after the hooded cloak as it slipped among the gathered people. Lindsay shifted the bundle of belongings slung over her shoulder and followed. But the crowd shifted around them and hid the fleeing man, so when Alex saw him next he was headed for a stand of trees in the direction of the river. The cloak fluttered as he hurried, and the man's feet appeared to be bare. But he skipped over cold, rough, rocky ground as if wearing boots.

"What's going on?" Lindsay trotted beside him.

"I don't know. I've got to find out something." It was a thin thread of possibility, but he now burned to find out who this guy was.

They plunged into the woods, close enough to keep sight of the quickly moving cloak but not close enough to catch his attention. Or maybe they did have his attention and he was only making certain they kept up without getting closer. Alex pressed onward, through dense bracken and prickly gorse. Finally they burst out on a glade by the river and found a small knoll. Perfectly symmetrical and conical, it was the strangest land formation Alex had ever seen outside of the Mojave

Desert. A stand of birch trees grew at the top, the winter-leafless trunks looking like white hair on a pointed mole. The hooded man was nowhere to be seen.

Lindsay, breathless from the run, said, "What on God's earth are you trying to do? I'm a pincushion from this gorse!" She examined a spot on her hand, in search of blood or a small thorn.

"There was a man in the crowd. I thought I recognized his face."

"There were a lot of men in that crowd you should recognize; you've been traveling with them for a week."

"No. I saw his face just before the plane went down."

Dry humor crept into Lindsay's voice. "We're running after God?"

Alex peered at her, annoyed, but a lift of the corner of her mouth told him she was joking. "Very funny. That guy is around here somewhere. I want to ask him some questions."

"All right, then, where is he?"

They went toward the knoll, skirting the foot of it. The hooded man didn't seem to be in the glade, and Alex searched for signs he may have gone back into the forest. But then Lindsay squeezed his hand and urged him to stop. He turned, and found her staring up at the knoll.

"Look."

It was a door, flat against the side of the hill about halfway up. Framed by mortared stones, it was made of gnarled, knotted wood bound and studded with iron. It had a heavy, wrought iron latch. A thin path switched back and forth up the steep slope between patches of heather.

Alex didn't hesitate, but went to climb the little hill. Lindsay hung back. "What are you doing?"

"I'm going to see if he's in there."

She made an impatient, clucking noise. "You're such an American. Just barge right in and look around."

"You have a better idea?"

"We could mind our own business and return to the coronation. We're probably missing the best part. There may be food."

He glanced back the way they'd come, for she had a point. The first thing he'd learned in this place was that missing an opportunity to eat—particularly for free—was always a bad idea.

But he turned back to her and said, "I thought you wanted to get home."

A shadow crossed her eyes, and he saw her game face slip. She lowered her lids for a moment, then looked at him again. "I do."

"Well, right now this is what passes for a lead in finding out what happened. We've had nothing better so far. I want to go up there and see what I can find."

She sighed and relented, then followed him up the slope.

The door was small, only about chest high to Alex. "Short people."

"Doors are always small. It causes intruders to bend over when they enter a house, so the unwelcome become vulnerable to beheading."

Alex nodded. That made sense. He knocked on the door, and it eased open on well-oiled hinges. He whispered, "Welcome to my parlor, said the spider to the fly." Deep within was a faint glow of fire, flickering against the sides of the entrance. He looked over at Lindsay, who was peering inside as if trying to see what was on the other side of the door without actually opening it. Alex gave it a shove, and it opened wide.

Through the opening they could see a short tunnel. Firelight flickered on its walls, from a chamber ahead. Quickly, before he could talk himself into prudence, Alex stepped inside with Lindsay's hand in his. She resisted, but followed him anyway.

The chamber was large. Much larger than Alex could have expected, from the size of the knoll that enclosed it. A lively fire danced on the hearth in the middle, its smoke rising to the ceiling and disappearing in a maze of large, gnarled, exposed tree roots above. Around the fire were cushions, silken mattresses for lounging and sleeping, and by the fireside were wooden platters piled with food. Fruits and vegetables, many of them not known to Europe in this century. Steaming corn on the cob and baked potatoes lay alongside the usual cabbages and lentils, bananas and mangos beside oranges and apples. An entire lamb was spitted over the fire, and appeared ready to be eaten. "We're expected."

"Or we're interrupting."

"That's a lot of untouched food." Alex picked his way across the floor between the pillows. "You think there were people here a minute ago, who heard us coming and just walked away from it?"

"Alex, let's get out of here."

"Wait." He reached down to one of the platters, where a tumble of brown chunks was piled. He picked up one of them, and found a word stamped on the side. "Hershey."

Lindsay came to look. "Really?"

He handed her the chocolate, then bent to take another and popped it into his mouth. "It's real, too. Someone here has tapped into our world." The chocolate was heaven on his tongue, and his eyelids drooped with pleasure.

As Lindsay savored hers and bent to take another, Alex explored the dim corners of the chamber. There was a corridor, and he gestured to her to come. The tunnel was dark and winding, nearly a corkscrew as it wended its way between tree roots and lumps of granite. There were whispered voices and giggling up ahead, almost musical, and tantalizing for its art, so he pressed onward quickly. But the voices stayed just ahead and out of reach, no matter what pace he kept or which way he turned. Shadows dashed away from them, and others crept up from behind to draw attention. A shift in direction only caused a shift in the traffic flow of the owners of those voices. Alex and Lindsay came to another chamber, this one empty. But as they crossed it, he caught a glimpse of the hooded man from the corner of his eye.

"You!" Alex turned, but the figure was gone. Perhaps he had never been there. Alex poked around the chamber and discovered another tunnel, and he followed it. The guy must have gone this way.

But no, it was another empty chamber. Nothing but a concave dirt floor and walls formed by thick tree roots that wound in and out and around like Celtic knots. There didn't seem to be another exit from this room.

Alex stopped in the middle of the floor, an area darkened by what appeared to be the ashes of an old fire. He said to the walls—to the roots and trees that made up those walls, "Hey! You! Quit hiding, I know you're in here!"

Silence.

Lindsay said, "Alex, how come we can see in here where there's no fire?"

He looked around. Good question. It was as if light were coming from nowhere. From the air. Or as if they were able to perceive without actually seeing. He waited, and when there was still no reply he pulled out the tin of matches from a pocket of his flight suit and said, "How about I set fire to this place? Lots of wood here." He wondered what light might do for their perception, and whether any of this was real.

The room burst into color, a high fire roaring in an enormous stone hearth opposite where Alex and Lindsay stood. A figure wearing a black cape trimmed in white fur lounged on a wide chair before that fire, elbows rested on the high arms of it. The face was dark with rage. His tunic was blood red, and he held a long, narrow, silver dagger in one hand gloved in fine calfskin. His tall boots were as fine, and splayed thighs were covered in black woolen tights. Almond-shaped eyes. Long, straight nose. Thin lips. Short, well-trimmed beard that sharpened his chin to a point. Also, if Alex wasn't seeing things, tips of pointed ears poking from shaggy, dark hair. Elfin, or something. A really tall elf. "I would strike you dead where you stand." The voice was smooth. Regal.

Lindsay's grip on Alex's hand became like iron, and he squeezed hers to give her reassurance. He was glad this guy was speaking modern English, with a broad, Scottish accent, for Alex had begun to tire of deciphering the language around here. "Okay, now we're getting somewhere. Who are you? You're a gremlin, right?"

Lindsay murmured, "Gremlin?"

"Yeah. Gremlins are little guys with goggles who damage fighter planes so they crash. They've been around since the Battle of Britain in World War Two." His eyes narrowed at her. "You're English; how come you don't know that?"

Her voice lowered so it was barely audible, as if he were embarrassing her. "Alex, this is 1306."

But he ignored her and addressed the elfin fellow. "So, where are your goggles, gremlin? Where's your drill? You're the guy who trashed my plane and brought us here to the past. I mean, I figure you're the one who did it. What did you do it for? What's the deal?"

"No deal. You're to die." The elf, or gremlin, or whatever he was, sounded tired as well as angry. It made for an implacability that gave Alex the creeps. He now knew for a certainty he was talking to an enemy.

"Die?" Lindsay's grip tightened even more, and she began pulling him away. But he stood his ground and swallowed his apprehension. "Why? What did we do to piss you off?"

"It was a costly spell." The voice trembled with barely controlled rage, and he leaned forward on his throne. "Too much power at stake to be thwarted by a single human. Too high above the earth. You had no business there. No right. *No place.*"

"I was flying my friend home."

Hatred seethed in the voice until it choked him. "*You should not have been there.* You were clumsy. Thoughtless. Humans are a scourge on the earth, just as the Tuatha Dé Danann, and always will be. Despicable creatures. You should all die. I should destroy you all."

"Then why haven't you done it yet?"

More silence, and Alex's heart thudded in his chest as he wondered whether the spell he'd interrupted had been to that very end. Finally he said, "Okay, listen man, how about you send us home, then do whatever it is you're going to do?"

"It was a costly spell." Each word carried a weight of trembling horror. Alex would swear the guy was about to cry.

He waited for Red Eyes to elaborate, but an explanation never came. Alex prompted him. "Yeah. It was costly."

"I will deal with you in my own time, for I rule it. Live with your terror. Steep in it. Meanwhile, leave my sight. You sicken me." Then, at a gesture from the cloaked figure, a hole blew through the wall opposite and a mighty wind from nowhere took Alex and Lindsay tumbling through it. Sunshine blinded them as they rolled and slid downhill.

They slowed to a stop on the rocky ground at the foot of the knoll, and Alex groaned as he lay still to assess the damage. No broken bones, and that was a relief, but he figured he was going to turn up black and blue if he ever saw his skin again soon. He reached for Lindsay. "You all right?"

She rose to her knees and looked around for the parachute bundle, which had rolled away. "Yeah." She located it a few yards off, and climbed to her feet to get it.

"What bug got up that guy's butt?" Alex sat up and looked back up the little hill. "The door is gone."

"Not very surprising. It was a wall he tossed us through. The door is probably on the other side."

But Alex knew they'd walked much farther underground than the other side of the knoll, and was puzzled how they'd ended up still at the foot of it. He climbed to his feet and looked around, and that was when he noticed the weight of his purse was gone. He slapped the pocket in alarm, dismayed to feel only the empty leather pouch inside. "Crap! It's gone!"

"What's gone?"

Fingers fumbling, he drew the purse from his pocket and opened it to find every penny, half-penny and farthing, every one of the jewels, was gone. "Our money. He took it." Alex turned and hurried up the side of the knoll in search of a way back in. But there was no sign of where they'd come out. "Sonofabitch."

"Are you sure you didn't just drop it?"

Alex showed her the purse and turned it upside down to demonstrate its emptiness. "He took the money, left the bag, and I didn't feel a thing."

Lindsay looked as dismayed as he felt. Then he looked around, and his stomach dropped as he noticed the local land-scape had changed.

Lindsay continued. "They've not just fallen out of your pocket?" Her voice drifted off as she also noticed the rolling hills around them. No forest, and the river seemed to have sunk into its banks.

Alex stared. "Where are we?"

Lindsay was turning, trying hard to get her bearings. "I don't know. This is definitely not Scone. Or anywhere near it, by that muir up there." She gestured to a flat-topped hill not far away. They moved away from the knoll, toward the river.

"It's not March anymore, either." The weather was warm, and more sunny than he'd seen in Scotland since the day they'd flown over it. When they entered the knoll, the weather had been over-cast and misty. Now there were mountains close in, where there had been none before, and the river was blue and ran freely, with no frost clinging to the sides. Alex began to sweat inside his chain mail and was glad to feel his bones warm, but it bugged him the weather had changed so drastically and so quickly. Last time that happened, they'd been displaced seven centuries.

"Think we're back in the twenty-first century?"

Lindsay, shielding her eyes from the sun with her hand, said, "No. I recognize this place. And you should, too. We passed through here about three days ago." She pointed, and Alex saw a cathedral perched above the river, surrounded by a cluster of thatched houses. He remembered this place, for it was the closest thing to a town he'd been to since landing. Not that it was actually a town. More like a loose collection of houses near a church.

"Dunblane," he said.

"And that," she pointed to the muir, "would therefore be Sheriffmuir. Three days' ride from where we were. There's no chance we could have walked it underground. We were only in that knoll for half an hour."

"Well, let's head on into town and see what ol' Murphy's got in store for us today." They began to walk toward the cathedral, but hadn't gone far when they turned at the sound of snorting horses behind. It was a large contingent of knights, commandeering the narrow track and raising dust for what seemed like a mile.

Lindsay took Alex's hand and was pulling him toward a copse of trees, but Alex held her back. "Look. It's Kirkpatrick." The banner of Roger Kirkpatrick flapped and snapped above the riders, and Alex recognized John's helm, riding in front with Roger. Alex's heart lightened at thought of seeing a familiar face, for it meant they couldn't have come too far from where they'd been. With a wide smile he trotted toward the column and held up his right hand in greeting, and John returned the salute, but with a gawking look of surprise and wonder. When Sir Roger recognized Alex, his expression darkened under his iron helmet and he gave the order for the column to halt. John pulled up his mount next to his cousin.

"MacNeil! You astonish me by this brazenness!" Sir Roger addressed Lindsay. "Squire, tell your master to explain your absence!" Roger's voice was ugly. Angry. John's face was impassive, but he didn't seem any more cheered at seeing Alex than Roger was.

Alex stood, speechless, with no clue what to say, until it dawned on him that these men had also somehow come all this way since the coronation half an hour ago. Something else weird had happened, and Alex began to wonder just how much time had passed since he'd last seen these guys. At the silence, Kirkpatrick drew his sword and ordered his men to take Alex and Lindsay prisoner. Four knights dismounted, and John also drew his sword. Alex backed off, not eager to let them have him but not yet sure enough of his moral ground to fight. When they grabbed him by the arms he surrendered, hoping to talk things out. Kirkpatrick's men took Alex's sword and dagger from his belt.

"Ailig," said John, "I hope you haven't spent these seven years past in England."

Seven years. "John, friend, what is wrong?"

"Where were you?"

Two of Kirkpatrick's men yanked Alex's arms behind his back. Pain shot through his shoulders. The others did the same to Lindsay, and she snorted rather than cry out. They were both tied fast, hands and feet, and the rough, hempen rope cut into their wrists. Casting about for a reply—any reply—Alex blurted the first thing that came clear in his mind, and he could only hope the story wasn't riddled with holes.

It was a struggle to make his voice casual, as if this were an easily cleared misunderstanding. He didn't bother with trying to speak directly, and let Lindsay translate modern English for him. "We sailed for the Continent. Had to. There was word my foster father had died, and my squire needed to return to claim his birthright. A stepmother gave him some trouble, and tried to have him murdered. It was an ugly business, and we're not entirely certain she isn't responsible for her husband's demise. And there were two sisters on whom to settle dowries, so complications kept us away." *For seven years.* Alex knew he needed to pad the story, and sighed as he continued. "On our return we were waylaid. Stripped of our horses and funds. It's only by perseverance and devotion to duty we made it back at all."

A horse was brought, and Alex and Lindsay were both lifted and heaved across its back like baggage.

"John, you've got to listen to me!"

John said nothing, and looked away as they proceeded into Dunblane. Secured to the horse's back, swaying with the gait, Alex watched the ground below go slowly past. He whispered to Lindsay in modern English, "You figure that guy in the knoll knew where he was sending us?"

"Haven't a clue."

"Reveal yourself."

"No."

"They won't kill you if they know you're a woman."

"You don't know that."

"I'll talk them out of it."

"Yes, we've seen your powers of persuasion. Besides, I'd rather die like a man than live as they would have me."

Helplessness overwhelmed him. Alex wanted to smack her sideways for being so stupid. He fell silent and pressed his face against the horse's salty-smelling flank.

The town lay on the slope between the muir and the river, its muddy street more like a hole around which stood a few earthen huts. A single stone building clung to the slope above the cathedral, and that was where Kirkpatrick took Alex and Lindsay. Knights, squires, and foot soldiers filled the area, staking out space to camp among the surrounding trees and between the thatched houses. It appeared an entire army was descending on the little village. Alex and Lindsay were hauled from the horses and their feet freed before they were manhandled up the hill and shoved through the door of the stone house. Alex was light-headed from riding upside down, and stumbled as he went.

The place was dark as a cave, the ceiling of arched stone, and light from the outside coming only from the door and one small window; it was furnished with a rough-hewn table and two chairs. As many Kirkpatrick men as would fit crowded into the rear of the place to watch. Others watched from the doorway, straining to see over each other. The men holding Alex stood him before the window.

They released his wrists, but the relief to his shoulders was short-lived. One of the men yanked Alex's mail shirt from him, and before he could stand upright again another ripped his flight suit down the front and off his back, then tore off the black T-shirt he wore beneath, exposing him entirely to the waist. Then each wrist was held by two strong men. The four pulled on his shoulders with all their weight, and he wondered whether they meant to dislocate the joints, or it would be an accident when it happened. In resisting them it was all he could do to keep his arms attached to his body. Sir Roger stepped before him, swinging a heavy chain from one fist, a twisted look of rage on his face. Fingers of terror skittered over Alex's body.

"All right, then, MacNeil, tell us where you've been." Lindsay didn't need to translate.

"I told you."

The chain jingled, then whooshed through the air and made a solid blow to Alex's side. His knees buckled and he cried out in astonished pain, then struggled to get his feet back under him so his shoulders wouldn't pull apart when the four men yanked on them again. A fiery throbbing licked across his belly, and the need to protect it with his arms was maddening. He yanked at the men who held him, but only succeeded in straining his own shoulders even more. The men hauled back against him until he stopped struggling. Ragged breaths snorted through his nose to contain the pain.

Roger said, "You told me naught."

Alex gasped to find his voice, then fixed his gaze on Kirkpatrick and croaked, "It's the truth. We were forced to leave. That's the plain truth."

Another blow across his belly. Alex grunted, and now there was blood trickling down his side into his flight suit. His mind scrambled for another story, or an augmentation of the one he'd told, which might make this stop, but nothing came. His knees trembled to keep him upright.

"You left your horses, but you left no word."

Lindsay spoke up on her own, her arms wrenched behind her back and her voice betraying the pain and fear. "In the excitement of the coronation we went unnoticed. I mean, the king is more important than a landless knight and his squire, yes? We couldn't take the horses. We sailed off down the Tay, on a boat too small for them."

"You sailed from *Perth*?" The ominous edge to his voice made it plain a "yes" answer would be a bad idea. One thing Alex had noted about knights in this century was that they were not very subtle. Easy to read. Besides, Alex knew they'd circled Perth the day before because it was English-occupied.

Alex of course replied, breath coming hard, "No. We were never in Perth."

"I don't believe you. I think you told the English—"

A voice boomed from outside. "What in the name of all that

is unholy is going on here?" The onlookers near the door shifted to accommodate the newcomer, who shoved his way in when the men didn't move fast enough. It wasn't the king's voice, and Alex was pretty sure it wasn't anyone he knew in this century. The accent was even weirder—broader and more rolling—than the ones he'd heard, but oddly more understandable. Less archaic. It sounded . . . Irish. Sort of.

"Hector!" Roger straightened, twirled the chain end in his hand so it jingled and clanked. A spot of blood from it flew and landed on his cheek, but he didn't appear to notice. He said cheerily, "It's good you've caught up with us. We've discovered your father's by-blow in a plot against the king, and you can come have a look if you like before we kill him."

Lindsay murmured the gist into Alex's ear, but he had understood on his own and panic fluttered in his gut. He struggled for breath. Lindsay's eyes were wide and frightened. They both believed for a dead certainty Kirkpatrick would carry out his intention.

A short, burly man with a dark beard elbowed his way to where Kirkpatrick stood, and peered at Alex held by the four men. "Who, ye say?" The man seemed half undressed, wearing only a loose tunic and a long drape of plaid wool slung over his shoulder, with nothing covering his legs. His feet were shod, but with leather shoes that resembled moccasins, not like the pointed-toed shoes worn by everyone else here. "What by-blow would this be?"

Alex's stomach flopped and his gorge rose. The jig was up. Even Lindsay wouldn't be able to talk their way out of this.

Kirkpatrick said, "The son your father sent to the Continent."

"Which one?" The man called Hector tilted his head as if trying to recognize Alex, but failing.

"My name is Alexander. MacNeil."

Hector laughed. "Alexander? One I've not heard of!" He turned to Kirkpatrick and Lindsay continued to murmur translation as he said, "Well, a pox on you, Roger! If he's a MacNeil, then he's my business! He's not the responsibility of a Lowlander such as yourself. Give him over!"

"I tell you he's the traitor who brought on the attack at Methven, seven years ago." Hector gave Alex another appraising stare. Kirkpatrick continued. "Nearly all was lost that night, for it was hard on that defeat the queen was captured and the king forced into exile."

Robert in exile? Alex threw Lindsay a faint, puzzled frown, and she responded with a shake of her head that said, *Don't worry about it. I'll explain later.*

Hector nearly bellowed, in high dudgeon, "Had he pledged his loyalty to Robert?"

"Aye," said Alex. "And I have never betrayed it." In Middle English he repeated, "I swear I've never betrayed the king!"

That brought silence. Then Hector said, "He swears an oath, Roger. Let him go."

"Easy enough—"

"If he's a MacNeil as you say, and he's my brother in the bargain, then he's of my clan and he's either a man of honor or he's mine to hang so he can be judged by God." He leaned in toward Kirkpatrick and spoke as if talking to an idiot. "Do . . . you . . . understand?" Kirkpatrick was much taller, but by force of personality Hector seemed to dwarf him.

Sir Roger didn't seem to have any reply to that, so he gestured to the four at Alex's arms to let him go. The relief was immense as they released him. He collapsed to kneel on the floor, crossing his arms and holding his aching shoulders so they might not feel as if they were about to fall off. He looked up at Lindsay and told them, "Let him go, too."

She was released from her bonds and came to help keep him upright.

Hector bent toward him to talk straight into his face, too close for comfort, and it took all of Alex's restraint to look him in the eye and not back away. "Alexander MacNeil is your name?" Alex nodded. "Do you know who I am, lad?" Lindsay murmured near his ear in case he missed an important word. Neither of them wanted to risk misunderstanding just then.

"Hector MacNeil?" Then realization struck. "The MacNeil Laird of Barra."

"Indeed I am. I'm also your half-brother. It seems my father when he was alive littered the countryside with bastards, and I must say the ones I've met have been a sorry lot. I've no patience for any of you, and if you give me aught for grief I'll cut your throat myself. Do ye understand?"

Alex nodded, and trusted wholly in his sincerity.

"Good. Now, restore your clothing and hauberk, and bring your squire to my camp. Have you any horses?"

Alex realized the horses he'd had, as well as the helmets that had been tied to the saddles, were now seven years gone, and shook his head, and Hector made a disparaging noise.

"Och. Do as I say, and be quick about it." With that, Hector left the stone hovel. The crowd began to disperse, and Roger and John moved toward the door. For one moment of madness, Alex had an intense desire to snatch his sword from the floor and whack Kirkpatrick across the back of his head with it. Alex's fingers gingerly touched the welts on his belly that raged fiery pain, and his gut clenched in anger.

Left to their own now in the little stone house, Lindsay retrieved the T-shirt from the floor and shook out some of the dirt from it, as Alex stood and pulled the upper part of his flight suit back on, then picked up his mail shirt he now gathered was called a "hauberk." Lindsay murmured over the T-shirt, assessing the damage, "It's torn only along the seams. I can mend this if you've still got that survival kit in one of your pockets."

Alex nodded, and knew she'd have to mend it no matter how badly shredded, for he had nothing else to wear. He climbed to his feet and pulled himself together as best he could with the zipper seam ripped at the front of his flight suit, restored his hauberk, and retrieved his belongings, then left the house with Lindsay.

The cathedral across the way dominated the town, all gothic arches and spires in brown stone, facing the little gray house of torture as if presiding over what went on there. Alex stared across at it and wondered. As he watched, ladders were raised against the cathedral walls. Men climbed them, and they set to work dismantling the roof and shoving huge pieces of metal from it onto the ground below. Someone shouted something about Robert wanting the altar to be spared, and the work proceeded. All organized, all strictly business.

Alex glanced around for the Kirkpatricks, and found them attending to business a few yards down the slope, near the enormous building. Carefully he watched them as he circled around toward a cluster of peat houses standing around the mud hollow at the foot of the rise on which the cathedral stood. There would be a fight, but he would choose his time. His account with Kirkpatrick would be settled when he was ready.

Lindsay asked around among the soldiers milling between the houses and found Sir Hector's camp farther down the slope, by the river. A path wended its way past the hollow and to the bank, where the MacNeil laird was surrounded by a couple hundred men. A few of them were knights, but most of them were foot soldiers, relaxing around cook fires here and there among the trees. Women and boys worked around the camp while men lounged in clusters and talked. They seemed no less boisterous than the privileged cavalry Alex had known under the king, and they all seemed very happy to be there. Snatches of conversation Alex caught were about recent battles and the rewards gained from them, and speculation about prospects to come. The fighting had brought a fair amount of glory and wealth, and everyone sounded as if they anticipated more of both. Alex found himself caught up in the enthusiasm, wondering if he might see some action after all, what with the conflict heating up over the past seven years.

He presented himself to the laird, and his elbow twitched to salute even though the sight before him was as unlike every commanding officer he'd ever had as anything he could imagine.

Sir Hector lounged against a fallen log before his tent, with his plaid cloth draped around him like a cloak, and he more resembled a dining Roman as he reached over to the fire to tear a leg from the game bird roasting there. A wooden plate stacked with small, round loaves of bread sat to the side. "Alasdair," he greeted, and gestured that Alex and Lindsay should sit and partake of the food.

"Sir Alasdair, if you please," Alex corrected as he seated himself and tore a chunk of meat from the bird with his fingers. The heavy eyebrows went up, and the conversation continued through Lindsay. "I was knighted by the king himself last . . . uh, seven years ago. Shortly before the coronation." Also with his fingers, he tore open one of the loaves of bread and stuffed it with the meat. Lindsay followed suit.

"And have you done anything of merit with your knighthood, wandering around as you have been?"

That put Alex at a loss for how to respond, so he took his

time chewing and gingerly pulling his clothing away from his bloodied and drying, injured belly. The pain was subsiding to a dull throb, and the blood-soaked flight suit was sticking to his skin. Finally he sidestepped the question. "I've been in battle." Never mind his weapon had been a jet airplane and not a sword.

"When? Where?"

Alex plundered his brain for a lie, but went with truth instead. "Not recently, but on the Continent when I was younger. In the mountains. The Balkans." *Quite true.* "I was squire to my foster father." *A lie.*

"His name?"

"Pawlowski. Uh . . . Igor Pawlowski."

Lindsay coughed, and it sounded like a disguised laugh.

Alex gestured to her. "My squire is his son, Lindsay."

Hector eyed her, then addressed Alex again. "Lindsay is a Scottish surname. Does his father have ties to Scotland?" Alex and Lindsay both said nothing, then Hector peered at Alex. "I've never heard of this Pawlowski."

Again struggling for words, Alex stammered some on his reply. "I'm told . . . I . . . apparently your father's encounter with my mother was . . . brief. My foster father was her distant cousin."

"And where is your mother now?"

"She died in childbirth."

"While bearing you, I sincerely hope, and not bringing forth yet another brat from a . . . brief encounter."

Alex's cheeks burned at the insult, though he'd brought it on himself. He responded, "Aye. I never knew my mother, any more than I knew my father." He thought of his real mother back home, and was ashamed of his lie. Neither of his parents deserved this. Despair crept in that he might never see them again. But he raised his chin and persisted because he had to. "My only brothers are you and yours. Even my foster father is dead, and aside from my squire I'm quite alone in the world." He swallowed, cleared his throat, and made himself add, "I've come here to learn what it is to be a MacNeil."

The light in Hector's eyes changed at that. Alex didn't know whether it was good or bad, any more than he knew why he'd said that last, but the man's voice did soften after that. "Well, then. Settle yourself among the men. I'll have horses and armor sent to you, and you'll repay me for them once you've captured some of your own."

Alex nodded and thanked his new brother, then said, "What's this I hear about the king being exiled?" He took another large bite of his bread.

"Och, it was a terrible thing. Not long after the coronation, the English caught him unawares at Methven while under a flag of truce, so he thought, and his forces were beaten and scattered. His queen, his young daughter, and the other women were seized at the sanctuary of St. Duthac. For four years the other women were held in iron cages like animals, immodestly displayed at Berwick and Roxburgh."

Alex's imagination took flight at what might have been meant by "immodestly," and he quickly decided he didn't really want to know. He didn't ask, but cut a look at Lindsay, who raised her eyebrows in a told-ya sort of glance.

Sir Hector continued. "The queen yet remains in the Tower of London, and the king's daughter is held in a nunnery. Though the king struggled mightily against the forces loyal to Longshanks, he had no recourse but to leave Scotland for a short time. But he's returned and now owns a greater part of the Highlands."

"Where is he now?"

"We have word he's with Angus MacDonald, bringing the Isle of Man into the fold. Over the past several years he's marshaled his forces, and taken Edward's garrisons at Perth, Dumfries, Dalswinton, Buittle, and Caerlaverlock. They've all been razed."

"He destroyed the castles?" That surprised Alex. Castles were the seats of military power in these times.

Hector laughed. "The better to not let them fall back into English hands, for he hasn't the men or money to garrison them himself. After the betrayal of MacDowall, he could do naught else, for there are few for him to trust as he does James Douglas. He holds the Highlands, for we Gaels have no love for the English king, the English people, or aught else that is English."

Alex glanced at the adamantly English Lindsay, great-great-granddaughter of a duke, who was picking crumbs from the end of her sandwich and eating them very, very slowly.

Hector continued, oblivious. "Now we're off to Stirling, to

join up with the king's brother in his efforts to purge the area of the English. He's surrounded the castle there."

"A siege?"

Sir Hector grinned. "If I know aught about Edward Bruce, we willnae be there long. He has no patience for sieges and would rather face the *Sasunnaich* in battle. He angers his cautious brother, who knows the English have more knights and more money than we Scots and are likely to overwhelm us if we fight on their terms."

"So Robert likes sieges?"

"He likes to be where he's least expected, and I think we would all prefer to take the castle and move on. But Sir Philip Mowbray, the garrison commander, is entrenched and stubborn."

"So Robert's strategy is the hit-and-run?"

That brought a short bark of a laugh and a fit of chuckling. "Aye. Hit-and-run. Excellent turn of a phrase. Hit-and-run. Also the destruction of the English garrisons, but we've not the siege engines King Edward has, either. It makes for a long, tiring effort to convince the English they're no longer needed here and to move along."

He emitted a long belch, then said, "Now, off with you. Rest yourself, for we move on in the morning." Dismissed from the company of his ostensible half-brother, Alex took Lindsay to look for a place to build a fire and pitch the parachute.

The river wasn't far, and some in the camp were washing linen garments that looked like drawstring drawers, then draping them over bushes to dry. "Bath," said Alex, smiling and savoring the idea as if it were food. "It's summer; we can take a bath." The thought lifted his heart and took the edge off the pain of the wounds from Sir Roger's chain.

Lindsay looked around at the woods crowded with people. "We'll need better privacy than these fellows are likely to give us." She took his hand. "Come. This way." They continued up the river until the voices of Sir Hector's encampment faded. Then they chose a flat, grassy spot in the midst of tall oak trees, Scotch pine, and thick underbrush where the water eddied behind some large rocks. She jerked a thumb toward the camp back the way they'd come and said, "You keep watch while I bathe, then I'll be your lookout."

For the briefest moment Alex wondered why he would need

modesty in a camp filled with other men, and opened his mouth to ask, but then he remembered what Lindsay had said about circumcision. He shut his mouth, and nodded. "Of course." He sat on a rock and posted himself with all the knightly chivalry he could muster, elbows on knees and facing away from the water. He bent to remove his chain mail, then let it thunk to the ground at his feet, and reached inside his torn flight suit to poke tenderly at his wounds. Anger rose again, and he imagined going after Roger Kirkpatrick with a chain. Let the sonofabitch see how it felt.

But there was no place for that anger to go. Alex was not yet ready to reply to this injury, so there was nothing to do but think other thoughts.

Lindsay. She was naked behind him, and the image that knowledge brought to mind leached the pain from his body like magic. His ears perked to hear every splash she made. Every little moan of pleasure at coming clean after more than a week of nothing better than hands washed in an icy stream. It would be so fine to be able to watch her. He imagined her wet, her breasts swaying as she moved, and savored the memory of her throwing away her bra. Her broad shoulders, her long, shapely arms, her very long neck atop which perched her most graceful head. His groin began to ache, as it hadn't when she'd slept beside him, and he knew he was in trouble.

To distract himself from his distraction, he talked. "So, what's this King Edward supposed to be like? How are we going to beat him?"

She thought for a moment, then said, "Well, by now it's got to be Edward II. Longshanks is surely dead, and that would explain Robert's recent successes. To the best of my recollection the second Edward wasn't nearly as formidable an enemy as his father."

"Is it true he's homosexual? He was the prince in that movie, wasn't he? The one whose boyfriend got tossed out a window?"

"Oh, yes. Definitely homosexual, though not at all the nancy boy. His preference of his boyfriend over others in his court is what will get him killed. They're going to murder him. The king, I mean. Rather horribly, in fact."

Alex found that intriguing. "Really? His own court?"

"Indeed. To the best of my recollection, his queen is going to have him abducted—"

"That French girl? The one who made it with William Wallace?"

She chuckled. "Yes, except that she was eleven years old when he died and more than likely never met him, let alone slept with him. And . . ." Her voice faltered. "Where was I?"

"The plot to murder the king."

"Oh. Right. They're going to kill him by shoving a pipe into his anus then running a red-hot poker through it into his guts."

"Oh!" Alex on reflex shifted his seat. "Ow! You're kidding."

"No, I'm not. Some think it was merely a way to kill him that would look like a natural death. No obvious marks on the body, you see. Others think it was considered a poetic justice."

"Very weird, sick poetry."

"People here don't think like you and I do. They were probably more concerned about being guilty of treason and regicide, and not so very queasy about how they went about it."

Alex knew she must be right, but fell silent, turning the image of such a murder over in his mind. What a horrible way to die! Then he shook off the thought and returned his attention to the splashing sounds behind him. There was a far better image to occupy himself, even if it did make him ache with wanting to look.

The temptation was too great. He ducked his head and peeked around his shoulder to find her laid back on the surface of the eddy near the shore, scrubbing her scalp under the water with her fingers, her breasts standing straight into the air, her nipples knotted with the cold. A sigh escaped him and he nearly moaned at the sight. Her torso floated on the water, and the surface lapped at a spot a few inches below her navel where he could see the dark patch of hairs just break the ripples. It riveted him.

She sighed, and her breasts rose and fell with unutterable magnificence. Each nipple was a tight, pink rosebud. He touched his tongue to his lip, then looked away as she righted herself and climbed from the water. He imagined her emerging from the water, dripping wet and glistening all over.

Once she'd pulled on her flight suit she said, "Your turn."

No way could he stand up just then. He pretended to search his pockets for something. "Where's that kit?"

"I'll just find it while you're bathing." There was a moment's pause, then she added, "And I assure you the water is quite cold enough to dispatch in a hurry any hard-on you may be cultivating."

He threw her an irritated look. "Turn away."

She chuckled, and obliged, and only then could he stand and undress. But she was right about the cold water. All warm, fuzzy thoughts of Lindsay fled as soon as he stepped into the river. It was so cold, he thought he might never exhale again.

Nevertheless, it was heaven to scrub the filth from his body and dig his fingernails into his hair and wash away the blood smeared across his belly. Huge, black welts swelled beneath the cuts left by Roger's chain, and other, smaller purple spots from his roll down the faerie knoll made him think he must resemble a bad banana. The cold water was soothing, but it didn't take long to put a chill on him, so he returned to the shore and his clothes where it was warm. Though they didn't dare wash the clothes and be caught out without them, he felt pounds lighter once he was dry and dressed.

That night they slept back to back inside the parachute tent, for Alex didn't dare roll toward her. Or even to lie on his back next to her. The relatively clean scent of her made his head swarm with ideas, his blood running persistently a little too fast for comfort, all of it wanting to collect in his groin. For hours, it seemed, he listened to her breathe before he finally was able to sleep.

CHAPTER 5

Stirling Castle didn't look like much. Square towers and a battlement perched atop a rocky hill. Plain and blocky, as strictly utilitarian as a mid-twentieth-century grammar school and no more aesthetically pleasing. It appeared to have been torched not long before, then repaired, for there were patches of new gray stone amid blackened expanses. The thing looked like a burn victim with skin grafts. A square gatehouse faced the town on the hillside that sloped to the valley floor. Along that slope, between the castle and its town, and on an arm of the hill that poked out to the east, Edward Bruce's army had erected earthwork ramparts topped with wooden barricades, behind which he set up the vigil.

Sir Hector and Sir Roger joined their men to those forces and they encamped, prepared to wait out the English just out of range of the alert archers on the battlements of the castle.

For the next two days of gazing at stone walls, the standoff—unmoving and stale—stirred something in Alex he'd not felt since Kosovo. Men came and went from the Scottish camp, some patrolling, some foraging the countryside for provisions, others merely hanging out or sparring with each other to keep busy and sharpen battle skills. Alex could see the camp settling into a sort of permanence that felt strange this close to an enemy. A complacency he found dangerous.

It gave him a maddening need to do something. Nearly anything would suit, but his military training took his mind in directions that would win the conflict. Thoughts tumbled, searching, working out scenarios, prodding for the answer. There were no orders from above, other than to sit and wait, so he spent his time thinking. And watching the gate from the rocky slope below. And thinking some more, plundering his memory of battles he'd studied at the Academy.

When Alex called for his horse, Lindsay hurried to comply and soon rode up with the steed in tow. As he mounted, Hector approached and said, "Where might you be off to, Ailig?"

"Just to have a look-see."

Hector smiled, amused by Alex's strange mixture of modern and Middle English. "Take care the archers don't skewer you."

Alex smiled and saluted, then wheeled away to kick his mount to canter with Lindsay following on her rounsey. He rode down to the valley floor and began circling the hill, weaving in and out between broken stone dikes, at a distance he figured was sufficient to keep him out of range of the bowmen lining the crenellated battlement of the castle high above. Along the northwest side, he slowed to a walk. The castle rock was steep here. Cliffs, from which the battlement rose as if part of the hill.

"What are you looking for?"

Deep in thought, he'd forgotten Lindsay was there. He absently replied, "Dunno yet." His courser tossed its head and danced to be let run. The inactivity of the past few days was showing in the animal, so Alex let it return to a canter. Lindsay urged her own mount to keep up. A short distance farther along, he pulled up again to examine the cliffs where they became a little less steep.

"What are you hoping to find?"

Continuing to stare upward, he said, "A way in. Or a way out. A sally port, maybe. Or a garderobe."

"What's a garderobe?"

"It's a latrine. Sometimes they hang over the side of the wall, and sometimes there will be a poop chute at the foot of a tower. But I don't see any."

"I should think they'd be well disguised, being openings and like that."

"Yeah, they would. And I should think our guys would know what to look for and have checked it out thoroughly. But I'm giving it a shot myself anyway. Fresh eyes, you know."

"Ah." She went silent as he fell back into his concentration.

It was a fair distance around the foot of the hill, and Alex continued to examine the steep ground away from Sir Edward's besiegers. Every so often an archer atop the battlements loosed an arrow, and boys on the valley floor raced each other to retrieve it, then hurried away before a hail of more arrows. They brought to mind ball boys in a tennis tournament, running in, snatching the arrow, then turning and running like hell to beat the aim of the archers, never slowing for a second, for that second could be fatal. Alex figured the kids—all less than ten years or so—were selling the ammunition to the Scottish side. The archers didn't seem terribly worried about running out of them; Alex was even more convinced they were obtaining supplies from somewhere.

He could see by the disturbed ground where the arrows' range ended, and he rode right up next to that line. Then he ignored the archers, and began checking out the rocky hill on which the battlement stood. It was almost entirely granite. On this side a sheer cliff dropped halfway, then came a steep, rocky, tree-covered descent to the valley floor. Some spots weren't as steep as—

An arrow whooshed downward, pierced the sleeve of Alex's hauberk, and lodged in the underside of his left arm. A bolt of pain shot to his shoulder, and with an angry shout he wheeled his horse and galloped away from the castle. Well out of range now, he wheeled back to stand, and shouted vulgarisms at the archers above. He was certain they were laughing at him, and that made him angrier.

Lindsay came to examine his wound, and he lifted his arm for her to see better. She said, "Can you take off the chain mail?"

"Not here. Can you get it out?"

She poked at it, and that made him clench his teeth. Then, without reply, she broke the fletching from the arrow and yanked the shaft through.

"Ow!" Alex jerked away, but the deed was done. "Dang, what're you trying to do, woman?" His horse stepped away, and he urged the animal back with his knees.

"Get the arrow out, as you requested, my liege. And, see," she held up the broken pieces, "here it is."

Alex glowered at her, then held up the arm to look. "How bad is it bleeding?"

"Hmm. Not terribly, I think." She lifted it to see better. "Can you move it?"

Alex demonstrated. "I think it's only nicked the muscle. Hurts like a sonofabitch. Damn, I didn't think arrows could pierce chain mail."

"I thought you knew."

Alex's head tilted and his voice took on an edge. "Oh. Hey, thanks for the warning."

She let go of his arm and set her hands on her hips. "I thought you . . . *we* were out of range. Surely you don't think I would risk your life on purpose. As I hope you would not risk mine. As I said, I thought you knew."

He had little to say to that. Then he looked at his arm again, and up at the castle. It didn't jive. "Look at all those archers."

Lindsay looked. "Right. What of it?"

"That's an awful lot of archers guarding a battlement on a hill that steep and inaccessible. Why do they think they're vulnerable on this side?"

"I think they're all just having fun, trying to pick off these boys."

"Maybe. Maybe not." Alex was searching hard the hillside.

Lindsay turned to stare in the direction of the hill. "Perhaps they're posted just on principle?"

Alex shook his head. "There aren't nearly this many on the western side. These guys should be taking their amusement with potshots at the earthworks out front. I think they're guarding a backdoor."

Alex examined the forests. Very still, he gazed at the scene, looking for anything that might seem out of place. Nothing moved below the castle. He continued to search, and stared at the cliffs, and the spots where they seemed a bit less steep.

And there was a line. A very thin, faint trail. It came from the lip of the cliff and traced ever so faintly down among a tumble of rocks and brush. Then it disappeared among the trees on the lower slope. He turned away, as if giving up on the search.

"I've found something," he said. Lindsay looked, but looked to him again when he told her not to stare. "It's a trail. Not worn, but like dots. Steps cut into the rock. Small, almost invisible. Come." He turned his horse and continued on his way around the castle rock, making his way back to the camp slowly, as if he were still looking for his way into the castle.

Finished with his circuit, he had Lindsay take the horses while he went directly to Edward Bruce who stood by the earthworks at the top of the castle hill, nearest the portcullis. Before he could approach, though, two high-ranking knights in silk surcoats blocked his way and demanded to know his business. They appeared amused to mess with him, and one was the knight who had accosted Alex his first day in Robert's service. Seven years older, but Alex recognized him.

"I need to speak to the king's brother. I think I may have found the route they'll take for sallies against us." He'd brought Lindsay, but didn't seem to need her for this conversation.

"Where is it?" The sneering, silk-clad knight crossed his arms over his chest.

Alex pressed his lips together. Where he came from, chain of command was nearly inviolate. Protocol was followed, and any deviation was treated as infraction, or at least frowned on by all concerned. But here things were more fluid. Most of the men were not only looking out strictly for themselves but also were expected to be that way. Landless and in debt, Alex was one of the lowest-ranking knights in this cavalry, and knew if he spoke to anyone but Edward about his discovery he would be left out of any action—and therefore out of any plunder to be had—resulting from the intelligence. Letting this guy get between himself and his commander would be the equivalent of having a fellow officer steal his paycheck. He said, "I must talk to Sir Edward."

The knights narrowed their eyes at him. The one with the sneer said, "I think you may come back tomorrow."

Alex muttered to the ground in modern English, "Great. I'm talking to the Wizard of Oz." Then he addressed Edward's man again and lied. "You won't find it. I have information from a local man. Furthermore, I know where their pickets . . . *guards* are. They'll kill you before you will find anything."

The shadow that crossed the man's eyes told Alex the knight surely would have spent the rest of the day looking for the sally port himself. There was a long silence, then Alex looked around as if he gave a damn who might be listening and said, "If Sir Edward should learn there was a delay in receiving this knowledge . . ." He shrugged and let the threat hang in the air.

The knight shifted his weight and finally said, "Very well." The two stepped aside and allowed Alex to approach Edward and bow.

"Sir, may I have a word?"

The king's brother had been engaged in light conversation with Kirkpatrick, and readily interrupted it for this diversion. "Who are you?" His tone was one of idle curiosity.

"Alasdair MacNeil, sir." Alex straightened to attention by force of habit. "I've found their sally port. That is, I've found the trail they will take from it when they will attack us. Give me men, and I'll assure nothing gets in or out for the duration of this siege."

"You've found their egress, you say?"

"Aye. And I'm certain they think it's secret. Also, the trail is well protected by archers."

"Then how do you propose to make the route secure without losing all your men to these archers?"

Kirkpatrick chuckled, and the urge to punch his lights out was maddening. Rather than explain his plan, which would have involved confessing to the study of seven centuries of war tactics that hadn't happened yet, Alex said simply, "By stealth. Trust me, sir. Let me have a contingent of ten knights and I give you my solemn oath I'll hold the ground or die trying."

Edward thought about that for only a moment, then said, "Very well. Pick five knights and as many squires. You may go."

Only five knights? Nevertheless, Alex nodded as his mind turned with adjusting his plan to new numbers. "Aye, sir." He took a step back to salute, but remembered to bow instead, then turned on his heel and withdrew to begin recruiting.

Hector, when he heard of the mission, recommended one of his own knights: a lanky, blond cousin named Cullan MacNeil, who seemed eager for action yet centered and experienced enough not to bounce on the balls of his feet like the younger MacNeil knight who also volunteered.

In spite of efforts to contain the intelligence, word of the mission spread quickly and John Kirkpatrick came to Alex and asked to go.

Alex stopped dead in his tracks, stood and stared at him, his eyes hooded and jaw clenched. The welts on his belly were now itchy scabs on their way to healing, but the memory of the pain and humiliation inflicted by the Kirkpatricks was still fresh. "No." He turned to continue on his way, but John held his arm and stopped him. Alex pulled away from the man's grasp.

"Ailig, you must understand, he'd have turned the chain on me, had I interfered."

Alex turned again, but John insisted and grabbed his arm. "Furthermore . . ." John blocked his path. "Furthermore, Ailig, you shouldn't have left the way you did. It was highly suspicious, and you can't blame Roger for being angry. Even if you did not turn traitor, neither should you have left. You're pledged to His Majesty."

"I had no choice. I was needed elsewhere by my foster family. I couldn't forget the Pawlowskis any more than I could betray the king."

John nodded. "I believe you. And I understand, as I hope you understand my hands were as tied as yours that day. But now, allow me to pledge loyalty to you and go with you tonight."

Alex considered that. A pledge from John would be a good thing, especially in the long run. He nodded. "All right, then, bring your best squire and leave your shields behind." John gave him a querying glance, and Alex elaborated. "Brightly colored and designed to be seen from a distance. Not the best thing for a stealth mission."

John nodded.

Alex continued on his way.

Also tapped were two of Edward's men along with five squires, and the contingent gathered after dark that night at the edge of the trees on the western side of the castle rock. Alex was pleased to have these volunteers, but when Lindsay presented herself he told her to return to their tent.

"Why?"

"Don't question my order. Just do it."

"Why?"

Stock still in the darkness, his anger rose and he was reminded she was an untrained civilian and had no business wanting to fight. He took her by the upper arm and hauled her far enough away from the group to speak in low-voiced modern English. "What do you think you're doing?"

"Going with you."

"No, you're not."

Her voice was a low growl. "You can't stop me."

He wanted to shake sense into her, but held his temper and funneled his anger into his command voice. "Yes, I can stop you."

"Why do you want to?"

Alex opened his mouth to reply, and only then did he realize he had no answer he wanted to admit just then. His desire was to keep her safe, but saying so would be a mistake, for she surely would react badly. There was no chance of telling her what was on his mind.

Lindsay continued, and spared him from lying. "If you send me back, it will become obvious to the others there is something different about me. Something wrong. There will be whispers that I'm not up to snuff as a squire. There may even be talk of cowardice, and that would destroy me here. I've *got* to be treated like a young man, Alex. You've got to stop thinking of me as a woman. Start thinking of me as a fellow soldier."

But she wasn't a fellow soldier. She was a girl in a dirty flight suit, leather-and-horn armor, and an elastic bandage. Never mind she was an attractive female and the only other person currently on the planet who could possibly understand his past, the bottom line was she wasn't trained to fight. Wasn't trained to think like a soldier, and he knew that lack would get her killed. Or somebody else killed.

But she was right. If he kept her from putting herself at risk, the men would perceive her as a coward and treat her with contempt. It could make life hell for both of them, for she was his squire, under his tutelage, so everything about her reflected on him. Wanting badly to insist she return to camp, he nevertheless acquiesced. "All right. Come, then."

Under cover of darkness, Lindsay and the others followed Alex on foot. Carrying swords and maces, moving slowly and silently near the trees at the foot of the hill, they circled to the spot on the far side where Alex had seen the faint trail. They approached in utter silence, daggers and swords at the ready in anticipation of encountering Englishmen, but there were none here. Up close now, he found the track among the trees below the cliff. Above, silhouetted against the night sky, were shifting shadows of men along the battlement. Well hidden in shadow despite the clear sky and moon overhead, Alex's detail settled.

The vigil was long and boring. Bugs crawled around in Alex's clothing, and he wondered whether they were ones he could shake out, or he'd acquired lice. It wouldn't have surprised him if he had; sleeping on the ground as he had been, he figured it was inevitable he'd be picking nits out of his skivvies by summer's end. Fleas and ticks, too. He scratched discreetly, flexed his aching, throbbing, wounded arm, and waited.

John, lying nearby, whispered to Alex under his breath, "Ailig, I must ask . . ."

Alex grunted for John to proceed with his question.

"How old is your squire? I was given to believe he would be a knight by now, after seven years away. But he seems little changed."

"Your memory is faulty, friend. Lindsay is nineteen, just turned. When you saw him last, he was twelve years old and newly made squire. He's still small, but will have his final growth soon, I'm sure. His father was a large man."

John nodded, and seemed to accept Alex's smoke-and-mirrors explanation. The night continued.

In the predawn, John whispered, "It's time we returned to camp, so we aren't caught by daybreak."

"Most of us will stay here. John, you and your boy go to the encampment to sleep, and return after nightfall. Each of the five of you will take turns sleeping in camp, and your squires will stay with you. Lindsay, you go back for some food, and bring it to us tonight after dark. The rest of us will sleep here through the day."

"Ailig—"

"Silence, John. If they hear us topside they'll know we're down here. We don't want that. Go. You, too, Lindsay."

She hesitated, and he hoped she wasn't about to give him more guff, but then she obeyed and moved down toward the valley floor to make her way back to Edward's camp. John signaled his squire and they departed also.

Alex whispered to the others, "Settle in, boys, and make yourselves comfortable. If you've got to pee or whatever, do it now before the sun rises. Once there's light, nobody moves a hair." And having reminded himself, he took the opportunity to step deeper into the trees for a leak and a good scratch. Then he reclaimed his position by the trail and settled in to sleep. His men also took turns stretching their legs, then the sun came up and they all slept.

Briefly in the afternoon, the warm sun high overhead, Alex awoke to hear voices above. Startled, he looked around, thinking his men were about to be discovered. But the voices were of archers on the battlements far above. And from their conversation it was plain they had no idea they had enemy Scots listening in. All that moved in the forest around them were leaves fluttering in sun-dappled breeze. So Alex laid his head down and fell back into his doze.

Darkness came, late this time of year and at this latitude. Alex began to listen for the return of John, his squire, and Lindsay, his belly now complaining for something to eat. The moon was high by the time the three arrived and took up position. The cold food was distributed, and the men of Alex's detail settled in for another night of waiting. Frequently, for the sake of keeping his muscles from stiffening, he approached the top tree line to note the positions of the archers, then made his way to the valley floor for a look before climbing once again to his position among the trees.

That morning before dawn another knight was permitted to take his squire to the encampment to sleep. Lindsay insisted on staying, and the following sunset the two on camp rotation returned with food. The watch continued.

"This is not knightly behavior, lying in wait," said John after nearly a week.

"This is the only way to be certain the English aren't sneaking out to attack us. Or to get messages to King Edward."

" 'Tis unmanly."

"It's what will accomplish our purpose."

"I wonder if the result is worth the means."

"Trust me, John."

The man fell silent, and another night wore on.

The following morning Alex insisted Lindsay return to camp

for the day. He could see the strain on her; she wasn't built for this, and a cough was coming on her. All night she'd been smothering her ticklish throat in the crook of her arm. This time when he ordered her away she didn't argue with him, but assured him she would be back that night.

After nightfall, before there was any sign of her, sounds came from above. Englishmen traipsed down the trail with barely a thought to the noise they were making, so certain the nearest Scots were on the other side of the castle. Alex's pulse picked up, his detail readied themselves for attack, and drew their daggers. Swords would be little help in the close quarters of these trees. Alex whispered with almost no breath, "On me."

The English coming from above made enough sound, but here on the north side of the rock, in the overcast, moonless night, they were shadows within shadows. They picked their way downward, then located the trail through the trees and made their way down it. The Scots kept deadly still as they waited for the signal. Alex let the Englishmen come, the shadows too numerous to count in the deep darkness. When their file was surrounded by the Scots, close enough to smell their filthy linens, Alex erupted with a roar and his men attacked as one. He plunged his dagger through a coif opening into the exposed throat of one shadow, then moved to another. The slope was steep, and several guys went tumbling, grappling with each other as they fell. Alex kept his footing and moved upward as English shadows tried to escape back to the castle. One turned to face him, and slashed with his dagger. Alex ducked and slammed him with his elbow, and the knight toppled and rolled down the hill. The next shadow was struggling uphill, and Alex chased. They burst from the tree line, and as the quarry scrabbled for foothold on the dark granite Alex thrust his dagger into his bare neck. One squeak of pain and despair, and the Englishman fell and rolled to the trees below. Another figure was already on its way up the faint trail, but Alex declined to pursue. It was time to beat hell out of there.

A hail of arrows pattered and whooshed among the trees, and all across the open ground around them. "Wait!" Alex's men halted, hardly needing to be told to drop and hug the ground. A Englishman raised up to shout, and Alex kicked him in the head to shut him up. Then he knelt to place his dagger at the man's throat, and promised he'd die on the spot if he uttered another sound. When the knight lay still, Alex looked around and listened to know whether any of his men were wounded.

Lindsay, Alex's heart clenched. Where was she now? Could she have been caught by the hail of arrows? A terrible sinking hollowed his gut and he yearned to search for her. But he couldn't take his men out into that deadly barrage until the archers tired of shooting aimlessly into the darkness and trees.

It didn't take long. When the silence came, Alex waited until a few more arrows were loosed. Then no more, and there was muttering from the battlement above. They were done. Alex hauled his captive to his English feet, then indicated the other men should strip the dead and move out. Three knights beheaded bodies, and carried the grisly trophies by the hair. Alex's first thought was to forbid it, but he thought again and decided to let them. He wasn't sure why, but tonight he didn't feel much bothered by it.

Again the Scots hugged the foot of the mound as they made their way back. Though it was a shorter run to be out of range if they went straight out from the mound onto the open ground, they would be sure to be seen in the moonlight then, and shot at in their race to get far enough away. By keeping to the trees they stood a chance of making it back to the encampment without being seen at all.

Keeping to the trees, they also stood a chance of finding Lindsay.

Alex did find her, crouched beside a cluster of rocks not far from their hiding place. He handed his prisoner off to John and let his men go on, then went to Lindsay. When he reached her he had to resist an urge to throw his arms around her in his relief, and to keep himself from it held his sword belt tightly in his fists.

"Are you all right?" he whispered.

"I'm fine. Not a scratch. What happened?"

"We surprised a foray. Killed all but two. One escaped, and the other we've taken."

"Bravo."

Alex grinned, and they continued to the Scottish encampment for him to relieve his prisoner of equipment, clothing, and ransom pouch filled with French gold and English silver. Then, having been ransomed so the Scots wouldn't have to guard him and feed him, the proud English knight was sent back through the portcullis without a stitch of clothing on him, accompanied by the hoots and catcalls of the Scottish army behind him. Alex grinned as he watched the pale, barrel-chested, spindly legged man run with both his hands over his privates, leaping and dancing as he stepped on rocks in his bare feet, calling out to his compatriots to open the portcullis. Archers on the battlement exchanged arrows with Scottish archers on the ground in covering fire as the castle gate was opened just enough to let the English knight squeeze under.

Far less in jest, the three severed heads were impaled and raised on spears in full view of the castle. Alex stared long and hard at the horrifying sight, and eased his qualms by telling himself it was a message the English garrison would understand.

That night a modest feast was provided by Sir Edward for Alex and his men, and Alex was happy to eat and drink himself into a royal stupor, laughing and joking with his comrades after the long, tense week. Around the cook fire, the men told and retold the story among themselves and to all who gathered to listen.

Every so often through a haze of mead, Alex glanced at the impaled heads lit by torches stuck in the ground near the pikes, blood and other fluids dripping and making strings toward the ground, mouths agape. The smell of flaming grease in the cook fire filled his head, and contempt for the enemy filled his heart. He knew he was lucky to be among the ones still alive. His skin tingled and his blood pounded with the understanding of the precarious nature of existence, and the knowledge that in this place there were only the successful and the dead. He looked around at the bright faces of the men who had gone with him, ruddy-cheeked in the flickering, firelight, and knew they must be thinking the same thing.

Sir Hector arrived, cut a chunk from the spitted haunch of venison, stuffed his mouth full with it, and announced as he chewed the enormous wad of meat, "We're leaving this place. On the morrow." Then he swallowed and immediately reached for another bite of the greasy meat.

Alex stopped laughing at something John had said, and struggled to focus on Hector. "No more siege?"

"He gave them a year." The laird let himself down to perch atop a felled log.

"He what?" There was a murmur among the others, and Lindsay bit her lip without saying anything.

Hector continued. "I'm told Edward Bruce made an agreement with Mowbray, that they would surrender without a fight if the English king did not send help within a year."

"So who's going to run to England and tell the king?"

"Mowbray is sending a messenger."

That stumped Alex. It went against everything that made sense to him about armed conflict. Several things came to mind to say and he opened his mouth to say each one, then shut it. Finally he was able to put together a coherent thought. "Is he nuts?"

Hector frowned, puzzled. "Nuts?"

Alex grunted, having blurted American vocabulary in the midst of his Middle English again. It took him a moment to dig the correct word from his inebriated memory, then he said, "I mean, is he mad? In a year King Edward could mass enough men to defeat us, and Sir Edward wants us to just sit here with our thumbs up our butts?"

Hector snorted laughter, but said, "The English king certainly has got the resources, and we do not. Apparently your thwarting of an attempt to obtain rescue and provisions has convinced Mowbray he needed to encourage us to move on. The king's brother has reasoned our resources are better used elsewhere than here. He wishes to oblige the English commander."

"What do you think will happen?"

Sir Hector frowned up at the torches along the castle ramparts, thinking. "I expect that we will wait and see."

"For a year?"

"Our commander will keep us amused and occupied, I think. I hear talk of raids into England."

"Raids?" Alex was accustomed to following orders that didn't make much sense to him at the time, but the word "raid" gave a heady sensation and a shiver up his spine. The adrenaline charge was kicking in before the last one had quite finished with him, making his skin rise in goose bumps and his blood surge. *Raid.* It felt the way it had the first time he had flown a Hornet and owned the skies at mach three. It felt . . . incredible.

CHAPTER 6

For his success in securing the sally port of Stirling Castle, and for his role in convincing Mowbray to make a deal with Edward Bruce, Alex was awarded a trained courser and tack from Edward's stable and the prisoner's personal effects, along with armor and cash.

Also, for the prowess he'd shown, he was approached by knights from Edward Bruce's army who expressed a desire to follow him. So Alex was allowed to lead a contingent of nearly fifty knights and their squires. It wasn't much more than a scouting party attached to the larger army, and flying the banner belonging to Edward Bruce, but Alex was well pleased nevertheless. Leading the small cavalry unit would be like being an officer again, and he liked the autonomy that came with being out in the countryside. Mobile and deadly. The fourteenth-century equivalent of a fighter squadron, and he was in command.

It was also good to have a nice suit of solid, English chain mail and bits of plate—no holes—and this outfit seemed fairly new and up-to-date. Now over his flight suit Alex wore his new hauberk and coif, and on his hands were fine leather gauntlets with iron plate riveted to the knuckles and fingers. The knuckle plates were adorned with short spikes that made Alex flex his fingers as he tried to imagine clobbering someone with those.

The thought was at once intriguing and horrifying, for it must be like stabbing. On his legs were quilted cloth cuisses around his thighs and saucer-shaped iron poleyns strapped over his kneecaps. They bound his tendons uncomfortably, but compared to the possible pain of being kneecapped by enemy infantry the discomfort was nothing. Alex figured he could deal with it.

Sick of Lindsay having to stuff his boots into his stirrups every time he mounted, he bought a pair of the softer ones worn by other knights. The toes were somewhat pointed, but not ridiculously so, and the leg cuffs when fully extended were just above his knees. When not wading through streams, he wore them folded over, where they slouched a little just below the knee. He knew he was going to miss the old steel-toed boots as soon as his horse stepped on his foot again, but these were high, lightweight, well oiled, and watertight, and just a little more practical in the long run for the life he was now leading.

He kept the Englishman's rowel spurs, selling his old prick spurs, and they added jingling to the metallic *shuss* of mail when he walked. A mail coif now covered his head and protected his neck, but the prisoner's helmet wouldn't fit. So Alex kept the one Hector had provided and paid back with the smaller one, and he sold the captured dagger, which was not as fine as the one Alex had won in his first victory.

The sword, however, was a treasure. A five-foot-long monstrosity the locals called a "claymore," it had a two-handed, leather-covered wooden grip and long quillons tipped with quatrefoils. The blade was the finest Alex had seen in this century, and so well balanced he found he could wield the weapon with only one hand if necessary, by hooking a finger over one of the quillons. To try it out, Alex took a stance, clear of everyone nearby, and swung the sword like a baseball bat. He could sure do some damage with this. A grin lit him up as he hefted the weapon. Yes, sir, he could sure do some damage.

The money from the sales of spurs and dagger, together with the helmet and the cash found on the person of the English knight, paid the debt to Hector for Lindsay's horse and scale armor shirt of leather and horn, and also bought a mace for her. Now they were free from debt, and as well equipped as anyone else of their rank on the field.

One final thing his new wealth provided him was a custom-
made saddle. He sold his hated battle saddle that stood high
over the horse's back with the stirrups straight down at the
sides, and bought a plain riding saddle that was a little more
along the lines of a modern English rig. Then he took that to a
leather worker in the camp and talked him into modifying it so
the stirrups were forward and shorter, and the seat situated directly on the horse's back. The resulting saddle was somewhat
crude and ugly, but his seat was now more normal and offered
better control over—and more sensitivity to—the animal. Not
to mention being far more comfortable on long patrols. Since
he didn't own a lance and didn't care to learn to use one, the
high, supporting pommel and cantle of the old saddle wouldn't
be missed.

The siege ended, Edward's forces moved onward, ever seeking to annoy Edward II and anyone loyal to him. Alex's knights
were deployed on scouting detail. Their first day out, Alex ordered them into a line and made inspection to take stock of his
manpower and their equipment. They totaled slightly over a
hundred men and boys—near to the same number of men-at-
arms as Robert had started with seven years before.

As Alex rode down the line on his prancing courser, he saw
wealthy, experienced knights well equipped with fine weapons
and armor, as well as poorer, landless knights who barely seemed
to be able to keep their horses fed. The sorriest of the lot was a
wary-eyed man named Sir Orrin De Ros, whom Alex could describe only as a "pencil-neck geek." He was painfully thin and
not very tall, but sat his horse as arrogantly as any of them. Orrin
was known to be an enthusiastic fighter, but he also had an ever-
present chip on his shoulder about his status. Word was Orrin
wasn't welcome in other units, and though Alex was aware of the
knight's reputation as a pain in the ass, he'd taken him on because
these days he needed every hand he could scrounge.

Alex took mental note of who needed what, so that when opportunities came to reward service he could make certain captured resources would go where they would do the most good.
In addition to the knights, there were green, young squires with
ruddy cheeks and soft faces, who seemed grossly out of place
among the battle-hardened warriors.

A few MacNeils had joined him, including Sir Cullan, and

Alex was glad to have them for they were part of his alliance with Hector and he could depend on their loyalty. The laird from Barra was turning out to be a good man to have on his side, and the MacNeil knights had a reputation for toughness. It made him glad to be one of them.

The unit was highly mobile, for they took no wagons or extraneous followers, and made do with a minimum of pack animals to carry provisions and gear, shelter and weaponry. A huntsman accompanied them, who provided the detail with meat from the forests. Anything else they needed Alex sent for from the main army or obtained from locals. And there was plenty to be had from locals who were loyal to the English king.

Shortly after they deployed, one late evening after Lindsay had finished with the horses she came to him and asked for some linen cloth.

Alex was in the tent with his broadsword across his knees, sharpening it. Lindsay's job, but he liked to do it himself because it was calming. He said absently, his concentration on the edge before him, "What for? You going to sew something?"

Her weight shifted, and he sensed irritation. "Why ever do you think I would be sewing?"

He shrugged and ran his whetting stone down the sword blade. "Well, isn't that what people do with cloth?"

"Alex." Now there was an edge to her voice that made him look up, and he saw he'd royally pissed her off somehow. Anger had darkened her already dark eyes until they were nearly black, and her brow was in a knot. "If one of the men came to you and wanted a piece of linen, would you assume he was going to sew something?"

Alex thought about that for a moment, then said, "Uh, no. Not those guys. They'd probably want it to sleep on. Or for a winding sheet to bury one of their buddies. But I know you don't want to sleep on a piece of linen; you've got a parachute for that. And you don't have any dead buddies." *Yet.*

She stared at him for a moment, looking as if she were assessing his reply and making a decision. Then she said in a voice so low he could barely hear her, "I've been trying to keep my monthly cycle a secret, you understand."

"Ah." He held up a palm to halt her explanation. "I do understand."

"I had a linen cloth I cut up, but I can't wash the rags and reuse them because hanging them out to dry would be . . . indiscreet to say the least. So I've had to throw them away once they became, you know, unusable." Her face was aflame with embarrassment, and she stared at a spot on the floor in front of her feet.

"I said, I understand. I'll get you some pieces of linen. We'll carry them as bedsheets and you can cut them up as you need them, then throw them on the fire or bury them when you need to get rid of them."

"No, you don't understand. I need help keeping clean. I can't . . ." She blinked back some tears, then continued when she'd brought herself under control. "It's extremely difficult to know I could be betrayed by a blood spot in the wrong place on my clothing. God knows what would happen to me if they found out."

He nodded. "Then we'll have to see about arranging more opportunities to wash. And the linen. I'll buy a big sheet of it." With conscious effort, he made his voice go soft, trying to soothe her. "Do you need it right now?"

She shook her head and sighed, and seemed to be calming down. Alex didn't feel so calm himself, and wished he didn't have to be involved in this. He didn't know how she felt, and didn't particularly want to know. He thought she was crazy to want to pass as a man. But he would do as she asked, just to keep her from flipping out. She cleared her throat, wiped her eyes, and said, "Thank you."

"You're welcome." She turned to leave, but stopped to listen when he continued. "And incidentally, Lindsay. If one of the men had come to me asking for linen, I also would never have assumed he wanted it to make sanitary napkins."

For a long moment she considered that, then nodded. "Point taken." Then she left the tent.

Soon another siege was under way, this one at Linlithgow Castle, and Alex's scouting detail was recalled and put to work on short, local patrols. Alex used the opportunity to drill his men-at-arms, and to learn how to wield a sword himself. Alex had never fenced, even at the Naval Academy, and now was guessing at what to do with his broadsword—which everybody called simply a "sword," because they were all broad. Rapiers, sabers, and such hadn't been developed yet. There were only "sword" and "great sword"—the claymore.

Especially, he was clueless about how to handle the claymore. Only the top half of the blade was sharpened, so it was apparent that it was not for close-in combat. But beyond that, Alex was mystified. Lindsay had taken fencing in college, but had never before wielded anything broader than a narrow, edgeless, foiled sport saber. She guided him through some basics with the sword, but her advice was skimpy. Practicing with the men was extremely dangerous, for there were no leather foils to cover the sword edges and Alex had to learn quickly or risk serious injury. At first he only watched his men, as if he were judging their skills. Nobody knew he sought only to improve his own.

Right away Alex observed why the claymore was sharpened only at the tip. He had been correct that the sword's strength was in being able to whack hard and fast with the tip at a fair distance from one's opponent, but there was far more to it than that. In the sparring sessions he saw guys use the blunt middle part of the sword like a staff. They held the blade and blocked with it, often hit with the pommel, and clothing could be snagged by the forward-tilted quatrefoil quillons to pull an opponent from a horse or yank him to the ground. That the function could be shifted so easily, sometimes without moving the dominant hand, made it a stunningly versatile weapon.

Later, in drill himself, Alex faced off against his best knight who pushed him hard. Sir Cullan was older and far more experienced with a sword than nearly anyone in the unit. Now Alex found himself pitted against an aggressive and merciless wild Island Scot, and had to step lively just to keep his skin intact.

Cullan had habitually angry eyes and a wicked grin as he sparred circles around Alex. "Ye fight like an Englishman!" He roared like a mad dog as he came at Alex and ended the exchange with a hard hit to the elbow with the flat of his blade.

Alex nearly dropped his sword, and his face burned for it as he stumbled over tufts of grass in the pasture and backed away from further assault until feeling would return to his arm. Then he came back with a fury. He was the commander of this bunch, and needed to be better than this.

Particularly with Lindsay watching him. Out of the corner

of his eye he caught her lurking by a tree, observing him with Cullan, and it blew his concentration all to hell. He staggered backward after a particularly painful "touch" that shook his entire hauberk and sent tingly numbness to his shoulder, then came back with an aggressive attack. He couldn't let this guy make a fool out of him.

But fool he was, for several days. Struggling to make his broadsword an extension of his arm, he kept at it for hours on end, every morning and evening, sparring with whoever wasn't on patrol at the time. His arm ached all the way to the center of his chest, and the pain kept him awake long into the night.

After some days of having his armor clouted until his arms were purple and his thighs nearly too sore to hold him up, he finally began to catch on to observing his opponent. Cullan's style was aggressive, but depended more on bluster than speed. Alex realized he had the reflexes to be quicker, and began to anticipate Cullan's attacks. He sped up, even to becoming reckless. More sure of himself, he began to set the pace and Cullan couldn't match him. Alex moved him across the practice field, and laughed aloud for the joy of winning. Now he hoped Lindsay was watching somewhere nearby. Glancing about, though, he didn't see her. His attention returned to the task at hand, and he forced her from his mind.

Over the weeks, as Alex got to know his men better, he came to realize they needed some instruction in discipline in order to respond to his modern command style. He also needed to adjust that style to recognize the men he was dealing with had no concept of "military" as he knew it. The fifty knights each had pride of position, however low that rank might be, and he had to acknowledge it or lose them. He also had to acknowledge that each knight had rights over his own squires. Each squire was a knight-hopeful and would do pretty much what he was told, but Alex had to be certain the protocol was observed. A messy and complex thing when the squires barely outnumbered the knights and were sometimes needed to function as a group. Often a knight would decline to pass along an order or would not make a squire available for a particular duty, and that would leave Alex pissed off and unable to respond effectively without starting a fistfight.

But men were men in any century, and commanding respect

as well as obedience was something he'd been taught in the Navy. Over the weeks the problems grew fewer as he earned the regard of his men and learned where their emotional buttons were.

Then there was Lindsay. She confused him. Not that he'd never seen a woman in a combat role before; women had been flying combat in the Navy since the mid-nineties and he'd flown with them since his earliest days of naval flight training. But this with Lindsay was completely different. No matter how hard he tried, he couldn't think of her as one of the guys. With every cell in his body, with every sense, every feeling, he perceived her as a woman, and she was the strongest, most fascinating woman he'd ever known.

Lurking during training, he sometimes watched her spar with her mace among the other squires, and the sight made him want to throw her to the ground and take her right there. Or at least to try, and the possibility she might hurt him for it made the prospect that much more intriguing. She moved like a panther, quick and lithe, in complete command of her body, and though the men she sparred with gave her no ground she held her own more often than not. Sometimes she bested them. Watching her struggle against the other squires turned him on in ways he'd never thought possible for a straight guy.

At night they shared a real tent now. It wasn't large, but it was well made of heavy material that caught the wind a bit less efficiently than the parachute and kept out more of the cold at night. The top was blue and its corner points ended in tethers for real pegs instead of rocks, and the sides were white with abstract blue designs. Alex thought it rather conspicuous out in the countryside, but his fellow knights seemed to consider it very stylish and it was certainly less obvious from afar than the red-and-orange parachute.

Alex and Lindsay now used both parachutes for bedding atop thin straw pallets, and so they slept separately. Though Alex took on a second squire to maintain his increasing number of horses, that squire slept in a second tent for the sake of keeping Lindsay's secret.

She'd relaxed about that, as well. The linen rags seemed to have done the trick, and Alex could see in the way she walked and carried herself she was no longer paranoid about spots on her clothing or other little things that might betray her. She began reading at odd moments a little book bound in leather and tied with a thong. He found her hunched over it one night, sitting by the fire and leaning in to see the pages by the flickering light.

Alex was on his way into the tent, but paused and said, "How come I never see you writing in that journal?"

She glanced up at him and held it out for him to see. "This isn't my journal. That would be a small spiral notebook I don't let anyone see for obvious reasons. This is a book someone gave me."

Alex looked, and found the smallish pages covered in fine, perfectly even script and illuminated by small but intricate drawings. "What is it?"

"Psalms."

"Someone just handed it over to you?"

Instead of the casual reply he'd expected for this small-talk conversation, she gazed into the fire for a moment before answering. When she finally spoke, what she said surprised him. "Do you believe in faeries?"

He sure didn't know how to reply to that. "You mean, as in effeminate men?"

She chuckled. "No. As in wee folk. Magical beings."

"Well, there was that one guy we saw. I assume he wasn't standard-issue human, what with those pointy ears and all." Alex sat on the ground next to her, the better to talk without being overheard, even though nobody in this century seemed to be able to catch on to their modern language.

"I don't have a clue about him, but I received this book from a woman who called herself Danu. She said she was what we would call a faerie."

Again Alex was at a loss for how to reply. It crossed his mind Lindsay had lost her sanity, but there was the book in her hands that had certainly come from somewhere. He pointed to it with his chin and said, "A faerie gave you a book of psalms? Isn't that a little weird?"

She shrugged. "Maybe she thought it was what I needed at the time. She didn't stick around long; I don't know very much about her. She simply handed me this, told me all would be well, then disappeared."

He reached for the book to see it and said, "You read Latin?"

She shook her head. "No, it's in English. Modern English, in fact. Though I'm certain it's copied and illuminated by hand. See?"

Alex was quite surprised to be able to read the page she'd held open. "Huh." Yet again he was at a loss for words and wondered if she'd slipped a gear. She must have had this with her when they crashed. "That's . . . something else."

"It was quite a shock, I assure you. So much has happened to us in the past couple of months, I hardly know what to think anymore."

"How come she didn't show herself to me?"

"I've not the slightest idea. How come that fellow we saw in the knoll never spoke to me? Nor even looked at me, as if I weren't even there. I can't say. I just know I'm glad to have this."

That was something, at least. If it made her feel better, he was all for it. "Good." A yawn took him, and he stretched out his sword arm to get rid of a kink in his back. "I'm off to bed."

"Good night." She opened the book and continued reading.

They acquired an oil lamp, so at night they were able to take turns in the privacy of the tent stripping to the skin and picking parasites from their clothing, burning each bug in the flame. For lack of real entertainment, Alex found himself relishing the way the lice and fleas and the occasional tick flared when they hit the lamp. A bit like a medieval bug zapper, and the thought made him grin.

One night Lindsay came to Alex with a comb. The thing was a nearly circular piece of hardwood, thick in the center and very thin toward the edges, cut with a fine saw into very closely-spaced tines. "Help me with this, would you please?" She handed it to him. "It's got a fine tooth that's supposed to remove lice. I think I need help getting them out of my hair."

"All right, come." He was sitting on his pallet, cross-legged. With her armor off and her flight suit unzipped and down around her waist, she knelt before him, and bent her head, but it was an awkward position. "No, here. Lie down and put your head on my knee." She did so, facing away from him with her back to his other knee, and he began combing out her thick, dark hair. It had grown some since she'd hacked it off, but was still much shorter than it had been the day they met. Its waves shone in the candlelight, and he ran his fingers through it perhaps more than necessary to comb out the nits. He did a very thorough job, making certain every little interloper went into the fire, and combing through every lock front and back.

He noticed there was a hole in the shoulder seam of her T-shirt, and he mentioned it.

"I know. I keep sewing it, but it's threadbare and it comes right apart again. You'd think it being so filthy, it would just hold together like a clump of dirt."

He chuckled, and then was silent as he combed.

After a while she said, "Do you think I'm fooling them?"

"The bugs?"

"The men."

For a long moment he thought about that, then replied, "Nobody has made a pass at you yet, have they?"

"No." Then she sighed. "But I'm often challenged. I can tell by the way they act they don't think I'm much of a man."

Alex hesitated, then said, "You're not one."

"Regardless, I need them to think I am."

He thought some more, then said, "What do you do when they challenge you?"

"I ignore it and go on my way."

"Oh. No wonder."

She said nothing and he figured he should drop it, but against better judgment he ventured some advice he figured wouldn't be well received. "You've got to challenge them back. Bust their chops like they bust yours."

"You mean, be an asshole?"

That made him chuckle as his fingers fiddled with her hair. "If necessary. Talk tough, even if you don't mean it. But expect to back it up with at least one fight. Then, even if you lose, if you've fought well you'll gain some respect. If you win, they'll respect you *and* fear you."

"What if I get hurt?"

"You'll heal. And if you're worried about getting hurt, give it up right now 'cause I don't want you going into battle behind me if you're worried about being hurt. In battle, you can't even worry about ending up dead, because the odds are excellent you eventually will be."

There was no reply to that, so Alex assumed she was thinking about what he'd said. He hoped she was. He hoped he was frightening her, and she would come to her senses and give up the charade. So he continued. "Whenever you're with just the squires, walk around like you own everything within a ten-foot radius. Just don't do it around guys who actually outrank you, or they'll take you down more than just a notch. But when the other squires mess with you, you need to give as good as you get. Give more than you get, and maybe they'll leave you alone."

She turned her head to look up at him, her brow gathered in a frown. "You understand these barbarians?"

He shrugged. "Guys are guys. These knights were born tougher than most grown men you and I ever knew, and I think the concept of 'gentleman' has a long way to go yet, but deep down they're no different from me and my brothers back home. If you're going to pass yourself off as one of them, you're going to have to think like them." Then he hesitated before adding, "And you've got to behave like them."

"I don't know if I can."

"Your other option is to wear a dress."

Lindsay fell silent, and laid her head on his knee again. He hoped she was considering the suggestion.

Eventually, though, when she broke the silence, he knew she hadn't been.

"What do you miss the most?"

"You mean, from the future?"

"Yes."

His fingers fondled her hair, and just then he missed nothing and nobody. But after some thought he said, "Going fast. I hate that it takes an entire day to cover ground I used to be able to drive across in a car in half an hour. Forget about the regularity with which I used to break the sound barrier."

"Is that all you miss?"

He laughed. "No. I miss my family, too. But I always missed my family. We try to make the holiday gatherings, but since Pete and Carl entered the service it's always been at the whim of the U.S. Navy. Military service is never conducive to family togetherness."

Lindsay sighed, and he could feel her relaxing against his

knees. "I miss people, too. My job frequently took me away from home, but I could always look forward to seeing them again. Now I'm afraid I can't."

Alex's only reply was a soft grunt, for another feature of military service was the knowledge that there were no guarantees of coming back from anywhere. He'd grown up in the shadow of death, where uncles and cousins were buried with flags on their coffins, where his mother spoke frequently of friends whose husbands had become casualties during the Vietnam War. He'd never known what it might be like to be certain of seeing his father or brothers again. Now he was certain the time had finally come he wouldn't.

The combing slowed. Became more of a caressing. Stroking. A finger traced the outside of her ear. He wanted to bend and kiss her. She was practically lying in his lap, and the desire to press his mouth to her cheek was intense. Movement stopped. His hand lay against her head, and he didn't dare go on lest he lean toward her.

"Are you finished?"

Alex blinked. The moment was broken. "Uh-huh."

She sat up. "Thank you. Do you need the comb?"

He shook his head and had to clear his throat. "I don't seem to have any 'wee creatures' there yet." His hair was still short from his military cut, and though it was grown out some and felt shaggy, it still wasn't long enough to make the bugs comfortable. They preferred his clothing and his privates.

Lindsay got up from the ground and moved to her pallet without a glance at him. As he watched her go, watched her settle in among the folds of her parachute, he wondered what was going through her mind. Did she know what she was doing to him? She must. Was it possible he was doing any of those same things to her? He doubted it, and that helped him look away. No sense in letting himself get all worked up for nothing. He extinguished the lamp, lay down, and rolled away from her.

After a while, her voice came in the darkness. "I expect I'll be required to kill someone eventually."

Alex rolled onto his back and replied to the darkness, "I expect so."

"How does one prepare for that?"

"You don't think about it. The more you think about what it means, the less likely you'll be the one left alive when the fighting's over. When you fight, the only thing you can be thinking about is making the other guy not kill you. And you do that by killing him first. Make it so he can't get back up and come after you again."

Her voice was soft, hesitant. "That sounds awfully cold."

"Don't expect warm fuzzies from the enemy. Never forget that he's there to kill you, and he'll do it if you give him the slightest chance." He looked over at her, but saw only darkness. There was no reply. Eventually he gave up waiting for one, and rolled away from her once more to sleep.

It was only the next day that Alex found out what Lindsay had taken from their talk. Shortly after dawn, after the men had eaten breakfast and while the squires were at work preparing the horses, there arose a clamor among the tents. Alex left his fire to investigate the uproar, curious who was going at it but not particularly surprised or alarmed. Fights here were frequent, and so long as nobody died or was injured badly enough to affect performance they weren't any of his business. He hovered near a tree to watch.

But he groaned when he saw the combatants were Lindsay and another squire, the largest man of his rank in the detail. "Crap." He'd hoped she'd back off from this nonsense, but she'd done just the opposite. Now she was getting her ass kicked. Though she tried to dodge the blows, the other squire was faster as well as larger, and whalloped her with ham fists. It didn't take long for him to knock her down.

"Stay down," Alex whispered.

Lindsay regained her feet quickly, and came back at her opponent. Bare-fisted and without her mace, the punches she landed were many but not very effective. She did little more than make the squire stagger, and he came back with blows that rocked her head back and knocked her to her knees. Blood ran from her nose and dripped from her chin.

"Stay down, Lindsay. Please." Alex's hands were fists at his sides.

But, no, she dragged herself to her feet again. The other squire circled quickly, too fast for her, and backhanded her head so she fell forward. Once again she struggled to her feet. Alex muttered a string of vulgarisms and began to pace among the trees, wishing the fight would be over.

The larger squire busted Lindsay in the face again so she went flying and landed on her back. Stunned, she lay there, but even half-conscious she was trying to regain her feet. Her opponent walked over and drew back a foot to kick her in the belly.

"No!" Alex pushed his way between the onlookers at a run. "Hold!" The squire stayed his foot and turned to stare. Alex strode in with all the authority he could muster, knowing it was an improper intrusion and he was going to pay for it later in terms of unit morale. "Leave huh—him alone. He's down and unconscious. You've beaten him."

She protested, "I'm not—"

"You're down, Lindsay. He's won. Let it go."

The other squire gave him a dull look, then glanced at his master, Sir Cullan, who nodded and indicated with a chin movement that he should get to work readying the horses. The squire stepped over Lindsay to obey.

Alex turned to the crowd. "Show's over. Nothing more to see, men."

The crowd dispersed, and Alex knelt by his squire. "How come you kept getting up?"

"I wanted to fight well." Her voice was a burble of blood and saliva, her lips swollen and purple. He helped her up, and she stood with her feet splayed like a colt to keep her balance. "Why did you stop him?"

"He was about to kill you. And how come you picked on the biggest guy here? Wait, don't tell me, you wanted to impress everyone."

"You said—"

"I said fight. I didn't say get yourself beat to a bloody pulp."

"I thought I could take him. I thought, being smaller, I'd be faster than he."

"You were wrong. And you were crazy. I think you may have bruised his face a little, but winning that fight wasn't going to happen."

"You still shouldn't have stopped it." She straightened as she regained her senses.

"It was a stupid thing to do."

"Seriously, Alex. Don't ever do that again." Her voice was

angry. She wiped blood from her chin, looked at it on her hand, then walked away.

Alex watched her go, and wondered if he should have just let that guy kick the wind out of her.

IN September, after the fall of Linlithgow Castle, the company moved on, ahead of the main Scottish forces and to the east. Without any of the impunity the English enjoyed, and without the manpower and other resources of King Edward, the Scots moved quickly, efficiently, scoping out the territory ahead and reporting back to Edward Bruce with squires on the fastest horses.

During this time, constantly on the move, Alex helped Lindsay keep her secret by trying to make their camps in places that would provide private access to clean water. Burns running through thick forest were easy to find in this era where towns were far between and farmland barely pushed back the wilderness, and so it was often Alex stood guard over Lindsay's privacy while she bathed. He liked a good scrub himself, and they usually traded off on guard duty.

One evening as the sun slanted quickly to the west, after his own bath Alex was taking his post on the path to guard Lindsay when he realized he'd left his hauberk on the bank. He declared his presence as he returned for it, but was quite surprised when he stepped into the clearing by the water. Lindsay, wearing only her T-shirt and panties, was struggling to get out of his heavy, slithery, chain mail hauberk. The forest was thick, and the clearing small. She danced around in it, unable to get the metal shirt to go on or off.

"What are you doing?" Surely she could hear the smile in his voice even through the rattling mail. It was a temptation to laugh out loud.

Bent over, trying to heave the metal garment over her head so it would slide to the ground, she grunted as she replied, "I just wanted to see what it was like."

"It's heavy."

"I can see that."

"It swishes when you walk."

"I know that. I wanted to know whether I could carry it."

"Can you?"

She quit struggling, the hauberk over her head and stuck almost halfway up her back. "Will you help me with this?"

"What if I hadn't come back for it?"

"I would have gone and found you."

"Like that?"

"Whatever it might take to get out of this. Will you *please* help me?"

He chuckled and went to lift some of the weight from her arms so she could back out of the mail. It crossed his mind she'd asked him to help her undress, and he decided he would be a lucky man if she might want him to remove her underwear as well. For that, he wouldn't even make her say "please" again.

Then there was giggling, and it certainly wasn't Lindsay. Alex immediately dropped the hauberk and went for the dagger at his belt, but there was nobody nearby. Lindsay let the mail slide to the ground, then tugged her T-shirt over her hips as she looked around. "What's wrong?" She hadn't heard it.

"Didn't you hear someone giggling?"

"No."

More giggling, then Lindsay said, "Okay, I heard that." She looked around and ran her fingers through her messed-up hair as she sidled close. "Who is it?"

Then Alex spotted it. A tiny person, perched on a moss-covered log nearby. She wore a brightly colored and belted sleeveless tunic the length of a miniskirt, and nothing else. Most of her was exposed through the gaping sleeves and neck of her garment, and it was not apparent why she bothered wearing the thing at all. "Who are you?"

"'Tis I who should be doing the asking, as you are the one walking all over my home."

"This is open forest."

"Typical response from a human trampling my ring. But if you would be so kind as to continue what you were about, I'll be entertained enough to leave you be until ye care to return to your own home."

"I beg your pardon?"

Lindsay said, "Alex, look." He looked, but saw nothing. "We have trampled her ring."

"What?"

"Look." She pointed, and he looked.

"Toadstools."

"Now look all around. The edge of the clearing."

Then he saw. All around the edge of the clearing was a line of large, brown toadstools. It encircled the log on which the little woman sat, ran up next to the water, and surrounded himself and Lindsay. "What is it? Ring?"

"A faerie ring. She's right; we're trespassing." To the woman she said, "You must forgive him; he's an American and has no manners."

Alex narrowed his eyes at Lindsay, then looked up at the creature, whose eyes were bright blue and hair was black as coal. She was awfully tiny, but no more faerielike than any other small, thin person. "Should we move? Will she leave us alone if we move outside her circle?"

"Don't be talking about me as if I werenae here. And besides, the energy the two of you have brought to me has caught my attention and there's naught to be done about it at this juncture. So just go about your business, and I'll watch."

"What business?"

"Ye cannae lie to me. I can see it all through the two of you. The maucht was so strong when ye both stepped inside the circle, I'll wager we'll have company from other parts of the forest soon to enjoy the show. So hurry, before they get here. Do it now."

"Do what?"

"Good God." Lindsay gaped at the faerie, and her face flushed darker than Alex had ever seen it. "I don't think so." At that she picked up her flight suit, stepped into it, and zipped it up, then began retrieving her belts and weapons.

"Hey," said Alex. "Is this that Danu faerie?"

"Hardly." Lindsay averted her eyes from his.

"What is she talking about?"

"I don't wish to talk about it."

"Lindsay—"

"Just . . . never mind." She hurried from the clearing.

Alex turned to the faerie. "What's the deal?"

"Ye could have had her, lad." Appearing disappointed, and mildly disgusted with Alex, she set her chin in her hand and rested elbow on knee.

"Could have . . ." Realization made him boggle. "Could have *had* her? You're not serious."

"Absolutely serious. She wants you, and I'm appalled ye cannae even see it."

"She doesn't."

"Does."

"How would you know?"

"I'm a faerie, ye sumph. We ken these things."

Speechless now, Alex looked in the direction Lindsay had taken. He picked up his hauberk, went to follow her, and caught up with her. She was looking for another spot in the burn to bathe. When she saw Alex, she crossed her arms over her chest and lowered her chin to look at him.

He said, "Ignore her. I think she's just giving us grief because she gets off on it." More giggling from behind, and he glanced back. "See?"

"Perhaps we should return to camp?"

"Nah. Just ignore her." But he couldn't help wondering whether the faerie was right. Might Lindsay have been open to an advance? Plainly she wasn't now, but had she been?

She looked behind him, where they both heard more giggling. "Do you believe in faeries now?"

"I believe in pointy-eared people, I suppose."

"You know, Alex, I don't know whether you noticed this, but you were speaking to that faerie entirely in modern American English."

Now he felt stupid again, not grasping her point. "Uh huh."

"And she understood every word."

His eyebrows went up and he looked back toward the clearing. She was right. The faerie knew modern English, just as that elf-looking guy had. The woman had the same connection to the future. He hurried back to the toadstool ring, but now there was no faerie. No wee folk of any kind, nor any giggling.

And suddenly he realized he didn't want to find her, even if she had the power to return them to their own time, which he doubted. He glanced around the clearing, a quick once-over and nearly dreading the sight of the faerie, then in the direction Lindsay had taken.

A strange lightheadedness came over him as he thought of the prospect of going home and what there would be to gain or lose by it. On the one hand, it would be sweet to return to the life he'd had, where seven centuries of civilization and technical advance pertained. On the other hand, he was coping well with his new life. He liked the autonomy of his new position. The prospects for advancement were nothing to sneeze at, either. Robert Bruce was going to win this war, and that meant advancement and wealth for everyone loyal to him. Alex now wanted things he would never have found in his old life. If they went home he would return to his ship, and Lindsay would return to London and whatever life she'd had there. Certainly he would never see her again.

Never see Lindsay again.

Without having looked all that hard, he returned to the tent and said he'd been unable to find the creature.

CHAPTER 7

One day while on patrol Sir Orrin, who had ranged ahead to scout, returned at speed. He galloped up to Alex, reined in to a skidding halt, and said breathlessly, "A column of knights flying the banner of Lord Clifford. Coming north."

"How many?" Alex asked.

The knight shrugged. "I didn't stop to count them."

"Why not? Did they see you and chase you?"

Orrin shook his head. "I wanted to report as quickly as possible." He seemed pleased with himself, and Alex wondered why. He peered at the excited man, and not for the first time wished for a modern military officer in his command. Just one man.

"But you have nothing to report. Do you remember where they are? How far?"

Now Orrin nodded eagerly. "Aye. Over that way." He pointed.

"Where is that way?"

"Through some woods, and across those hills that way."

An impatient sigh escaped Alex. "Take me there." When the eager knight wheeled and kicked his horse to a gallop, Alex whistled for him to stop. He turned, puzzled. "I said, take me there. Wait for me to come with you."

Then Alex called out to one of his more reliable knights,

"Halt here. Don't make camp; I'll return shortly, and we may have to move out in a hurry." He gestured to Sir Cullan to come with him, and Cullan rode over with a squire. When Alex turned to go with his scout, Lindsay kicked her horse to follow.

Alex reined in and turned. "No, not you." He waved her to a halt.

"But, sir—"

"I said, you stay."

She pressed her lips together, but said nothing further. Alex spurred his horse to a canter and the three knights and a squire hurried off to find the position of the English.

They watched the enemy from a vantage point among trees on a hillside, hopefully hidden from the English scouts. When Alex learned how near the column was, what it carried, and its size, at once alarm and excitement surged in his blood and a smile rose to his face. It was a provisioning train, herding livestock and pulling lumbering wagons filled with food and equipment. By simple body count his small company was outnumbered by nearly double, but the English had fewer men-at-arms. The rest seemed to be women, children, and unarmed peasant workmen. They were making good time, considering their burdens, so decisiveness was called for on Alex's part. He couldn't be certain whether the English knights knew of his presence and position, but he doubted it. This wasn't an army, only a guard for the provisions, and probably they were hurrying to garrison rather than looking for a fight. A whispered conversation with Sir Cullan supported the idea.

"Castle Galashiels lies up the river." Cullan pointed with his chin. "They're more than likely going there," said the knight from Barra. His flowing, white-blond hair spilled from his helmet and lifted in the breeze.

"Is it close enough for them to make it by nightfall?"

The man thought for a moment, grimaced, then nodded. "If they keep this speed, they could arrive by then, or shortly after. We'll need to apprehend them by midday, or they'll be close enough to the castle for the garrison to be a danger to us."

Crap. "All right, then, let's go."

They hurried back to rejoin the company, and Alex had his knights form up to intercept. The provision train seemed to be following the river and would have to ford at a particular spot to attain the castle in question, so that was where Alex took his men. He cantered over the land on each side of that ford and wasn't entirely pleased with what he found. It would be best to place his ambush on the far side to catch the convoy while it crossed, the way William Wallace had skunked his enemy at Stirling Bridge, but here the ford was too generous and the land after the crossing was too open. There would be no way to contain the English while they crossed or once they were on the other side, and Alex didn't care to be outflanked.

His best bottleneck was before the ford. The land just short of the crossing was a narrow field, hemmed in by the river on one side and a steep slope on the other. They were well away from the train's intended destination, and blocked the only route to it, atop a long, low hill that overlooked the field. This was where they would await their prey.

Alex and others who owned coursers retired their rounseys and mounted the larger horses trained for battle. Squires supplied their knights with lances, then fell back to ready themselves at the rear. Alex himself declined to use a lance. He knew their value in battle was not worth the risk in wielding them, particularly to himself for he was untrained for them. But he didn't discourage his knights from them. So long as the English were carrying lances, he needed men who had them also.

Scottish knights arrayed across the hill, and squires waited behind it. The reserves would be out of sight of the English until they were needed, a surprise tactic the Duke of Wellington would hone in his struggles against Napoleon a few centuries later.

There the detail waited, each man taking the opportunity for a drink of water—or to relieve himself of some water—as needed. Alex stared at the track by the river, down the slope where the train would first show themselves, and occupied himself letting go of all that mattered to him except to win this battle. He readied himself to die. It was a difficult process at any time, but especially now, for Lindsay kept rising in his thoughts. She was at his back, mounted and waiting with the other squires, and just as likely to die today as himself. More likely, perhaps, for she wasn't as aggressive as the men and had doubts about this job. He hated that she was involved, and was far less sanguine about what might happen to her than about his own possible fate.

The excited scout came at the gallop, his mount dancing as he reined in before Alex, and reported the approach of the English convoy. The trap was ready to be sprung. Alex's pulse picked up as he realized he was about to fight his first pitched battle as a knight.

The wait was not long; by the standards of the day, they'd made their position barely in time. The band of Englishmen came over the rise in the distance, then halted at sight of the Scots ranged on their rise. Their apparent surprise made Alex wonder if the train had even bothered to employ scouts. It was entirely possible they hadn't, what with the state of military matters being so slipshod these days and the arrogance of those loyal to Edward II so prevalent. But the English knights hurried to make up for their mistake. Quickly they came forward from the wagons and arranged themselves across their end of the ground, foot soldiers to the rear.

The Scottish line began to creep forward, a forest of lances already beginning to tip to front for the charge. Alex spurred his horse before them to put a stop to that. "Hold!" he called to them, loud enough to hear but not enough to carry across to the enemy. "Don't give yourselves away. Show the English you're not afraid; don't let them see you fidget like shy girls before a suitor." He rode along the line, looking each man in the eye as he passed. "You men are Scots. A fighting force superior to any in the world. Know those coddled southerners are afraid of you. Know they will see your calm and be the more frightened for your confidence. And when I give the order to charge, you will assault them. You will overpower them. You will ride through them like . . ." a smile touched his mouth, ". . . like crap through a goose."

There was a cough from the rear, and he thought it might have been Lindsay, who had surely seen that movie, too. The rest of the men nodded, in complete agreement with General Patton.

"On me, men." Alex returned to his place in the line. Horses all through the ranks fidgeted with the tension of their riders, but there was no more jostling for the front line.

And so they all waited. The English waited for Alex to charge, and he waited for them to make the first move. Sir Orrin bellowed a challenge, and Alex ordered calmly, "Silence." His men eyed him sideways, but obeyed. "Be still," he commanded. His courser shifted weight impatiently, eager to run, and Alex held him with his knees.

One of the English rode out to the middle of the field under a flag of truce, apparently to parlay. Alex remained where he was. He wanted those supplies and knew they were worth a fight, for the Scottish army was chronically underprovisioned. The train had no choice but to come this way, for if they turned back the Scots would charge immediately and take them from behind. No deals for the English today. Alex only sat his horse and stared.

Everyone continued to wait, then finally the negotiator returned to his line. Across the way there was a great deal of putting heads together and agitated gesturing, and Alex figured he had his opponent good and pissed off now.

"Wait for it," Alex urged his men.

Finally the English arrayed themselves to charge. Alex again told his men to wait. The English began their charge, and still Alex said to wait. The attackers rode nearly the length of the field, and were halfway up the slope to the Scottish position before Alex finally drew his sword to brandish it over his head, and bellowed as he spurred his mount, *"Charge!"*

His courser surged forward and he rode with his men toward the oncoming English lances. Alex galloped at speed, his sword held high, and he saw he was chosen by a man opposite. He aimed himself. *Steady,* he told himself. *Speed and distance . . . speed and distance . . . steady . . . sword high, let him think you're a yahoo. Let him think all Scots are idiots.* Each stride of his horse was measured in his head. Every wobble of the English lance observed. Closer he came. Like flying a dogfight in slow motion. At the last moment before his opposing number would touch him, he ducked and slipped sideways in his saddle to press against his horse's neck, let the tip of the lance past, and swung his sword behind himself to catch his attacker in the face. The English helmet flew.

Immediately he righted himself and reined in, then wheeled his horse. The English knight held his bleeding face in one gauntlet, his horse loping and stalling under no control. Alex spurred his mount to finish the guy off with a blow to the back of his now bare head, then turned for a fresh opponent.

Horses and men all around screamed and shouted, amid the crunch of metal on metal. Swords flashed against mail and plate with the dull thud of banging pots under which could be heard the grunts of exertion.

Alex faced off against another enemy and engaged him. Their horses circled as they went at each other, each trying to reach the other's off side. Then Alex gave that up and crowded in an attempt to get inside the sword length. He knocked his opponent with his pommel, but for his trouble was clouted by a mace in the English knight's left hand. Alex saw stars, and had to parry madly the sword that followed the mace. He shook his head to clear it, and renewed his effort at gaining an advantage with his sword. The horses circled once more.

In a flail of legs and head, the English horse went down, screaming, hamstrung by an unhorsed Scot who then dispatched Alex's opponent as casually as swatting a spider. Alex saluted his follower, then wheeled his horse and spotted Lindsay whacking hell out of a foot soldier with her mace. Mounted, she had a terrible advantage of height, but the infantryman slashed at her leg. She kicked him, and when he turned back she clobbered him in the head with her mace. When he stood again, without his helmet, she hit him again. This time he fell and didn't get up. Alex smiled.

Then across his chest he took a surprise hit from nowhere. The hauberk held, but his breath was knocked nearly away. He gasped for air, in remarkably little physical pain as he cursed himself for losing his focus. The horses danced away from each other and Alex swung to oppose his attacker, then the riders charged again to clash swords and circle once more. At another approach, Alex took the off side and had his horse crowd the other. Close in, he drew his dagger quickly to stab his opponent under the chin. The Englishman dropped his sword to grab his neck in a hopeless attempt to save his own life. Blood gushed over his gauntlet, and he quickly slumped over his saddle.

Alex turned to survey the waning struggle, and found Lindsay on foot now, swinging her mace at an English knight who had her at a disadvantage with his sword though he was also on foot. In an instant Alex was on him, attacking from behind and swinging like a polo player, and broke the knight's back with a heavy blow. The English knight swung as he went down, and caught the underside of Lindsay's arm. She shouted in pain and fell to her knees. Alex wheeled his horse, then leapt from it to go to her.

"Are you all right?" He reached for her arm.

She jerked it back and struggled to her feet. "Get away from me!"

"Lindsay, give me your arm." But she ignored him and tried to stanch the bleeding herself.

The clamor about them was dying, and Alex glanced around to find the tatters of the English detail were fleeing, back the way they'd come, leaving their pack train and wagons to the pursuing Scots. He flagged down Sir Cullan and shouted orders to him over the din.

"Send your squires to chase them a short distance, but only far enough to keep them from trying to reclaim their goods. Then the squires should give up the chase and return. You and the knights take charge of that train immediately, and start moving it off toward Linlithgow. We'll keep moving so long as there's moonlight tonight to see by."

"Aye, sir." The knight hurried to obey.

Then Alex turned to Lindsay, who was pressing a hand to her wound with little success. The hand was entirely red with blood. "I said, give me that arm."

"No! I want you away from me!" She shouted in anger, and her voice cracked with the pain of her wound. Her eyes glittered with rage. Dark hair spilled from her helmet and stuck to her face from the sweat. She shoved it away with a bloodied hand, and left a smear across her forehead.

"I saved your life." The battle high was still pounding in his ears, surging in his veins, and he was gasping for breath. There was still much to do, and in a hurry. He had no time or mental energy for this.

She squared off with him. "And who asked you? Are you going to be following me around the rest of my life to make sure I never have to do anything I'm supposed to? Why can't you just let me do this? How come I've got to be something different to you from what I am to everyone else around here? However in hell am I going to make a reputation with you following me around, fighting my battles?"

"I just want you to be safe."

"No, you don't. You want to fuck me. And I'm telling you right now, MacNeil, that's not going to happen." She let go of her wound and raised her mace. "If you come near me again, I'll bloody kill you. I mean it, Alex. You will not touch me. Ever."

Words stuck in his throat. He was so shocked he couldn't even tell her how wrong she was. All he could think was that he wanted to knock her out just then. So he stared, his mouth dropped open. Finally she turned and walked off, blood dripping from her fingertips.

Once she was far enough away he could trust himself to move, he thrust his sword into the sod with every bit of strength left to him. Then he threw back his head and bellowed his frustration and anger so it echoed off the slopes around him. A few well-chosen expletives were added, and only then could he think about looking for his horse. Through the darkness of his rage, he found the thread of thought for what was needed next. He focused on that.

First he searched the dead knight's body for his ransom cache and slipped the leather drawstring purse into a pocket of his flight suit. Then he remounted for the work ahead, taking the provisions to Edward Bruce. They hurried, and rode straight through to Linlithgow. Alex posted Lindsay at the rear of their column, and so never spoke to her the entire way. The rage festered in his gut, and he had to contain it as best he could.

The plunder was rich, more so because a good half of the English contingent was left dead on the ground while Alex had lost only five of his knights and six squires. When they reached Linlithgow Castle, Alex was paid appropriately for the cattle and supplies, the money for which he distributed to his men according to rank and seniority, himself taking the lion's share, which was his due as commander. Then, in addition to Lindsay's share, he tossed her the purse from the knight who had cut her. She glowered at him, but he could tell she was nonplussed by the gesture.

Then he walked over and stared straight into her face, leaning in the way he used to when impressing his ire upon ill-behaved enlisted seamen. She pulled in her chin and leaned back, but otherwise held her ground. He said, his voice a low, ugly, pissed-off growl, "Now hear this, soldier. If at any time any man in my command finds himself in a position to give aid or support in battle to a comrade, he will give it." He paused briefly for that to sink in, then continued. "We are a unit. We are not a cluster of yahoos flailing at the enemy. We work together, we give support, and we accept support. Any deviation from this policy will be met by immediate disciplinary action." Another short pause, then, "Am I coming in loud and clear, soldier?"

Her reply was prompt. "Yes, sir."

"Good. See that you don't forget it."

"Yes, sir." Anger still flashed in her eyes, but he thought she understood. Alex turned on his heel and walked away.

That night they encamped just outside the castle walls. He had one of the hunters slaughter and spit an entire cow for his men to feast on, and in addition provided them all with bread, cheese, mead, and public women from among the camp followers of the larger army.

The fire was high, throwing sparks and flaring at dripping grease from the roasting carcass. Now that they were all relatively safe, well fed, and well on their way to being drunk enough to not care how ugly the whores were, the men of Alex's company relaxed, lounging around the fire, telling and retelling of the skirmish to each other and to the women, and to anyone else who would listen. Others from the castle and Bruce's men came to share in the food and festive mood, and Sir Hector came to hear the exploits of his half-brother Ailig and cousin Cullan.

Musicians began to collect. First a guy with a lute wandered in to serenade and accept whatever coins might come his way. He was a rangy, rawboned character, with a bright eye and a quick wit as he improvised his ribald lyrics. Soon he was joined by a midget with a small, wooden whistle and a boy who played a flat drum with a two-headed stick. Now the soldiers, most of them drunk enough they had no business even trying to stand, were moved to get up and dance to the lively tunes with the women in their company. The lute player sang songs of love, of knights giving service for the regard of great ladies. Of romance and devotion, pure and chaste.

Romance. Love. The words gave Alex a knot in his gut that felt the size of a cannonball, and he sucked down an entire bowl of mead in one draught. Maybe if he could get drunk enough, the knot would loosen and stop annoying him.

After a while, after more than his share of mead, he decided he felt pretty good. His purse was fattening, and quickly, considering he'd only been at this a few months. He'd come through this battle with no worse wound than a deep bruise across his chest and a slight hitch to his breathing, and that bit of luck surprised him as well as relieved him. It brought a weird feeling of immortality at the same time he knew the odds were against him living a long, full life. Since Kosovo, each time he lived after having prepared to die was like a reprieve, and the joy of it was heady.

The alcohol in his brain made the world swim, and the sharp edges of reality blurred so there was no pain. Anywhere. Even when he looked at Lindsay and saw her sulking and bored, the sleeve of her flight suit rolled up and a bloody rag wrapped around her forearm, he was able to shrug it off and not care. Let her sulk. He didn't care. She didn't want him to help her; he didn't care.

Damn straight, he didn't care. He didn't.

What he cared about at that moment was the woman who plopped herself down next to him and snuggled up. "Hello," she greeted as she pressed her breasts against his arm. Her waist was cinched and laced, but he could feel the cushion of her bosom against his flight suit. She was warm and eager, and soft. Very soft, everywhere. He decided he liked women whose breasts weren't bound by elastic bandages.

"Hello, yourself." He knew the grin on his face was an idiot's, but he couldn't wipe it away. It just wouldn't go.

"You're a handsome one."

That gave him a charge of pleasure, though he couldn't return the compliment. Her hair was frizzy, brown, and uncombed, and her round face was completely free of chin. But just then he figured all cats were gray in the dark, and if she thought he was handsome then that was something at least. She placed her hand on his upper thigh and squeezed, and that made him more than smile. He took a glance at Lindsay, who was frowning at him from the other side of the fire, then he leaned down and kissed the whore.

The woman eagerly accepted, and moved her hand straight to his crotch. She leaned back, pleased at what she'd found, and said, "Oh, but you're even more handsome than I'd thought!"

He laughed, and kissed her again as he grabbed her chest. She fumbled with the front of his flight suit, then began to take a closer look at it. "What sort of garment is this, then? I've never seen the like!" She tugged at the flap over the zipper and tried to pull the teeth apart, then held it to the firelight and ran her finger over them.

Rather than explain to the creature, who wouldn't have understood anyway, he stood, took her by the hand, and drew her away from the fire and into the tent he shared with Lindsay. He didn't want the whore hauling his equipment out into the open, which by observations of the other pairs pawing each other around the fire he knew was more than a possibility, and so he guided her onto his straw mattress and parachute. Her giggling and silly chatter about her good luck to be with such a handsome man was so enthusiastic, it was almost endearing.

The act didn't take long, particularly since Alex couldn't allow the woman to see him or handle him, and he was out of his mind horny and drunk besides. He could only unzip his suit and lift her dress, and there was barely enough sense left in his brain to pull out the one condom he had, put it on, then climb on and start banging away. It didn't take long at all, and when it was over he rolled off her, zipped himself, and gave her a pearl before telling her to leave the tent. Consciousness remained just long enough for him to watch her go, thrilled to squealing with her enormous tip, then he collapsed onto his parachute and passed out.

The morning sun woke him, entirely too high but cold in the late September. Alex's head felt like he'd been clobbered with a mace, but the rest of him was warm and relaxed from last night's encounter. He looked over at Lindsay, sitting on her mattress, and caught her frowning at him again. She looked away, and he wondered what the hell she expected from him.

"You were right," he said through a throatful of phlegm, then coughed to clear it. "All I needed was to get laid." There was something cold and clammy stuck to his thigh, and he reached into his flight suit for the condom that was now loose in there. Not sure what to do with it, he threw it into a corner where it would at least be out of the way until they moved on. It caught and dangled on a tuft of grass.

Lindsay said, "You used the condom? Whatever for? The diseases those things were invented for don't exist here yet. Not till Columbus's men pick them up from the red Indians and bring them back."

He looked over at the limp bit of latex, grunted and shrugged, then adjusted his skivvies before zipping his suit again.

She continued, "Leprosy on the other hand . . ."

Oh boy. He glanced over at her, then looked away and shut his eyes. Something new to worry about. "Thanks for the trivia lesson." He lay down on his mattress and tried to go back to sleep. But he was awake, his head was pounding, and his stomach felt like it had been kicked by a horse. He needed food. Maybe some more mead to take the edge off this. He struggled to his feet and made his way to the tent door and called for his other squire, who was a fifteen-year-old boy and not just pretending. He was a big kid, though, and looked older.

"Colin," he said, "bring me a plate of cold meat and some mead."

The boy gaped for a moment, unaccustomed to being told to do anything not involving the horses, and his gaze went past Alex into the tent. Alex turned to find Lindsay behind, staring at him. He turned to Colin and said, "Go, boy. Now."

"Aye, sir." Colin went.

Alex returned to his mattress without a glance at Lindsay, lay back, and put his arm across his face. There was a horrible, sinking feeling as he realized he still wanted her.

CHAPTER 8

Quite naturally, the garrison at Galashiels Castle was the Scots' next target, for they knew that castle wouldn't be receiving supplies or reinforcement anytime soon. Edward Bruce's army approached with as much stealth as possible, and encamped in a hollow some miles from the town before sending scouts to reconnoiter.

Impatient with long sieges, and inspired by the imprudent proximity of forest to the outer curtain of the fortress as well as a nearly moonless night, Edward grasped firmly those advantages and decided on a quick and daring approach to defeating this garrison. He took his best knights, including Alex and his forty, and bearing rope ladders slung over their shoulders, crept up on the ramparts on an early October evening.

Squires remained in the forest with the horses and infantry, but Alex allowed Lindsay to accompany him, a risky decision among men for whom being first in was a matter of spoils as well as reputation. To quell the objections of the privileged knights as well as the squires left out of the action, he had her carry a bucket of urine in case they were discovered and set upon by greek fire. Urine and vinegar being the only things that would put out the oily, napalmlike concoction, it behooved them to bring some along, and carrying the evil-smelling bucket was a degrading job nobody else wanted. Lindsay wanted to play with the big dogs; he figured he'd let her.

In black cloaks, and faces smeared with ash, several hundred Scots crept through the forest toward the castle, carrying with them large rocks and sacks of earth with which to fill a part of the moat so it would be shallow enough for crossing. The work went carefully and silently as the night deepened.

Once the moat was defeated and the Scots began to cross single file, Alex led his men, intensely aware of the watchmen above bearing crossbows. Edward's men spread out along the curtain wall, and Alex was ordered to take his to the side of the castle nearest the portcullis. Once assembled beneath the walls and surrounding the castle, they all dropped their cloaks to the ground and with long rods began raising the grapnel hooks of the ladders to the battlements. It took immense strength to lift the rod-and-rope ladder to such a height, and with enough dexterity to set the hook silently on the stone above. Even with the support of two other knights, Alex's arms began to ache before he could pull the rod vertical, and nearly gave out by the time he was able to find an adequate niche in the dark and set the grapple three stories above his head.

As commander, he was first up his ladder, with his best men close behind him. Lindsay came last, carrying her bucket up the unanchored, stretchy, swinging rope ladder, and that bothered him. He would rather she had been ahead of him, but he could no longer treat her differently from the men. Instead, he put her from his mind and told himself she wanted it this way. She'd barely spoken to him since the skirmish with the provisions train, and it was plain that the more he tried to demonstrate to her his concern for her safety the more convinced she would be he was only making moves on her. Damned and damned.

He climbed the ladder, and paused just under the parapet to listen.

In a distant part of the castle a cry of alarm rose, and Alex cursed as he climbed the rest of the way and hauled himself over the stone wall. Quickly he ran, drawing his broadsword, but he pulled up when he saw nobody to oppose him. Torches flickered along the battlement and in the bailey below, and a dozen figures were hurrying toward the door. The watch on this side was gone.

He grinned. *Cool.*

Alex ran toward the gatehouse, his men close behind in single file along the parapet. They found only one defender at the raising mechanism, that man outnumbered, surprised, cowed, and quickly dispatched. "Come!" Alex waved his men into the room. Several of them gathered at the mechanism and pulled mightily to raise the gate, and the rest hurried down the stairs toward the bailey. In the torch-lit dimness Alex saw Lindsay straining at the bar, and he remembered the bench press back on the ship. This task was one he knew she was quite up to, and that enabled him to ignore her and concentrate on what else was at hand.

English knights came, wielding swords and maces, and shouting curses. Alex and some others broke away to defend the gate-raisers, and he found himself challenged by a large knight whose blows rattled him to his boots. Alex staggered beneath their force, but gave no ground. There was very little ground to give in that space. His men had the gate moving, then a little faster. At the first crack wide enough to accommodate a man, Edward Bruce's infantry and the cavalry squires pressed in and joined the fray with an elated cry. At the sound of shouting Scots below, the English knights fighting in the gatehouse broke off to flee to the parapet.

Alex's opponent shoved him off, then turned and fled for the stairs. Alex chased him, and shoved him forward hard so he toppled head first down the spiral in a clatter of plate and mail. Alex followed and finished off the moaning knight with a dagger to the throat, then hauled him on down the stairs so the body wouldn't block the passage of Scots through the gatehouse.

In the bailey Alex took on another challenger as fellow Scots ran past. His single-handed broadsword was at a power disadvantage against the other knight's longer two-handed cross-hilt sword, and so he had to be light on his feet. Speed was a small equalizer, but all he had, and he concentrated on not being where he was expected. The English knight's sword clanged and clattered against a stone wall one second, then pavement underfoot the next. Alex concentrated on getting inside the slower blade to break the man's joints through the mail, and finding exposed skin he could harry, his blows as heavy as he could make them and still be quick.

But he was tiring. He needed to put this guy away soon, or be the one to die. He took fewer swings, dodging to catch an extra moment between blows. The other knight was forcing him backward. Alex's strength was flagging. He had to do something different. His gun was in his right thigh pocket. He reached with his left hand to unzip it, but his hauberk was too long and he couldn't take the time to bend and reach it. He transferred his sword to his left hand to reach for the gun with his right, but now his speed was gone and he found himself staggering beneath the other man's assaults. His shoulder felt like it would drop from its socket, and breathing was such a terrible effort it felt as if he were only exhaling over and over. Alex's sword went back to his right hand and he pressed his opponent to keep from being backed into a wall. Then he circled and backed some more, not entirely certain where he was headed. But he made his opponent chase him, throwing his rhythm off. Alex began to catch a second wind.

Then he feinted to the left, swung his weapon like a windmill, and attacked to the right. The Englishman was forced to parry with his arm, and Alex felt the satisfying give of broken bone under the mail. Again he feinted and attacked, and was parried neatly by his opponent's sword. But at the same time he drew his dagger with his left, stepped in, and stabbed the English knight in the throat.

The snarling knight only shouted in pain, coughed, and spat blood, renewing his vigor with the sword.

Alex cursed, then backed and circled some more, hoping there would be enough blood to weaken the guy. Swords clanged, and the Englishman cursed him and his unborn progeny, blood spraying from his lips as he spoke. Alex's aching arm slowed, and desperation came.

"Die, dammit!"

The knight wouldn't obey, though blood streamed over the neck of his coif and soaked into his surcoat, in a spreading, black stain that glistened in the torchlight. Alex erupted in an impatient roar and slammed his sword harder with each blow.

Finally the other knight stumbled, weakening with the bleeding. He began to stagger. In an instant Alex hauled back, gripped his sword with both hands, and with all his might delivered a blow to the head. The helmet dented and the knight collapsed, his head caved in on one side and blood streaming from the metal casing and across his face.

Gasping for air, Alex turned from the dead knight and looked for a spot to take a moment's respite and regain his breath. He slipped into a dark corridor nearby and collapsed against the stone wall, gasping, chest heaving in the cold night air that was like knives in his lungs. Every joint in his upper body felt pulled apart and jammed back together like a child's abused toy. But there was only a moment to rest, to bring the gasping under control, then he found some stairs and followed them up to the parapet where swords still clashed and echoed from the castle curtain.

He came out of the stairwell to find himself behind an English knight engaged with a Scot, and ran to take him, sword raised. But then a torch on the battlement revealed the knight's opponent was Lindsay. She was fighting with mace and dagger, a fire of determination in her eyes. There was nobody else on the parapet; the rest of the fighting was in the bailey or within the castle chambers. Alex stood, sword raised, behind the English knight. Never taking her eyes from her opponent, she shook her head and bared her teeth. Alex shifted his weight, wanting desperately to kill the man but knowing Lindsay would hate him for it if he did it too soon. Like the rest of his men, she wanted the glory of having fought well. In fact, she needed it to appear the man she pretended.

The gun. He scabbarded his dagger, shifted his sword to his left hand, and reached down to draw the SIG M11. Calmly he chambered a round and pointed the weapon at the knight's back.

"No!" Lindsay's voice was hoarse and angry. Her adversary tried to look around to see what was behind him, but she kept him occupied and focused on her. The parapet was too narrow for him to do anything else.

Alex winced and groaned and flexed his fingers against the grip, wanting to pull the trigger but only pointing the muzzle.

"I said no!" Lindsay wailed hard on her opponent, and as she backed him up Alex also backed up. The knight trying to kill her was grunting with the effort, and red anger colored Alex's vision. More than anything he wanted to blow this sonofabitch into the next century. Though he held his fire, he also kept the gun trained on the knight's back and looked for the slightest sign Lindsay might be in trouble enough to make her change her mind. Even the tiniest suggestion she might falter.

But she was smart. She was varying her rhythm, and setting the pace of the fight. Just a shade quicker than the knight, she kept him off balance. Her dagger parried, her mace struck elbow and knee, and the knight was weakening. Staggering. Finally she was able to get inside the sword and whack his head with her mace, stunning him enough to make him lean against the battlement. Now it was a simple matter to hit him again, then again from the other side so he draped over the inner wall, and Alex helped her shove him over the side of the parapet. The knight landed on his head several stories below, then lay still in a crumpled heap.

Both Alex and Lindsay looked over the wall to the bailey ground, silent. Lindsay gasped from exertion, wavering, then sank to her knees. Alex restored the chambered round to the clip and pocketed his pistol, then leaned against the battlement and watched her as the noise of clashing weapons began to die in the castle. The fight was nearly over, and the victorious voices were Scottish. Lindsay stared hard at the dead man, and slowly regained her breath.

Finally, still staring, she said, "You lied."

"Huh?"

"Killing people who want to kill you doesn't feel like a job."

"This isn't the first time you've killed a guy."

She turned to peer at him. "It is."

"No. The provision train. That one you whalloped is dead, I'm sure."

Her mouth gaped, and she appeared to want to speak, but didn't. Then she looked down at the body below.

He sucked air between his front teeth. "No, you're right. I lied. It doesn't feel like a job. But at the time it was the only answer you would have understood."

For a long moment she stared into the middle distance, thinking, then she nodded. With a deep breath she then turned to him and said, "Thanks for watching my back."

He slapped her on the shoulder, and said, "Bravo Zulu, soldier." She had only a blank look for that, and he elaborated. "Well done."

Her response was something between a laugh and a sigh, but she didn't smile. "He was a fellow countryman. They're all my countrymen, Scots and English."

Alex's reply was immediate. "That guy was your enemy, trying to kill you. Make no mistake about that. Countryman or not, he was your enemy."

She thought about that for a moment, then nodded again. He turned and led the way down to the bailey, where Scots were herding disarmed prisoners into a cluster, shouting and jeering at the cowed men. The prisoners stood motionless, sullen and quiet, staring at the ground and not at their captors. One young squire was in tears, and sniffled pitiably among the more hardened knights as they were herded away to the detainment cells in the gatehouse.

Alex found Sir Hector, who told him the garrison commander had retreated to the keep and was now entrenched there.

They all stared at the small tower to the left of the gatehouse. It was accessible by only one door, near the parapet, reached by a span of wood that had been withdrawn so the invaders couldn't get to the door to beat it down. There were no windows in the keep, only tiny arrow loops. Alex said, "How long do you think he'll hold out?"

Hector shrugged and turned to Alex with a twinkle in his eye. "Perhaps he believes there will be relief soon."

Alex and Lindsay turned to look at Hector, and Alex snorted a laugh through his nose. "He's going to be a seriously disappointed sonofabitch, then. Think we should tell him?"

"Edward has already, and the commander isn't of sufficient trust to believe him. They will hold us off for a while, then succumb when they become hungry enough and thirsty enough. The relief will never come as expected." A smile then brightened his face. "Come. The prisoners are safely tucked away in the gatehouse and under vigilant guard. We've caught the garrison during supper, and there's plenty to eat for everyone."

Alex and Lindsay went with him to the Great Hall and sat with the rest of the victorious Scots for a good supper of meat and wine. Among the many tales of the night's exploit, Alex regaled the room with the story of his young squire's skillful kill. Lindsay, her cheeks ruddy with wine, the heat of the room, and the excitement of the evening, grinned and bore the praise, but the haunted look was in her eyes. Alex had seen it before in men he'd flown with, and had most likely worn it himself during times when the ugliness of the world tore his soul. He figured all Lindsay needed was to toughen up. Surely she'd be fine once she learned to partition her emotions and keep the horror contained.

Meanwhile, they all ate till they could hold no more, for nobody ever knew for certain when the next meal would be. Most of them, including Alex, tucked away pieces of bread and cheese in their clothing for later.

As the excitement died down, exhaustion swept over the Scottish army of Edward Bruce, and the party didn't last long. Soon the talk petered out, and the knights each found beds and bunks to claim. Alex went looking for a spot, with Lindsay tagging behind, but without the keep and its bedchambers for their use, the warm areas of the castle seemed full up with Scots claiming corners. Snoring bodies lay scattered across the Great Hall like logs on a river. Everywhere, it seemed, there was already a Scottish knight or his squire occupying.

"Maybe we should return to the pack train and pitch the tent in the woods?" Lindsay was pale and looked as if she might collapse any second from her adrenaline letdown, and Alex felt close behind.

"No. It's too far and too dark, and I'm too tired. There's got to be a corner here somewhere." Looking to where the fires were, he found the kitchen by the smell of burnt bread. The complex of rooms, in which stood heavy tables laden with iron utensils and food scraps, was filled with dancing shadows from the dwindling fires. Stacks of meal sacks and crates stood in haphazard array, some having been moved to make room for the sleeping bodies. Alex took Lindsay's hand and stepped over men and around stacked bags of grain and onions, and ducked beneath smoked meat and game carcasses hung on racks. Then he spotted a corner not far from the fire, beneath a worktable where it was dark and warm. "Here. Come." He drew her there.

They settled in under the table, chain mail and leather-and-horn armor clinking and scraping against stone. He hauled in a sack of oats, which they used for a pillow, and wished there were enough such bags to make a mattress. Hard as the floor was, though, the kitchen was far warmer than the tent would have been. They stretched out side by side in their cubby and closed their eyes.

But, exhausted as he was, Alex was unable to sleep. Lindsay still had his hand, and was holding it tightly in hers, their fingers interlaced even as she slept. Her palm pressed his, and she gripped as if afraid to let go. It made his blood sing, and his head turned so his mouth would be nearer her face. Not a kiss, but as close to it as he dared. Something inside him far more insistent than his loins was stirring, and he had no idea what it was. All he knew was he'd rather stay awake than sleep through this time with her. It wasn't until the smallest, coldest hours came that he finally dropped off from exhaustion.

No wonder he felt like crap the next day, surly and irritable as he and his fellow knights supervised the plundering of the English and the burial of dead. It was all very businesslike but competitive, the way the personal belongings and property in the castle were collected, tallied, and doled out to the Scottish victors by those in command. Arguments arose. In the bailey, Alex witnessed another altercation between Roger Kirkpatrick and his cousin John.

This time Alex didn't care what the issue was. He was in a mood to fight, was sick of Sir Roger's attitude, and had been waiting for an opportunity to retaliate. He was almost gladdened to hear the raised voices. As soon as Roger began slapping his cousin around, Alex strode over to intervene.

"Leave him alone."

The Lowland knight gaped at him for a moment. "Cheeky of you."

Alex hauled off and clobbered him. The spikes on his gauntlet cut two deep gashes in Kirkpatrick's face. Stunned, Roger staggered back but quickly regained himself and drew his dagger. Alex drew his as well, and they circled.

"I was wondering when you would take your revenge." Blood trickled down his cheek and dripped from his jaw.

"You need to learn some manners, Kirkpatrick." A cluster of onlookers began to gather.

Roger laughed. "The Hungarian by-blow is going to teach me manners!"

"Yup." Alex took a swipe and Kirkpatrick dodged. His voice took on a tone of patient instruction, like a kindergarten teacher. "You're going to leave your cousin alone, and you're going to pay for the scars on my belly."

Kirkpatrick touched the swelling gashes on his face and his countenance darkened. "I'm going to kill you."

"You going to lay blame on the king like you did with Comyn?"

With a roar, Kirkpatrick came at Alex. His rage made him clumsy, and Alex easily sidestepped to help him along and into a stone wall. Kirkpatrick collapsed and dropped his dagger, which Alex kicked to the side. Then he knelt beside his surprised opponent and held his own dagger to the man's throat. "You'll leave John alone, or next time I'll kill you." He grinned. "And I'll let King Robert take the credit."

Then he let Kirkpatrick go and picked up the dropped dagger for a prize.

The excitement over, the crowd dispersed and returned to the business of the day. Burials were quick and efficient, nobody eager to dwell on deaths that could just as easily have been their own. Only one of Alex's own knights and three squires were missing after the battle the night before, and Alex and Lindsay walked past the row of corpses lying by the graves being dug, to verify who had not made it. Lindsay gasped when she saw, and laid a hand over her mouth. "Oh, God. Brian."

Alex leaned over to see, and sure enough it was one of Cullan's squires. "Brian. That's the guy who beat the snot out of you a few weeks ago."

"Oh, God." Lindsay knelt by the body. "No." Both hands pressed to her mouth, and she began to sob.

Alex went to a knee beside her and murmured, "Hey, take it easy."

"He was a friend."

"Friend? He nearly killed you."

She stood and turned away, as if looking for a place to hide or a hole to crawl into. He followed her.

"Lindsay, don't be so upset."

"He was my friend. After we fought, he began to talk to me like he respected me."

The question arose for Alex as to how good a friend Brian had become, but he refrained from asking, and tried to counsel Lindsay in this. "Well, I told you that might happen. So now you've lost a buddy. Mourn in private. Making a big deal out of this is a bad idea." The several friends Alex had lost during his years in the Navy rose to mind, and he shoved them all back into their compartments for now was not the time.

She threw him an evil look, bleary with tears. "He was my friend."

"Wipe your eyes, soldier," his voice was soft but his words were firm, "and carry on." He stood. "I guarantee he isn't the only friend you'll lose before this is over."

With angry swipes to her face she obeyed, and stepped behind him where he couldn't see her. "I hate this." Alex ignored the comment and continued his examination of dead faces to take note of who was gone from his unit.

Though tears were not forthcoming, the loss of four men darkened the edges of his soul and hatred of the enemy churned in his gut. He went quiet and spoke very little, even to Lindsay, for saying anything at all would reveal parts of what he was feeling. It was a vulnerability that appalled him.

The following night tents were pitched in and around the castle, and normal sleeping arrangements resumed as the English commander went through the process of realizing relief was not on its way.

For the next three weeks life settled into a tedium of patrols. Though Alex hated to, he made certain Lindsay rode as often as any of the other squires. He saw how the constant anticipation of fighting now wore on her, and how she despised carrying her weapon anymore. The wan paleness of her cheeks and the dark, haunted look in her eyes told him she was only sticking it out by virtue of her stiff upper lip—he had to give her credit for never complaining—and it was only by his understanding that she would refuse to comply that he refrained from ordering her to stand down from patrol.

Of course, she quit holding his hand when she slept, and probably didn't remember having held it in the first place. How he wished she would take it again.

Finally the garrison commander surrendered the keep, and he and his fellow holdouts joined the rest of the prisoners in the gatehouse to await ransom.

One morning Alex found Lindsay eating alone, at the far end of the board in the Great Hall when everyone else had finished

their breakfast and gone. She wore only her now very threadbare flight suit, and no armor. At the front of her suit he could
see her black T-shirt was full of holes, now almost more like
lace hanging from the neck than like anything meant for
warmth. His was a little worse, and he thought it might be time
to go looking for indigenous clothing. They could afford it. He
sauntered over to straddle the stool opposite her, and she
smiled. "Isn't there a rule against fraternizing with the lesser
folk?"

There was, and in the military there always would be. He
hated that she was one of those lesser folk, but he couldn't say
it out loud. "You're eating late."

"I woke up feeling ill this morning. I don't really want
breakfast, but around here you eat when you can and hold it
down as long as possible." She picked at a cold joint of mutton
that was already mostly clean.

"You're sick?" He reached out to feel her forehead and
found it hot and clammy. She leaned back to avoid his touch,
but she was too slow to keep him from knowing. "You've got a
fever." Now it was his turn to go clammy, for illness was serious
stuff here and one never knew what bug might happen along to
kill one.

"I don't have a fever. It's just warm in here."

"It's freezing in here. You're the one with a high temperature."

"No. Not a fever." Her voice was sounding panicky, and she
glanced around as if for someone to agree with her she wasn't
sick. "I can't have a fever, not here."

"Maybe it's just a cold."

"It's nothing. I'll ride today. No problem."

"Problem. You're not riding."

"I must."

"Bring that with you." He gestured to her plate. "We're going to the tent, and you're going to rest."

"It's nothing."

"Right. And it's going to stay nothing. Come." He rose from
the table and headed for the kitchen. The workers there were
surprised at his intrusion and stopped work to watch him come
down the steps into the hot, smoky, and thickly scented room,
but said nothing as he rummaged around among the smaller
utensils near the center fire and came up with a small pot. Then

he picked up a bag with a few onions left in the bottom and slung it over his shoulder. "You got a chicken here somewhere?"

A kitchen maid's gaze went to a stack of wooden cages against the wall, all thickly coated with poultry dung. Alex reached into one for a nice, plump hen who squawked and fought until he could grab her by the neck and break it. The bird went limp. "Okay, now, how about a cabbage?"

That brought looks of surprise, but he said, "Cabbage. Now." The girl went to a bin and pulled out a sad-looking leafy thing that obviously needed to be eaten soon or go to waste. Alex took it gladly.

"Thanks. Have a nice day, y'all."

"Is your squire ill, sir?" The young kitchen maid's eyes were wide with concern, and her pretty face troubled as she regarded Lindsay with soft, dark eyes. "He doesnae look well at all." She tucked a stray bit of her hair behind her ear and bit her lip to moisten it and redden it as she stared at Lindsay.

Alex glanced at his squire, who avoided the gazes of everyone in the room. "Aye. He's sick. You'll want to stay away or you might catch it yourself." He waved to Lindsay. "Come along, boy."

Lindsay's head ducked, and her cheeks were red with more than just fever as she hurried away from that girl. She followed Alex to where their tent was pitched, just outside the castle gatehouse. Their small fire was barely alive, having been neglected that morning, so Alex set down his burden and bent to tend the flame.

Lindsay asked, "What are you doing?"

"Chicken soup." He straightened and looked at her. "Get in bed."

"Alex—"

"I said, get in bed. Stop arguing with me, or I'll send your ass back to your father in disgrace and you'll never become a knight."

A grin spread across her face, and she shook her head as she went into the tent.

With his dagger, Alex cleaned the chicken, cut the meat from the carcass and browned it in the pan they kept, then threw it all in a pot of boiling water, along with chopped onions and cabbage. A dash of salt and a little costly pepper finished it, and he let it cook. Then he donned his armor and weapons and saw to the evening's patrol assignments. Once his men were deployed, he returned to the tent and found Lindsay asleep. When he felt her forehead she was still warm, but no worse than before. He took that as a good sign, and hoped he wasn't as clueless as he felt. She stirred when he touched her, but didn't awaken, so he dumped his armor onto the tent floor and for the next half hour divided his attention between her and the pot on the fire.

It was sunset when she awoke, and her temperature was still up. "Here, take this." Alex put a shallow cup to her mouth and she drank some soup.

"It's too hot in here. You've got the fire too high."

"The fire's outside."

She had no reply for that, thought for a moment, then took some more soup. Alex was able to get her to empty the cup, then she lay back down to sleep again.

The pretty, young kitchen maid who had been so concerned earlier came with a cup, and curtsied at the entrance of the tent. "Pardon me, sir, but perhaps it would be good for him to drink this here tea."

Alex took the cup and looked into it. The liquid was a yellowish color, and smelled like wet wood. "What is it?"

"Willow tea, sir. 'Twill ease his fever." She brushed a wisp of hair from her forehead and looked over at Lindsay with the unmistakable eyes of hopeless infatuation. Alex struggled to hide a smirk.

"What does it do?"

A tiny frown creased the girl's brow. "Do? As I said, it will make him well. Ease his pain."

Alex looked into the cup again, then at the girl. "Okay. I mean, very well. Thank you."

She curtsied again, then left with a lingering look in the direction of her heart's desire.

Once she was out of earshot, Alex murmured, "That girl's hot for you."

Lindsay grunted. "She's going to be terribly disappointed, then, because—trust me—size does matter."

A laugh snorted through Alex's nose and he looked into the cup. "I don't know if you should drink this."

"I keep drinking things, I'll have to pee. I hate having to pee in this damned suit. I wish it had a trap door."

"All right, never mind." He started to toss the liquid, but Lindsay stopped him.

"Give it to me anyway."

"You sure?"

"Willow bark tea. Everyone knows willow bark tea is the next best thing to aspirin. Same stuff."

Alex looked into the cup. "Really?"

"Really. Give it over." He complied and she drank, made a face at the taste, then returned the cup to Alex and lay back on her parachute. He felt her forehead, and her temperature seemed neither worse nor better than before. He sat on his own pallet and watched her for a while. It quite surprised him when she spoke, and she sounded half asleep. Her words were slurred.

"Seriously disappointed."

That was certainly out of the blue. Not sure what he should say, he said only, "Okay." He wondered if she was having a dream.

There was more silence, then she said, "Alex, are you married?"

Not a dream. Puzzled now, he said, "You mean, will I be married in about seven centuries?"

A pause, then, "Right. That." She sounded sleepy, drifting in that netherworld just before unconsciousness.

"No. Not married. But you knew that, because you interviewed me."

There was a pause, then she said, "Oh. Right." After some more silence, she asked, "Girlfriend?"

"No girlfriend."

There was a deep sigh, as if she were annoyed by his reply. Her voice was almost petulant, comical, when she spoke again. "Why ever not? No, don't tell me. You're married to the Navy."

He had to smile. "No, I just haven't had an opportunity to become serious with anyone. Been too busy, first with school, then training, then deployment."

One limp, wobbly hand waved in the air. "Do you mean to say, girls haven't been flinging themselves at your uniform like bugs on a windscreen?"

He chuckled. "They did, but none of them stuck."

There was a weak laugh from under the parachute, muttering and very drowsy now. "The Teflon Lieutenant."

That amused him even more, but not so much that he didn't fear she was slipping into delirium. He reached over to feel her forehead again, and found it cold and damp. She captured his hand in hers and held his palm against her face.

"Fever's broken," she muttered.

Relief washed over him.

Then she said, "Why didn't any of them stick?" Her hand still held his.

This was way too personal, and he debated for a moment evading the question, but went ahead and answered it honestly. "I haven't met anyone who could handle being a military wife the way my mother did."

"How Freudian of you. Derek would laugh himself sick."

He didn't reply to that, and she was wrong, this Derek person notwithstanding. The truth was, he'd wanted someone as dedicated to him as his mother was to his father. Almost nobody existed for her but Dad, and he wanted that. It was so hard to find, he was beginning to think Mom was the last one and there would be no others like her.

Lindsay didn't speak for a long time, and Alex thought she must be asleep, until she uttered yet another non sequitur. "Anyone ever tell you you've got the most incredible green eyes in the entire gene pool of humanity?"

He chuckled and closed those eyes for a moment, then admitted, "Yeah. I've been told." His crystalline green eyes had once been described by a former girlfriend as "spooky."

"Piercing." A long pause, then, "They zap me right behind my navel."

Alex couldn't help laughing to himself, and at the same time he peered at her, wishing she weren't delirious. Or whatever the hell was going on with her. Aspirin couldn't have been the only thing in that cup. He waited for her to go on, but she didn't. After a while, her breathing settled into genuine sleep and he retrieved his hand. Then he sat back on his own pallet and watched her face until it was too dark to see.

CHAPTER 9

Winter was closing in, and activity on both sides of the conflict slowed with the harshness of weather and shortness of days. It seemed the sun never poked its nose above the horizon enough hours even to call them days anymore. While not on patrol, Alex spent his time hanging out in the Great Hall with his fellow knights, hearing news of exploits of other Scottish forces, often playing chess with Hector, but rarely winning.

"How a man can be so skilled in battle, yet so addled before a chessboard, is a mystery to me," Hector crowed as Alex yet again tipped over his king in defeat.

"It's good to be a MacNeil, so I'll never have to face you on the field."

Hector laughed well and long at that, as Alex began setting up for a new game. "It is good to be a MacNeil. Barra is the most beautiful island in the Hebrides. I'll be glad to go home soon."

Alex glanced up, but said nothing and returned his attention to the game. He hadn't thought about Hector leaving; he'd be sorry to see him go.

The laird continued. "I haven't seen my children in six months. I hope they're all still living. Two have been lost already, and some of the others are young yet." His voice lowered and softened. "It would be a great shame if I were to find any more missing on my return." But then he grinned again. "Or, perhaps, I'll even find a new one. Wouldn't that be something, eh, Ailig? To find I'd left my wife with a new one?"

Alex's mind slipped away from the game as he contemplated Hector's attitude. He sat back in his rickety, wooden chair and examined his friend's face leaning over the game board. To speak so casually of dead children was beyond Alex's ability to comprehend. "How did the two die?"

Hector shrugged. "The one was frail and sickly, and wasted away before she was two years of age. The other, just last year, died of the pox. He was five." His voice was soft again, but otherwise his demeanor was unchanged as he spoke of his loss. Alex thought it strange the children's names weren't mentioned.

"How many do you have still?"

"Och, I never count my children, bless them." Hector crossed himself, as if attempting to ward away evil.

Now Alex thought he understood. Too much pain, and too much attention paid to it, and a man was crippled. The only defense against the deaths of others was to not feel the grief too much.

Later that evening at supper Hector and Cullan came to sit at the table opposite Alex. Without preamble, Hector said, "Come with us, little brother."

Alex paused in chewing a mouthful of beef, and felt a flush of pleasure at the appellate. For the first time in his life, Alex was the younger and he found he liked having a big brother, for Hector was not nearly so intimidating as his father. It felt as good to be a MacNeil in this century as it had in his own time.

"Where?"

"Barra, of course. Come home with us for the winter."

Deep in thought, Alex shredded a piece from the chunk on the wooden plate before him as he mulled the suggestion that had been presented as a command. He said, "To Barra?" Ostensibly the illegitimate offspring of the previous laird, he couldn't imagine being welcome there. Suddenly it occurred to him to wonder whether Hector's mother was still alive.

"Aye. Come to my castle. Leave your men to winter here under the king's brother, or go home as they will. There will be little to do here until spring, and they'll be glad for the respite."

"Disband my company?"

"They'll follow you again when you return to the fight. If they don't, they were never truly your men in the first place. But you're a MacNeil, so there will always be men to follow you." That made Alex smile. Hector always assumed every MacNeil had special qualities of bravery, intelligence, and loyalty, and apparently Alex hadn't yet disappointed him on any of those counts.

"James Douglas is still out making raids on the Marches."

"James Douglas is daft, and fights for vengeance besides," said Cullan. "Come with us. Come see your home. Every man must find his true home before he dies, and if you're a MacNeil yours is on Barra. It's the truth I'm telling you."

Lindsay threw Alex a look though she wasn't part of the conversation, and he looked away. *Home.* His home, if he ever had one, seemed an eternity ago and a million miles away. And as he glanced at Lindsay, and remembered she wasn't part of that former life, it fell in his estimation. Barra was what there was for him now. "All right. We'll go."

Hector grinned and laughed, and it warmed Alex's heart to matter so much to this man who had been a stranger less than six months ago.

Hector's army of clansmen were mostly infantry, and traveled on foot. The march to the western coast was slowed by snows that marked the beginning of winter, and it took them through mountains higher than any Alex and Lindsay had experienced since coming to Scotland. Mountains that closed in and towered over their column like neat stone walls. After two weeks of travel they reached the rocky shore of a sea loch and boarded large boats that took Sir Hector, his men, and their horses across the gray, choppy sea from the rocky Highland shore. It made Alex smile to feel the swell of ocean beneath him again, though this was far more violent bobbing than he'd experienced since leaving the Academy. For days they sailed, in such damp and cold that it made Alex think he'd never suffered until now. He hated to think what it might have been like in stormy weather.

Then, just when it began to seem to Alex they would never

reach Barra, he spotted something on the horizon to starboard. He went to the gunwale to see if they were about to pass by the land they were seeking, but the thing he'd seen was gone.

Then it was there. Then gone. He frowned and shaded his eyes from the overcast sky, and suddenly there were two low, dark mounds in the water. Then one.

Tingling covered his skin. As he watched, the single object became three. Then two. "Hector . . ." Now there were three again. "*Hector.*"

The laird came to see. Alex pointed. Hector gazed, then he jumped, startled, and uttered something guttural that sounded like a curse. Others came to look, and as they all watched the distant object undulate on the surface there arose much excited Gaelic chatter.

"Hector, what is it?"

"Can you not see?"

"Looks like . . . floating debris." Great, huge, wobbling piles of it.

" 'Tis a sea monster." By his voice, Hector wasn't kidding.

"A herd of whales?" But the mounds were rising awfully high from the surface for that.

"No. As I said, a sea monster. A single creature, and if we dally we'll be its supper." He looked up at the sails, then back at the island from which they were taking their position, and snapped an order to his men. Immediately the ship heeled onto a different tack, away from the thing to the north.

Alex didn't think it was a sea monster, though he refrained from saying so to Hector. But he stared. The more he stared, watching the rising and falling of the mounds, the more it looked like a single, huge, swimming thing.

Eventually it sank beneath the waves and didn't rise again, but the MacNeil ships continued their course away and took the long way around to Barra.

It was with deep relief Alex finally saw the dark line of land on the overcast horizon. There the MacNeils debarked below a castle perched on a rocky cliff and surrounded by more rocks. It was not huge, but squat and solid like its master, and was the first castle Alex had seen that appeared whole and never razed and repaired.

"You built this?" Alex stared upward as they climbed to the portcullis.

"Nae. My great-grandfather built it. And at great cost to his people, but the only way to keep his land from invaders was to keep a ready garrison. The village is not far, tucked in that glen there you see." Hector pointed to what looked to Alex like more rocks, and he took the man's word for it there was a village down there.

"Where are your livestock? I see pasture but no animals."

"In byres for the winter. The cold being too bitter for animals to stand in these parts."

"Ah." Alex nodded as if he understood all about island cattle and sheep. They reached the castle portcullis, and entered, their horses' hooves thudding on the ground inside the bailey. People came to greet the returning soldiers. Wives in ragged plaid clothing rushed to their husbands, parents to their sons, and Alex followed Hector through a maze of animal pens, hay wagons, and more clusters of people. Barefoot women and children crowded the horses, and Alex kept an eye out, concerned they might be stepped on. Before a large, heavy door, Hector pulled up his horse and dismounted.

"Fiona!" He called out, then continued shouting in what Alex could only assume was Gaelic. A woman came and curtsied to him. He spoke to her some more, and she looked to Alex slantways then asked Hector a question. The laird laughed and replied, then shouted to Alex, "Ailig! My wife says you're too tall to be my brother!"

Alex smiled, but didn't know what reply to make other than to wonder why Fiona would greet her husband with only a curtsey. So he said nothing.

Hector continued. "I told her you're Hungarian on the outside, but Scottish on the inside!" He tapped his forehead to indicate what he meant by "inside." Then he said to Alex as he gestured toward a wooden building that stood back the way they'd come, "Have your squires take your horses to the stable, and they can sleep there in a stall."

Alex said, "Lindsay stays with . . . Lindsay attends me, and I'll need him close by. Colin," he gestured to the boy, "Colin, you take the horses, see to them, and stay with them." As he dismounted he looked to Lindsay for an objection that she should go with the boy in order to be one of the guys, but she was remarkably silent now. A tiny smile crept to the corners of his mouth; maybe she was coming around on things finally. She dismounted and fell in behind him as Alex followed Hector into the castle structure, his spur chains and rowels jingling as he walked across the stone paving.

The rooms were small and close, but a little less messy than some of the castles Alex had seen lately. Perhaps because it probably housed fewer military people than the English garrisons in the Lowlands. The residents here were a family, not soldiers far from home.

The corridors were a maze to Alex. One thing he'd learned about these stone fortresses since he'd been here was that it was nearly impossible to keep a sense of direction while inside one. Arrow loops were not a light source worth mentioning, particularly in winter, and many rooms didn't even have those. So Alex and Lindsay were guided from one cavelike space in stone to another, up some stairs, and down another corridor until they came to a heavy wooden door strengthened with diamond-shaped studs. Hector shoved it open. Alex and Lindsay followed him in.

"Here's where you will sleep." The hearth was huge and the fire high, so the room was warm in spite of the stone all around and the frosty temperatures outside the castle. Tapestries hung on the walls, and thick animal skins covered the floor: bear and wolf and deer. It was a level of comfort Alex hadn't experienced since he'd joined the Navy.

"A cauldron," said Alex to Hector. "Would it be possible to have a cauldron of water to put over the fire?"

"Och. If it's soup you're wanting—"

"Just water. Plain, clean water."

The laird gave a puzzled pause, then said, "Very well. I'll have it brought. And fresh clothing, for the two of you don't seem so well equipped for living where there are no English to fight."

Alex nodded. "Thank you."

Hector eyed Lindsay, then Alex, and said with a slight edge to his voice, "I'll also have Fiona send up your supper. No need for you to search out the Great Hall this evening."

Alex wondered what that was about, but said nothing and nodded his thanks. Hector then left them alone.

Lindsay, looking around, let the bundle of their personal

belongings slip to the floor while Alex went to the middle of the room to survey their new digs. The bed was as large and roomy as the fireplace, and had a tall frame hung with heavy curtains and great expanses of sheer silk in shades of wine and gold. The feather mattress seemed deep enough to smother in, and an enormous expanse of light brown fur covered it. He couldn't tell what animal, but it was matched skins that might have been a wild cat of some sort.

The tapestry behind the bed was nearly too dark to see, but it appeared to be a hunting scene. Another hunting scene that was a bit more visible graced the next wall. Trunks, and a washstand bearing a plain ceramic bowl and a stack of linen cloths, lined the wall by the door. Through a door beside the far tapestry, Alex found a one-hole garderobe that smelled of dank stone, ammonia, and methane, overlaid with wintergreen. "Oh, look. En suite latrine."

Lindsay snorted. "Far better that than squatting in the woods every day, I say."

Alex looked for a screen of some kind, something to provide some privacy from each other, but there was nothing other than the tiny garderobe. A couple of chairs stood against the wall near the fireplace and a straw mattress lay in a wooden bed frame on the other side where Lindsay would sleep, but that was all.

"Looks like we'll be taking turns getting dressed again."

She nodded, but didn't reply and neither did she move.

A knock came on the door, and Alex went to let in Fiona and a serving girl, who delivered a cauldron filled with steaming water. The girl scurried across the floor with the heavy pot, and hung it on the hook over the fire. Then Fiona turned to Alex and said something in Gaelic, eyeing him with a look that struck him as odd.

"I'm sorry, I don't speak Gaelic."

Then she spoke again, and in the midst of it he picked out the word *Sasunnach*, meaning "Englishman," so he realized he did know at least one word of Gaelic. But he held up his palms and apologized again.

She smiled, curtsied, and the two left the room.

He watched them go, and when he was certain they were gone he murmured, "I wonder what that was about." Then he returned his attention to the hearth and said, "The water looks like it's already hot." A thin cloud of steam rose slowly from it.

"They probably have a big cauldron of heated water they keep in the kitchen. A bit like having a full hot water heater in the plumbing at home."

Made sense. He turned to Lindsay and gestured to it. "Go ahead. You first."

She eyed him, and humor colored her voice. "Trust me, Alex, you need it more than I do."

"I know. That's exactly why you should go first. That water is going to be a biohazard once I'm done with it."

For a moment she looked as if she would say something, then changed her mind. "Very well, then, turn around."

He pulled one of the chairs away from the wall and turned it toward a tapestry so he'd have something to look at while he waited. It was awfully big, and the intricate design appeared capable of holding his eye for a while. Flat-looking dogs leapt upon a stag. Big-nosed hunters with staring eyes let fly their arrows in perfectly even flights. In the corner one distraught hunter held a thinly bleeding wound, apparently inflicted by the stag in flight. Another part of the scene showed a man with a long knife who appeared ready to butcher the animal for meat. Stylized trees and branches with leaves wove in and out between the figures, and though the drawing seemed flat and childish to Alex's photography-spoiled eye, he could still see the workmanship in the cloth was finely detailed in ways he'd never seen even in manufactured things.

Another knock came on the door, and he rose to receive a platter filled with steaming meat and small, flat loaves of bread. There was also an earthenware jug filled with mead, but no cups. He set the food atop one of the trunks, took a piece of bread and stuffed it with meat, then carried his sandwich and the jug to the chair where he sat, ate, and watched the tapestry. His eye traveled over the scene, caught here and there by small details and the flow of the story. It was remarkable how much action could be crammed onto a single piece of fabric.

Lindsay bathed quickly, and her voice came from near the bed when she told him it was his turn at the water.

Hot water. Alex marveled at the luxury, then found himself shocked he could consider it a luxury. He rose from the chair and stripped to the skin, dropping all his clothes and armor in one smelly, threadbare, metallic pile, and picked up the towel Lindsay had brought from the washstand. The heat from the fire and the water seeped into him and warmed parts of him he'd thought would be cold forever. Muscles relaxed, joints loosened. He scrubbed crud from places he'd forgotten he had, and rubbed dirt from skin that turned red because the filth had become so embedded. Then he took his knife and cleaned his fingernails thoroughly for the first time in six months. Gradually he began to feel human again.

Once clean, he looked at his filthy gear on the floor and knew he didn't want to put any of it back on. But the clothes promised by Hector hadn't yet arrived, so he went to the washstand for a dry towel to wrap around his waist.

When he turned around, figuring by now Lindsay had also wrapped herself in a towel, his heart nearly stopped. She stood by the bed with one of the sheer silk drapes drawn around her like a toga. Paying no attention to him, she was adjusting a length thrown over her shoulder and apparently unaware—or uncaring—that the very thin fabric was entirely translucent. It hid nothing, but instead gave her lean, athletic body a blush of red. Orange light from the hearth flickered across her skin and gave her the appearance of a magnificent human flame. Her dark, shoulder-length hair was drying in a mass of waves and wispy curls around her face. The high cheekbones and aquiline nose of her aristocratic face was set gracefully on her most elegant neck.

The smooth muscles of her broad shoulders belied the strength he knew she owned, and her arms were long and straight.

And, oh, her breasts. *Oh, yes.* Freed from their bondage, they were full and soft and round, and he ached to touch them. Then his eye was drawn to her sleek belly, and onward to the dark patch below. There it rested, for he was unable to move, or even think. His hand gripped hard the ends of the towel at his waist.

Her glance went to him, and when she found him staring she took a step back toward the bedpost, where she laid a hand against the wood. But that was all. She seemed uncertain what to do next, but it was plain she didn't mind him looking, and she watched him. His pulse surged, and he could barely find his voice and his gaze found her face again. "You can't possibly not know what you're doing to me."

She cleared her throat and said, "I might guess."

"On purpose?"

"You make it sound like I'm being mean."

"Are you?"

"Not on purpose."

There was a silence while he considered his response to that. Then he said, "If I were to kiss you, would you hit me?"

Now she smiled, as if he'd made a joke, but he hadn't thought it funny at all. Her chin lifted. "Are you man enough to try it and see?"

Uh-oh. One of his many buttons that sent blood rushing to his loins, and he stepped toward her. "How much danger am I in? Where's your mace?"

"With the horses and your swords. Colin has it." She took a step toward him, and closed the distance. He could smell her now, beneath the earthy stone of the castle, a thread of feminine skin that was unlike anything else on earth.

A smile twitched his mouth. He tucked the ends of his towel at his waist, then leaned in to kiss her. It was the sweetest moment in what seemed forever, her warm lips friendly and alarming all at once. He murmured in her ear, "How long have you had this change of heart?"

A kiss on his cheek, and she whispered back, "Not a clue. I still don't know whether this is at all a good idea. But somehow you've gotten under my skin." She sounded breathless, and as surprised as he.

"I haven't been anywhere near your skin." He touched a reverent finger to the fine silk covering her shoulder. Beautiful skin. "It's my eyes, I know. You can't resist my piercing green eyes that get to you behind your navel."

She leaned back to search his face, her own eyes wide with surprise. "What?"

"You don't remember saying that?"

"No." She shook her head slowly, as if struggling to recall. "I only remember thinking it. I dimly remember thinking it."

"Out loud."

"Oh, God."

He kissed her lips again, then brushed aside the silk and touched his mouth to her shoulder. "It's all right. I've got other parts that can touch you there, too."

"I expect you do." With a smile, she tugged his towel loose and let it fall to the floor, then ran both her hands over his flanks to the backs of his thighs. He slipped his arms around her and held her to him, suffused with joy and delighting in the feel of silk and skin, and the scent of her hair, and the feel of her hand on his—

Oh . . .

The caressing sent his brain tumbling. He found her mouth again and took it with his tongue, claiming every part he could reach. When she broke away and drew him toward the bed, that was all it took. He reached down to lift her in his arms, and carried her. The silk lay about and under her atop the coverlet as he parted the folds. They were deep in feathers and fur, and then he was deep inside her.

The feel of her overwhelmed him so that he had to hold still a moment to let pass an intense urge to end this in a few quick, hard strokes. As much as he wanted her, even more he wanted this to last. She looked straight into his eyes, and he smiled as he began to move again. Slowly. He pressed hard, insistent and slow, and she responded in kind. Her hips met his; her eyes never left his face. He could see in them all she was feeling, everything he was doing to her, and it was more exciting to him than anything he'd ever felt. Each sound she made, each tilt of her hips, and each touch of her lips to his skin, surged through him. Her legs wrapped around his waist to bring him to her, and her ecstasy drew him in even more. Time lost meaning. Reality dwindled to only their bodies, and even in release Alex knew there could be no release. Ever.

He didn't stop, but slowed, not wanting to quit but unable to keep on. Breaths came hard, panting, and finally he collapsed to lie at her side, exhausted. Sleep. He needed to sleep. Lindsay was gasping also, and whimpering next to him. Shivering. He rolled toward her, a hand slipped over her belly to pull her close, and she came to his arms. There they held each other, and he kissed her forehead, and their legs entwined, and she kissed his chest before settling in under his arm with her head on his shoulder.

When breathing slowed, he took a deep breath and let it out slowly. He murmured, "Why did you change your mind about me?"

She twirled a bit of his chest hair around her finger, and he waited patiently for a reply. Finally, though, he had to nudge her to get her to speak.

"You'll laugh."

"I won't laugh."

She leaned back to check the sincerity in his eyes, then said, "I feel safe when I'm around you."

A smile grew on his face, and though he'd promised not to laugh the grin widened and his amusement crept into his voice. "Safe, you say?"

"Yes. Over the past weeks I've come to appreciate you."

A warmth filled him, a sense of rightness that made him feel whole in a way he'd only ever imagined. He pressed his lips to her forehead and his heart soared that she'd finally come to her senses.

And he to his. This would never be over, he knew. For the first time in his life, he knew he was entirely lost to another and it was like freefall that would never end.

CHAPTER 10

"Well, I can't say as this isn't something of a relief."

Alex snapped awake and rose to an elbow to look around, startled and confused to find Hector standing at the foot of the bed in a gap between the curtains, leaning on a post, his arms crossed over his chest. Alex sat up, blinking and struggling for something to say. Lindsay stirred, and groaned to be awakened so precipitously, but when she opened her eyes and saw Hector she reached for the edge of the fur coverlet and drew the far corner over them both. Alex's voice went low and angry, trying to hide his embarrassment. "What are you doing here?"

Hector laughed. "I thought something must be afoot, the way the two of you rarely ever speak to each other though you're almost never out of each other's sight. And the sidelong glances were plain enough." The hilarity rose in his voice. "I confess, *Ailig mór*, I'd assumed you had a taste for the boys. Which, of course, would have meant you couldnae be a Mac-Neil after all, for the man who sired me was a hound for the women to such a degree as to make inclination to sodomy dead impossible in his sons. I might instead have assumed without question you were hiding a woman, and I beg your forgiveness for my error."

Alex was not amused and his face flushed hot. "Your error was in—"

"But," Hector raised a finger, "in my own defense, allow me to point out how extremely well she plays the role of young man. She's a far better fighter than any woman I've ever known from the Continent; are you certain she's not Scottish?"

"She's not."

"What would her real name be?"

"Lindsay Pawlowski."

Hector's eyes went wide with sudden realization. "Please tell me Kirkpatrick was mistaken about you, though your absence after the coronation could not have been to claim an inheritance for this woman."

Alex shook his head as his mind flew to reconstruct the blown story. His heart thudded in his chest. "Lindsay is her father's only child. There was no inheritance, but we didn't know that until we returned to Hungary. By the time we got there, the stepmother had allowed her own son to squander what there was, and she had arranged a marriage for Lindsay to an unsuitable candidate. It was a long, complicated chore to free her, and the result is that she can never return to Hungary." He thought for a moment, then added for the heck of it, "And neither can I."

"Och, there's a story I'd love to hear in detail one night at *céilidh*."

Alex ignored the comment and continued. "We made our way back to Scotland without funds to speak of. It was an extremely difficult journey, but I'd pledged myself to the king and couldn't stay away. It's only by bad luck we didn't arrive sooner."

Hector's genuine relief was evident. Alex took the upper hand now. "I asked you why you're here." Lindsay was sitting up, staring at an anonymous point on his chest, avoiding Hector's gaze and saying nothing while waiting for this exchange to be finished. Alex took her hand beneath the coverlet and held it tight as he drew in his knees and draped his other arm over them as insouciantly as he could manage.

The MacNeil laird shrugged. "I'll nae lie. I came to learn the truth about the two of you. Also, I wished to deliver these clothes." He indicated with his chin a stack on the trunk where Alex had set the platter of food, "and make certain ye both were settled in properly. I can see now you have no need of my presence or my opinion. So I'll be wandering off, and a good night to the both of you." He shoved off from the bedpost, but paused when Alex spoke.

"And what will you be saying to the others?"

Hector's grin never faltered. "I'll be saying naught but that my brother, *Ailig Mac Dìolain,* is a great fighter." He moved toward the door, strolling backward as he continued to address Alex. "Also that he's taught his squire well, and that young man will be a fine knight one day, for he's the toughest lad in twelve parishes." He reached the door and laughter burbled into his voice so he could barely contain it. "But between us, and I say this from my heart, do take care you don't make him a mother first." With that, he succumbed to chuckling, left, and closed the door behind him.

Lindsay was trembling. "Ballocks," she said.

"Yeah." Then Alex said, "What did he call me? *Mock jeelin?*"

She shrugged, then said, "He's going to blurt everything."

"No, he won't." She looked him in the eye, and he nodded to affirm his statement. "He won't. He's not like that. If he says he won't, then he won't. If he was going to have an issue with this he would have said so just now, and more than likely would have thrown us out of the castle. He's the laird, and the law around these parts. He won't give us trouble if he hasn't already."

"Why did he wake us up, then?"

He cut her a sideways glance and grinned. "To bust our chops for fun, I expect." Then his smile faded. "And to warn us. He's not the only guy in Robert's army who has eyes, and he knew what was happening even before we did. We need to be more careful."

She nodded, and threw off the cover to slip from the mattress. "Indeed. Perhaps I should sleep on the—"

Alex kept his grip on her hand and tugged her back toward him. "No. You'll sleep here." He laid his palm aside her cheek. "I couldn't stand to have you not here. Not after tonight." He kissed her, then murmured with almost no voice, "Not ever again."

"Alex . . ."

Decisive now, not taking any guff, he rose from the bed,

pulled her toward him, and lifted her over his shoulder. Then he hauled back the heavy covers and dumped her back down inside them before slipping in himself and taking her into his arms. "No," he said. "I won't let you go." He kissed her and brushed a wisp of hair away from her face. "And I'll never let them hurt you. I swear it."

With a sigh, Lindsay kissed him back then settled in by his side, there to sleep. Alex lay awake for another hour, feeling the rise and fall of her breathing against his side, thinking, reviewing the events that had led him to this. It seemed they were adrift in a sea of time, out of control. Free fall. But at that moment he didn't want to grasp too firmly what was happening, as if to trap and hold his heart would be to crush it.

Finally he slept, and dreamed of ejecting from a fighter jet.

WHEN he awoke, he was alone. For one deeply disorienting moment the soft, lonely mattress made him think he was at home, in his own bed in Virginia. Then he drifted close enough to consciousness to smell peat smoke, stone walls, and the faint whiff of the garderobe beyond the door on the other side of the room. He groaned as awareness came but the horrible grogginess wouldn't lift. He didn't want to wake up; he wanted only to roll over and continue sleeping. Maybe he would have done that if Lindsay's voice hadn't come from across the room.

"You're awake."

He grunted. "A relative thing." Sitting up seemed the thing to do, so he did, and was now able to see between the bed curtains Lindsay standing by the fire, feeding it.

"I didn't sleep long, and so have been maintaining the fire since nobody has been in here all day to do it. I imagine Sir Hector has told the castle staff to keep away. A mixed blessing in this place, for these fires don't tend themselves and meals are served in the Great Hall, which is quite a walk from here."

Alex stared stupidly at the fire and struggled to make sense of what she'd said. Then he mumbled, "All day?" There were no windows in this room, and the arrow loops were covered by tapestry. It felt like night, and he was sleepy enough for it to still be.

"It's late afternoon. The sun's about to set. You slept about twenty hours."

He grunted. "No wonder I feel like crap." And no wonder he'd awakened thinking he was back home. The last time he'd slept like this was on return from his first deployment. Six months on combat duty, being shot at by day and sharing a stateroom with three other guys by night, and on his return to Virginia, when the noise and adrenaline quit, he'd crashed and burned like the Hindenburg.

He sat on the edge of the bed and looked around. Lindsay was wearing clothing Hector had brought, looking very boyish in a tunic of black and green. He hated it. He wanted her to lose the clothes and look like a girl again. Her chest was bound, and he could see she'd solved the problem of having no bulge in her pants, which hadn't been an issue when she'd worn the zoom bag. Now, wearing a dark-colored something or other that was sort of like tights but sort of not, a bulge in the front was making her tunic stick out. Whatever she had in there must be huge.

His head tilted and he regarded her crotch. "Think it's big enough?"

She looked down, then at him. "I wanted it to be noticeable."

He chuckled, and coughed to clear phlegm from his throat. "Well, you're thinking like a guy at least. We all wish they were noticeable, but they usually aren't so much. Besides, the thing you're after is to *not* stand out in a crowd. I'd lose at least one of those socks, or whatever you've got in there."

She reached under her tunic, fiddled some, then drew out a wad of cloth, tore it in half, and returned one of the pieces to her drawers. "Too bad codpieces haven't been invented yet; that would have solved the problem quite neatly, to have a stuffed and decorated artificial penis strapped to my front."

"Oh, yeah. That would be just adorable." He pointed with his chin. "What're those, tights?"

"They call them 'trews.' Precursor for 'trousers,' I suppose. Not nearly as tight as tights, but not near as baggy as pants. Your clothes are over there." She gestured toward the trunk where Hector had left them. "Mine are rather plain, but your outfit is quite nice, I think."

"How did you know which was which?"

"Well," she faltered, as if hesitating to state the patently obvious, "You are, after all, the knight. I am but a squire, so your clothing would be the nicer set. Besides, yours are bigger."

"Ah."

"I've arranged to have our flight suits, underclothes, and armor cleaned. There was some commentary about the cotton-knit T-shirts, but I convinced Fiona it was the way they make cloth in Hungary. She seemed somewhat envious of the stitchery, and I pretended not to care." There was a pause, then she said, "Actually, I didn't have to pretend, because I don't care."

Alex stared at the clothing and knew he should get dressed, but couldn't bring himself to move.

"Get dressed, and perhaps there will be something to eat downstairs. Dinner is past, but I'll lay odds they won't let you starve. You're the hot topic down there today; if you go down they're not likely to let you alone at all."

"What are they saying about me?"

"Oh, Hector is going on about your exploits, telling what a great warrior you are, how mightily you vanquished the sally from Stirling Castle, and how you stopped the supply train from England last month."

"I did all that?"

"You led the company, and so the story is about you. Apparently he's very impressed with your skill in strategy."

Alex grunted a wry laugh. "He clobbers me regularly in chess; it's probably more like amazement I haven't lost my entire company yet." Some faces of the men who had died under his command rose to confront him, but he fought them back and tucked them away in the dark recesses of his mind for later, when he might feel strong enough to think of those things. Suddenly, getting dressed seemed like a welcome distraction, so he slipped from the bed and went to see what Hector had brought.

A linen shirt, some linen drawers, a pair of those "trews" things, which turned out to have feet in them like kiddy pajamas, and a fairly fancy-looking tunic with elaborate embroidery in dark green and blue against wine red. The design was Celtic knot involving horses and stags. A pair of leather shoes had severely pointed toes that tipped up some, and Alex bypassed the munchkin shoes to wear his knee-length boots. Less fashionable, perhaps, but far more practical.

Carefully, with his dagger, he shaved in the cold wash bowl, then he donned the borrowed clothing. There was a leather belt to hold up his drawers and trews, and the shirt and tunic fell almost to his knees. His dagger he hung at his waist by his sword belt, minus the sword and scabbard, which were with Colin, Now he felt well and comfortably dressed, more so than he'd felt since parachuting in. "How do I look?"

"Your hair needs combing."

He ran his fingers through his hair and realized it had become quite shaggy in recent months. It would have made him happy to cut it short again if for no other reason than to discourage nits, but everyone he met these days assumed he'd had his hair cut off to get rid of a bad infestation of lice. It was hard to tell which was worse: to have lice, or to have people think he had them.

"Come here," he told Lindsay. She complied, and he slipped a hand behind her neck to kiss her thoroughly.

Her response was to kiss him back, but then she said, "What was that all about?"

"Just checking to make sure you're still in there." He looked at her wet, darkening mouth and smiled. "Still female."

That didn't seem to amuse her as he thought it should have. She blushed, then turned away toward the door. "Come and eat if you're going to," she said as she left.

He watched her go, puzzled, and let her get well away before following her.

Usually the quickest way to the Great Hall in any castle was to follow the smell of food and the sound of conversation. Alex wended his way through corridors, and finally was dumped out from the hallway through a wide, rounded arch. There stood three ladies, apparently in amiable conversation until they spotted him. They then stopped cold, and stared.

"Good evening, ladies," he greeted with a smile. A quick glance around failed to tell him where Lindsay had gone, so he returned his attention to the women before him.

The two younger murmured replies in kind, but the oldest of them gaped at him with wide eyes, looking as if she'd been slapped.

"Ma'am?" Had he done something?

She pulled herself up, mustering her dignity, and said, "You look not at all like him."

"Like who, ma'am?"

"Like your father."

Oh. He drew himself to respectful attention and said, "You're Hector's mother?"

She nodded.

Struggling for a soothing comment, he said, "It's very kind of you to welcome me into your home."

"'Tis my son's domain now. He welcomed you."

His cheeks warmed at the rebuff, but it faded to unimportance as, to Alex's appalled surprise, red eyes appeared over her left shoulder. He tensed to see the vague outline of the elfin guy from the knoll, his cloak hood dropped back onto his shoulder. The pointy-eared face was staring thoughtfully at the old woman, and Alex could almost see the gears turning in his head. A narrow glance at Alex, then the image disappeared entirely.

Alex faltered, speechless for an interminable moment. Finally he gathered his wits and replied to the dowager, "I mean no disrespect, ma—"

"You're very presence—"

"*Mother!*" One of the younger women, a pretty version of Hector, gently interceded. "Mother, he cannot help the circumstance. Please."

The older woman pressed her lips together, the pain in her eyes making them shine. "I'm told you are a skilled fighter and a man of honor."

"Aye."

"I pray you will pledge your energies to the clan, and not the clan to your own ends."

That puzzled him, but he worked out in his head what she probably meant and was able to formulate a reply he thought might make sense. "I make no claim beyond whatever regard I might earn."

Her face smoothed some at that, but she said, "What you earn is all you will receive, and if Hector is blinded to your merits—or lack of them—I will not be. Take care." With that, she turned and made her exit to the corridor from which Alex had just come.

The other women said nothing, but glanced apology at him and left also.

Alex watched them go, then sighed and turned his attention

to the next batch of MacNeils he needed to win over. He hoped for better luck with the men.

The Great Hall, where most castle residents ate meals, was alive with folks coming, going, cleaning up after dinner, and lounging about the fire. Hector was holding forth among the men, as usual the loudest man in the room, and when he spotted Alex he raised his hand and shouted, "Ah! Ailig Mac Dìolain! Come! Come sit by me and tell us about your adventures in the war against the Sasunnach king!"

Alex glanced back at the archway through which the laird's mother had disappeared, and for the first time since his arrival in this century was glad to be living in a place where the men and women didn't mix much.

Hector and Cullan sat among a group of several men gathered at the hearth in the far end of the room, some wrapped in yards of plaid cloth over their tunics and trews, some with only the plaid and shirt with no tunic, and one sorry-looking fellow at the fringe had nothing but a belted shirt, and his feet were shod with the sort of shapeless moccasins Hector had worn during summer in the Lowlands. The rest of the men, even Hector today, had pointy-toed shoes like the ones Alex had been given.

Hector proceeded to introduce him around, and Alex learned why his name when Hector said it always had some sort of qualifier attached. Of the seven men sitting before the fire, he was the fourth with the name "Alasdair." Hector's full brother was "Alasdair Og," for, as Hector explained, their father had also been an Alasdair and that made the brother "Young Alexander." In addition were cousin Ailig Dubh MacNeil, named for his dark hair, and the son of Ailig Dubh, Ailig Neil MacNeil, who went by both first and middle names.

Alex asked, "Then what does 'Mac Dìolain' mean?"

"Illegitimate son."

A groan rose, but he stifled it.

Hector rattled off something in Gaelic to a passing woman, who hurried away, then returned his attention to the gathering. "I want the lot of you to know I value my new brother and I'm pleased he's found his way home. I've never seen in battle a man such as this one, who stands up to a beating and thinks naught of it, who fights with his head as well as his arm."

The woman who had hurried off now hurried back with a

plate of meat and a wide, shallow cup of mead. Alex was famished, and ate eagerly while listening to Hector tell the story of how he'd rescued Alex from the Kirkpatricks who had been about to beat him to death with a chain. The memory was not a pleasant one for Alex, but Hector told the tale with such fervor and drama, it was hard not to be entertained by it. Hector made him come off like a hero for his stoicism, and as Alex listened the pain and scars of the beating began to seem no big deal.

Throughout the evening the men talked, in English for the sake of their foreign visitor, mostly shooting the breeze, but Alex pulled nuggets from the conversation he figured would help him get along with these MacNeils. He noted the brother of Hector—Ailig Og—accepted without question the presence of a younger half-brother. His scrutiny was thorough, and Alex felt his eyes on him the entire time he was in the room, but his tone suggested he'd accepted Hector's assessment of their father's *mac dìolain*. He also seemed to accept Alex wasn't there to claim a birthright. Hector's surviving children included two sons, one of them in his early teens and in fosterage in Ireland. Alasdair Og had four young sons and a pregnant wife, so more than likely they both felt the MacNeil succession was secure from any illegitimate interlopers. Alex certainly didn't want anything from these guys, and perhaps Hector had sensed that over the past several months. Perhaps that had gone a long way toward making them secure in bringing him here in the first place.

Or perhaps bringing him here was an effort to keep him under observation and control. In any case, Alex knew to tread lightly and make clear his lack of agenda.

By the time the fire in the enormous hearth began to wane, Alex was feeling sleepy again and the voices around him were blending into a dull murmur. He'd only been awake for a few hours but already wanted to return to bed. He looked for Lindsay, but she wasn't anywhere around. A yawn took him by surprise.

"You look worn, Mac Dìolain. You should go to bed," said Hector. It was nearly an order.

"Where's my squire?"

A bright flash of amusement lit Hector's eyes and he looked as if struggling to not crack a joke, but instead he said, "Certainly he's where any squire would be at this time of the evening: in his master's quarters waiting to serve. Go. We'll see you in the morning."

Murmured partings were given, and Alex had little choice but to rise and return to his chamber.

When he arrived, Lindsay wasn't there. He turned to head back out to find her, but hesitated. It wouldn't do to go wandering about the castle, asking after his missing squire. He'd have to wait for her return. So he poked the fire and put another log on it, then began to undress. He laid his shoes, tunic, belt, trews, and drawers on the trunk by the wall, and as he gathered the voluminous linen of his shirt and hauled it over his head, a pair of hands slipped over his hips to his privates and startled him. He jumped.

But he knew whose hands they were, even as his body jerked. "Hey!" He turned and untangled his arms from his shirt to remove it, and found Lindsay behind him, wearing only her shirt. "Where were you?" He glanced at the door, but she couldn't have come from there. Not dressed like that.

"I was in the garderobe. These stone walls are great soundproofing, you know. It's like a tiny little cave in there, and it's so quiet you can hear . . . well, things *fall* quite a distance." There was laughter in her eyes, and it made him smile. He kissed her, and sleepiness fled. It was time for bed, but there would be no sleep for a couple of hours at least.

He made love to her, and even more important she made love to him, very slowly, gently, mouths exploring, hands tracing contours, hips pressing, he trying to put his entire self inside her, and she doing her best to enfold him. Then they slept, entwined in each other.

As consciousness returned slowly, the darkness of the windowless room gave no indication of the time of day or night. Alex felt rested, and hoped he hadn't slept through another entire day. Only dim outlines could be discerned by the embers in the hearth.

Lindsay was at his side, her hand on his chest, fiddling with the hairs there. It had awakened him; she was fluffing them and arranging them all neatly in a sort of coif all the way to his navel and a bit beyond. He lay as still as possible, for he knew the instant he moved she would stop. It was hell to not laugh while she tried to make swirls of hair around his nipples. She patted and pressed and stroked, but the hairs wouldn't stay down, so she fluffed them again. He focused on controlling his breathing so it wouldn't betray him.

But then his heart ran away with him when she touched her lips to his skin and spoke in the barest of whispers, thinking he was unconscious. "I love you, Alex MacNeil." Her voice was nearly inaudible, but the words pierced his soul and filled him with warm joy. "God help me, I do love you and don't know what to do about it."

The need to see her face was overwhelming. He couldn't help turning his head to look, but when she realized he was awake she stopped fiddling and sat up to leave the bed. His heart sank, and he reached out for her hand to keep her there. "Don't go." The light was too dim to read her face, though he sat up to try.

"I thought you were asleep."

"I know. You woke me up with all that 'I love you' stuff." He held both her hands in his, and his pulse skipped around in his ears. "So how come you can't say it when I'm awake? And what is it you think you need to *do* about it?"

Her eyes had that haunted, slightly angry look she'd had off and on for weeks. "No. You shouldn't have heard that, and you shouldn't take it seriously. I'm sorry I said it."

"Why?" His heart made an uncomfortable pace, and he wasn't sure he really wanted to know, but no way was he going to let this one just go unanswered. It took a long time for her to reply, and he waited.

Finally she said, "You don't know anything about me, Alex."

"I know everything important."

"No, you don't."

"What, are you a serial killer, or something?"

She sighed, and her voice took on a bitter edge as her eyes narrowed at him. "You've killed more people than I have, so don't you dare go there."

Quickly he blinked and backpedaled. "I mean, Lindsay, I don't care what it is; I want to know what's wrong."

"No, you don't. Trust me, you don't want to know." She stared hard at his hand holding hers.

"Is it true what you said?"

She sighed. "You think I'm normally in the habit of telling unnecessary lies to unconscious lovers?"

"Lindsay—"

"I mean it. You don't want to know." She yanked her hand from his grasp, and slipped from her side of the bed.

"What? What is it you think I don't want to know?" He got out on his side, grabbed his linen shirt, and drew it on as he said, "I do. Tell me. What's going on with you?" He met her at the foot of the bed and held her arm. "Tell me. 'Cause I love you right back, and if there's something wrong between us I want to know. And I want to make it go away."

"You can't make it go away."

"I don't believe you. Tell me what it is."

She gave it another long think, then said through a clenched jaw, "Very well. Revive the fire, and we can talk."

Fair enough. He went to put wood on the embers while she pulled on her shirt, drawers, and trews. Then she came to stand beside him by the fireplace and stare into the struggling flame as its tendrils licked the new logs and slowly grew. He waited patiently, only gazing with her.

Finally she said in a low, flat voice, "I never told you that when we met I was engaged to someone. Derek and I were to be married a month after my voyage on your carrier."

A surge of alarm sickened Alex. He said nothing, but felt the need to sit, and slowly let himself down into one of the chairs behind him. The past several months paraded past in his mind. Every time she'd cried, every flicker of her face. The perspective this information brought changed the picture entirely, but he wasn't certain exactly how. *Derek.* The guy she'd said would have laughed at him. Would have laughed himself sick. Alex slouched in the seat, the long tail of his shirt draped between his thighs and his arms leaning on the chair arms. He looked up at her, and she continued to stare into the fire, unmoving.

"Why didn't you tell me?"

Her voice was soft, almost dreamy. "At first it wasn't any of your business. After a while, when I realized your attraction to me, I thought if you knew you wouldn't try to find a way home. And now . . . now, I didn't want to tell you because I don't want it to matter."

A laugh tried to come, but it stuck in his throat. "Yeah, it matters. You were *engaged*? You were in love with someone else." A long, dark pause fell, then he said, "Possibly you're still in love with someone else."

"Possibly."

His stomach knotted. Anger rose, and he stared hard into the fire. When he could trust his voice, he said, "You being here is the only thing that has made my existence in this place anything better than miserable."

"I don't believe that."

Now he peered at her, frowning. "Why would I lie?"

"I think you're deluding yourself. I think you like it here far better than you're willing to admit."

He snorted. "Yeah. I love being in the saddle all day and sleeping in a tent for months at a time. I get all gooshy inside at the thought of carting around on my body thirty pounds of chain mail, or wiping my ass with dead leaves." He pointed to the garderobe door. "Which, you know that wad of hay in the head? That's as good as it's going to get in our lifetime."

A sigh hissed from her, and she returned her attention to the fire. The silence drew out for a very long time, and as Alex's anger subsided he wished to return to the moment before she'd told him her secret. She'd been right: he really didn't want to know.

He broke the silence. "You said you loved me."

She nodded.

"But you'd rather be with him."

"I'd rather be home."

"With him."

"Not necessarily."

Hope rose, but he tempered it. "You would stay with me? Or are you saying that so I'll try to find a way back?"

Finally she turned, with a frown on her face. "It's not as if we're in any danger of finding it, is it? That strange fellow didn't seem terribly inclined to help us, did he? So how do I know what I would or would not do?"

At least she was being honest. And this explained quite a bit of her behavior during the past few months. "So . . . now what?"

Another sigh, and the crease in her brow relaxed. "I do love you, Alex."

"But you'd rather be with him."

"Nevertheless, I'm with you."

"You have no choice." He looked away for a moment as a terrible thought came. "Are you certain this isn't just some sort of Stockholm syndrome thing? You've convinced yourself you love me because you think I'm all you've got?" The thing she'd said two days ago rose to mind and the joy of it soured. "I make you feel *safe*."

"You do. I thought you wanted that." A smile lifted a corner of her mouth, and she ducked her head to peer at him. "I'm not your prisoner. And you are all I have. Unless you would like me to start banging Sir Cullan."

That landed in his gut, hard. It was absolutely the wrong thing for her to say. He stood. "Maybe you should." Suddenly he had to get out of there. No more talk. This was doing nothing more than pissing him off. So he rose and went to get dressed, then he left the room. She said nothing to stop him.

He spent the day avoiding her. It wasn't difficult, since squires never socialized with knights. Winter weather raged outside the castle, while Alex hung out with Hector, Ailig Og, Cullan, and the others by the fire in the drafty Great Hall.

Images of Lindsay with Sir Cullan swarmed in his brain. The rangy, raw-boned Scot sat among the men in the Great Hall, and Alex couldn't help throwing glances at him. Why had Lindsay mentioned him in particular? What did she see there that made her think Cullan would be her alternative? Did she think the guy was handsome? Alex couldn't see it. Cullan was better at hand-to-hand combat—could that be it? Did that turn her on? He sure didn't know. He figured he didn't know much of anything for certain anymore. And Lindsay didn't seem very forthcoming with information. Had what she said been truth? Alex was wary of accepting she loved him, for he knew how easy it would be to believe what he wanted to be true.

If only it were true. If only he could be certain of her.

As the day wore on, Alex became bored and fidgety. He wanted to do something. Anything. In mid-afternoon—sometime after lunch and before sunset—he wandered away from the Great Hall and took a walk through the castle.

The place was a labyrinth. It would have been nice to get a sense of which way was north, but the deep overcast sky and constant drizzle made it impossible to get his bearings even when he found a window or arrow loop. He wandered through narrow corridors that were like tunnels, chambers that were like caves. He found the kitchen, and hoped he could find it again when he wanted to. Smells were strong, and the scent of wood and dried peat burning permeated everything. The odor of burnt meat and bread under the smoke was relatively faint, even near the kitchen.

At one point he came through a door that deposited him in what appeared to be a meeting room, or sitting room of some sort. Or it had been at one time, but now it had fallen into severe neglect. Heavy wooden chairs with wide arms, old, brittle, and discolored, stood around a cold hearth. The only light in the room drifted in from a small window opposite the door. The walls were free of decoration other than cobwebs heavy with dust. Alex idly wondered what this room might have once been used for, then his thoughts slipped easily away to looking for the stable. He thought he might have his horse saddled in the morning if the rain would stop. Some physical activity might take his mind off things.

But just as he began to withdraw and pull the door closed, the room suddenly blossomed and glowed with candles. Gentle light filled the corners, and the hearth leapt to life. A bearskin rug covered the hard, stone floor, and a tapestry hung across the entire wall opposite the fire. The chairs were smooth and new, their leather seats supple and the studs attaching them shiny.

Alex went cold, and his first impulse was to shut the door and get as far away as possible. But if this was that elf guy's idea of an entrance, the thought occurred that Alex had a score to settle with the sonofabitch. He stood his ground and opened the door wide enough to see if the elfin creature was anywhere around.

"Come in, lad."

Not the elf. It was a Scot, speaking Middle English. Curious, Alex took a single step forward and looked, but saw nobody.

"Come inside and shut the door, young man. We've business to attend to." The voice was commanding, accustomed to obedience. Alex complied. The door latch clacked shut behind him.

He turned to look at it and hoped the feeling of being locked in was only his imagination.

He still couldn't see the source of the voice, but when he came around to the front of a high-backed chair he found an old man lounging in it. Small, wizened, and gray, he nevertheless gave the impression of having once been powerful both physically and socially. In these times those things went hand in hand.

The old man peered curiously at him. "I know who you are."

A shiver came over Alex, and he briefly wondered where his grave was that someone had just walked over it.

The man who couldn't exist continued. "I also know who you are not. You are not my son."

Alasdair MacNeil the Elder? "They said you were dead."

"And so I am. Lucky for you." There was no anger in the aged countenance, and the bright eyes held only curiosity. Perhaps a glimmer of amusement. "However, beware my wife, for you're not the first to seek his birthright here. She is a danger to you. She loves her sons and will do her best to bring you low. She is highly skilled. You'll note that none of the three who came before you remain, and each of them had a valid claim where you do not."

Three? "I claim nothing, and I don't mean any harm."

A sly light came into the ghost's eyes. "And you would be the first *mac dìolain* of mine to even say so, were you my son. Even at that, every man, at some point in his life whether he means it or not, brings harm. And receives it without deserving it. The priests and those who command them will tell ye otherwise, but those of us who live genuine lives ken the truth." He gestured to a chair on the other side of the hearth, and Alex carefully sat, eyeing the ghost in hopes it wouldn't suddenly turn into a decaying corpse.

"You know a lot about truth?"

The former laird smiled, showing a ragged mouth of blackened and missing teeth. "Aye. Ever so much truth, I can hardly contain it! I know where ye come from. I know, though you're nae my son, you are descended from Niall of the Nine Hostages, and that makes you a clansman. And your sons. And their sons."

"Niall of . . . what?"

"The first true king of Ireland. Let Hector tell the story; he has the gift I never did. But let me tell ye, lad, I can see you're a MacNeil for true."

Alex raised his chin. "I knew that."

"Ye did not. What you knew was only that you are your father's son and his father's grandson. You understood only that much because your people have forgotten how to tell stories. They only tell of their own lives and never of those who came before."

"That's good enough—"

"That is nothing."

"I took history in—"

"You know naught of the first MacNeils. You know naught of the blood that came down to you through more than a millennium and a half of brave men and women. Ye havenae the first notion of clan loyalty."

Alex's ears began to warm. "I care about my family, and would die for my country. I've pledged myself to the Scottish king, and have put myself at risk for the cause."

"A cause you still think of as someone else's."

"I wasn't born here."

The laird's eyes went wide; he gripped the arms of his chair and leaned forward. "Och, but ye *were* born here! Centuries ago. You were formed by this land, as were all your ancestors before you. You were made for this place. You're part of the blood of my people. Not my son, but descended from the clan."

Alex's interest perked. "I have ancestors living here now? Who? Who are they?"

The old man sat back and gazed hard at him. "All of them, Alasdair. Every man, woman, and child currently living on this island who will leave descendants. They will live their lives and you yours, and most of them will never know you. But know you are part of them." He nodded to affirm his words. "They are a part of you."

"So . . . you don't mind if I tell people I'm your son?"

"Have I a choice? No, I think not. And there is that you're a tall, well-formed lad with a will for fighting and enough sand in your craw to not embarrass me."

That made Alex smile, for the old man suddenly reminded him of his real father. "Aye, sir."

The former laird waved him off. "Now, lad, go ask Hector

for the stories. Learn who ye were, decide who ye are, then become who you will be."

Then he was gone. The fire was gone, the candles, rug, and tapestry. Alex found himself sitting in a cold, dark room, staring at an empty, decrepit chair covered in spider webs.

He jumped up to slap away the webs that clung to him from his own chair, his back, his fingers, and picked the tendril pieces from his clothing. Once he'd made himself presentable, he left the room as quickly as possible. Outside in the corridor, he took a moment to gather himself and wonder if he'd hallucinated all that. It sure had seemed real, and he'd seen enough whacked-out stuff since coming to this century to think just about anything might be possible. He ran his fingers through his hair, checking for more spider webs, then went on his way.

Wending the route back to the Great Hall, he found the Mac-Neil clansmen lounging around still. So he planked himself down in a chair and listened to their talk of past battles.

He waited until there was a break in the storytelling, then said, "Hector, you know I'm new to these parts, and came to learn more about my father's people. How about telling me about Niall of the Nine Hostages?"

Hector's face tightened. "You've never heard tell of the first of our clan? Who is also the first high king of Ireland? Och, it's no wonder ye had to leave the eastern mountains, as deprived as you were. Did your foster father tell you nothing?"

"I don't think he knew."

More clucking from Hector, and chuckling from the others, then Hector took a deep breath to begin. It was plain he loved telling such stories.

"Well, 'twas more than a thousand years ago. The Irish king Eochu Muigmeadón had four sons, and a fifth was Niall, whose mother was a Saxon slave named Cairenn Chasdub."

"Niall was the *mac díolain*?" Alex asked with raised eyebrows.

Hector paused, a slight smile turning the corners of his mouth. "Indeed, he was. And there's something to be learned in this story, so I hope ye take the correct message."

Alex sat back. "Pardon the interruption."

"So, as I was saying, Eochu had five sons, the fifth well despised by his wife, who forced heavy labor on the lad's mother so that he was born out in the open. Nobody, not even his own mother, would have aught to do with the child, for fear of the queen. Finally the poet Torna came and took the child to fosterage until he was of age to be king."

Hector paused here, and glanced at Alex as if expecting another interruption, but Alex kept still, his expression only of bland interest.

"Well, then, when Niall rescued his mother from her servitude and dressed her in a purple robe, the queen was furious. She demanded her husband determine immediately which son should succeed him, for she saw it as the way to ensure it would be one of her own sons."

Now Alex did interrupt. "Wouldn't it be the eldest?"

The cluster of men murmured a collective grumble, and Hector said, "The English King Edward I brought that notion here, and we Scots are unaccustomed to the idea. 'Tis an invitation to weak leadership to deny position to the most worthy candidate."

"But you're the eldest in your family."

Hector straightened in his chair and drew himself up in offense. "I am laird by merit, not mere birthright. I lead by strength, by wit, and by the loyalty of my clan, and don't need the *Sasunnach* law to award my position to me."

"Ah." Alex nodded, and slowly began to understand some of the attitudes around here. "Forgive me. You're right, and I should have seen that."

Hector nodded and continued. "So, the king turned the choosing over to the blacksmith, who contrived to test the five brothers by setting fire to the smithy where they were all at work. One son rescued the hammers, another a pail of beer, a third the weapons, and the fourth of the queen's sons brought a bundle of kindling. Only Niall was strong enough to carry the anvil.

"Next the five sons went hunting. When they wanted water, the first of the queen's sons found a well, guarded by an ugly old hag. He asked for a drink, but she would give it only in exchange for a kiss, which he refused and went away thirsty. The second son then went, then the third and fourth. Each failed to take a drink, for they wouldn't bring themselves to touch the hag.

"Finally, Niall went to the well. When the hag asked for a

kiss, he was pleased to lay with her, whereupon she became the most fair and beautiful lass he'd ever seen. Her name was Sovranty, Goddess of the Land. She named him King of Ireland, and told him his race would be kings forever. Because Niall accepted Sovranty with all her imperfections, he was deemed worthy to rule over the land with all its troubles."

Alex smiled and nodded, agreeing with the sentiment though he was certain it was the part about the pissed-off queen Hector wanted him to take to heart. "Aye," he said, "it's not a job to be taken lightly, nor to go to the wrong man."

The other men murmured agreement.

By then it was late, and the people still awake began to drift off to bed. Alex returned to his chamber and lit a candle stump at the hearth to find Lindsay asleep in the bed. Part of him had hoped she would take the servant's mattress by the fire, but he was also relieved she'd not. Then it crossed his mind she might have expected him to sleep on the other bed, but it was a fleeting thought for there wasn't a chance in hell he would ever do it. He set the candle on the trunk by the wall and slipped out of his clothes, letting them all fall to the floor.

As he slid between the covers, he watched Lindsay's face. She seemed undisturbed by his presence, and he settled in. Lying on his back he closed his eyes to go to sleep, but he couldn't help himself from looking over at her. So beautiful, her sleeping face on the pillow, her nearly black hair fanned out across it.

He should have known she'd been spoken for when he'd met her, but he'd been utterly clueless. All this time it had never occurred to him to ask—or even wonder—whether she was available. Not when he'd thought about asking her to lunch that day of the crash. Not ever. Her voice echoed in his mind, what she'd said to him that day on the battlefield. She'd been right; he had wanted her. But he had her, and still wanted her. He couldn't imagine ever not wanting her.

His hand moved, just enough to rest on her hip. She stirred and raised her head from the pillow. For a bleary moment she blinked at the candle that was already guttering on the nearby trunk, then focused on his face. He expected her to roll away from him, perhaps to leave the bed, but instead she slid over close to him, under his arm, and rested her head on his shoulder.

His fingers lightly touched and stroked the hair that lay across her forehead. He said, "You meant what you said?"

"I love you. You're all there is left for me, Alex."

Not what he'd hoped to hear. But for now he was willing to accept it, because it was all there was for her to give.

Then she asked, "Why do you love me, Alex?"

He struggled for a reply, then finally had to admit, "I don't know."

"I turn you on somehow. Me and that pie-faced whore who smelled like a tuna boat."

"You know that's unfair."

"Then, what?"

His lips pressed against her head as he considered an answer, then he said, "I used to want someone as devoted to me as my mother is to my father. But I don't seem to have found that."

The comment was received with only silence. Without letting it go on too long, he continued. "Maybe it's because I can admire you. Maybe . . ." he thought hard, ". . . maybe it's because you're the most beautiful woman I've ever known."

She made a skeptical "hmm" sound.

"Maybe it's because you understand me in ways nobody else here ever will. If I meet someone else, no matter how long I might know her, she'll never be able to understand those things about me I can never reveal."

"So I'm all there is left for you, as well."

"I wouldn't put it—"

"It's true. We're together because we're stranded together in the midst of a sea of people who can never truly know either of us."

"Relationships have succeeded on less."

"Now you're seeing my point."

He sighed. "I guess so." Then he hugged her close, kissed her head, and closed his eyes to sleep.

CHAPTER 11

Over the winter months, when weather permitted, Alex, Hector, and Alasdair Og rode to the village and visited around the island. Hector said it was to improve Alex's Gaelic, and that turned out to be true because even the few words he picked up here and there were an improvement. With Hector's help, pretty soon Alex could tell whether the subject at hand was the weather, the fields, or the livestock.

The nearest village was shockingly small and poor. The people were even dirtier than the knights Alex had come to know in this century, and their clothing seemed to consist mostly of long tunics and lengths of plaid wool draped around them. Most of the men wore shoes, but none of the women and children did, even in the cold.

The men who came from the peat houses to greet Sir Hector and talk with him seemed not to notice their abject state. Unlike the vassals in the south, they spoke in proud voices and looked Hector in the eye. In return he listened to what they had to say, and spoke to them in a tone that suggested they were equals. The relationship between Sir Hector and his clansmen was far different from the vast chasm of culture and regard between the aloof Lowland nobility and the people who worked their rich lands, not to mention the downright pompous airs of the English knights of every rank Alex had encountered. Hector's regard for his kinsmen and their sense of participation in his rule seemed almost a whiff of home to Alex, and he admired the laird for it.

So strange to be in a place where nearly everyone for miles around had the same last name as himself. The entire island population considered themselves related to him, however distantly, and treated him like a cousin. The ghost of Hector's father had been right; he hadn't known what it was to be a MacNeil. But he was finding out. It made him wish his brothers could be here to see this.

As the weather worsened toward January, he and Lindsay were more and more glad for the warmth of their room deep within the walls of the castle. When the ugliest storms raged, and even the high fires of wood and peat failed to entirely hold off the invading cold, Alex and Lindsay bolted their heavy, iron-studded door and retreated to their bed and to each other. They comforted and warmed each other, entwined and joined, surrounded by fur and feathers, the scents of stone, wood, and crushed reeds scattered across the chamber floor, permeated by peat smoke that smelled like the spirit of the earth itself. He moved slowly, rocking with care, at once part of her, she a part of him, and both part of this place, at home in the shadows and surrounding walls like a cave.

Alex did his best to make her forget what had gone before.

Other days, when the weather stilled to ice-locked cold, they spent hanging out in the Great Hall, where folks gathered from all over the island to visit with each other; the MacNeils called it *ceilidh*. Sometimes there was music, and often dancing accompanied the music. Not as exciting as football on television, but far more interesting than gazing at tapestries.

The local music sounded a little like the entertainment he'd heard in the army camps of Robert and Edward Bruce, but only a little. What Alex heard on Barra was closer to what he might have expected to hear in a St. Patrick's Day parade. Though he'd seen pipes during his months fighting in the south, the ones in the household of the MacNeil laird were larger and louder than those. One of the bags looked like an entire lamb filled with air. The castle piper did make lively music with it, though, and he was obviously skilled.

But what really interested Alex were the stories. Tales of
Scotland's past, of Scottish kings and the glories of Gaelic culture, brought visions of tough, brave, and resourceful men. Men
who were his own forebears, and that made them all the more
exciting. More and more, awareness of his Scottish blood stirred
and it was no longer the vague perception he'd had of kilts and
whiskey. Now he knew why he was coming to identify himself
as a Scot. Lindsay had been right, and so had the old ghost: a
couple of centuries was not a long time, and two hundred years
of American history was only a thin veneer laid over the millennia of his Celtic heritage. He listened, rapt, to bloody, violent stories of glory won in battle by MacNeils against other
Scots and all Scots against the English, and before them the
Saxons, and before *them* the Romans, told with a relish akin to
sports announcing.

The MacNeils taught him of the recent English atrocities
that had led to the war they now fought. Of the massacre at
Berwick led by Edward I. Of Scots disinherited and their lands
given over to Englishmen. Of entire towns put to the sword,
where women and children were chased down by knights and
cut open to lie, dying, in the streets before their homes. Of the
weak reign of John Balliol, who had been the puppet of Edward
I. Of the bravery and martyrdom of William Wallace, who had
been tortured to death for standing up to the foreign king.

Wallace was a favorite subject around the MacNeil fire, and
Alex learned every detail of the depraved execution from Alasdair Og, who had been there to witness it. It had been an imagi-
native torture thought up by the English king, so brutal the
telling of it made even the sturdy MacNeil men go pale and
quiet. Alex glanced over at Lindsay, who listened from the
fringes with others of her rank, and saw her face pale. Her fingers pressed to her lips as if she might vomit, and a sheen of
sweat covered her forehead. Quickly, he reached for the cup that
was making the rounds, drained it, and raised it high to be re-
filled. Lindsay leapt to her feet in service of her master, took the
cup, and hurried from the room. He didn't expect her return until this particular story was finished, and it was well over before
she came back with the cup filled with mead. As she handed it to
him, the soft look of gratitude on her face warmed him.

He knew how she felt; the story had been hard on him as

well. The horror in Alasdair's voice had brought home to Alex the reality of the death in a way the depiction on film had not, and he had found himself wanting to follow her from the room for some air.

At the same time that the story made him queasy, it also fired his blood with anger. The movie he'd seen as a teenager had told a story distant and unclear, and, he realized, in many ways inaccurate. Now he realized the horrible execution had been an offense not just to one man, but to all of Scotland.

If the ghost of the former laird was correct, that included himself, and for it he wanted retribution. After six months of battle against forces loyal to the English crown, he hated the English as much as the rest of the MacNeils did.

In fact, as winter wore on he itched to get back to the fight. Occasionally he'd see men working in the frozen fields of the island, spreading manure behind small carts pulled by tiny horses led by wives or children, and he counted himself fortunate to be a knight. Soldiering was his profession as it always had been, and fighting was all he was expected to do here. In fact, he was honored for it in ways he'd never experienced back home. Frequently in the evenings, he was asked to tell stories of his battles and of the blood he'd shed. Nobody here ever asked him how it felt to kill someone, probably because most men already knew and the women knew they didn't want to know.

However, as much as he enjoyed hanging out and telling stories, after a couple of months sitting he was ready to return to the fray against King Edward.

He knew James Douglas was more than likely still harrying the Borderlands at every opportunity, and that sounded like where he wanted to be. Alex thought long and hard about riding into England. Besides the wealth to be had there, he was now aware of the need to protect Scotland from incursion from the south. He was pleased to have sent Lord Clifford's men to their maker where they belonged, for they certainly didn't belong in Scotland.

"What are you doing?" Lindsay returned to the bedchamber from somewhere, where she'd been doing squire stuff Alex didn't care much about. Probably grooming the horses or cleaning the tack, for though it was Colin's job, she liked to get out of the living quarters from time to time and needed something to do.

Alex was sitting in one of the chairs by the fireplace, with a piece of paper and a board rested on his knees. "I'm drawing a coat of arms. I've been carrying that English shield around for half a year; I want to stop looking like a lime . . ." He glanced up at her, then quickly slipped his foot from his mouth. "I want to be identified as myself on the field." He wanted the English to know who they were up against, and hoped they would be frightened.

"You want them to think you're Scottish."

He gazed blandly at her for a moment, then said, "Aye. I do."

"Even though you're not."

His attention returned to the drawing before him, and he ignored her remark, saying, "Hector tells me I can base my design on the one he inherited from his father. That's it there." He pointed with his chin to the shield leaning against the foot of the bed.

Arms crossed, standing hipshot, she was about to tell him something he didn't want to hear. He was sure of it. "You realize if you do that you'll have to indicate your illegitimate status."

Oh, good. He already knew that. He sighed. "Yeah. Hector made certain I knew how to do that. Blue-and-silver border. Got it. My father must be turning in his grave. I mean, if he were born yet, and then . . . you know . . . died. I can't even imagine what Mom would say." He held up the paper. "So, see what I've got."

It was a simple design, the better to not have to draw a lot of pictures. Inside the border of alternating silver and blue, which he'd made as thin as he figured he could get away with, the interior was divided into two parts. Below was a sailing ship of black on a background of gold, and above was an eagle with wings spread, gold on a background of red. He liked that the red and gold happened to echo the colors of King Robert's arms as well as those of MacNeil. "See, I used the ship from Hector's shield."

"Nautical and aeronautical. That's you, all right." Lindsay pointed to the eagle's neck, where the color of the body ended in a jagged line, and the head was an outline not filled in. "That's a bald eagle."

"It is."

"They don't exist here. Nobody here has ever seen one."

"Yup."

She chuckled. "You're such an American."

He sat back and grinned at her. A smile twitched on her lips, and her eyes shone so his heart swelled. "You love it. It gives you something to rag me about." He took her hand, and drew her close so he could kiss her.

Alex had his shield painted by the armorer, then hung it on the wall of his chamber with his swords until he would need them. Gazing at it, all gold, black, and red, he almost trembled with the urge to get back to the action in the south.

But winter hung on, and the Sea of the Hebrides was too dangerous to cross to the mainland. February passed. March came, rainy and as cold as February. Days were gray and boring, but nights were filled with warmth and comfort. Alex had never been married, nor had he ever lived that way, and now he wondered how he'd ever been able to stand sleeping alone. Even the nights when they only slept, to have her there, warm and breathing beside him, eased his soul in ways he didn't truly understand. He knew only a need to touch her before sleep. To touch her, hold her, make love to her, or just to have an arm against hers, and then he could rest.

She seemed to need it, too, and reached for him as often as he did her. Sometimes when he rolled toward her, he was quickly pressed over onto his back again and told to lie still for her to take him into her mouth. It happened only twice before he figured out why, and when he realized it was the only form of birth control available to her, he also realized his feelings about it were mixed.

She was right, of course. Pregnancy would be at best difficult to explain. But on a level deep inside, where lurked the uncertainties he never let show, he wondered whether it was children she didn't want, or only *his* child. When he let himself think about it, the absent and therefore idealized Derek rose to mind and he knew how out of luck he himself would be if Lindsay was ever able to return to the fiancé.

But now was not the time to press the issue, for the question was moot. They were each faced with the lives given to them and the likelihood one or both would die in battle one day. He was pleased enough to let this winter pass in the comfort of Lindsay's body and not think about the future until it would arrive.

Then as spring blossomed, drill with swords resumed. An expanse of pasture outside the castle was given over to lines of men, some whacking at each other with blades covered in leather, others with pikes or maces. Alex was glad to be active again, for the relentlessly greasy and starchy food of this century was catching up with him. He felt horribly out of shape, and his body made him regret sitting around by the fire all winter. Softness had set in around his middle and he could no longer find his abs without poking with his fingers. On Lindsay a little extra flesh was okay, for he liked her soft and giving in his hands, but for himself the flab had to go.

The aching muscles of the first few days were nearly a pleasure, for the pain made him feel alive. Overcoming it made him feel capable and strong, able to master whatever the English— or anyone else in the world—might send against him.

Today he worked with Lindsay in the castle bailey, taking the afternoon to spar with maces. She was quick, and slung the wooden haft and its curved flanges with deadly accuracy. A smile came as she backed him up against an animal pen. He set his teeth because she was refusing to pull punches, taking advantage of her knowledge he would lose rather than hurt her. He knew it, she knew he knew it, and there was nothing he could do about it short of actually hurting her. And that he wouldn't do.

"I'm gonna come back at you," he said, breath coming in gasps.

"So come."

"Be ready."

"Listen to you, warning your opponent you intend to fight him."

"I'm not going to hurt you. You know it."

"I know I'm beating you." She hauled back and swung harder, but he dodged and she only whacked an upright pole. Thatching overhead rattled, and bits of straw and dried bracken fluttered down like snow.

As she yanked the mace flanges from the wood, he came around behind and tried to goose her with the spiked end of his mace, but she was too quick for him and parried. Laughing, he danced backward, then bounced on his toes, his weapon at his side to invite careless attack.

Lindsay hauled back to swing, but only feinted. When Alex tried to parry, she lunged to the side to goose him and succeeded.

That made him roar with offended dignity. "You limey!" he teased.

"You Yank!"

Then he laughed and lunged to goose her as well, taking the both of them into a whirling, circling flurry of trying to poke each other in the rear with the mace heads, laughing so hard they could hardly stand.

"Limey!"

"Yank!"

Finally they both dissolved in laughter and gave up the contest. Lindsay laughed so hard she doubled over, and Alex reached to steady her. Her eyes were bright with amusement, and he looked deep into them to share it.

Then they stepped back from each other, and Alex's heart froze to find the Dowager Lady MacNeil watching from an open window above the pens, entirely too intrigued by what she saw. The old woman's face was set hard, her chin pulled in and her eyes alive with hatred. For a brief, appalling second, Alex thought he saw the hooded, elfin figure standing beside her, leaning in to speak near her ear. But the image blinked out too quickly for him to be certain what he saw, and it left him staring into the face of a woman who by her expression would be happy to see him dead.

He then realized what this looked like to those who thought Lindsay was a boy, and said a bit more loudly than necessary, "Enough play. The English won't be so amused, and will kill you for your lack of discipline."

A puzzled look of betrayal crossed Lindsay's face, then he muttered, "Curious onlooker, six o'clock high. Don't look, just let's drill." Mace raised, she fell back into drill mode. Alex faced off with her once more, and hoped he'd caught the situation in time to keep Mama MacNeil from thinking unclean thoughts. However, he knew what he'd seen. She hated him too much to let this go, and so did that elf. Alarm fluttered in Alex's gut.

It took only one day for Hector to come to him, cantering up behind him as he took a ride along the cliff overlooking the rocky shore. Eschewing the French circumspection of the Lowland nobility, the laird came right to the point, his voice of firm command that would brook no argument. "You must reveal your squire, and quickly."

Alex laughed, imagining what Lindsay's reaction would be to that suggestion. Probably laughter, as well.

" 'Tis no matter for hilarity. My considered opinion is also that you should marry her straight away."

"She won't have me. Besides, wouldn't it appear strange if I married my squire?"

"You think it's less strange to be making eyes at him?"

Alex lost his smile, and reined in his horse to gaze seaward as he thought of what to say. None of this was up to him. Lindsay would never reveal herself as a woman. He said, "One indiscretion."

Hector's horse nervously circled Alex, picking up the tension between the men. "One is sufficient, I think. It's my opinion you must either convince her of the need for honesty in this, or else force her into a dress and then into wedlock."

Alex turned to peer at his kinsman. *"Force?"*

"Aye. Distasteful, but ye must do it." Hector seemed completely in earnest.

"Are you nuts?"

A wry smile lifted the corner of Hector's mouth. "Nae. Are ye nuts yourself? You run a high risk here with the men. And with His Majesty, were he to learn of the rumor. As pious a man as he is, he'd not only give the order for ye to be burned, but he'd light the wood himself."

"I can't force her to marry me." He boggled at the idea, and wondered if Hector might be having him on. Forced marriage? Rape he could comprehend, but the mechanics of forcing marriage to an unwilling woman were impossible to grasp. It couldn't possibly be something people ever actually did. Or even *wanted* to do.

But Hector showed no signs of humor. "She's no brothers, nor father. Has she any male relatives at all? Uncles? Cousins?"

Alex shook his head, not sure if that was a wise thing to admit but unwilling to start up yet another lie he might have to lay cover fire for.

"If she's without kin I don't see why you hesitate, nor why you think she'd object. Get her to a priest, and make her yours.

You want her, that's plain. It's so plain ye cannae hide it from a woman who doesn't even know you well."

Hector's mother. Alex wanted to ask what lies the old bat was spreading, but the woman was the laird's mother and argument there was a minefield.

Hector continued, his voice flat with authority. "It's plain you don't want to simply reveal her as your mistress, or you'd have done it long ago. Your path is clear."

"But she doesn't want to get married."

Hector laughed, a short, derisive bark. "And how should that matter? A woman must marry, or be a burden on the world. It would be a blessing to you both, as well as to everyone around you."

"You don't think she's pulling her weight as a squire?"

"Oh, aye, she's pulling far more than her weight in that. You being a MacNeil and all, I'm dead certain you keep her busier than any squire on the island, particularly at night. But that's neither here nor there. She is in fact a woman, and as such is causing trouble among the men."

"I think it's your mother who is causing the trouble."

Hector fell silent and glared a warning, then replied, "The Dowager Lady MacNeil is concerned for the welfare, and for the immortal souls, of her people. Further, she's not the only one who has noted your attraction to the imposter. She tells me she's been visited by a man who has voiced concerns about you."

"What man? Who?"

"He is called Nemed, after the ancient king. He came to my mother to speak to her of rumors he'd heard of you and your squire. Said he knew the two of you at Galashiels."

"Do *you* remember anyone called Nemed in Galashiels?"

Hector grunted. "Nae."

Who was he, then? "Where is this man? I'd like to confront my accuser."

Hector shrugged. "He hasn't lingered. He came only to tell what he knew. By now he's gone on his way."

That was fast. And convenient timing. Realization crept in, and Alex's heart went cold. "He wears a hooded cloak?"

"Aye."

"Did your mother see his ears?"

"I cannae imagine what his ears might have to do with aught, but of course not. 'Twas a *hooded* cloak."

The elf. "How did he get onto the island? I thought the water was not yet passable."

Again Hector shrugged. "A determined man who feels he has something important to say might take risks I do not. But this is all unimportant, and I'll tell you what is of consequence. Your squire is causing trouble for you, and without anyone even knowing her sex. She's no right to dress or behave like a man. God made women the way they are for good reason, and trying to cheat Him of what He's decided for her is sinful and wrong. It can do naught but end badly. Take away her man's clothes, take her to a priest, and make her know who she really is. Once she's settled down, and realizes it's where she belongs, she'll be a good wife to you. But even if not, you'll at least be alive. And any wife is better than none at all for a man's comfort."

Alex's chest tightened as he struggled to assimilate all he was hearing. The idea of forcing Lindsay to marry him was appalling, but at the same time strangely attractive. And the fact that he found it attractive was in itself appalling. As he realized that within this society he had such power, his mind cast about for the pitfall. There had to be a catch, and he figured he knew what it was.

She'd hate him forever. No matter how she felt about him now, if he forced her to marry him she would then hate him with all the intensity of the love he now enjoyed. And she would never forgive him.

He shook his head. "I won't do it. I think it's dishonorable to force any woman into such a contract. Just as it would be dishonorable to force a man into a business agreement. Where I come from, we don't do such things."

Hector shrugged. "'Tis certainly not the best thing to have to do, but when it's the only choice—"

"I said, I won't do it. I don't believe in it."

"Och, the courtly love." Hector nearly spat the words. "Folly from the Continent, and an invitation to cuckoldry, in the eyes of all who would see. Surely you're not trying to tell me you're in love with the wench."

Alex gaped a moment, for he'd thought that was the subject of this conversation. "Of course, I am."

Now it was Hector's turn to gape. Finally he found words to express the shock in his eyes. "That, my brother, is foolishness even our father never committed. Sex and love can never mix. It can only end badly. Not to mention she's hardly unattainable, and not nearly so comely a lass as to inspire devotion in a strong heart."

That made Alex bristle, and he shifted his seat in the saddle. "I don't know. I think she cleans up rather nice."

"The woman is no lady, let alone a great lady worthy of the love of a knight. As a mistress she is pretty enough, and as a wife she might serve well enough, but to devote yourself to her the way ye have . . . 'tis unseemly in the extreme."

Alex peered at him, puzzled. "What are you talking about?"

"She's unworthy of ye, lad."

"But I should marry her?"

"As easily as she's let ye between her legs, I'd say marriage is better than she should expect from you. And I dinnae ken how you could say you love her so deeply when you've indulged yourselves so freely. She cannae possibly love you, and I doubt your sincerity as well."

Now Alex had a dim idea of what Hector was trying to say. That this "courtly love" thing only worked if a knight admired from afar. Anything else was disrespectful to the lady and qualified as neither "courtly" nor "love." He boggled at how screwed up that was. He could hardly find breath to say, "I love her more than if she were a queen, and will stand my devotion against any knight declaring himself for any lady."

Hector gazed at him as if sizing him up. "Perhaps, Mac Dìolain. It could be you're a better man than any knight in Christendom and have devoted yourself so fully to a woman so unworthy. But I'm telling ye, lad, she'll be your downfall. You need to face up to the real considerations of your situation. Reveal her, then marry her if you wish to continue bedding her and protecting her."

"I won't. I can't. Not against her will."

Hector made an impatient sound in the back of his throat. His face began to redden, and irritation showed in his wild, gesturing hands. "Your life is at stake, lad. One way or another, she's got to be shown for a woman. I don't wish for the king to lose such a strong knight as you, or the clan either, and I don't think you'll go so far as to let that happen."

Alex blinked as he realized that was the third time Hector had referred to him dying. *"Lose?"*

Hector's voice took on an *of course* tone that rose with the frustration of having to explain the obvious. "I wouldn't want to see you burned, lad. Nor your lover, for that, but especially yourself."

Cold sweat covered Alex. "Burned? You mean, at the stake?"

"Aye." Hector was silent for a moment as the information seeped into Alex's shocked brain, then he said, "Am I to believe where you come from you never burn sodomite heretics?"

Alex shook his head and said, "Never."

Hector made a disgusted noise in the back of his throat. "Are you even Christians in the eastern mountains, or have ye all gone heathen?"

There was no response to that but a look of impatience. The implications raced through Alex's mind, and something occurred to him. He peered at Hector and asked, "That first night we were here. If you'd not learned Lindsay was a woman—if you'd found me in bed with a boy—would you have had me burned?"

"Och, nae." Relief loosened Alex's chest, but Hector continued. "I would have killed ye both myself on the spot. More merciful, and far less public."

Alex remembered him backing toward the door that night. "You had your sword behind your back."

"Nae. 'Twas a mace hung on my belt. Tell me, lad, what were the chances of me finding you in bed with a boy?"

Alex gazed at him as anger rose, struggling to think of what to say that wouldn't involve drawing his sword. Finally he said, "I'm my father's son." That seemed to satisfy Hector, and Alex added, "I'll find another way to keep the men from talking."

"'Twill mean a fight."

"Then I'll fight." Killing that Nemed would be ideal, but he knew the elf would not be around for a challenge. "Who repeated your mother's words to the men?"

"Sir Cullan has taken up the banner for her. He means to

curry favor by purging the clan of your presence. He does not ken the truth as I do."

Alex blinked, and his stomach dropped. Cullan. His jaw clenched until the muscles stood out. "Very well, then, I'll fight him."

"He'll kill you."

"I'll teach him a lesson."

That brought a snort of laughter. "Teaching Cullan. Och, Mac Dìolain, ye make me laugh. Mark me, young Ailig, it will all end badly if you don't make it right with the Lord and return Lindsay to her womanhood. Do what you will, but do it quickly." With that, Hector wheeled his horse and returned the way he'd come. Alex watched him go, thinking hard about the thing laid before him. *Cullan.* His gut churned.

The next morning he wasted no time challenging the blond knight. During breakfast, with the entire castle complement at board, he walked into the Great Hall, straight up to Cullan where he sat, and whacked him across the back of the head with the palm side of his gauntlet. "Get up, Cullan!" He tossed the spiked glove onto the stone floor.

The knight was already on his feet, and reaching for his dagger. "What do you mean by this?" As if he didn't know. Everyone in the room moved back, scooting their benches and stools out of the way, making a circle around the two. The breakfast meat was forgotten.

Alex drew his own dagger. "You'll stop spreading lies, or I'll kill you."

"Try me. I'll kill you, then say what I like."

No point in wasting words. "All right, that's it." Alex attacked with his dagger. Cullan parried, and the two circled, each sizing the other and looking for an opening.

Cullan took the opportunity to make certain everyone in the room knew what rumor was being contested. "The entire castle knows you're more than just friendly with your senior squire."

"It's a lie, you sonofabitch. Take it back."

"There is a witness."

"Witness of nothing. And I mean to prove you a liar." He intentionally let down his guard, and Cullan took the bait. A lunge, and Alex sidestepped and tugged on his opponent's sleeve to help him along. As Cullan passed, Alex stabbed his side. He didn't want to kill, and so let the quilted tunic foil the weight of his thrust, but there was a surge of satisfaction as the knife went deep enough to make Cullan cry out.

Wild-eyed and growling in his rage, Cullan rounded on him and swept the air with his dagger. Alex wasn't anywhere near, but stepped in after the knife passed, and punched Cullan in the mouth.

The blond Scot staggered back, then with a roar attacked. Alex backpedaled to throw off his aim, but his heel caught a bump in the stone floor and he toppled backward. With a shout of victory, Cullan knee-dropped him in the gut and stars burst in Alex's vision as he tried to roll away and draw in his knees. But Cullan held him there. For a long moment he couldn't breathe, and Cullan had his dagger arm, kneeling over him. A punch to his side, and there was an odd, metallic pain. Cullan had to twist his dagger to get it out, then was ready to stab again. Afraid for his life now, Alex yanked hard, rolled, and brought his opponent with him to the floor, but Cullan held him from behind, still holding the dagger arm. Alex was pinned facedown, and pain radiated from his side as he struggled to free himself.

Then, instead of ending the fight, Cullan began moving his hips against Alex from behind. "You like that, eh, Mac Dìolain? Do you submit to your squire? I think you like it that way, taking it like a woman."

Flaming rage filled Alex's head. He roared as he wrested his arm from Cullan's grasp, then twisted beneath him and knocked his face with the knife hilt. Cullan grabbed for the dagger, but Alex was already stabbing. He caught Cullan in the neck, and blood burst everywhere. Cullan stood, grasping at his neck with bloodied hands, and Alex rose to follow, stabbing again. The dagger cut Cullan's tunic, and this time went in to the hilt. Alex hauled back and deliberately stabbed again, then followed his opponent to the floor.

No longer thinking in terms of teaching a lesson and letting the man live, he was no longer thinking at all beyond making certain the entire MacNeil clan knew the consequences of messing with Alasdair Mac Dìolain MacNeil. He raised his dagger and stabbed yet again, and this time it was an unconscious, helpless man he violated.

Another stab was halted by Hector, and Alex struggled

against him before relinquishing his blade. Hector said calmly, "Aye, Ailig, you've shown us the truth. Now let the man rest in peace."

Alex stared at Cullan as he climbed to his feet, then faced Hector. "Return my dagger via my squire. And announce to the castle that I'll do the same as this to anyone else who wishes to besmirch my name." Alex could see in Hector's eyes he was sorry to lose his cousin, but just then Alex couldn't give a damn. Though a wide puddle of blood was creeping across the stone floor, at that moment Alex wished Sir Cullan would not bleed out but rather die a lingering, agonizing death from peritonitis.

He glanced over the stunned crowd, and his gaze rested on the impassive face of the dowager. Her posture was stiff, her body perfectly still. Just then he wished the bitch was a man, so he could fight her as well. With a glare he hoped expressed his rage, he picked his gauntlet from the floor, then headed for the nearest archway that would take him back to his chamber.

By the time he got there he was limping and the pain in his side was so excruciating he thought his guts might fall out. He fell to his knees before the fire, where the light was strongest, and gingerly removed his tunic and shirt. A great, purple mound covered his right side, and the wound was leaking a fair amount of blood that seeped into his trews in a large, dark patch of purple. He poked at the wound, and could see how the blade had not gone straight in, but rather had penetrated the muscles from his side to his belly, then the tip had poked out near his navel. Another small cut added a smear to the ugliness. He lay back on the rug and stared at the dark, wooden ceiling, holding his shirt against the entry wound to stem the bleeding. Nothing to do but bear the pain and wait for the swelling to go down and the wounds to heal.

Lindsay came in. She'd seen the whole thing. "He's dead." She threw down Alex's dagger so its bloodied point stuck in the chair arm.

"Damn. I wanted him to last a while and then die."

"He wasn't your enemy."

Alex's voice went low with his rage. "He was, by God, my enemy. He was telling anyone who would listen that I was banging a boy. A lie that would have gotten me killed—us killed—if I hadn't made him stop."

"But he believed it to be true."

Alex looked over at her. "Your point?"

She came to kneel beside him and drew away the wadded shirt to poke at his wound. Bolts of pain shot all the way to his chest and he made a face. Her voice was very tight as she said, "I should think you'd be a little more regretful than this."

"He could have killed me just as easily, and damn near did."

"You're the one who challenged him. He was defending himself."

"He didn't have to do what he did. He didn't have to fight; he could have retracted the lie."

"He didn't know it was a lie."

Alex sighed. "Lindsay, do you even get that they would have executed both of us if I'd let him keep shooting off his mouth? Not just executed, but burned at the fucking stake. *Burned alive*, Lindsay. Never mind that this could have been entirely avoided if you weren't so afraid of being a woman."

There was a very long silence. Then she said, "I do get that. My point, as I've already said, is that you don't seem to regret any of this. Hector's cousin has been destroyed, and you don't seem to think it's anything more than a problem solved. Hector, who you profess to have accepted as your brother, and that makes Sir Cullan your kinsman as well. But you aren't the least bit sorry for his death."

Alex fell silent, fuming, and stared into the fire. She would never fully understand. There was no use talking to her anymore about this. He said nothing as she brought the wash bowl to clean the blood from him, both his own and Cullan's.

CHAPTER 12

There was no more talk among the MacNeils about Alex's masculinity. The castle guard seemed to relax, pleased to have been shown the rumor was false. Trial by combat. The clan knew, with the certainty of piety, that if Alex had been guilty God would never have let him win the fight. Alex figured, since he wasn't guilty, he couldn't naysay that view, and for all he knew they could be right. He tried not to think too hard about what Hector had said about God not wanting Lindsay to dress like a man. There were many questions he didn't want to ask himself these days, and whether there was a God was one of them. Hector's contention that God wanted him to force Lindsay to marry Alex made him more than uncomfortable.

In late March, weather permitted the MacNeils' return to the mainland and Sir Hector and his men made the journey to Castle Galashiels in the Lowlands. There Alex rejoined Edward Bruce's army and reclaimed his command.

Alex's flight suit was history now, having disintegrated nearly to lint during the winter. For months he'd dressed as his kinsmen, in linen and wool in addition to the chain mail and plate, and now wore a "plaid" or blanket slung around him that often provided warmth on long, cold travels. Though it was called a plaid, the many-colored wool bore little resemblance to the intricate and organized tartan patterns of the future. In a given such blanket it was enough for the colors to balance from one end to the other, for often they didn't. Alex's was various shades of green—which Lindsay had once said brought out the color of his eyes—splashed with random stripes of dark blue and black. He'd chosen it for camouflage value in a shady forest.

Without pockets now, he carried elsewhere the items that remained of his survival gear. The knife was in a scabbard at his waist next to his dagger, the first aid kit—which had dwindled to a couple of adhesive bandages and a crumpled tube of antibiotic ointment—was in his saddle bag, and the gun he now carried in a leather pouch attached to his sword belt. At first he missed the pockets, but as he grew accustomed to the new arrangement he decided he was just as glad to have the pistol where he could reach it easily.

At Galashiels Alex found many of his former company ready and eager to return to his service. Many had gone home to stay, some had been killed in service to Douglas during the winter, but a number of men joined his company from other units. During his time on Barra, apparently, his reputation had grown and spread. The group Alex now commanded was slightly larger than the one he'd disbanded in the fall. Sir Orran De Ros was back, surprising Alex he hadn't been killed by now. Cullan, of course, was gone, and Alex shoved the memory of his former second in command into a mental compartment where he could do no harm. Another knight rose to fill the vacancy: Sir Henry Ellot, who was young and had done well as a fighter for Alex before. That his clan was known to be steadfast in their loyalty to Robert was also a huge point in his favor.

Lindsay had been quiet since the day Alex killed Cullan. Now when he moved to her pallet in the tent at night he sensed a reluctance in her he wished he could dispel. But no matter how he made her laugh, or how he distracted her in other ways, he could see in her eyes she was drawing away from him. Finally he asked, "What's wrong?"

He sat naked on a grassy bank after bathing in a sun-warmed eddy about a mile upstream of the castle. The late afternoon was fading to orange in the southwest, and the earth smelled rich with fertility and growth. After the long, cold winter on Barra, there was a joy to seeing the sun and smelling the earth again. Chilly burn water swirled around his ankles. He took her hand and drew her down onto the bank between his knees, where he slipped his arms around her and hugged her from behind. "What's bothering you?"

"Nothing is bothering me." But she looked away and said, "This is dangerous." Her eyes glanced around to indicate there could be voyeurs nearby.

"I risk my life every day; at least this is something I enjoy." He nuzzled her neck and took a bit of skin gently between his teeth.

Catlike, she tilted her head away to let him kiss her neck, then higher, then he took her earlobe. She said, "Alex, have you given any thought to trying to get home?"

"Home where?"

She drew away to turn and look into his face. "Home. To the twenty-first century."

"Of course, I have." Not recently, but he'd thought about it a lot back when he'd imagined it possible. "I don't think that guy is going to help us out."

"Why are you so certain?"

"He just didn't strike me as very cooperative when we saw him. Or any other time."

"What other time?"

"When he was whispering into the dowager's ear about you and me. Didn't you see him?"

"No. I didn't." A skeptical edge to her voice sounded as if she thought he hadn't seen the elf with Hector's mother, either. He figured anything he might say just then would be a waste of breath, so he said nothing and stroked her neck with his fingers. Her collarbone, where the skin was taut and smooth. Her shoulder. The valley between her breasts, and he watched them jiggle when he pressed with his fingers. Pink marks showed where the elastic bandage bound, and he made a futile effort to stroke them away.

"This place is changing you, Alex."

Uh-oh. "No, it's not. I'm still the same guy I always was."

"You haven't mentioned Cullan since that day."

"Why are you so bunged up over him?" Alex pressed his mouth to the back of her shoulder, and wished she'd drop this.

"He was a human being."

His lips still touching her skin, he murmured, "Death is everywhere. I have no control over it."

"You had control over that death."

"Let it go, Lindsay."

"Some remorse, Alex. Just a hint."

He looked away, toward the setting sun. "All right, I'm sorry. I'm sorry he's dead; he was a good fighter, and we're going to miss him when we get to the action. He was a MacNeil, and that makes his death a loss to every MacNeil."

"You're not a very good liar. I know lip service when I hear it."

Irritation blossomed and grew. "How come he matters so blasted much to you?"

"Specifically him? He doesn't. It's you who concerns me. You're the one I worry about, who has become so callous."

"Callous?"

"And you hate the English. You don't give a damn about Cullan, who was a MacNeil, so you must have even less feeling for the English who are your declared enemy."

He sighed. "Don't do that. I love you."

"In spite of my being English."

"I don't think of you as . . ." No, that wasn't the approach to take. He cast about for possible replies, but all of them took him to pitfalls. So he repeated, "I love you. No matter what."

She stood to face him in the knee-deep water. "I don't think you really know what it means to love." Then she climbed to the bank to retrieve her clothing, and began to dress. He let her leave before climbing the bank also, and told himself it was only because they shouldn't be seen returning to the castle together.

From the castle at Galashiels, Alex's detail sallied south, having been directed to raid border towns loyal to King Edward. But their first objective was in a shambles before they arrived, and they were greeted with the stench of burning and blood. Smoke from houses reduced to ashes blew every which way in the blustery spring weather, under a slate sky that promised rain soon to put out the remaining fires that flickered in the ruins. Whoever had done this couldn't be gone long.

"What's going on?" Alex reined in his horse and the company halted behind him. He gestured for Henry and Orrin to ride out a short distance as pickets, then looked around at the destruction and muttered mostly to himself, "What happened here?" Animal pens stood empty and the enclosure dikes lay broken. Off near a shelter of trees by a burn, a cluster of townspeople stared at the force of armored men on horseback. Frightened and confused, they were ready to scatter like birds if startled.

Alex urged his mount toward them and ordered his men, "Stay here, and don't disturb anything." There was a bit of grumbling about the lack of looting potential, but Alex reined in, wheeled, and shot back a look of warning so nobody would destroy or steal whatever was left. He would decide what to do once he'd learned what had happened here. He then spurred away toward the cluster of people.

When the villagers shifted to flee, he called out, "Don't be afraid. I've come to ask questions." They obviously had already been stripped of anything he or the other knights might have wanted, and he was under orders to not harm anyone who gave them no trouble. "Resist and I'll retaliate. Stand fast and answer my questions, and I'll leave you unharmed."

The cluster shuffled some more, the more timid moving behind one man who became their spokesman by default. He was the biggest guy in town, it appeared, a heavy-boned man with a shaggy mop of reddish hair and thick features that were almost apelike. But there was a light of intelligence in his eyes that was decidedly not simian.

Remaining mounted, Alex bent his head to look the man in the eye and asked, "What happened to your village?"

"Who are you?"

Right. Definitely not stupid. The man eyed Alex's company, probably looking for the banner they would ordinarily have carried. But, like the captain of a pirate ship, Alex had chosen to keep a low profile and kept the red-and-gold banner of the king rolled up until necessary. Alex glanced around as if unconcerned, and said, "Would my reply determine what happened here?" When the man didn't answer, Alex continued. "The truth, please, then I'll tell you who I am."

The red-haired man considered that, then said, "Edward's men did this."

"Which Edward?" Alex wasn't stupid, either.

The man hesitated, then said, "King Edward. The English king has ordered the destruction of anyone who pays tribute to Robert."

"I was told you're loyal to the English king."

A light of alarm flashed in the man's eyes, and he replied slowly, carefully, as if watching Alex's reaction to know whether to run. "We've not betrayed our pledge to Edward."

"Playing both sides?"

Bitterness rose in his voice. "Wishing to be left in peace. But instead we're attacked by both sides when we pay tribute to both sides."

"Has anyone loyal to Robert harassed you?"

"Not since a year ago."

Alex glanced off to the horizon and sucked air between his front teeth with an irritated hiss. He said to the red-haired man, "They won't anymore, if you will cease giving tribute to Edward. I'm Sir Alexander Joseph MacNeil from Barra; my allegiance is to King Robert of Scotland. You're Scottish; yours should be, too."

"We expect protection in return for payment."

Alex leaned over in his saddle to peer into the man's face. "Well, then, it's clear the English are not your best bet, are they?" He sat up and gazed around at the terrible destruction all around, and thought what a stupid sonofabitch Edward II was. That guy was going to win the war for them. Meanwhile, though, he was also trashing the countryside. There would be little left for the Scots once they'd reclaimed the country. He said to the red-haired man, "How many did they kill?"

Now tears welled in the big man's eyes. "They've murdered many men, and several women. They took all our livestock, and the grain as well. We've no seed for the planting." He nodded toward a patch of ground scattered with straw, where Alex guessed dregs of winter haystacks and stacks of last fall's oat harvest had been earlier.

This was bad on so many levels, Alex couldn't even consider all of them at once. Scorched earth was a valid war tactic at first glance, but only in retreat. This was sure to weigh against Edward in the hearts of those he would claim to rule. One thing Alex knew for certain about armed conflict: deliberately killing noncombatants always backfired. In addition, Edward II was putting Robert's army in a position of providing PR–boosting succor. Good for Robert, except the Scottish army were ill-equipped to support anyone. Alex's men knew how to make war, and little else. He was at a loss to know how to help these people who, half an hour before, he'd only expected to fight.

He cleared his throat, gathered his reins, and said, "As I told you, I won't harm you. We'll be on our way."

But the man reached out for his stirrup. "What will we do?"

"I've nothing to give you."

"Tell us what clans have got enough to eat."

Alex figured the plan would be to steal from neighboring clans, but he shook his head. "Our enemy has hurt all of us. I'm sorry, but there's nothing I can tell you. If you want to make a raid, you'll have to reive in England if you don't want reprisals from us."

The man nodded that he understood, though Alex knew that didn't mean the villagers wouldn't head right out and rustle a herd from the next village over.

Alex started to rein his horse around to leave, but Lindsay rode over and said loudly for everyone to hear, "Sir, I beg you to allow me to stay behind to hunt that forest yonder for some venison to give these people."

The word "no" rushed to his lips, but he bit it back. He stared at her, angry at her impudence and appalled at the idea of letting her out of his sight this far into enemy territory, then said, "Your skills—"

"If my master would be so kind as to loan me his special weapon . . ."

"No." She wanted his gun. *Not just no, but no way in hell.*

"But sir, these people are desperate. Some of them may die if there's no relief for them."

He knew that. He wished he didn't, but there was no denying it. There was a very long moment when he couldn't speak, knowing that no matter what he said next he would regret it one way or another. Finally he called to his huntsman. The man rode up and saluted.

"Sir!"

"Hunter, I need you to take some deer from the forest over thataway." He indicated with a nod an area among the rolling hills that was thick with moss-covered trees.

"You wish me to poach?" The query was only for clarification, for poaching was nothing the huntsman hadn't done for Alex in the past.

"Aye, and it's probably the English king's personal preserve, or something, and crawling with sanctioned huntsmen. So be careful. When you've taken three deer, give them over to this man, then make your way back to Galashiels and await us there."

"It would be simple enough to catch up with you."

Alex thought that over. The man was a skilled hunter, and more important, he was also experienced at evading capture by the English king's men. He nodded. "Very well. Meet us at Lochmaben."

"Aye, sir."

"Dismissed."

The huntsman hurried to his task.

Alex ignored Lindsay, for he was very angry with her. He turned back to the villager, whose gratitude was plain on his face. Alex expected to feel good about what he'd done, but all he could think of just then was that the English raiders had cheated his men out of a fight that was their livelihood. He remembered what Lindsay had said about how Edward II would be murdered in a few years, and just then he would have paid well for the privilege to be the one to stick that hot poker up the king's ass.

"That will tide you over until you can find seed corn." Or steal it.

With a nod good-bye, he swallowed his anger at Edward, and ordered his men on toward England.

"Who was that masked man?" Lindsay rode beside him, her voice heavy with sarcasm. "You were going to just leave those people to starve."

Alex bent his head toward her and said in the lowest, angriest voice at his command, "If you ever ask for my gun again in front of people, I'll throw you in irons and leave you for your beloved English king to find you. Or not."

"Alex—"

"I mean it. Question my authority all you want when we're alone, but by God if you ever pull a stunt like that again I'll be forced to do you damage."

She fell silent, and they rode for a while. Then she said, "I'm sorry."

"Just don't do it again."

"Yes, sir, *Lef*-tenant, sir."

They rode in silence for a while before she spoke again. "What's on the agenda now?" The word *agenda* was heavily emphasized, and Alex gave her a sideways glare.

"We're to join up with the king's brother at the castle in Lochmaben. Our objective now is Carlisle, where they haven't been paying tribute to Robert. At least, by last report they haven't. I never know for sure what's going on anymore, it takes so long for news to get anywhere." *My kingdom for a radio.*

"We're going into England?"

"Yup. The closer we get, the better I like it."

"Less chance of finding people paying tribute to Robert, because they're English. Better chance of finding something worth taking."

"Aye."

"They teach you that at the United States Naval Academy? Plunder 101A?"

Alex cut her another sharp glance, then continued riding without reply.

With a heavy, acidic tinge to her voice she added, "Well, so long as you remember: first you rape, then you pillage, *then* you burn." With that, she slowed her horse and fell behind to ride with the others. Alex turned to stare long and hard at her, appalled.

"What is that? Python? You're quoting *Monty Python* now?" She wouldn't look at him, so he faced forward and kept riding. "How's your Harpo Marx impression? Can you do Harpo for me, please?"

They rode on in silence.

LOCHMABEN was crawling with Robert's knights, the castle well stocked and so far undamaged by King Edward's army. Or for that matter, by King Robert's. Word was the English king was busy with personal problems within his court, and he fought the war in the north with only half his attention, but Alex knew if the decisive battle of Bannockburn was to take place in only two months Edward II must already be preparing for it.

The mood here was nearly festive. The men were eager to ride into England, kill their hated enemy, and take back the wealth and the pride that had been wrested from them over the past decades. Hanging out by the cook fires, Alex listened to men speak of what had been done to them—the wrongs they were out to avenge. Some had been disinherited and hoped to win back their families' lands. One man had lost his entire family, uncles and cousins included, in the massacre at Berwick nearly a generation before. The fellow had been a small child then, and now wished to make England pay. Most of the men simply were eager to free their land of meddling English so they could prosper.

All through this war, Alex noticed, economics seemed to be foremost in everyone's mind. Revenge came second, cultural considerations third, and nobody seemed to think that was remarkable. These guys were the warrior class. They never did anything but fight, and so battle was a given in their lives. Necessary to their existence. As a professional soldier it was a natural state he recognized, and there was something attractive about not having to justify it. Everyone here understood the need. Anticipation of battle surged in his blood. Even the thought of death the next day didn't dampen it, for what else could he do with his life that would be more worthwhile? Or even as interesting? Give up his knighthood and plow fields for a living? No, thanks.

He shrugged his plaid up around his neck against the evening chill and looked over at Lindsay, who sat on the wall of an animal pen, just inside the circle of light from the fire. Heels set into a niche between stones and elbows leaning on knees, she leaned forward, hunched over, looking very wan. Tomorrow she would fight well, but tonight the anticipation of blood seemed to weigh heavily on her. Thoughts of death crept in on himself, and he looked away. His own death was a given in his mind. Hers would be unbearable.

IT was a large force from Lochmaben that descended on Carlisle. Hundreds of Scottish knights swept into the town, cutting down anyone who resisted. They were under orders to spare those who offered no fight, but amid the shouts of men, screams of women, thundering of hooves, battering of swords and maces, it was always hard to determine who was a combatant and who was trying to flee or surrender. Difficult to say exactly what happened, or what would have happened if one hesitated. Alex figured it was enough to limit the killing to men, and assume any man who showed himself in the midst of a fight was asking for it. For the better part of the day, the Scottish army battled the English garrison and townspeople. Buildings were torched; thatching burned merrily, throwing ash and smoke everywhere. Alex's men stuck with him, and he led them through the streets in search of men with weapons. Lindsay rode dutifully by his side, but he never saw her lift her mace. Alex assaulted and cut down every man who raised a hand to him.

Only one he saw surrendered. Tall, thin, middle-aged, he ran from a house with a war hatchet in his hand. Alex spotted him and spurred his horse to ride down on him, but on sight of the Scottish knight, the Englishman dropped his weapon and held up his hands. Sword cocked to swing, relishing the sure coup de grace, Alex nearly swung anyway. It took enormous effort to stay his hand and ride on past. When he wheeled to be certain the townsman left the hatchet and ran away, Alex was nearly disappointed to see him do it. Then with a roar of frustration he wheeled again in search of another opponent.

Finally, sometime later, as the din of weapons and shouting gave way to the weeping of women and bawling of children, Bruce's men began gathering livestock and valuables for transport. They were quick and efficient, rounding up wagons and loading them with whatever they could find worth taking. When the roar of attack dwindled and became shouts of organization and industry, Alex reined in his dancing mount and looked over the streets.

Women cried over their men. Children watched wide-eyed as the town's wealth was herded away or packed into sacks, tucked into shirts and saddlebags, and in some cases chewed up and swallowed on the spot. Alex gazed around him, exhausted from the fighting and covered with the blood of many Englishmen, and felt nothing more than gentle relief he was still alive.

But when he looked over to see Lindsay, her horse standing fetlock-deep in mud, she was wiping tears from her eyes. He nudged his horse to a walk and went to her.

"What's wrong?"

"Nothing." She mopped her face with a patch of leather between the horn plates of her armor coat, but only left a smear of mud and blood.

"Tell me."

Her gaze avoided his, but finally she said, "These people don't deserve this."

"Let their king worry about them. He's responsible for the welfare of his people. He's a lousy king, and it's going to get him killed."

"They don't deserve this."

"Did those people up north deserve it?"

"Of course not."

"Then tell me what we're supposed to do."

"You're thinking like one of them."

"One of who?"

"Them. These medieval people who don't know any better than eye for an eye and might makes right."

"It's an ugly world, Lindsay. I didn't create it." The green wool wound around his body had loosened, and he tugged it tight again with a yank.

"But you're certainly making the most of it."

"What's that supposed to mean?"

She stared at him, long and hard, her jaw muscles working, then said, "Have you ever tried to contact that elfin fellow to see if he would send us home?"

Dread filled him. "Have you?"

"Of course I have. But there's not been so much as a glimpse of him since that day. He won't speak to me. Even that day in the knoll, he never looked at me. Not once. I think there's something very wrong here, Alex."

"And what's *that* supposed to mean?"

For a moment she looked as if she might blurt something in anger, but she snapped her mouth shut and lowered her chin. "Nothing. It means nothing." Then she reined away and spurred her horse to a gallop. He wanted to chase her down and make her explain, but didn't, lest she ask questions he'd rather not address.

In subsequent days on this raid, three other towns were plundered and two churches burnt, then the Scottish army returned north with their booty to Lochmaben, where supplies were assessed and allocated, and rewards distributed. Alex found himself in possession of a large herd of cattle and some jewelry consisting of a necklace and some loose stones. After slaughtering one of the cattle for his men to feast on in the safety of Lochmaben, Alex then sold the rest of the livestock to a landed knight who had use for them. However, he kept the jewelry: a gold necklace set with rubies, two unset sapphires, and a small handful of pearls. Jewels were lighter to carry than would be their worth in coin—pounds of silver pennies that were currently the largest English denomination.

Besides, in the back of his mind lurked a hope he might one day give the necklace to Lindsay to wear. As a woman. Someday.

Shortly after their return to Lochmaben, Edward Bruce's army was summoned north to join Robert in Torwood Forest, near Stirling Castle and alongside the Bannock Burn. It was time.

CHAPTER 13

The battle was a month away and Torwood, just south of Stirling Castle, was filling up with tents belonging to the knights of the Scottish army. Cook fires sent smoke all through the trees, and the sharp smells of grease and charred oat bread wafted everywhere. Paths became trampled throughways, particularly as one neared the king's pavilion, where knights, squires, and pages came and went in increasing numbers as the king went about the business of mustering every resource at his command. A large clearing in the midst of the trees was made muddy by horses charging back and forth in drills, carrying knights bearing lances and swords.

Alex was drilling with his sword opposite one of his men when John Kirkpatrick rode over to hail him.

"Mac Dìolain!"

Man, he wished they would stop calling him that! He lowered his sword and wheeled to face him. "Aye, John?"

"I hear tell of a trick you have against the lance."

Alex nodded. "I don't need a lance to defeat a man who uses one. I don't even like using them myself. Everybody knows that." A cluster of men on horseback was drifting near to hear.

"Will you show me?"

It was a flattering thing to be asked that by a tried knight, particularly one as experienced and lauded as this one. Alex smiled and opened his mouth to agree, but hesitated. The move was dangerous, even with the lance blunted. Screwing up could get him killed, and he couldn't expect John to particularly care if it did. But men were listening, and he couldn't appear fearful or his leadership of his company might weaken. In an instant he decided he had to do the demonstration but would at least relieve himself of concern for hurting John. "Yes. But I won't use my sword, or I will kill you."

John made a harsh, disparaging noise in the back of his throat. "Don't be so certain."

"Aye, I am. If I carry my sword to show you this, I will end up killing you. So I'll use a stick." He called out to his men, "Someone bring me a straight stick the thickness of my thumb and the length of my sword!"

Quickly a branch was torn from a tree, stripped of leaves, and brought to him. He gestured to the opposite end of the field for John to face off against him, then spurred his horse and cantered to his own position. The steed was eager to go, dancing in the mud, so without delay Alex raised his stick and urged the animal to a gallop. John started off toward him.

Long, smooth strides. Alex's horse was a steady runner. Keeping a careful eye on the opposing lance, stick raised in his right hand away from John's lance, he gave no indication of what he might do until the very last. Careful . . . careful . . . He ducked and swung. And connected.

John's helmet flew from his head. The lance hadn't come near Alex, who regained his seat and wheeled to see Kirkpatrick drop his lance and grab his face. Blood poured from under his gauntlet and over his chin. Alex had broken his stick and the man's nose.

Nevertheless, when John lifted his hand, he was grinning. "Brilliant!" He didn't seem to care his nose was flattened, and he sprayed blood from his lips as he spoke.

"It only works once, though. You have to sucker in the knight so he thinks you'll sit still for him to stab you."

"Sucker?"

Alex shrugged as his horse circled and pranced. "Uh . . . deceive."

"Oh, aye. I thought I had you there." John laughed. "I'm glad you didn't have your sword!" That brought a round of laughter. "By my lights, a man wouldn't live long enough to face you twice!"

"Well done!" It was the king, sitting his horse at the edge of the clearing, and everyone fell silent. "You're a man who is there, but not there! You make me pleased I made you a knight those years ago, Alasdair an Dubhar!"

Stunned, Alex gaped for a moment, then removed his helmet, thanked the king, and bowed his head before restoring the headgear. *An Dubhar.* That was a new one on him. He wondered what it meant.

"Return to your practice, all of you." Robert made a gesture to include everyone in the field. "You'll not want Edward and his minions to catch us unprepared!" The men responded with gestures of obeisance, then obeyed and resumed practice while Robert watched.

In addition to the cavalry, archers and other foot soldiers trained everywhere about. Practice ranges had been set up, where men with bows shot straw-filled dummies to pieces over and over. Drills with mace and dagger carried on in clearings made the woods echo with the ping and clang of metal on metal. During this time it was a challenge to walk anywhere without stepping in front of someone wielding a weapon of some kind. Knights on foot sparred with each other in preparation for what they knew would be the deadliest affair since the beginning of the war. Word had come that Edward II was marching from Berwick with thousands upon thousands of English cavalry, Welsh longbowmen, and Irish conscripts, bringing along a pack train that would sustain them in Scotland for a very long time. It was now or never to make the English king understand he had no place in Scotland.

Lindsay was barely speaking to Alex now. Still forced to share his tent, for moving in with Colin would be to risk discovery, she nevertheless made it clear Alex was no longer welcome in her bed. In keeping with the social conduct of knights and squires, they rarely ate in proximity to each other, particularly if there were other knights around to socialize. Alex found himself missing her, though she was there every night.

He sure didn't know what he was supposed to do, or be, for her. She thought he was fitting in too well with their new circumstance. How that was a bad thing, he had no clue. He saw himself as merely successful at his job. He fit in because he was good at it. His men respected him, and he liked that. There was no downside he could see. Especially when he saw how his wealth was accumulating. Lately he'd been one of the most successful knights of his rank, and the rewards had been generous. Lindsay's vague dissatisfaction with his attitude made no sense. He tried to ignore it.

Aside from the bewilderment over Lindsay, Alex was delighted to learn Hector and his MacNeils had come from Galashiels to join the excitement, and it was a grand reunion though they'd been apart for only a month. The brothers MacNeil caught up on gossip, drinking, and talking by Alex's fire well into the night.

Alex asked about the name Robert had given him: "An Dubhar."

Hector's face lit up. "He calls you that, does he? *An Dubhar?*"

"Is that good, or bad?"

"Apparently the king thinks you're dangerous. A shadow. Darkness."

"Darkness?"

"*An* Dubhar. *The* darkness. The shadow of death. Robert, who is known throughout England and Scotland as the most skilled fighter in all the islands, thinks you're a deadly and dangerous man, *mo caraid*. I commend you."

Alex decided he liked the name very much. In these times it was good to be thought deadly. And it beat the snot out of being called *mac dìolain*.

Hector and Alasdair Og told stories about raids in Lothian, where landholders were being punished by Edward II as had been the towns in the south. They all agreed it would be a wonderful thing to rid the area of English presence and bring peace to all concerned.

"Ailig an Dubhar, come join us in Robert's battle," said Hector. "Come fight under the king's own command. We Gaels must stick together. Watch each other's backs around the Lowland race. Bring your men and fight alongside your own people."

"My men belong to Edward Bruce. They all fought with him before they came to me."

Alasdair Og snorted, and Hector chuckled. "Your men will follow you if they're truly yours. They've followed you thus far; they'll go with you to fight directly under Robert and be glad for the privilege."

Alex thought about that. Hector was right. Leadership and obligation here were more by personality and opportunity than by law. Most of his men would stick with him, he was sure, and the ones who didn't he was better rid of in any case. He nodded. "All right. I'll go."

It was late and the sounds of activity throughout the forest were dying away. Alex didn't think about wondering where Lindsay was until she returned. Without her mace she wandered into the firelight, backlit by other cook fires beyond the trees, as if she'd materialized from the other moving shadows.

Alex held up a hand to stay the conversation with the men and addressed her. "Where did you go?"

She gave him a bland look, then replied, "James Douglas's camp. There was a contest. I didn't win."

"Where's your mace?"

"It wasn't that sort of contest. We were wrestling."

Now he frowned and tilted his head as if to ask the question she must know he couldn't ask in front of Ailig Og. But she ignored him and asked to be dismissed. He was forced to let her go rather than let Hector's brother know something was amiss between them.

He returned to the conversation, but Hector was peering at him as if to ask that same question. Alex shrugged, and shifted the subject to the sacking of Carlisle. Hector and Ailig Og both were eager to hear that story, and so immediately forgot about Lindsay.

But Alex didn't forget. Later, after the MacNeils had returned to their own camp, he sat on his pallet in the tent and pulled off his boots in preparation to sleep. His voice went very low, though he knew his modern American dialect was as incomprehensible to the medieval Scots as would have been the Hungarian they believed it to be. "Where were you really?"

"Wrestling."

"And nobody could tell?"

"I told you, I didn't win. That's why I didn't win. I threw

every last bloody match. It was either that or explain why I didn't want to participate."

"What were you doing in Douglas's camp, anyway?"

"Socializing." She fixed him with a hard gaze. "I am allowed, am I not? Colin invited me to get to know some other squires. Some of them were fairly senior and could teach us a lot, he said. And he was right. You know how those guys are, the senior ones. Damn near as old as I am, just aching to get their spurs and a few of them pissed off because they don't have them already. It's all any of them care about; earning the right to carry a sword into battle and ride at the front." She was silent for a moment, then added, "I feel rather sorry for them."

"Why?"

"It's awfully pathetic, don't you think? Their entire existence hinging on which weapon they get to cart around."

He thought about that, then said, "I don't know. Doesn't sound that much different from wanting to fly fighters instead of lesser aircraft. Combat experience makes all the difference in a military career."

She rolled toward him as if to say something, but said nothing, and turned away once more.

An irritated sigh blew through his nose, and he pulled his plaid around him and rolled into his parachute to sleep. But he was awake for a long time, thinking about how much he didn't want Lindsay hanging out with other men.

Eventually he spoke. "Lindsay?"

There was no reply, and he figured she was asleep, but finally she said, "What?"

It nearly killed him to ask this, but he forced himself. "Why did your feelings change?"

"Which feelings?"

He looked over at the shadow that was her, and wished he could tell whether she was serious or just messing with his head. "You once said you loved me."

The silence unwound, but at length she murmured, "It's entirely possible to love someone and not be happy with them."

His heart sank, and he rolled over again, not to sleep for a very long time.

The next day after breakfast, instead of taking his horse to the drill field, Alex wandered in the direction of James Douglas's camp. He wanted to see where Lindsay had gone.

And there she was, standing among a cluster of squires in the shade of gnarled Scotch pines, chattering away. A bright smile lit her face, and then she laughed at something one of them said to her.

Dark anger rose from his gut and swarmed into his head like black flies. His ears buzzed and the day was suddenly too warm even for June. Deep breaths took the edge off, and he muttered to himself, "They think she's a boy . . . They think she's a boy . . ."

But she knew she wasn't, and what mattered most was what she thought when she looked at them. And he could see in her eyes she enjoyed their company. She leaned against a tree, thumbs hooked into her belt, as relaxed and jovial as he'd ever seen her.

One of the men was Sir James himself. The tall, thin, dark-haired one. He'd been only a teenager in 1306 when they'd first seen him, but now he was eight years older and had grown to a healthy, energetic, and flamboyant manhood. Alex hated him. He was known as the Black Douglas, partly for the color of his hair, but also for his ruthlessness and skill in battle. He was the king's favorite. An extremely rich and influential man, who would more than likely become even more so if Bruce achieved his goal of removing the English from Scotland. And Alex knew he would.

So did Lindsay.

Alex was about to step back into the shadows of the trees, when Lindsay looked in his direction. She fell silent and a shadow crossed her eyes. Her lips pressed together. She looked down at the ground. Alex faded into the trees and went on foot to watch the sparring in the drill field.

Today was not a day for him to pick up a weapon.

Later on, Alex went looking for Lindsay and found her taking a drink from the burn that ran past the forest. She was the one kneeling, but he immediately said before he could think better of it, "Marry me."

Startled, she looked up and her *Are you mad?* look lit her eyes. "Is that an order, sir?" She stood to face him, wiped her mouth on her sleeve, and shook water from her hand.

"It's a plea. Please marry me." He hooked his thumbs into his sword belt and tried to appear casual, but he knew he was failing. His stomach clenched, and his pulse was entirely too quick. He hated feeling like this.

"What, and give up all this?" Lindsay gestured to her leather armor and trews.

"I know you don't like to fight."

"I would like being hidden away and treated like furniture even less. As a man, even a small, effeminate one, I get to go where I want. I get to keep the money I make, and I get to decide whether or not I want to marry. I can be a merchant if I want. Or a farmer."

"No, you can't. You're a soldier."

"Which will make it difficult to do something else, to be sure. But not impossible. Which, being a woman would make those things impossible."

"Marry me, and I'll let you do what you want."

"No, you won't. You're one of them now. I don't even know why you're bothering asking me this."

"You love me."

"I do. So, what?"

"I want to protect you. I see you wandering around this place, and I know how dangerous it is. All it would take is for someone to pick a serious fight with you, and it would be all over. Even your buddies would kill you in a heartbeat if it was in their best interest to do it."

"There's the voice of experience."

His cheeks warmed and he gripped his belt with both hands. "What's that supposed to mean?"

"It's easy to hate, isn't it?"

"You tell me."

She sighed. "I don't hate you, Alex. I wish I did, for that would be easier than loving you and seeing you like this."

"Like what? What do you want from me that I'm not doing?"

Her shoulders sagged with frustration. "Alex, you haven't been listening to me. I'm horrified at the changes in you. When we first met, you were a gentleman. You were clean, polite . . . You shined your shoes, for God's sake. And you had the good grace to understand that what you did for a living was not truly comprehensible to most people. But now . . ." She welled up and looked away for a moment, blinking, then she looked him in the eye again. "Now you look at the world as if killing were sport and everyone who doesn't think like you is silly and naïve. You're like them." She waved a hand to encompass the entire army camp. "You think war is business. You never look toward ending it, only toward getting what you can out of it."

"The world—"

"*This* world, Alex. Not our world. This world is that way. I am not, and I don't want to be. I don't want you to be, either."

"I'm not like that."

"Don't kid yourself. You are. Take a good look at yourself. You have become one of them."

Rage colored his vision red. "Wrong. If I were one of them, I would have forced you to marry me in Barra."

Her eyes went wide. "Forced?"

"I can force you to marry me. Did you know that? Hector told me I should do it. He wants you to stop pretending to be a boy, and after Cullan's death I tend to agree with him."

"You killed Cullan, not I."

"I killed him defending you. I was trying to keep from exposing you as a woman. It wasn't his fault. It was ours."

"No, Alex, I saw that fight. You killed him because he embarrassed you in front of the others. You lost your temper when he humiliated you. I had nothing to do with it."

Alex choked on his next words, unable to say them because she was right and didn't deserve what he would say next. Instead, he said, "I'm sick of this crap. You want me around because I make you feel safe, but you won't marry me because my armor isn't shiny enough to suit you."

"I'm sorry, Alex, but I won't marry you."

That did it. He blurted, "I'll expose you."

"You're threatening me? For that, why don't you just haul me before a priest and force me to marry you as you said? The end result would be the same." Then she sighed and passed him to return to the forest and camp.

He watched her go, and realized he'd lost her.

CHAPTER 14

A s the time drew near when the English would have to rescue its garrison at Stirling or lose it, the Scots prepared the
ground chosen by King Robert: a bit of land just across the
burn, hemmed by forest on one side and marsh on the other.
There were only two routes for the English to Stirling Castle: to
cross the Bannockburn and fight in the meadow below the forest, or to cross the stream to the east and fight on the clayland
between it and the marshland to the north. Workmen were sent
to dig holes on either side of the road approaching the forest,
and they felled trees across paths within the forest to impede the
enemy. James Douglas took a small contingent of riders to
scout the approach of King Edward.

On June 22 word came that the English army was nearing
from the south. An army larger than anyone present had ever
seen. Officially, the Scots were told the English were in disarray, disorganized, but murmured rumors circulated quietly of
the many columns of foot soldiers, mounted men displaying
banners, and a wagon train that stretched into the distance. Alex
knew the alarming rumors were true, for he'd once studied this
battle as history. But he also knew his people would prevail, and
encouraged his men to believe the lie.

Now the Scottish army moved into position. The pack train

was gathered and hidden far back in the forest with the reserves of "small folk" who were mostly unarmed locals, poorly trained, and whose value lay entirely in their enthusiasm for the fight. The cavalry armed and armored themselves, and mounted to ride into position.

Alex's men, attached to the king's battle now, stayed behind at Torwood to guard while the rest of the army prepared in the forest below Stirling Castle. It wasn't until very late in the day they mounted to make the two-mile trek to the battlefield. There they took up their position on a forested hill between the two open fields, a deployment they knew and understood well, for the king had drilled them thoroughly.

As they arranged themselves atop high ground, just inside the tree line, Alex noticed a cluster of men ride up to the king. Something about them struck him, but he wasn't sure who they were or what it could be. They seemed familiar, but he couldn't put his finger on why. The four newcomers, all shadows within the forest shade, chatted briefly with Robert, who then gestured to the north where the "small folk" awaited. The four then saluted and rode in that direction, quickly joined by others wearing identical surcoats. The entire group went to wait with the reserves.

Then it hit Alex why the surcoats looked strange yet familiar. He'd only seen them in history books and movies. "Templars."

"Where?" asked Lindsay, who hadn't noticed the four.

"Those guys, they went that way." He pointed with his chin. "They're Knights Templar. Red cross on white, right?"

"You've gotten pretty good at identifying people. Yes, that would be the Templars."

"What're they doing here? I thought they were outlawed."

"Well, for that, most of us are if you're talking about anywhere outside Scotland. The Templars were betrayed by the French king and condemned by the pope, and most of them were tortured and executed. Robert was excommunicated by that same pope. I say that makes him a natural ally for the Templars who escaped France. Especially since they probably still have plenty of cash to give in support of a king who would refrain from burning them at the stake."

Alex grunted in agreement, then turned and peered at her. "And you call me cynical."

Her eyes narrowed at him. "You know better than they. You were born to a better world and know it's possible."

"Was I? You're sure the future was a better world? You think our century isn't filled with people motivated by self-interest, greed, hatred, or just plain love of violence?"

She fell silent, and looked away toward the burn.

Alex looked the other way, and made himself stop thinking about her, to focus on what lay ahead.

Then, as always, came the waiting. Alex's pulse picked up some, but today he had little care for anything other than pitting himself against the English. Whether he lived or not was irrelevant; all he wanted was to live or die in glory. With Lindsay lost to him, it was all in the world that was his anymore to give a damn about.

That night the Scots slept in their positions, propped against trees, with their mounts nearby. The next morning they heard Mass, breakfasted on bread and water, then armed themselves and took up the wait again.

It was afternoon when, from a rise among the shadows of the forest, Alex looked out through the scattering of trees and saw movement in the distance. The English had arrived. Plate armor glittered in the sun, and brightly colored banners waved. Alex shivered, for it was like gazing at a tiger that was beautiful but deadly, approaching with murderous intent. Robert's own battle, including Alex and his men, watched as the enemy approached. Lances waved and wobbled, a thick forest on the English vanguard. Each knight was ready to assault the Scots enemy.

Robert rode forward, still riding his rounsey, as yet not fully armed and carrying only a battle hatchet. The circlet of gold on his head with its points of fleur-de-lis glinted in the occasional patch of sunlight as he walked his mount back and forth. He inspected his lines of Highlanders, spoke encouragement to his men as he went, and rode out to observe the ponderous approach of the massed enemy. His horse felt the excitement all around and fidgeted. The king seemed unruffled, calm and confident, and held his mount without apparent effort.

A shout rose from the front of the English column, and the man who rode at the head broke away, lowering his lance as he went. He was headed for the Scottish king, and nobody was close enough to defend Robert, who had no lance. Roger Kirk-patrick shouted for the king to withdraw, but went ignored. Instead of fleeing the onrushing lance, Robert faced off and kicked his horse to a canter. Alex leaned forward on his stirrups and watched with sickened heart, fearing history might change, knowing if the king were killed the entire campaign would be over and they would all be outlawed or executed.

Down the road through the forest Robert rode, straight at the English attacker, then the instant before the wobbling tip of the long enemy lance would have touched him he slipped sideways in his saddle. As the Englishman thundered past, Robert straightened and with a throaty roar slammed his axe into the English helmet, where it stuck. The handle shattered in his hand. Blood and brains splattered. The English knight toppled and his horse galloped on in confusion. Silence fell among both armies.

Then a wild, fearsome war cry went up among the Scots, and the Highland foot soldiers charged, running through bracken and climbing over felled trees to get at the enemy. Robert's infantry raced down on the English column struggling to negotiate the hole-riddled field below, and routed them. But as the enemy retreated from the burn and circled to the northeast, toward the field where Moray, Douglas, and Edward Bruce waited, Robert halted the Highland charge and recalled his infantry to the forest.

For the rest of the afternoon infantry lines were reestablished to face the enemy's new position and attack, and Robert's cavalry watched the struggle from the forest as the foot soldiers fought. Alex fidgeted, wishing Robert had sent knights, though he knew the king's tactics were valid and would win them the battle. He wanted to fight, to be part of the action. His horse sidled with the tension in Alex's knees against its flanks.

To the east of his position, the English main body was now engaged by Moray's infantry, and Alex edged himself and his men in that direction along with the rest of Robert's cavalry, keeping just within the cover of trees. Down on the field within the bend of the burn, the Scottish pikemen had formed a schiltron—a tight circle of men with spears and shields facing outward—against which the English knights threw themselves in futility. Alex witnessed what appeared to be suicide as knights charged the pikes, and he was boggled that they didn't just stand down and let their archers lob arrows into the tightly packed cluster of Scots. The archers of Edward I had defeated Wallace's schiltrons at Falkirk; Alex knew it, every Naval Academy midshipman to attend the class *HH381. The Martial Heritage to 1500* knew it, and certainly even the half-naked MacNeil infantry from Barra knew it for the story had been told in the castle at least once last winter. But the son of the man who had given the order at Falkirk apparently did not. The schiltrons held.

Then Douglas's men charged from the trees, at a run and with voices raised to the sky, and that was it for the English that day. They broke and ran. Some headed toward Stirling Castle and safety, and others back across the burn, there to camp. The Scots let them go, and retired to the forest once again to eat and sleep. Everyone knew, though, the fight wasn't nearly over.

It was a short, fitful night as the Scots waited for daybreak, the midsummer darkness lasting only four or five hours. Men slept lightly, and everyone knew the enemy could attack if they had a mind.

The sun was barely turning the sky a lighter black when word came via running, whispering pages to mount and assemble in battles. The sun topped the horizon, warming the landscape from a cloudless sky, when King Robert rode to the front to address the army. He began calling names, and those men went forward to kneel before the king.

Alex heard his own name, and with a thrill of surprise and a little alarm, looked toward Lindsay to know what might be going on. She only shrugged as he dismounted to go before the king. When he knelt with the others, he found himself next to Sir James Douglas. Alex allowed himself only sideways glances at the king's favorite—and possibly Lindsay's favorite. Douglas was calm, focused on the ground before him as he waited, a smile curling the corners of his mouth. So smug. He obviously knew what was going on, and Alex resented him for that, too.

Then Lindsay's name was called, and it was all Alex could do to not turn and watch her come to the line. In the corner of his vision he saw her kneel on the other side of Douglas, but Alex couldn't see her face. His jaw clenched as he struggled to keep his attention on the ground before him.

Then the king began tapping guys on the back of the neck with the flat of his sword, declaring them knights, and Alex understood. It was a mass knighting ceremony. But he and Douglas were already knighted, so he wondered what was in store for them. More sideways glances, but Douglas's face told him nothing he wanted to know. He heard Lindsay murmur her allegiance to Robert, and he felt adrift. She was a knight now, and no longer his squire. All his ties to her were gone.

When the king reached Douglas, it turned out he, Alex, and the knight to Alex's right were to become knights banneret. The three were promoted nearly in the same breath, as Robert pressed on with the ceremony.

Knight banneret?

After the blessing by the Abbot of Inchaffray, and the newly minted knights were sent back to their units, Alex remounted his horse and went to Lindsay to congratulate her though his heart wasn't in it. Her cheeks were flushed, and the slight curl of her mouth showed she was very pleased with herself in spite of the killing her new job would entail.

Then he whispered, "He made me a knight banneret."

"I don't know what that means."

"Neither do I." He thought for a moment as they awaited their orders, then said dryly, "Maybe it means I'll go to a different part of heaven if I die today."

Lindsay didn't reply. The flush of her face reduced to small, hot roses in her cheeks. She looked stricken. He was sorry he'd said it.

Orders came, and the infantry began to move. Contrary to custom in which knights had always formed the front line, foot soldiers were placed in front again. Pikemen and archers left the forest and formed schiltrons in the clear before the English, whose cavalry flung themselves against the pikes exactly as they had the day before. And with no better success. As the schiltrons advanced from the forest toward the burn, they trapped the enemy on their narrow campground, for the tide from the firth had come in and the swollen stream was no longer passable.

The Scottish knights, cheated of their right to first attack, waited, grumbling, as they watched the bloody exchange between archers. It was a horrible embarrassment to be left behind in the fight, and Alex burned with the longing to charge. Difficult enough to work up the mindset to fight and possibly die, without having to maintain it while waiting and doing nothing.

The schiltrons advanced, stabbing horses as they went and causing confusion amongst the English knights, who thwarted their own archers simply by being in the way.

Alex watched Douglas's infantry troops attack, and ached to take his own men into the fray. It was all he could do to obey his king and wait for his orders. The day wore on.

Finally the moment came. When English archers ran from behind their knights to take the fore, trumpets called Robert's knights to descend on them. Alex drew and raised his sword, and with a hoarse shout kicked his mount to a gallop and led his men into the fight.

No longer could he see what was happening beyond his own reach, and he no longer cared. Cross-hilt sword cutting a swath, he plowed into the line of English archers. The dull clanking of metal on metal, mixed with wails of dying men, was deafening. Wounded horses screamed and lunged. English infantry collapsed under Scottish cavalry. A crossbow bolt found Alex's thigh, but he felt nothing more than a brief, metallic sensation. Then he was slashing the face of another archer and turning to make certain the man was dead. There was more blood than Alex had ever seen, covering the ground in pools, and the primal rage urged him onward to shed more.

Then he turned. His eye fell on a scene that made him go cold. An unhorsed English knight had faced off against Lindsay, also unhorsed, and he cut her down, his sword making a solid hit to her side. She collapsed with a shout of agony Alex could pick out from the din of death cries.

No thought, his action was automatic. He dropped his sword, reached for the pouch at his belt, and drew the pistol. In an instant, before the Englishman could deliver the coup de grace to Lindsay, Alex shot him.

The report was a pop amid the noise and confusion. Alex urged his horse toward where Lindsay lay struggling, and as another enemy knight raised his weapon to her, Alex shot again. The knight fell, still alive but looking around in terror to know what had hit him. Alex dismounted as he rode up, strode over to the guy, put the pistol's muzzle between his eyes, and fired.

Six more men met their deaths by Alex's gun, then he was out of bullets. He returned the pistol to its pouch, then ran to Lindsay's horse and pulled his claymore from her saddle scabbard to continue defending her where she lay. He fought with all his strength, and with every bit of skill he'd acquired with the weapon. Men were cut down like wheat before a scythe, and Alex's only thought was to kill anyone who came too close to Lindsay. Until the noise died and the English were seen to flee the field, he vanquished all comers. Then, when the surviving enemy fled, he collapsed to his armored knees in the blood and mud, gasping, exhausted, and quite surprised to still be alive.

He turned to Lindsay, terrified of what he might find, and crawled to her. "Lindsay. Breathe. Be alive. Don't be dead." Her breathing came in desperately short and shallow gasps, and she'd gone pale and clammy. Her heart beat, but she was bleeding horribly. The leather and horn armor she wore was cleaved across her side, and blood soaked her body, her bloodied hand over the wound.

"Can't . . . breathe . . ."

"Don't talk." He drew his dagger to cut the leather between the horn plates, and found a long slash in her side. The armor had taken the brunt of the blow, but the sword had been sharp enough to make it through her padded tunic and shirt, and still it had opened up her side and caved in the bottom of her ribcage. If not for her armor, she would have been sliced in two.

Fear filled her eyes, and he knew the question she would ask if she could. He said, "You're bleeding, but not so bad as to kill you, I don't think. I'm betting you've got broken ribs, but I'm not seeing any bubbles. Do you taste blood?"

With her tongue she pushed out her lower lip, where he saw it was badly split, swelling and purple, covered with blood.

"Oh. Okay, we'll just wait to see, then, if you've punctured a lung. Just lie still, and wait until I can get someone to help me carry you back to camp."

She nodded, then as he sat next to her she pointed to the bolt sticking out of his leg. It made him laugh. "Thanks, it hurts now. I didn't feel it until you reminded me." The pain radiated to his hip, and he knew it wouldn't do anything but get worse until he pulled the thing out. No time like the present, so he grabbed the shaft as close to the wound as he could grip, took a deep breath, and yanked. A grunt blew out his nose, then he looked the bolt over once and threw it away. He poked at the hole in his cuisse, bleeding nicely now, and figured he'd live.

When he looked back at Lindsay, her eyes were closed but she was still breathing. He drew his plaid from around himself and laid it over her.

Hector came. His nose was neatly cut across the middle and bleeding merrily down past the corners of his mouth, where the blood dripped from this chin and splattered his woolen plaid. He looked around at the bodies lying in a rough circle around Alex and Lindsay. Some had faces blown away, others displayed large, bloody holes through chain mail. "Och, it's a fearsome warrior ye are, Ailig. I can't say as I've ever seen the like of this."

Alex kept his head down and said nothing. Just then he didn't care what anyone thought about what he'd just done.

Hector then looked down at Lindsay. "Is she dead?"

Alex shook his head.

"Give thanks to God, then. And pray she never does anything this foolish again." There was a strained look about Hector that made Alex ask, "Who did you lose?"

Tears began to glisten in the laird's eyes, and he looked off toward the horizon for a moment before he could turn back to Alex and reply, "*We*, Ailig. We lost our brother. Alasdair Og fell, toward the last."

That hit Alex harder than any loss he'd had since coming to this time. Many of his own men had been killed in battle, but Ailig Og had treated him like a brother, and in many ways Alex thought of him as one. He thought of Ailig's wife and young children back on Barra, and had to swallow his own tears.

So instead of dwelling on the loss, he said, "Here, help me take her back to the forest. Both together; careful, I think she's got a broken rib." They knelt on either side and slipped their arms under her, then lifted her and carried her like that all the way into the forest. Colin was already there with the horses he'd retrieved or captured from the field, having come through the battle himself with only a badly bruised face. "Go get my tent from the pack train," Alex ordered. Colin ran to obey.

Alex and Hector laid Lindsay on a thick, grassy patch near a tree then when Colin returned with their pack horse the three

erected the tent over her. Inside it, Alex and Hector shifted her
to her pallet. Alex then told Colin, "Go and bring some water in
the pot. Build a fire, and set the water on to heat."

"Aye, sir." Colin ran once more to do his master's bidding.

Hector helped Alex remove Lindsay's cut armor, then left
him to do the rest. Alex unbuckled his sword belt and let it drop
to the ground in the corner, then pulled off his helmet and coif,
and dumped them as well before kneeling beside Lindsay. Her
padded tunic was history, as was the shirt underneath. He removed those garments as gently as he could, then drew his dagger again to cut the bandage that bound her chest.

"No."

He paused. "Why?"

"I . . . need . . . that."

With a sigh, he pulled the pin she'd used to secure the thing
since the demise of the flimsy clips months before, and with ut-
most care unwound it from around her upper chest. The wound
was long and ugly. He could see rib bone between the edges of it,
cut but not through. The bleeding had slowed, and the bone was
stark white inside the purple gash. "This'll have to be sewn up."

"Hurry . . ."

He looked at her, and she elaborated. "While . . . it . . .
still . . . hurts. 'Cause . . . it's . . . gonna."

That made him chuckle. "Okay."

Outside the tent, Colin had lit the fire and put the pot on to
boil. Alex went to wash his hands of the battlefield dirt and
blood. It took him half an hour to walk to the burn and back. His
leg was beginning to stiffen, and by the time he returned he was
limping badly. When the water was heated, Alex took a needle
and thread from the kit and dropped it in. Once he figured it had
been in there long enough to do some good, he picked it out
with his dagger and dangled it so the needle would cool.

Inside the tent he sat on the ground next to Lindsay. "All
right, young knight, ready yourself. And remember to breathe.
If you don't breathe, you'll pass out."

"Sounds . . . like . . . idea"

Alex grinned and shook his finger at her.

The wound took twenty stitches. Alex worked carefully but
steadily, drawing the skin together as he went, trying not to
press on the fragile bones beneath. Each poke of the needle

brought a sharp breath, then panting through her nose, but she never cried out. Toward the end, tears began to run from her eyes down the sides of her face, but there was never a peep. He finished up, then cut the thread with his knife. For several minutes afterward Lindsay lay, panting quick, shallow breaths. Then gradually they lessened until she was breathing more or less normally.

Alex ripped off a piece of the linen he kept for her, dipped it in the hot water, then sat again, dabbing dried blood from her, just as his adrenaline crash came. Suddenly it was all he could do to keep on through the overwhelming, bone-deep exhaustion, washing away blood that turned to pink rivulets and colored the cloth he used. This was Lindsay's blood, and the horror of it blew through him. Her hand was crusted nearly brown. This should never have happened. She should never have been in any sort of battle. She hadn't been meant to even see such things, let alone participate.

He bent his head and raised her hand to his face, kissed her palm, held it there for a moment against his cheek, and the relief she was still alive swarmed in on him. That she was still part of his world, still on the earth, breathing, able to speak to him, meant more than his own life. More than anything or anyone else in his life. The thought of how close she'd come to leaving him forever choked him so he could hardly breathe, and a tear ran down the side of his nose.

"Don't . . . cry."

He sat up. "I'm not crying."

"Uh-huh."

Gently he finished cleaning her hand and laid it on her belly. Then he rubbed his eyes dry with the heel of his hand as he stood to go search for something to eat, but his legs would hardly hold him up.

"Lie . . . down . . . before you . . . fall . . . down."

"I told you not to talk."

"Sleep."

He looked at his pallet, and considered. Sleep or food? Suddenly his body felt too heavy to carry itself, and his wounded thigh would hold no weight. He eased himself onto the parachute to drop into unconsciousness like a rock in a pond.

When he awoke, still with the loud and drunken voices of

celebration all around though it was sunrise, he was dismayed to find he'd slept in his armor. "Aw, jeez." Every part of him ached, and his legs were numb from the poleyns strapped to his knees. His feet felt swollen inside his boots, the leather tight where it shouldn't have been. He groaned as he sat up and struggled to unbuckle the poleyns and cuisses, and wriggled out of his hauberk. His wound was throbbing, and he let down his trews for a moment to poke at it. It was purple and swollen, but still had feeling and showed no sign of infection. He restored the trews.

Lindsay was still sleeping, and he let her. Tottering on sore feet and a bad leg, moving like an old man, he left the tent and went in search of food. But first he had to see to his men and find out how many had survived the fight.

Sir Henry was among the group camped nearby. Alex went to sit with them, and cut a piece from the remains of a haunch they'd roasted the night before. "How many of us are left?"

Henry reported only five of the knights had been killed, but fifteen squires had lost their lives. Alex allowed as those who had died had all been brave men and had given their lives to the cause of freedom for Scotland, and it was true. Nobody else knew it yet, but yesterday's battle meant the end of English control in northern Scotland for the next three centuries or so, and that meant a firm foothold for King Robert over the next decade and a half of finishing the job in the Lowlands.

Together the men rehashed the battle, each telling his story and Alex only listening. He had no desire to tell what he'd done, and so encouraged everyone else to speak. They all laughed about the English being cowed by the lowly infantry, each of them certain the defeat would have been even more overwhelming had the cavalry been the first to charge. Alex knew better, but still said nothing.

Then the conversation turned to what was going on with the higher-ups. Rumors had been flying since yesterday, as they always did among soldiers who were rarely told anything beyond the very next set of orders. One had it that the king had kept watch all night over the body of the Earl of Gloucester, and another had it Robert was treating the English prisoners as guests while arranging ransoms from Edward II. In general, Robert's behavior in victory was well admired by both armies. Some prisoners had even been released without ransom, a gesture that would surely go far to turn the hearts and minds of both English and Scottish nobility in his favor.

And tales of the booty taken from the English baggage train were boggling to the point of incredibility. Word was that many of those who had come north with Edward II had brought wagonloads of rich goods with them, expecting to occupy captured castles after the fight.

That was good for a long, hearty laugh among the Scotsmen.

Belly full of beef, Alex requested some for Lindsay and was granted a large piece, which he carried back to his tent. She was awake.

"Here, eat."

She tried to sit up, but he wouldn't let her.

"Nah, nah, nah. Stay still. I'm a lousy doctor, and you'll pull your stitches if you do that. Wreck all my hard work. Lie back." He sat down next to her and began tearing pieces from the meat and handing them to her.

"I'm starving." She ate as fast as he could feed her.

"Good sign. You're breathing easier, too, it looks like."

"It still hurts, but not as much."

He fed her some more, then said, "You're lucky."

A glance at him, then she said, "I had you to protect me."

"You could have taken him."

"No, I couldn't. I'd be dead if you hadn't come."

His fingers twiddled a piece of meat for a moment, then he placed it between her teeth and said, "Are you mad at me?"

"No." Her reply was unequivocal. "Are you *nuts*, as you say? Sorry you saved my life? I don't think so!"

A smile came, and his heart lifted. He fed her the meat. Then, though he knew it was foolish to mess with this moment and ruin it, he said, "You shouldn't be a soldier."

There was a large wad in her mouth, and she swallowed it quickly to reply. "Because I'm a woman? I'm not as brave as the guys? Not tough enough?" A tense edge crept into her voice, and warning lit her eyes.

"No. You're as brave as any man I've ever known. And as tough." He paused, thinking hard of how to put this, and glanced at her sideways before he added, "But not in a way that makes a good soldier."

"Why?"

"You don't want to be one, for one thing."

"I want to do well. I train as conscientiously as anyone."

"But you don't want to *be* a soldier. I've known women who were as good, or better, than most of the men I've fought beside. Women tougher than me, and some as skillful. But those women have something you don't, and that's a willingness to make it a life. Without reservation. You're doing it because it's what you fell into, and I can tell the things you've had to do are eating at you."

"I did them nevertheless."

"And you're to be commended. But I wonder if it's worth it for you to continue struggling against your nature. You're not built for this."

"But you are."

For a moment he considered his family's long history of military service, and further what he'd learned of his MacNeil ancestry and traditions of Scottish bravery in battle, and knew it had been bred into his bones for millennia. "Yeah." He nodded. "I am."

There was a long silence, then she said, "I hate myself."

"You've got no reason to hate yourself. I, for one, love you to distraction. Marry me."

At first there was no reply, and Alex braced himself for what she would say. But then she said, "Let me think about it."

He blinked, not certain he'd heard right, and tilted his head at her. "Think about it?"

"Please."

She would consider it. Hope rose, and for the first time since the crash he thought there might be a future for him. She'd think about it. A grin widened on his face. "Cool."

All that day and the next Alex attended to Lindsay. It attracted some comment for him to wait on such a junior knight, but there was nothing for it and at this point he didn't care much what anyone thought. Lindsay, with her broken ribs, couldn't bind her breasts, so letting anyone into the tent other than Hector wasn't going to happen. Alex looked after her, and waited as she thought over his proposal.

On the evening of the second day after the battle, Alex was told by one of Robert's pages of a summons from the king.

"Our king?"

"Aye, sir." The boy was small and skinny, and had been running back and forth through the forest the past couple of days, summoning other knights. As young as he was, there were shadows of exhaustion below his well-bred eyes.

"You're sure he meant me?"

The royal page laughed. "Alasdair an Dubhar MacNeil, he said."

Alex nodded. That was him, all right.

The kid ran off, saying, "Promptly, he said, sir."

Alex didn't know what to think. A smile touched his mouth, but he suppressed it. *All right. An audience with the king. This is special.* Quickly he slapped some of the dust and crud from his tunic and donned his sword belt. No self-respecting Scot ever went anywhere unarmed, and he would feel undressed without the sword. Then he ran his fingers through his rather longish hair, and scratched his chin, wishing he'd shaved that morning. No time to do laundry or bathe. "Promptly," the king had said. Damn.

He told Lindsay, "I'll be right back."

"I'll leave the porch light on for you."

That made him chuckle.

The king's tent was huge in comparison to the tiny piece of cloth that sheltered Alex and Lindsay. It had several rooms, hung with rich curtains and tapestries, and lit by colored candles in gilt stands, and bejeweled oil lamps. All of it recently arrived from England, Alex was certain. He was escorted into a remote end of the complex where stood a heavy, wooden chair on a dais, surrounded by the king's ministers. On it sat Robert, his face aglow beneath his royal dignity, for it surely had been a pleasant few days for him to bask in a victory so complete and unexpected. Alex couldn't help but smile with him, though he had no clue why he'd been summoned.

"Alasdair an Dubhar!"

Alex knelt and bowed as gracefully as his stiffened thigh would let him. In front of the king, he never let the pain reach his face. "Your majesty."

"Rise." The command was perfunctory, as if the king were eager to get the formalities out of the way and proceed with his busy day.

Alex stood.

"Alasdair, I understand your performance in the late conflict was exemplary. More than exemplary, it is reported to be heroic among men who rightly consider themselves heroes."

Good. He wasn't going to be chewed out for something. Alex took a deep breath and said, "All the men fought well, your Majesty."

"Indeed, they did! But I'm told that when all was finished and the English had turned tail, you stood on the battlefield, surrounded by no fewer than ten dead men, all of which they say you killed on foot."

Uh-oh, Alex raised his chin so as not to appear guilty. "Aye. Ten." He'd actually killed more like twelve or thirteen if one counted the ones he'd put away before drawing the pistol, but he wasn't going to volunteer that information. Bragging at this point would be unseemly, and apparently unnecessary, and might attract too much scrutiny as to how he'd killed so many.

"That is an amazing thing. To wound is difficult enough, but to dispatch to hell so many in so short a time is magnificent! Prowess beyond compare!"

Alex had no idea what to reply to that, so he said, "Thank you, your Majesty."

"No, it is I who thank you." The king stood and waved away Alex's modesty to get down to business. "The English pack train was large, and well laden. There is now the means to thank all the men who have fought so well and with such loyalty. In particular, the men whose talents have proven so valuable in the struggle, for the fighting is not ended. I'll need skilled commanders. *Loyal* commanders." Then he paused, as if waiting for a reply, so Alex obliged.

"Aye." He figured his loyalty was without question.

The king proceeded. "Now that you are knight banneret, you will need lands commensurate to your standing, and where you will have the means to maintain your following."

"Following?" It was as if Alex's brain had gone for a walk. *Huh?*

"You already command men who are loyal to you. And you deserve the estate for your actions here and in the past. It's not an excessively large piece of land, and it is remote, but it's enough to support your status and enable you to maintain a garrison."

"Estate?"

"Eilean Aonarach. In the Sound of Canna off Rhum. The castle barracks there can house fifty men, I'm told."

Suddenly the king was speaking gibberish. It sounded like he was handing over an entire island. Stupidly, Alex said, "An island?"

Robert laughed. "Aye, Sir Alasdair. A lonely one, if it's well named. But they say it has plentiful pasture and there are some farms. Your vassals are hardworking, pious folk. Exactly as everywhere else in Scotland." That caused a ripple of laughter in the room.

Vassals. Holy crap.

But the king seemed in a hurry to get to the next beneficiary, and so proceeded, reading from a paper. "From the English pack train I award you four horses, ten cattle, fifteen sheep, a pair of goats, twelve pieces of linen and the same amount of silk, a hundred and twenty pounds in coin, and this ring for your finger." The king produced a gold ring set with the most enormous pearl Alex had ever seen. He took Alex's hand, and slipped the ring onto the pinky finger. It was entirely too large there, threatening to fall off, and Alex shifted it to his index finger. There it stuck out like a gumball nestled in filligree. "Also, a wagon. You'll need a wagon."

Alex nodded. Indeed, he would.

Robert lowered his chin and peered into Alex's face. "Are you well, man?"

For one more moment of stupidity, Alex only blinked at him, then he decided for now to pretend this was business as usual and sort it out later. "Aye, your Majesty. I'm quite well. And well pleased by the largesse."

Robert smiled. "Good. I was concerned for a moment I'd been too generous and could have had your loyalty for less." Another ripple of laughter took the room, and Alex smiled.

"My loyalty is not for sale, for I pledged it to you eight years ago. But if my king wishes me to live in comfort, how should I disagree?"

Again the tent erupted in laughter, and the king's guffaw was loud, long, and happy. He handed Alex the paper from which he'd been reading, and a small chest of iron-bound wood, filled with coins, wished him well, and handed the case over to one of his retainers. Alex bowed and withdrew as the next recipient entered.

The king's minister directed him to find his livestock, and showed him the wagon containing his goods, then told him he would be summoned from his estate when next the king needed his services. Until then, he was free to go about his business.

Indefinite leave? Honorable discharge? What had just happened, and now what? Apparently he was supposed to maintain and command a garrison, and would have to figure out what that meant in terms of men, money, and logistics. He folded the letter and stashed it inside his shirt.

Alex paid a page to hitch two of his new horses to the wagon, and while that was being done he took his chest heavy with cash and returned to his camp and his men. The thing felt like it weighed a ton, but it was too small to hold a hundred and twenty pounds of silver. He guessed about half the money was in gold. The chest landed at his feet in the camp, with a loud, rattling *ca-chunk*. He brought the folded letter from his shirt, then announced to all present, "You're now looking at the new master of a place called Eilean Aonarach." A pleased but unsurprised murmur riffled among the men. Alex continued. "I'd like it a whole lot better if I knew where that was." That brought laughter, then Henry spoke up.

"'Tis among the Inner Hebrides. If you cross the sea to Barra, and halfway there turn north, there it is, exactly where they left it."

"Good. All right, then, who of you wants to serve in my garrison, and will be loyal to me and the king?"

Twenty-three men volunteered for garrison duty, and the rest had lands of their own they were eager to see again but pledged their loyalty if called upon. Alex could hardly blame those men for wanting to go home, and for a brief, wistful moment he wished he were returning to his own home. But he shook that off as impossibility and counted out to each of the knights and squires a pound in silver coin. The men who would stay as retainers he assigned to collect his livestock and bring the wagon around. They would leave for Eilean Aonarach in the morning.

Alex's pulse picked up as he went to the tent to see Lindsay, and he stopped just inside the flap. The oil lamp hung from the roof burned merrily in the midsummer twilight. Her eyes opened.

"Where did you go for so long?"

"I was summoned by the king."

"What for? Did someone see the gun and he wanted you to explain it? You didn't show it to him, did you?"

Alex shook his head. "He gave me an estate in the Hebrides and he expects me to maintain a garrison there."

Her eyebrows went up. "You know property ownership isn't like it is where we come from. The king can take back the land whenever he wants to; that's how James Douglas was disinherited by Edward."

He nodded. "I reside at the pleasure of His Majesty, I know. But I'm perfectly happy to keep the king happy, and it's a place to go where we'll be relatively comfortable. No more sleeping on the ground, and no more wearing the same clothes every day for weeks. I'd be willing to bet I can even find a blacksmith there who'll build us a bathtub."

A smile widened on her face, and it lifted his heart. "A bathtub? Honest? I think I'd do anything for a bath."

He grinned. "Yeah. So marry me."

The silence that followed landed hard in the pit of his stomach and his smile died. Rather than let the silence go on, he said, "Okay. Don't answer that. Not yet. Think about it some more. Think carefully."

Lindsay nodded, but said nothing more.

CHAPTER 15

"Were I to accept your proposal, how would I change my gender?"

The ship rose and fell in the choppy, foggy Hebrides sea. Alex's heart leapt in his chest as he leaned close to hear Lindsay's question, spoken in a low voice under the wind. He'd not mentioned marriage since that day a month ago, and this was the first Lindsay had brought it up. Struggling to control his excitement, he hooked his thumbs into his sword belt, looked out over the water, and said, "This is a yes?"

"Still thinking."

Now he didn't know where to look, and stared at the deck planks. "What have you been thinking?"

"That you may be right, that I just don't have the mentality for soldiering." Now he looked over at her, and she was examining a frayed spot on her tunic sleeve as she continued. "All year I'd thought the victory at Bannockburn would help me to understand. I'd thought it would let me in on the whole glory concept you fellows seem so keen on. But all I learned from having my chest cracked open was that I don't want to die."

"I don't want to die, either."

"But you've accepted the probability. I've learned I can't do that. I want too much to live. And it makes me a poor soldier."

Her face turned toward his, though she didn't look him in the eye. "Does that also make me a coward?"

Had anyone else asked that, Alex would have said yes. However, this was Lindsay and her life was even more precious to him than it was to her. He said, "No. Not a coward." Loved. Lovely. Treasured. Not coward.

"So . . . I'm open to other ideas. I have two choices now: to accept your proposal of marriage, or go off on my own and make my way in the world without you."

Alex's heart lurched, and he searched her face. Leave? "Don't leave. I think you should become your own sister."

"My what?" Lindsay lowered her head and peered over at him.

"Remember when we explained to Kirkpatrick where we'd been for seven years? I told him your father died and there were sisters to settle with dowries, so now everyone thinks you have sisters. You can go away as the boy, and return as the woman."

"And stay away for another seven years?"

He waved away the thought. "Nah. We'll produce a letter and say it's from your sister, telling us to expect a visit. Then we'll go across to the mainland to 'meet' her. Once there, Lindsay will . . . die, or something. He can have an accident. Maybe he can be shanghaied, or run away. Eaten by wolves, maybe. That way we don't need to return with a corpse. In any case, once the kid is gone I can fall in love with his poor, abandoned sister, whose paltry dowry has dwindled since it was settled on her."

Lindsay made a disparaging noise in the back of her throat, a habit she'd picked up from her fellow squires. "I sound fairly pathetic, don't I?" She gazed out into the mist, staring forward.

He eagerly dropped that idea and went for something she would like better. "Well, I guess the dowry part might be overkill. Maybe instead you'll be a terribly pampered rich girl who will fall for me because I'm a war hero of great renown, an up-and-coming knight who is a royal vassal and possibly in line for a peerage title of some sort." A smile curled the corners of her mouth though she wouldn't look at him. "Hey, you never know," he protested. Then he continued, warming to his invention. "Or maybe you'll be a great beauty of comfortable means, who will graciously consent to marry me because I've fallen head over heels in love and you can't stand to watch me suffer. Which would be more or less the truth."

Now the smile came in full, and she looked at him. How he wished he could kiss her then!

But her smile faded, and she looked out across the water again. "And if Lindsay dies, what would his sister be called?"

Alex grunted. He hadn't thought of that. "Name change. Right." There was a long silence as he thought it over, then he asked, "What's your middle name?"

"Thelma."

He grunted again and kept thinking. "Okay, how about a relative you admired? Someone you knew back home and would like to honor?"

She looked down at her hands and her eyes began to glisten. It took a very long time, but he waited in silence. Finally, she said, "Marilyn. It was my mother's name."

Alex picked off a hangnail on his thumb, then said, "I miss my family, too."

"Not your fault." Lindsay straightened and took a deep breath.

He started to tell her how much it would mean to him if she would become his new family, when her eyes went wide at something out on the water. "Oh, look! Is that it?"

An island had materialized from the fog ahead. A fairly good-sized one, several miles across. It was hard to tell yet, but there seemed to be cliffs at one end, then rolling hills studded with patches of granite, that descended to the sea at the other end. A single peak thrust up from the center, a crown of bare gray rock surrounded by green.

Alex's heart thudded in his chest as he beheld his estate. Eilean Aonarach. *Lonely island.* Moving from place to place throughout his childhood, then also traipsing around the world after joining the Navy, there had never been a place he'd thought of as home. No attachments to places, and no special people other than his immediate family. Now, for the first time in his life, though he'd never set foot here, he felt a tug from this bit of land. It was already his home, more than any other had ever been. As the island came clearer in the mist, there was a sense of belonging to it. Not it belonging to him, for only the king owned property in these feudal times and even that ownership was always bought and maintained by force of arms. But he belonged to it, and the nearer he came the stronger the pull.

A smile lit his face, and he could hardly wait to arrive. He began looking for a place to land.

Half an hour later, as the ship negotiated a rocky breakwater to approach a stone quay, Lindsay said, "Look."

Alex glanced over at her, then up to where she was staring. High above, built into the rock face of the cliff, was the castle. Gray stone like the rest of the island, it blended in so well Alex hadn't noticed it until now. At the water, a high stone wall dotted with arrow loops backed the quay, the only entrance guarded by a square, blocky gatehouse that was empty of gate.

As the ship sidled along the quay, Alex vaulted the side to investigate. Chain mail and spurs jingling, he hurried to the unmanned gatehouse, where the opening gaped. "What happened here?" Not that he expected a reply, but the sight did not please him. The gate was blackened, and partly burned away. Dark burn marks covered that end of the quay, and it was apparent there had been an assault of some kind. Perhaps a siege. Arrows lay here and there, lodged where the weather hadn't blown or washed them away.

Men followed him, and Alex turned back to count volunteers and give orders. "You five, come with me. You, too, Lindsay. The rest of you start to unload the livestock and bring them through the gate." Then he returned his attention to the castle.

Alex strode through the gate, making mental notes of what repairs would be needed to make this a viable garrison again. First on the list: find wood and a blacksmith to build another gate. Immediately.

Inside the barbican, his heart sank. There had once been buildings here, but like the gate they now were nothing more than burnt remains, crumbling to black mush in the weather. There was nothing salvageable, and now his mind flew with assessment and calculation. These were less important than the gate, and the barbican would hold the livestock well enough for the time being. He'd need to have all this removed, and that would take manpower. Now he wondered what sorts and how many vassals he had at his disposal, and what would be required in payment for their labor. His knights would be no good for this; none of them would be caught dead doing manual labor.

Against the face of the cliff, a long, zigzagging stair leading to a doorway had been carved into the rock. He started up at a run, but quickly slowed to a more reasonable pace when his breath shortened. The stair took him and the others halfway up the cliff face, then disappeared into a doorway in the side of a rounded protrusion of the castle wall.

Inside was a spiral staircase, lit only by arrow loops that shed little light in the misty day. Alex climbed some more in the dimness, struggling for breath now. After a couple of turns he came to a broken door that looked as if it had been cleaved with an axe. Who had been here? English? Or had Robert's army done this? It could even have been the assault of a feuding clan from a nearby island.

Alex entered a small anteroom and smelled cold ash and death. The darkness was nearly complete, for this room had no windows or arrow loops. He removed his right gauntlet and felt around for something to light. There was a candle sconce on a wall close by, and on it hung a striker.

"Give me a piece of cloth, someone." He held out his hand to the shadows behind him, and there was a tearing noise. A bit of someone's shirt was placed in his palm. With the striker he threw a few sparks onto the linen, then gently encouraged the ones that caught. Soon the cloth was aflame, smelling sharp yet welcome in this dank place, and he touched it to the candle in the sconce. Now they could see the door to exit the room.

With that candle he lit others his men took from sconces, and they ventured from this anteroom into the castle proper. It led directly to the Great Hall, a cavernous place overarched by huge beams and dimly lit by smoke holes in the ceiling. The enormous hearth ran down the middle of the room, a great, long pit filled with damp ashes, where spits for roasting entire animals appeared intact. Some of the tables and benches also looked whole, but the floor was scattered with broken pieces of others.

There was also the familiar stink of old blood and feces, but it appeared the bodies had been removed. Alex assumed there would be nothing of real value left behind by the attackers, whoever they had been, and he found himself grateful any of the furniture was usable. That the place was still standing, the beams and ceilings untouched by flame, was a miracle, given the king's penchant for tearing down castles as soon as they were in his possession. The fortresses at Edinburgh and Stirling were probably both casualties by now, and neither would be rebuilt for a long time.

He began looking for candles and lighting them, but the small flames did little to dispel the woeful atmosphere of the place, so he dispatched Sir Orrin De Ros to find some firewood and light the hearth.

"I'm no laborer, sir."

Alex peered at the man and briefly wondered why he hadn't died at Bannockburn. "Do you want to eat tonight?"

"Of course."

"Then do as you're told today. Until we get some villagers in here to help us, we're on our own."

"The squires—"

"Do you have a squire of your own to delegate this detail?"

Orrin shook his head.

"Then do as you're told and stop giving me guff."

Orrin hesitated, then said, "Aye, sir." He obeyed his orders.

It was plain Alex needed to find some locals and put them to work, or he'd have a mutiny on his hands. "Anyone have an idea how we're supposed to get our livestock up from the quay?"

Sir Henry said, "I observed a hoist at the rampart above us, sir."

That perked Alex's curiosity. "A hoist?"

"Above us, on the east side. It appeared undamaged."

This sounded promising. Alex found a door to a spiral stairwell at the northwest corner of the hall. Two more flights, hurrying up wedge-shaped stone slabs in the dark, and he came out on the roof of the Great Hall. He lit the candle in the top sconce of the stairwell, then said, "Save your candles, men." They blew out their lights and tucked them into belt pouches. Over the north battlement, they all looked out over a narrow, winding, overgrown bailey hemmed in by slopes of solid granite topped by stone walls. He led his men past two cisterns to the south side, where the vista was the misty sea that isolated the island in gray silence. As Robert had said, this place was well named.

More stairs along the east side of the building descended to something that appeared to be a wooden platform where a huge wooden crane arm reached out over the side of the cliff. Beside it, Alex recognized the same sort of mechanism that lifted heavy castle gates, a rope dangled from the end of the hoist, and

Alex looked down to find a leather sling hung from it. The barbican below was coming alive with the cattle, horses, sheep, and goats from the ships. Behind them on the land side, a narrow track descended along the side wall of the keep to a bailey beyond, a killing ground beneath arrow loops and oil sluices in the battlement above. Outside the gates, the countryside appeared deserted. Though the island was small, it was still large enough they'd need their horses.

Alex shoved on the hoist arm to see if it was solid. It swung nicely on a well-oiled pivot. He smacked the joints and found them tight, the wood not badly weathered. Then he climbed onto the arm and walked to the end. No give. He bounced, and the wood held as steady as rock. Last time he'd weighed himself he'd come in at one-eighty-two, and in his armor he figured he was over two hundred pounds, but his weight didn't even begin to bend the hoist. It might handle a large animal, and the sling suggested it had in the past. He would find out soon, for they needed their horses.

He turned to his men and hopped from the hoist arm. "All right, let's get some horses up here first." He pointed to Lindsay. "Go down and ready five of them. Be sure to blindfold them before putting the sling on." He turned to the remaining four men. "The rest of us will turn this hoist." He saw no pulley at the end of the crane, only an iron bar over which the rope was draped; this wasn't going to be an easy task.

Over the course of the afternoon they hauled five horses, then a load containing tack and armor, up and over the face of the castle keep. It was a monstrously difficult task, for though the hoist was of solid construction it was badly designed and the rope was a disaster waiting to happen. The men sweated and strained, and Alex kept a sharp eye on the rope as it stretched and twisted under the weight. Once the horses were lifted to the platform then led to the bailey, Alex ordered no more use of the hoist until the rope could be replaced. He counted himself lucky the thing hadn't let go today with a valuable animal hung from it.

Squires presented themselves in the bailey to saddle their masters' horses, a small beginning of activity in this empty, rugged place. The area outside the Great Hall was a maze of outcroppings of rock, and buildings of stone and wood. Situated between two rises in the cliffs, the castle was nestled and carved into the granite like the cliff dwellings of the Anasazi Indians. The layout was asymmetrical, the curtain walls following the peaks of the narrow, precipitous rock all the way to the flat ground of a glen beyond. There two curtains spanned the ravine, guarded by two ugly, square towers.

Once Alex and four of his knights were mounted in full armor, with surcoats and flying his new banner, they sallied out of the bailey, along the narrow outer bailey between curtain walls, then out the landside portcullis in the outer curtain, and finally onto the island. Pasture surrounded the castle for a couple of hundred yards or so, then gave way to thick forest covering rolling hills. Alex was relieved to find a cluster of low, peat houses near the forest edge, for that meant some centralization of the population. He wouldn't have to ride all over the island to find someone who could give him information and act as liaison between himself and his vassals.

Vassals. He was still having trouble getting used to that idea.

The five cantered toward the huddled houses that passed for a village, and as they approached, people came from their homes to see. Alex adjusted the plaid thrown across his shoulder and slowed his mount to a walk. The villagers were dressed exactly like the MacNeils on Barra, in tunics, shirts, and plaids and very little else. Being summer, none of the men wore trews and many of the smaller children were entirely naked.

Women and children hung back, letting the men form a line between them and the strangers. Alex reined in his mount and spoke first.

"The English have been vanquished in Lothian." His banner with the bald eagle waved gently in the early August breeze.

He'd expected a reaction, but didn't get it until one of the men turned and repeated his words in Gaelic. Then came the bright smiles and cheerful chatter, the gist barely comprehensible to Alex. He could see he would need to do some more studying up on the language if he was going to accomplish much here. Now he addressed the man who apparently knew English, but loudly enough for everyone to hear his voice and the tone it carried.

"I'm the new master of Eilean Aonarach. I've come to claim this island and its castle as my award from King Robert."

Instead of translating, the man asked, "And what might be the new master's name?"

"Sir Alexander an Dubhar MacNeil, Knight Banneret and royal vassal to His Majesty, King Robert of Scotland."

One of the women exclaimed, "A'mol Dia." She sounded thrilled. "MacNeil!" The other women began to chatter, and Alex gathered they were debating whether they would be displaced by Barra MacNeils. The English-speaker silenced them.

He explained to Alex, "She is your kinswoman, and comes from Barra." Then he hesitated before continuing. "An Dubhar, you say?"

"That's what they call me."

The man nodded slowly, then said, "Are there many kinsmen with you?"

Alex shook his head. "No. Only my knights. I don't expect much to change around here."

That brought a wide smile and an air of relief from the man. He translated to the villagers, and a ripple of that gladness moved through the gathering. Alex realized this was going far better than he might have hoped, had he given it much thought before now. He asked, "How many people live on this island?"

The man shrugged, and asked the question of the rest of the villagers. Nobody knew.

"Are there many more than are here now?"

The English speaker looked over the crowd and said, "I think, perhaps, there are as many more living elsewhere on the island as are here before us."

Alex thought a moment. His mount, fidgeting under the excitement of the day and the new surroundings, shifted weight and pawed the ground. Alex calmed the horse with a word, then said, "All right. I need workers. Anyone who will come to help clean the castle and make it livable can join in a feast when the job is done. No work, no food. The sooner the place is habitable, the sooner we all can celebrate." He threw a look over his shoulder at the early evening sun slanting to the west, and said, "In the morning, come. Everybody come tomorrow, and spread the word to the rest." He reined his horse around, but the English-speaker stepped forward.

"There is other work to be done tomorrow."

Alex turned back and nodded. "Aye. This isn't an order. Nobody is required to come. Only those who wish to participate in the feast."

The man blinked at him for a moment, then nodded and said, "Aye. Fair enough."

Alex lowered his voice and leaned down, to speak more or less privately. "What is your name?"

"Donnchadh MacConnell. We're mostly MacConnells here, and a few Betons."

"Who was your master before?"

Now the man's hesitation gave Alex the willies, and suddenly he wasn't too sure this was going to go so well. Donnchadh said, "We pay tribute to MacDonald. And MacLeod."

This couldn't be good. "Both of them?"

"Nae both at once, you understand. They take turns fighting over the island. 'Tis been a feud now since the time of my grandfather."

"Who built the castle?"

"The English king. The father of the sodomite." Alex noted that, for a backwater island, the natives were remarkably aware of current affairs in the south. But from his time on Barra he knew the interisland fishermen's gossip was an efficient information system to rival the Internet. Donnchadh continued. "And old Longshanks, he handed it over to a crony from the south, who fancied himself a laird though he'd never seen a Gael in his life. Both MacLeod and MacDonald showed the usurper exactly how much he is not a Scot, and now his knights have fed the fish and the two true lairds are tending to other concerns for a time."

Alex said slowly, "But they'll be back." That would explain why none of the important parts of the castle had been burned. The guys who had stormed the place together each expected to occupy it later.

"I'd wager my life on it. They'll be wanting their tribute." And Alex couldn't tell by his neutral tone whether Donnchadh thought that was good or bad.

"I see, then." The new master of the island straightened and called out over the crowd, Donnchadh translating. He took care his voice didn't give away his concern. "Now hear this! You will no longer pay tribute to MacDonald, MacLeod, or any other laird who would lay claim to this island! I am the law here now, allied with MacNeil of Barra and Robert of Scotland! Any man here who fails to come to my keep and pledge loyalty to me within the fortnight will be evicted from his property and banished from this island!" He took a moment for that to sink in, then said, "Am I understood?"

His vassals gave a murmur of assent.

"Excellent. Come tomorrow, and we'll get to know one another."

A bald look of surprise at the change of tone landed on Donnchadh's face, and a smile began on Alex's. He was about to leave, when Sir Henry whispered to him, "The gate."

Oh, yeah. "Donnchadh, one more thing. I need a blacksmith. Is there a blacksmith in the village?"

MacConnell turned to shout, "Alasdair Ruadh!" Alex wondered if there was any place in this country that wasn't crawling with guys named Alasdair. A skinny, red-haired man pushed forward from the pack.

"Aye."

"The barbican gate at the quay needs replacing immediately. Will you do the work?"

Donnchadh spoke to him, and Alasdair Ruadh nodded as he replied. Then Donnchadh said to Alex, "He'll come to look at your gate in the morning."

"I'll need a translator—"

"I speak Gaelic." Sir Henry spoke up and nudged his horse forward.

Alex peered at him for a moment, then said, "Very well." To the villagers he said, "Good day to you all. I look forward to seeing you tomorrow." With that, Sir Alasdair turned his horse and kicked him to a walk. His men followed.

Sir Orrin called out to him, "That may not have been wise, sir, to be so informal with the lesser folk."

Alex grunted and waved him forward. Once Orrin was riding beside him and out of earshot of the others, Alex told him calmly, "Thank you for your opinion, Orrin. It's a calculated risk I think worth taking. And from here on out, I'll ask you to remember your pledge to me and take care in what you say in front of the others. As you might well see, I can ill afford insubordination at this time. One more outburst will call for punishment. You're on shaky ground, De Ros."

Orrin thought that over for a minute, then said, "Aye, sir." Then he fell back to ride in the ranks.

Alex's mind turned with all the ramifications of what he'd just learned, sorting out where he stood and what he needed to look out for, but there were too many unknowns. Too much to do all at once. Suddenly he wondered whether Robert's gift was the blessing he'd thought.

CHAPTER 16

At the castle, a handful of squires had cleared space on the floor of the Great Hall for the men to lay out their pallets around the small fire that burned at one end of the long hearth. Ellot posted the watch, the men cooked and ate the rations, then, while they lounged around the fire in preparation for sleep, Alex took a candle to explore the keep.

Unlike the rambling castle on Barra, there wasn't much to it. The impossibly narrow bailey was crowded with outbuildings for the kitchen, brewery, bake house, stable, barracks, and chapel, jutting this way and that and separated by narrow alleys or bulges of rock. So the keep probably held little more than the Great Hall and the laird's living quarters. The spiral stairs upward from the Great Hall led only to the roof, and the spiral stairs from the anteroom led only to the barbican. The main door at the entry of the Hall led outside to the bailey, and a single door at the rear led to a small chamber lined with toilet seats. A many-holed garderobe. Strangely, the smell in here was a little less rank than elsewhere in the keep. Alex looked around the room and figured it was because nobody had died in here. Not recently, anyway.

Having scoped out the main level of the keep, Alex took his candle down a wide flight of stairs at the west end of the hall.

Below, he found himself in an oblong room, with a stone ceiling curved like a quonset hut, even more dark and cavelike than the Great Hall above. The oppressive dankness was unrelieved by openings of any sort, and there was only one small hearth on the long north side. Two doors opened from this room at the southeast corner. One of them led to a dead-end chamber equally close and dank. No windows. The second door led to a similar chamber, and beyond that anteroom was another small chamber in which he found an arrow loop. Finally, fresh air.

Alex leaned into the loop to breathe for a moment the salt air from outside, the stench of death in here was so thick. He'd become used to bad smells, and rotting corpses were nothing new to him anymore, but this was like a tomb, where such things dominated. It seeped into his skin and he could taste it in his mouth, an oily, sweet, gagging thing. The air seemed thick with the souls of the departed who hung about for jealousy of the living, and who might in their numbers and their misery even gather enough energy to reach out with cold, unseen—

"Alex."

He jumped nearly out of his skin, and his chain mail rattled. "Lindsay!" His heart flopped in his chest, and as he turned to her he pressed his fist against it to make it stop stuttering. "Dang."

She stood in the doorway with a candle, chuckling. "There you are. You disappeared on me."

"Sorry. I didn't think you would be up to a lot of stair climbing yet." It had been only a few weeks since the battle, and her wound was still bothering her enough to make her fold her left arm close to her side as if holding her ribcage together.

"I wanted to see the place." She looked around, "It's a bit of a dump, isn't it?"

That was putting it mildly, but he didn't want to dwell on it. Finally alone with her, he went to kiss her but stopped to stare when his candlelight fell upon a human skull atop a dark pile behind her. Alex had assumed the high stench in this room was strictly from body fluids left all over the floors after the recent fight, but here among the rags thrown on the floor in this chamber was a sunken-eyed head. Most of the flesh had rotted or been eaten from the face, and a mass of yellow hair stuck out like dried grass. Something grew from the dark mound on which it sat; a fungus of some kind, strange and shimmery in the dim light, and the corpse appeared to have become part of the wall behind it. Alex gawked, at once appalled and fascinated. He'd never seen such a thing before.

Lindsay turned to follow his gaze, looked down, and stepped back. "Oh, God!" She backed through the door to the other room, moaning in terror, "Oh, God, oh, my God . . ."

Alex didn't know who the dead guy had been, but now he wished him to hell for scaring Lindsay. "Wait, shhh." He left the room with her and yanked the chamber door closed behind him. It closed on reluctant hinges and scraped over gunk on the floor. "Lindsay, calm down. It's just a body they missed when they cleared the place out." He put an arm around her and held her as close as he could without hurting her, and she was trembling. "Don't worry about it. We'll get them to take him out in the morning and give him a proper burial."

She pressed her face against his plaid.

"Don't be frightened. You've seen dead guys before."

"Yes, but they're starting to add up, and it's getting to me. I don't know if I can stand to see another mutilated person." She looked at his face. "I don't understand how you can take it anymore, either."

He shrugged. "It's not like I have a choice."

She sighed and settled into his arms, holding him around the waist with her weak arm. He let her warmth and her living presence bolster him, for the corpse had rattled him, too. Then he forced his voice to a cheerful tone. "Hey, there's one more chamber. Let's see what's behind door number three."

"More rotting flesh, I imagine."

"Dunno. Maybe not." He took her hand and drew her along.

The third door led to a chamber much larger than any of the others. At one end the ceiling of mortared stones was curved, as were those in the other rooms directly below the Great Hall, but then the room widened and there the ceiling was wooden. Beams ridged it as they did in the Great Hall, and part of one wall was living rock that bulged slightly into the room. The hearth was deep in the wall opposite, large enough to spit half a deer. A door near the hearth opened to a private garderobe with two holes.

Alex slapped the rock wall. "Check this out. You couldn't buy décor like this back home."

Lindsay ran a hand across it, then they both noticed at the far end was a glazed window rather than an arrow loop. Small, but still larger than a loop.

"Look, glass." Lindsay went to tap on it, as if doubting it could be real. The glass was terribly wavy and only a little more transluscent than a frosted bathroom window, but there would be light through it even in winter for it faced south. When she opened it, fresh summer night air wafted in from the sea below. She set her candle among the many stones that made up the very deep, slanted ledge, and turned to survey the room. "Must be the lord's chamber."

"If it wasn't, it is now." He went to kiss her, and this time succeeded. He did it gently, so not to hurt her, and she breathed carefully. But also he kissed her gently because she was the only soothing thing left in his life. She was soft voice, bright smile, and yielding breasts when they weren't all bound up out of his reach. Her mouth was sweet and welcoming, kissing him in return with all the enthusiasm he could hope for. It was moments like this he thought she really did love him the way he wished, and his heart ached that he might think it all the time.

Lingering, tasting, wanting never to stop, Alex finally had to take his mouth from hers when the blood in his other parts began to pound. *Not now.* He said, "You need to go back upstairs, so the men won't start muttering ugly things about us again."

"Right." She reached behind his head to steal another kiss, then took her candle from the room and went upstairs to the Great Hall.

Alex watched her go, then stood by the window for a few minutes and gazed out at the water, restless in the moonlight, thinking about how he wished she were safely his wife. No more watching her ride into battle, no more seeing her cut open, no more terror of being discovered. She'd relax, then, he was sure. She'd be happy, and that would make him happy. If only she'd agree to marry him.

He closed the window and returned to the Great Hall to find a place to sleep the night.

The next morning the sun was well into the sky when Alex was awakened by the call of Sir Henry. "Sir Alasdair! Come see!"

Alex struggled awake in a hurry, and his body ached from too little sleep. Patches of sunlight from the chimney holes above lay across the stone floor, and he wondered if he would ever get used to dawn coming so early in the morning. Then he figured he'd be used to it by the time the days became shorter and he wouldn't see the sun till almost noon.

"Sir Alasdair!"

He climbed to his bare feet and found Henry calling him from the roof stairwell. As he picked his way across the floor, he was glad he hadn't seen much of this crap strewn everywhere the day before. All sorts of broken and rotting things were lying about: chicken bones, leather pieces, wooden bowls, and rodents skittering in and out of it. It was like a garbage dump in here. Henry disappeared up the stairwell, and Alex followed.

On the roof, Henry pointed across the bailey and past the curtain walls. "Look."

People were coming. From all over the island, it seemed, but especially from the village. They carried buckets and brooms, and there were far more of them than Alex had even hoped for. More than twice the number he'd seen yesterday, he was certain.

He muttered to Henry, "We'll need two cows slaughtered today. Get the spits going. And bread. See if we can rustle up some bread. Snag a couple of the women and put them to work at it if you have to." Henry went. "And mead! We'll need mead," Alex called after, then returned his attention to the approaching villagers.

Vassals.

MacConnells and Bretons swarmed over the castle, sweeping, scrubbing, and hauling dead people away to be buried. In addition to the corpse in the family quarters, there were three more dead guys stinking up the kitchen, and one that had fallen in a crevice between a stone slope and the rear wall of the servants' quarters in the inner bailey. Alex set his twenty knights and squires to work bringing wood from the forest, and he himself spent the day going from one villager to the next, meeting people and monitoring the work.

Women carried water from the well in the bailey to the Great Hall, and threw it across the keep floors to loosen up the dried blood. Then they set to scrubbing, some singing as they did so. Alex took a few moments to help carry a bucket, and it was suggested he dump the water down the garderobe.

Then he went down to the barbican to see about the gate on

the quay, and found ash-smeared village men hauling out the burnt remains of outbuildings and throwing them into the sea. Pieces of charred wood floated across the surface of the sea and bumped up against the stone, some tossed onto the rocks along the shore to the west.

Alasdair Ruadh was there, taking measurements on the gatehouse with a knotted cord and the efficient movements of an experienced workman. He was not a bulky man, but had strong, ropy muscles worthy of his craft, and his bright red hair cascaded over his shoulders to fight for attention with the yellowish linen shirt he wore. When the blacksmith saw Alex, he straightened from his work and began talking in Gaelic, but stopped when Alex held up a hand and shook his head. Too fast; Alex wasn't even picking out the words. He looked around for an interpreter, but Henry was off with the woodcutters looking for deadfall and Donnchadh was nowhere near.

Alasdair Ruadh pointed to the burnt gate lying on the ground and shook his head, making a gesture to indicate the thing was useless. "*Neo-fheumail,*" he said carefully so Alex would understand. Okay, Alex had figured that, and nodded. He knelt and pointed to the iron fittings in hopes of salvaging them, and Alasdair crossed his arms and repeated, with strained patience, "*Neo-fheumail.*"

The iron couldn't be reused. So Alex stood and asked, "How much to build another?"

That got a blank look, so Alex drew out his purse from his belt and took a silver penny from it. "How much?" He plundered his memory and attempted it in Gaelic. "*Dé a' phris?*"

Alasdair again shook his head. Then he held up one finger and made a baa like a sheep. "*Caora*"

No money. He wanted livestock. That made sense in a place where there were no shops. Alex put his hand near the ground to indicate the size of a lamb, but Alasdair shook his head again. He put his hand farther up, to indicate a full-grown sheep. Then he put his hands out in front of him to suggest a full belly.

"A pregnant ewe?" *Highwayman.* "No. *Cha bhi.*" Alex shook his head and looked over his livestock. He had plenty of sheep, but he wasn't going to feed Alasdair's ewe until she was bred then hand her over. He pointed to a good-sized animal, then to Alasdair.

The blacksmith thought that over, then nodded and immediately picked up a big, black hammer and began wailing on the twisted iron on the gatehouse. Alex moved on, and decided he really needed to learn to speak better Gaelic if he was going to live here.

As he approached the stairs, he noticed a thin, brown stream coming from a hole at the bottom of the keep wall. It was slow and sludgy, and so far had only made it to the barbican floor, but he could see the old runnel where it would eventually wend its way across the flat and spill out the gate and into the water. It smelled of sewage. He looked up at the keep, visualizing the inside behind that hole, and realized where it was coming from.

"The garderobe." He groaned. Open sewers were okay for other folks here, but he didn't want his bedroom window to look out over this. He'd need to build a duct of some sort and run it out past the wall, away from the quay. He added that project to his growing mental list of things that needed reconstruction.

Then he went looking for Donnchadh, and found him stacking pieces of broken furniture in the hearth, where dried peats were already smoldering atop wood coals. Two beef carcasses had been spitted, and the fire was just beginning to burn well. The hearth ran nearly the length of the room, and could accommodate five such roasts if necessary.

He asked Donnchadh, "Where are the hides?"

The vassal faced him, nearly at attention. "Being made ready for tanning. You'll have them in a few days, sir. The entrails, heads, and hooves are in the kitchen."

"Excellent. Thank you. Donnchadh, is there a rope in the village I can buy? A new one? Long enough and strong enough to replace the one on the hoist outside."

Donnchadh nodded. "I'll need some eggs for it."

"I haven't got any eggs yet." Chickens, from Glasgow where he'd spent most of his gold on supplies and furnishings, but no eggs.

"A single chicken, then. I'll get you the rope you need."

"Perhaps the beef livers waiting in the kitchen?"

Donnchadh's eyebrows went up. "I'll have ye your rope tonight, personally, and a good one."

"Tomorrow will be soon enough, and if it's a heavy rope I'll be pleased. And another thing. How good is Alasdair Ruadh at building things from a diagram?"

Donnchadh frowned. "I'm afraid I dinnae ken the word 'diagram.'"

"A picture. If I drew a picture of something, could Alasdair build it?"

"Oh, aye. He'll make you the best armor you ever had, sir."

"Not armor. I want to redesign that hoist out there. Make it work better."

Donnchadh hesitated, but then nodded. "I think our blacksmith can give you what you desire. He's a talented lad, that one."

"Very well. Tell him when he's finished with the gate I'll want him to come to me about the hoist."

"Aye, sir."

The work about the castle went quickly with so many hands. Alex recruited Donnchadh as his interpreter and began going from villager to villager, learning names and asking questions. He wanted to know who was who, and what was what, and certainly got an earful. Having seen how Sir Hector ruled the people of Barra, he knew his new role included settling disputes among the vassals. Some of them recognized MacDonald as laird, and others recognized MacLeod, but it became clear in the course of the day that they all understood Alex was the guy currently with the power, and both factions did their best to gain his ear.

The MacConnell women complained about the Breton women seducing their men. The Breton women complained that the MacConnell women declined to trade to them goods they needed. The MacConnell men bad-mouthed the Breton men and vice versa, even though most everyone on the island was related on one level or another through intermarriage. It was an incredibly weird network of alliances and enmities.

Each family on the island also seemed to be related to folks on every other island around as well, distantly and not so distantly. Donnchadh spoke to Alex at length on it, spinning out the web of relations, but there was no untangling it all in one day. In addition, Donnchadh had opinions of his own regarding everyone who brought complaints to Alex, and the new master recognized a man with an agenda, for the Bretons rarely came out looking very good. He couldn't put his finger on exactly what lurked there, but there was surely something underlying Donnchadh's helpfulness.

Alex looked into who had worked at the castle before the fall of the English lord, and began recruiting a small staff of people who seemed experienced in the work. Kitchen maids, chamber maids, stable boys, and shepherds came first. He would eventually need specialists for brewing and baking and such, but that could come later.

Tomorrow he would need to sit down with each of the householders in the village and work out whether and how much this labor would figure into the tribute owed to him by his vassals.

"*Vassals.* I still can't get used to it," Alex murmured to Lindsay as they stood in the lord's chamber and watched two village men hammer together the bed he'd had made in Glasgow.

She murmured in reply, "It's not really such a thing as you're making it out to be. In another few centuries they'll be called tenants. Same thing, basically. Just be glad none of them are serfs. Then you'd be a true slave owner and you couldn't hold your head up in America when you returned home."

He grunted and looked at her as he realized she still expected to go home eventually. Was that what was taking her so long to answer his proposal? She first wanted to be certain she wasn't going to see Derek again? His heart crumpled at the thought, and he returned his attention to the workers so she wouldn't see his eyes.

As the workers lifted the feather mattress onto the box frame before hanging the curtains, she asked, "What are you going to use for sheets on this bed?"

You, she'd said. He cut his eyes at her that she didn't sound as if she anticipated sleeping there. "Well . . . I've got twelve humongous bolts of silk. How about silk?"

She smiled. "I suppose the fact you think like them is in some ways a good thing."

He turned to her. "Why do you keep saying that? That I think like them?"

"You do. You fit right in here. It's practically seamless."

"Okay, so I have excellent coping skills."

She appeared amused and irritated at once by his difficulty in seeing her point. "You revel in the system, Alex, and you've become as dark as the times. I even doubt you're as uncomfortable about having vassals as you say you are. I know you get off on being called 'sir' all the time."

"I was an officer in the United States Navy. Of course I like being called 'sir.' Don't you?"

"*Was.* You just said 'was.' You don't think of yourself as a lieutenant anymore. I don't think you even think of yourself as an American anymore."

"America doesn't exist yet. Besides, I should think you'd take that as a good thing."

"I'm not so sure these days."

Then she fell silent and looked away, and Alex didn't know what to say. Finally he said, "But you love me and want to marry me anyway."

She gave him a glance sideways. "Don't, Alex."

Now it was his turn to go quiet.

After a while, she murmured, "I do love you."

He tried to believe it, but just then it was a stretch.

By sunset late that night the castle was livable. Though furniture was scant, it was sufficient for the time being. Alex's bed and its fluffy feather mattress were sheeted and hung with silks of deep red and black. Some tables and benches lined one wall of the Great Hall. Hearths everywhere in the keep blazed with fires that began to work against the dank air, throwing the welcoming scent of wood and peat all through the chambers. The enormous fireside in the Great Hall, aided by torches lined along the walls, made the cavernous room visible, if not exactly cheery.

Like every other castle Alex had been in, the flames threw dancing shadows across walls, furniture and faces, and gave the place a gloomy, cavelike atmosphere. The stench of decayed body fluids was gone, replaced by wintergreen, peat and wood smoke, and burnt grease. The bare walls echoed every spoken word, but the floors had been strewn with reeds that acted as a sort of air-freshening carpet. The green smell they loosed into the rooms when crushed was as pleasant and earthy as mowed hayfield. Alex gazed across the Great Hall filled with people, and felt a part of it: the shifting darkness as well as the fiery light, the strength of stone, and the fragility of the lives now placed in his command and care.

As promised, the master of the castle provided a plentiful

feast for the workers. Partiers spilled from the Great Hall into the courtyard outside, eating and laughing and talking. Rustic music echoed from the steep, rocky hillsides surrounding the castle, and there was a great deal of dancing and singing. Alex understood little of the talk, but Sir Henry assured him he'd made a favorable impression on his villagers.

The party was well begun when the blast of trumpet from the watch heralded an approach from the water. Alex climbed to the battlement to look, and found off in the moonlight a sail, making its way toward the quay. It was a small fishing vessel, not large enough to give him concern for attack, so Alex only stood and watched until the boat was about to dock. Then he hurried down the stairs, wended his way among the guests through the Great Hall, then down the rest of the way to the barbican. Sir Henry followed him without being asked, and they picked up the watchmen at the barbican gate on their way to the quay. Alex strode onto it with four men behind him and his broadsword hung at his side. It might have behooved him to don his armor, but he realized when he saw the boat up close he probably wouldn't even need his sword.

The pilot of the boat stayed on board, and the only passenger to venture onto the quay was a black-robed priest. The man was armed, a cross-hilt sword hung from a belt that bunched his robe around his hips, but his broad smile and otherwise empty hands were reassuring.

"Good evening, my son!" The priest was young, and appeared happy to have arrived at his destination. Alex crossed his arms over his chest and wondered if the guy had found the island he'd intended. Two days earlier, and there would have been nobody here but villagers. "Welcome to Eilean Aonarach, Father. I'm the laird here. What might I do for you?"

The priest blushed and glanced around. "Forgive me if I've taken you from your supper, my lord—"

"Sir. Alasdair. I'm Alasdair an Dubhar MacNeil."

"Indeed, sir, I'd heard there was a new master of this island, and I've certainly heard your name before. I've come to offer myself for your chapel. If the post isn't already occupied, I mean."

Behind the priest, the fisherman on the boat threw a satchel, then a wooden trunk, onto the quay. It thudded with the weight of a well-packed box. Plainly the priest was quite ready to move in, and the ferryman was impatient to be on his way.

Alex said to the priest, "Where are you from?"

"The Isle of Man." He added hopefully, "But I'm educated in France."

Alex knew it was rare for a priest to be educated at all, but also knew the credential could be a two-edged sword, depending on what he'd been taught so far from Scotland. "You're very young."

"Wise beyond my years and eager to serve." His hand rested on the pommel of his sword, which gave him more of a mercenary look than spiritual. Oddly enough, Alex found that comforting. Good attitude, but the temptation to decline was nevertheless strong. Alex was not religious and felt the church stuck its nose into far too many corners of a man's life for anyone's good.

On the other hand, he understood that a priest who was "eager to serve" him would be an important asset in maintaining control of his island. The people of the island had a need—even his knights, who never openly admitted dependence on anyone or anything—for a religious presence among them. Lack of a priest in his employ was a power vacuum he could ill afford to ignore. He said, "Release your boatman. Come eat with us, and you and I can talk. If we fail to come to terms, I'll return you safely to Man and no harm done."

The priest's smile widened, turning even more boyish, and the tension in his body released. Alex counted the young man's transparency as a point in his favor. "Thank you, sir!"

Alex gestured for his men to pick up the priest's belongings, and as the fisherman shoved off they made their way into the keep.

The priest's name was Patrick, and it was apparent he'd not eaten that day. He fell upon the plate of meat offered to him, with nary a word of thanks to God or anyone else. Then, his mouth crammed with food, he made his case to Alex about the need for a priest to guide the people in the way of life pleasing to Jesus Christ the Savior. For Alex it was enough the man was young and hungry, and apparently sincere in his eagerness to serve. He let the talk spin out, nodding in the right places, then allowed as Patrick was right about the need for someone like him on Eilean Aonarach.

He offered the rectory in the chapel, and explained that due to the condition of the castle and his recent arrival, the priest would be on his own for cleaning, furnishing, and maintaining the accommodations for the time being. The joy and gratitude on the young man's face was so effusive and heartfelt, it made Alex wonder if providence may actually have been at work in the man's life today.

Patrick, having eaten, was given leave to his new rectory. As he went, Alex glanced over at Lindsay, who sat at a far table with the lesser knights, and noted she was watching the priest leave, a look of wariness on her face. Then she turned toward Alex with a question in her eyes. He looked away.

The evening continued, and nearly everyone was slipping into drunkenness. Alex, though, had stayed sober, watching Lindsay and taking glances at her whenever he dared. When she made her way to the public garderobe off the hall, he rose from his table and headed there also.

The small room was empty, and Alex jammed a stool against the door to make certain nobody followed. Lindsay, untying her trews, turned to see who had come in behind her. Alex took her face between his hands and kissed her.

One hand held up her pants, and she murmured against his mouth, "You've brought a priest so you can force me to marry you?"

He leaned back, surprised. "No."

"He just showed up here, out of the blue?"

"Yes." Alex stepped back to search her face in the flickering sconce light.

"Fairly stiff coincidence, I'd say."

The accusation caught Alex flat-footed. He blinked and gaped, then said, "Maybe it's God working in mysterious ways."

"Suddenly you're a believer?"

"You're not?"

"I am. But don't you dare use that to—"

"No. I'm not. I swear."

"That doesn't work on me. I know bet—"

"Hey." He placed a finger over her lips. "The guy showed up because he'd heard we were coming here. He'd been on the look-out for a flock, and heard through the ecclesiastical grapevine

there was a castle chapel with a new master. It wasn't even coincidence."

The question left her eyes. "Oh. Very well, then."

"You don't want to marry me?"

"I don't wish to be forced."

Irritation rose. "If I were going to do that, I would have done it already."

"That's a relief."

Now he wasn't certain whether she meant that, or if she was being a smart-ass. He kissed her again, and she let him. He slipped a hand inside her open trews, and she let him do that, too. She pressed against him so he stroked her, but when he tried to shove the trews from her hips, she balked.

"No."

"Yes." It had been far too long. He was quite ready to lift her and take her against the stone wall.

"Not here." She held his hand and drew it from between her legs. Reluctantly he obeyed and stepped back again so she could restore her clothing.

"Then, when?"

"I don't know. But someplace that doesn't smell like a latrine and with people outside waiting to get in."

"Marry me."

"I'm thinking."

"Think hard."

"I am. But I'll have to start sleeping with the men now."

Alex's mind slipped a gear, and he gaped at her. *"Excuse me?"*

She gazed across at him, blank for a moment, then realization of what she'd said struck. Her eyes went wide and she laid fingers over her mouth. "Oh. No. I mean, I need to reside in the barracks now that there is one."

He blinked. That was better, but he was still puzzled. "Why?"

"Do you want a recurrence of what happened with Hector? Or worse, with his mother?"

He made a face. "No. But how are you going to keep them from seeing? Your . . . you know, bandages."

She shrugged. "I'll manage."

Alex hated the idea. No way did he want her sleeping among

the men, away from his protection, where a bad slip might mean disaster and she could be attacked if the truth were discovered. The urge to make his case for marriage was nearly unbearable. But he'd already done that. Now he kept silent, waiting for the reply she'd promised.

CHAPTER 17

For several days Alex was kept busy attending to the business of making his castle functional. One by one the men of the island came to pledge their allegiance to him by kneeling before him and reciting an oath. Alex kept track of who had pledged, by carrying around a sheet of parchment and a charred stick with which he wrote their names. Later he would make a permanent record with quill and ink, and that would be the basis of an island census once he knew how many children each man had. He was already on his way to mapping out the social structure among the vassals.

He'd noticed the villagers and the island farmers didn't seem to have suffered much from the lack of a garrison, and surely didn't miss the English garrison commander who'd lost his life there at the hands of the MacDonalds and MacLeods. It made him think his own men were as unwelcome, but one day he made a comment to Donnchadh to the effect that the village folk were bearing up well under the burden of a castle full of men to be fed. MacConnell's reply was bland.

"With all respect, sir, ye noblemen have your purpose. Better you and your men to be the ones protecting the island than we bearing naught but pitchforks and dirks. We small folk being allowed no swords, we're happy enough for the presence of them as are skilled in fighting."

Alex asked, "From whom do you need such constant protection? MacLeod? MacDonald? Someone else?"

Donnchadh looked at him as if he'd said something incredibly stupid. "See who comes first to claim this island from you, or to reive our livestock, and you'll have your answer. See who wants the garrison for himself."

"Do you hope for one of them to come?"

"I hope to tend my land and raise my family."

"A man of peace?"

"A man of prudence."

"And if MacDonald or MacLeod were to come? Who would you support?"

Donnchadh grinned. "Why, my liege, of course. I've pledged my allegiance to you, have I not?"

Alex nodded, but he wondered.

He hardly saw Lindsay that week. She lived and worked with the men, ate at the other end of the room, and socialized with knights closer to her own rank, most of whom had also been knighted at Bannockburn. During those meals he would sit at the head table and try not to stare at her, but his eyes frequently drifted to where she sat. He never caught her looking at him.

As with the priest in search of an empty chapel, it didn't take long before there were visits from folks who'd heard a young, handsome, unmarried knight with good prospects had taken possession of Eilean Aonarach. Alex had been in residence only five days before a large, nicely turned-out boat came, bearing the hopeful father of a young maiden. A Mackay, from the far north, and he had come a long way.

"Crap," Alex muttered when he learned who awaited him in the Great Hall and why. At the moment he was occupied with the installation of a pulley on the hoist over the barbican, and was neither in a mood for company, nor was he dressed for it. He'd seen the boat coming, but had hoped it carried only a messenger who could be fed then sent on his way with a reply.

Trusting Alasdair Ruadh to continue the job without him, Alex went to the Great Hall to greet his not particularly welcome guest, and decided he was as well dressed as he was going to get today and too bad if the visitor didn't like it. "Good morning to you, Mr. Mackay," he greeted as he emerged from the stairwell and strode across the stone floor.

Standing about, looking as if they were appraising the building, Mackay and his entourage turned at the sound of his voice to offer smiles and greetings.

Alex sent a maid to the kitchen for some mead and cold meat. "You must be hungry." Nobody ever turned down food in this country, even if they weren't hungry. Neither would Alex, anymore. "Come and sit." He directed his visitor's servants to follow the maid so they could eat in the kitchen, then waved a hand at one of the plain chairs nearby, and pulled up another for himself. "If you'll excuse the poor furnishings, I've been here less than a week and don't expect to be so lacking for much longer."

Oddly, Mackay seemed pleased by that. He was the shortest, roundest man Alex had ever seen in this or any other century, and his tiny, dark eyes seemed magnetically drawn toward his own long, pointed nose. Alex shuddered to think what the daughter must look like. Surely this was a waste of time, and he hated to lead this guy on, but the aspersions cast on his sexuality in the past made him too cautious to dismiss this overture out of hand. He entertained himself with a fantasy that the daughter might be a beautiful and sweet and terribly unappreciated stepchild.

Mackay settled himself and adjusted his seat with care so he might not tumble out of the chair as he said, "Sir Alasdair, I hope I bring you good news." His toes barely touched the floor, and he balanced himself on his perch with the balls of his feet.

"Perhaps you do."

The man beamed and looked around at the hall. "I have it you are well thought of in certain important circles."

"I'm a royal vassal, on good terms with His Majesty. I'm glad to hear my reputation is what I thought."

That brought a chuckle. "A confident man, as well. I expect you're a very important knight in Robert's service."

The buttering was thick and enthusiastic. Alex wished this guy would get to the point, say his piece, and get the hell out. "I'm told . . ." Food was brought from the kitchen, and a table moved from against the wall to serve them where they sat. "I'm told you are here to speak to me of your daughter."

"Indeed. My beautiful daughter. A fine girl, sheltered like a princess her entire life. Disposition sweet as honey, and never a harsh word for anyone." Mackay picked up a bowl of mead and drank from it.

Alex pictured a spoiled, fat, beady-eyed little girl without the slightest clue to life's realities. But he said only, "I'm sure she's very charming." Noncommittal. This was a negotiation. Alex already knew it would come to nothing, but he needed to make it look good for a little while.

"Och, more than charming. The birds come to roost on her shoulders."

A sudden flash of a Disney movie made Alex nearly burst forth with laughter. He blinked it back and bit his lip, then said, "How sweet."

"You certainly must be looking for a wife, now that you have an estate. And with the north secured from the English I see prosperous times ahead."

Alex saw them, too, but with Lindsay. "How old is your daughter?" It occurred to him the girl's name hadn't yet been mentioned.

"She'll be twenty-three on her next birthday."

Damn. Neither too old nor too young. No quick rejection there. Alex cleared his throat and said, "And what about her father? Tell me about yourself."

Mackay was pleased to launch into a recital of his own accomplishments as a merchant. He was apparently quite wealthy, and heavily connected to the widely known MacKenzies. His son was married to the daughter of another royal vassal in Sutherland. Alex listened with an ear for something he could use, and as Mackay talked the meat and cheese on the nearby table disappeared. It was astonishing how long a man could go on about himself. Alex was yawning long before it was finished. Very early on he'd noted the man's family tree and figured he knew how to get rid of him.

When Mackay finally led the subject back around to his daughter, Alex made a show of thinking hard and preparing to say something difficult.

"Well, you see, as you said earlier it's true my prospects for the future are excellent." Mackay smiled, but not as brightly as before. The guy was a salesman, and surely could smell the rejection coming as Alex continued. "Most excellent, in fact. I have money, land, and my influence is growing. Also, I don't know if you're aware, but my father was a nobleman."

"Aye." The eyes were wary now. "I would point out that I am also aware you go unacknowledged."

"But I am acknowledged. I arrived from the Continent too late to know my father; nevertheless his sons call me brother. And so you can see that I might have higher hopes than to marry into the merchant class."

Quickly Mackay pressed on. "Let us at least arrange a meeting."

That gave Alex pause. Apparently the girl was pretty enough her father thought her presence could sway this decision. So he said, "It's early yet. I'm only just beginning to settle into my new home. Perhaps in a few months—"

"My daughter does not grow younger."

"Nor any of us. And were she to find happiness elsewhere in the meantime I would wish her all good fortune and many healthy children. But if in six months neither of us is married to someone else, then I will meet her."

Mackay now smiled, apparently relieved to have salvaged that much. "Very well. Six months, then."

Alex gestured to a maid standing by. "Mary will show you to the guest quarters."

"I'm afraid I must hurry on my way." Mackay stood. "Business never slows, you see." He puffed up his chest and took a tone as if Alex should be impressed by his industry.

"I do see. Then have a safe and prosperous journey." Alex stood, and Mary escorted Mackay and his entourage toward the barbican and Mackay's boat. Alex watched them go.

"That was graceful."

Alex turned to find Lindsay standing behind, just within earshot of his conversation with Mackay. "You heard all that?"

She nodded and approached him. "Am I to take this as an ultimatum? Six months?"

There was a long silence as he gazed into her eyes and she searched his face. He thought of how much he loved her, but that he couldn't bear to be left hanging forever. Or even six more months. Finally he decided.

"Yes."

There was no expression on her face. No apparent reaction

at all. Then he turned on his heel and left the Great Hall to see
how work was coming on the hoist, and hardened himself to
what she might be thinking now.

He didn't see her for the rest of the day, not even at dinner.

That night as he retired to his quarters he found a sheet of
parchment folded in thirds slipped under the door to his inner
chamber. He looked back to the residence antechamber, but nobody was near, not even the maid. Then he stared at the thing as
it lay there by his feet, wondering whether he really wanted to
know what it would tell him. His pulse picked up enough to
make him uncomfortable, and his hands felt cold. Finally he
took a deep breath, picked up the note, and closed himself into
the bedchamber. He bolted the door with a heavy bar as was his
habit. Then he sat on the edge of the bed to read the page by the
light of his candle.

It was a formal letter. The words were odd but legible, and he
could make out the weird spellings in the Middle English. As he
deciphered, his puzzled frown dissolved and he smiled, for it
was from a Marilyn Pawlowski, expressing her intent to visit
and placing her estimated date of arrival in Glasgow at a week
hence. The maiden Pawlowski suggested a desire for her brother
to meet her there, and further expressed pleasure at the prospect
of seeing once again her foster brother, Alexander MacNeil, to
whom the letter was addressed.

Warmth spread from Alex's belly to every extremity, and
his heart tripped madly in his chest. The joy of it nearly made
him laugh out loud, and he said to himself, "Okay, we'll call
that a 'yes.'"

The very next day, Lindsay was dispatched on a fishing boat
to Barra. There she would place herself under the care of the
laird and request help with their plan. They needed her to travel
with him and some carefully chosen MacNeils to the shore of
the mainland, where the retainers would remain on the boat
while Hector and Lindsay went alone to stay with some MacIan
cousins for a day or so. Then on the way back to the coast,
Lindsay would make her change and return to Eilean Aonarach
as Marilyn.

While she was gone, Alex occupied himself with organizing
his castle, training his horses, improving his Gaelic, and jogging for exercise. It felt good to run again; it had been an aw-

fully long time since he'd run for pleasure. As he exited the outer bailey and headed out onto the pasture and toward the forest, the peace of being alone settled in and he was glad to rediscover what his body could do for itself.

As he passed a small patch of farmland, a shout went up and he saw the farmer wave a pitchfork at him. Alex waved back, but the man took off at a run to intercept him, plaid flying. So Alex slowed to find out what the man wanted.

"Whatever is the matter, sir?" The MacConnell farmer ran up to him, breathless and holding his chest.

The language, of course, was Gaelic, and Alex took a moment to regain his breath and decipher in his head. Then he constructed a reply in the local language.

"Nothing. Nothing's the matter."

"Why do you flee?"

Alex chuckled and shook his head. "Not fleeing. Running. I like it." He jogged in place a few steps to demonstrate how much he liked it.

The man stepped back and looked at him with a light of distrust in his eyes, as if Alex had confessed to being in league with the devil. "You enjoy it, you say?"

"Aye. It's good for my heart." He stopped himself from suggesting the farmer should try it himself, for he figured the guy probably got plenty of exercise every day. "It keeps my wind good. I can fight long."

That was something a Scot could understand, and the farmer nodded. "Aye. Then by all means run far and fast. Never let me stop you."

Alex grinned, waved farewell, and resumed his jog.

Farther on, another farmer stopped him, and he repeated his explanation, then chuckled to himself as he ran onward and into the thickest part of forest along the north side of the island.

It was very thick, and dark. The track here was barely discernible, and took him over fallen logs covered deep in moss. He almost felt like a horse in a steeplechase, there were so many obstacles in the path. Then he hopped over a row of toadstools.

Toadstools. He skidded to a halt in the grass, panting hard. Sweat trickled down his back and along the sides of his jaw so it tickled, and he wiped it with his sleeve. Turning, he saw the fungus made a circle. Like the one where he and Lindsay had seen the faerie. He wondered, and looked around. The faerie folk were real. He knew it. Had seen it. Could one be living here? Could it be the same one? But there was nothing and nobody about. The forest was quiet, the fauna gone still and silent at his intrusion. *Nobody home but us chickens.* He shook his head and continued his run.

From the time Lindsay left Eilean Aonarach, the journey took a little over three weeks. By then summer was waning, the weather had begun to lose its warmth, and the days were normalizing toward the equinox. After many days of keeping an eye out to sea in hopes of spotting Hector's boat, Alex heard a shout from the south of the keep. There was a boat.

He ran to an arrow loop over the barbican to find a sail approaching the quay, and his pulse surged. He shouted to the servants to present themselves to aid Hector and his entourage, then amid the scurrying ran down the stairs and out to the barbican. Breathless with excitement, he arrived at the quay just as Hector was helping Lindsay from the boat. He came to a halt, stunned, and stared.

She was gorgeous. Light rust-colored silk to her ankles, the sleeves tight to her forearms, where they widened so dramatically they nearly brushed the ground. Over that was a tunic of red wool so dark as to be nearly black, shorter and short-sleeved. At her neck were the rubies from Carlisle, glittering gold and blood red against her pale skin, and a headdress the color of her dress covered her hair and framed her face in reddish-brown silk and a drape of gold chains. Her naturally red lips picked up the color of the stones in the necklace, and he barely resisted the urge to kiss them then and there.

For a year she'd been a convincing boy, had moved like a boy and had sounded like one. But now, dressed as she was in silk and gold, and layered with linen beneath, she displayed an innate elegance. An aristocratic grace so refined she put to shame even the king's mistresses. Alex marveled, and knew everyone who saw her would admire her as much. While her belongings and Hector's were unloaded from the boat he said, "Miss Marilyn."

"Sir Alexander."

He reached out to take her hand and kiss it. Then he straightened and looked into her eyes. She gazed back, her eyes the softest and deepest blue of any he could recall seeing. Her happiness was plain. It made him smile. "How was your journey?"

"Tiring."

Hector said, "Greetings, brother. My journey was tiring as well; I thank you for asking. Never mind me. I'll go find my way around and eat whatever I might discover."

Jerked back to himself, Alex greeted his nominal brother with great, sincere joy. It was good to see him, for he was what passed for family in this century, and Hector had proven to be a good friend as well as a stalwart brother. "So, Hector, did all go well?"

"Smooth as morning milk. And you can see the results are remarkable."

Alex looked at Lindsay. "Indeed they are."

His former squire blushed.

Inside the castle, they were met by the head chambermaid. Alex said, "Mary, take Miss Marilyn to the guest bedchamber."

"Off the anteroom?"

Alex hesitated. It would be so sweet to put Lindsay in one of his private rooms where she could come and go to his bedchamber unseen. But the very proximity would cause everyone on the island to assume she was sneaking into his bed at night. Even now, the light in Mary's eyes seemed to assume his intention. The assumption was correct, but that was beside the point. He wanted to at least appear to do this by the book. So he said, "No. The larger one off the receiving room. Let Sir Hector take the private bedchamber."

"Aye, sir."

"And see Miss Marilyn is made comfortable. I notice she's traveling without attendants of her own. Assign one of your girls as her maid. Whatever she wants, see she gets it.

"Aye, sir." Mary peered at Lindsay as if trying to place her face.

Alex explained, hurrying to guide her perceptions before the recognition would be complete, "Miss Marilyn is Sir Lindsay Pawlowski's sister."

Mary's eyes lit and she smiled. "Aye. A strong family resemblance. Welcome to Eilean Aonarach, Miss."

Lindsay murmured thanks. Mary hurried to comply with her master's orders, and Lindsay glanced back at Alex with a slight

frown as she followed the maid. He knew she wouldn't like
sleeping in that windowless room, but there was nothing for it.
Regardless of what they might actually do during this courtship,
she couldn't openly stay in the lord's suite until she was married
to him.

Soon. Soon everyone would know what she meant to him.

Meat was on the hearth and smelled nearly ready, so Alex
went to his own chamber to clean up. Then he met Lindsay and
Hector in the common room in the apartments to escort her up
the stairs to the Great Hall. As they ascended to the room where
Alex's knights awaited dinner, heads turned at the sight of the
woman on Alex's arm.

As one, the assemblage stood and bowed. Alex struggled to
disguise his pleasure at the wide eyes of the men who gazed
upon Lindsay. He couldn't allow anyone to see him smile, for a
whopping lie had to be told before he could let anyone know
how he felt about her.

Lindsay reached out to snag the sleeve of his tunic. Her tension was palpable, and there was good reason for it. This could
go very badly if she were recognized.

Alex stepped forward, composed his face into the most
somber expression he could manage, and hoped he could pull
this off. Lindsay was right; he wasn't a good liar. "Men, I'm
afraid I have some bad news. Sir Lindsay, our youngest knight,
is no longer with us."

Complete silence fell, and Hector filled it. "Allow me to tell
the story, brother, for I was there and saw the terrible thing with
my very eyes."

Alex nodded and gratefully stepped back to stand with Lindsay so Hector could continue. He gazed at the floor in what he
hoped was a somber posture.

"After meeting the poor lad's young sister on the mainland,
and on our way to bring her here, during our travels over steep
terrain we were beset by robbers. They were enormous villains,
strong and determined to have us." Hector gestured to indicate
just how big and terrible those men had been, and his voice rose
and fell with the drama of his tale. "In the struggle on the high
path through the mountains, the brave young knight lost his
footing. Though I reached for him, and nearly caught him, I
couldnae hold him. His fingers slipped from mine and he went

over the cliff, falling to the bottom of a deep gorge where it was impossible to descend to retrieve his poor, broken body."

The utter seriousness of Hector's demeanor nearly made Alex laugh. He bit the inside of his lower lip until he thought he could taste blood. A dark murmur riffled through the gathering at Hector's news, and the laird let it die before going on.

"He was a brave young man, and we'll miss him terribly. He fought well and killed many enemy in the fight against King Edward, was wounded and nearly died in the crucial battle for freedom from the English at Bannockburn, and he was a good and true squire, and loyal knight, to my brother and his own foster brother, Alasdair an Dubhar. Let it be known he died protecting his sister from a foul robber, who, I assure you, fell with him in the struggle and now burns in hell. Sir Lindsay Pawlowski surely lived in grace and resides in heaven." Heads nodded.

"As for his sister, though her heart was broken to lose her brother, and she would have ended her journey at once to return home, I've convinced her to visit with her foster brother for a time. So sad to come all this way and not see the delightful and comely castle of Eilean Aonarach." The knights, squires, and kitchen maids laughed.

Alex smiled at Lindsay and said, "For which I am mightily grateful. It's been so long since I've seen this woman, who was very young when I left the eastern mountains for the last time. So, all of you, I wish you to make the maiden Marilyn Pawlowski feel welcome."

A murmur riffled through the room.

Sir Orrin muttered something, just loud enough for the men near him to hear and laugh. Alex figured he'd better call him on it. "What did you say, Orrin?"

The knight stared at Lindsay for a moment, then shifted his weight like a chastised schoolboy and said, "A woman traveling alone. I welcome her with body and soul."

Nobody in the room moved, not even Hector. Everyone knew it had been said only partly in jest and also that it was a deadly insult any way one looked at it. They waited to see what Alex would do.

The lord of the castle stared hard at Orrin, sauntered a few steps toward him, then said with a keen edge to his voice, "Miss

Pawlowski's father was my foster father. He was as fine a knight as I've ever known, and his daughter's reputation is utterly above reproach. Her escort turned back toward home at Lindsay's death, and so now she is under my protection. Make no mistake, I take that responsibility most seriously and will dispatch without hesitation any man who suggests Sir Lindsay's sister is less than pure of heart, pristine of body, and of perfect grace in the eyes of God." He looked around the room and found nobody willing to challenge that. "And the first man to treat her as other than a lady of finest breeding will taste my sword. Orrin, I say you should look to your own state of grace rather, and not be slandering an innocent woman."

Again, no reply.

Alex's voice suddenly light and cheerful, he called out across the room, "So. Someone bring us our meat. Miss Pawlowski has had a long, tiring journey and needs to refresh herself and rest."

The knights, and their squires standing by, returned to their seats and their private conversations, and glances at Lindsay made it clear many of those conversations were about the dead knight's beautiful sister. Alex, Hector, and Lindsay took places at the head table at the end of the hearth. Alex looked around at the admiring stares in the room, and he smiled. If only he could tell them all she was already spoken for.

Lindsay seemed relaxed in the relative safety, away from the men against whom she had always been on guard. Now she was able to laugh and joke, and when she looked at Alex it was with the eyes she had once dared not show when others were around. His attention could be fully on her, and throughout the meal he feasted his eyes. For the first time since they'd met he was permitted to look at her in public without guarding his expression, and he reveled in it. The smiles came easily this evening.

Over the next days as they established their relationship, they spent long hours in the public areas of the keep and on walks along the seaside cliffs, talking in low voices of the future and of the past. Alex found himself opening up in ways he never had before, and told stories of his flight training and shipboard practical jokes, of buddies who had died and of the prospects he'd had back home. Those were all gone now, and flying seemed like a dream he'd had from which he'd awakened. Lindsay spoke of her ambitions as a writer, also gone.

"You can still write," he told her. They were on the battlement atop the keep, looking out over the silver water to the south. Alex leaned against the stone and turned to drink in the beauty of her profile as she stared into the distance with a stillness he found astonishing. The September sunshine peeking between clouds was golden on her skin, slanting even in mid-afternoon and precious for its scarcity.

"Write what? Who would read it? And who would bother copying it to be read? There's no printing press. And nobody here would take seriously anything written by a woman in any case."

"You could write it for posterity."

She snorted and glanced at him, then returned her gaze to the horizon. "And have it destroyed as fanciful nonsense immediately upon my death? There's something to work toward."

"Why do you need it to be read? Why not just write it?"

Her voice took on a *duh* tone he'd learned over the past year to ignore. "There's no point if nobody reads it. For that, I might as well just sit around and think. That's no way to live."

"There are worse things."

"Like bashing in skulls with a mace for a living."

That stung. "It got us where we are. More important, it's kept us alive."

He waited while she thought it over. Then she said, "I suppose there are even worse things than being a soldier."

There was another very long silence, then Alex said, "I wish you could be happy."

Now she looked him in the eye. "Don't expect me to love this place the way you do. I don't understand these people, and hope never to understand them. They're dirty and rude, and they frighten me." She looked down at her hands, which had knotted together with her tension. Slowly she unclenched her fingers. "When I was fighting, sometimes I found myself glad to kill them, they disgust me so. And I hate myself for that."

He had been as glad to kill his enemies, and hated only the enemies. It puzzled him she could be so confused about something so simple. "You think folks in the twenty-first century were more pure of heart? More honorable?"

"They didn't smell nearly as bad."

Alex chuckled. "There is that, I guess. If you think smelling bad is a capital offence."

Lindsay chuckled and shrugged. "What I really mean is that I don't know these people and I don't think I'll ever know them or understand them. I just don't get how they can stand to live the way they do."

"Look around, Lindsay. How else would they live? For most of them life is a contest to see who gets to eat."

"I've gone without eating since we've been here, and I haven't turned into a barbarian."

"But, as you have pointed out to me in the past, you know another life is possible. They don't."

"You're right, I do. I know I'm not like them, and I can't be like them."

Slowly, carefully, in a voice as scarce as the fall sunshine, he said, "I guess it's a good thing you're going to marry someone from your own time."

There was no reply. She only continued to gaze out over the water.

AFTER the equinox, a boat came from the mainland carrying four knights wishing to pledge loyalty to Alex. Also, they brought news of MacLeod's intentions against Eilean Aonarach.

"The MacLeod claims your island," said one as he planked himself atop a table in the Great Hall. His chain mail shussed and rowel spurs jingled. He was a Ross, cousin to the woman who had married Edward Bruce several years before but nevertheless quite landless. By his poverty, his attitude, and his manners, Alex pegged him as a very distant cousin.

"So does MacDonald," replied the master of Eilean Aonarach.

"But MacLeod is gathering an attack even now."

Alex sat up. "How do you know this?"

Ross pointed a thumb toward one of his men. "Fearghas here. His wife is a MacLeod and her brothers boast they will have land here by Samhain."

Halloween. The attack would be soon. For a moment, Alex wondered why he was being warned, but then quickly answered his own question. Ross was landless, and would expect gratitude. But Alex feigned naïveté to force the knight to state his position in words. "What is it that brings you here, then?"

Ross blinked and stammered that the answer should be obvious. "I and my men will fight them with you. We hear you are a man of good sense and know the value of loyalty."

"Loyalty must be proven."

"It must also be fed, or it will die."

"You would be my tacksman?"

Ross nodded.

"And if the attack doesn't come?"

"It will. The MacLeods will not let this land fall to the Mac-Neils. The attack will come. After Samhain, after Martinmas, after Christmas, but it will come."

It didn't take a rocket scientist or a crystal ball to know the man was probably right. Alex said, "Very well. Take your men to the barracks. Once you've proven yourself, we'll talk again."

"I would like—"

"I'm a reasonable man, as you said. We'll talk later."

Ross accepted that, nodded, and took his men into the bailey.

Hector stayed on during these weeks, enjoying the same hospitality he'd extended to Alex the winter before. Alex and Lindsay needed him to aid the game of making it appear the friendship between Sir Alasdair and Miss Marilyn had become a marriage negotiation.

There could be no courtship in the sense of hearts and flowers, for the sort of marriage that would make sense to the people around them was arranged only according to benefits of property and status. Alex and Lindsay let his knights and the villagers think she was considering marrying him for his money, his authority as royal vassal, and his prospects for the future as a knight in Robert's service. But it was impossible to hide his joy in engagement to Lindsay. More than once over the next few weeks Alex was cautioned by Sir Henry to beware of his heart leading his head.

After three weeks of courtship, Alex and Lindsay became publicly engaged to be married. The wedding ceremony was set to take place in the chapel of his castle.

Alex found Hector in the quarters anteroom and invited him

to sit before the fire. "It's settled. We're going to be married as soon as the banns have been said." Another three weeks, and Alex thought he would lose his mind with the waiting.

Hector smiled wide and slapped Alex on the back. " 'Tis the wisest thing for the both of you, lad. You'll keep out of trouble. Also, a woman like that will give you strong children."

Children. Alex realized they would not only be possible now, but expected. It struck him breathless for a moment as he rubbed a finger across his chin, hard, as the future seemed to widen before him. He said, "Aye. She's nothing if not strong."

"So long as you're the stronger one, lad. Never let her control you, or you'll be a sorry man in your household and on the field." Meaning, of course, that Alex's men wouldn't respect him if he appeared henpecked.

"Lin . . . Marilyn has a sensibility other women do not. She behaves reasonably and thinks rationally. I'll do well to attend to her counsel."

"But always within limits."

"Of course."

"And you would do well to temper your feeling for her as soon as possible."

That brought Alex up short. "Temper my feeling?"

"I've seen the way you look at her. You've the dewy-eyed look for her seen only in men who will have a broken heart. For no woman ever loved a man in return. It's naught but your protection and your position she wants."

"You don't know what she wants."

Hector laughed. "I do. It's what every woman requires in marriage. Safety and comfort. She doesn't need your love at all, and you're a fool to give it to her for her to abuse. Give her your rud only, and keep your heart for your own, so you willnae end up hating her when she breaks it."

Alex considered his next words for a moment, then said, "I admire her. She reads and writes, you know."

Hector fell silent and stared. "Does she?" Alex nodded. "Do you?"

"Of course, I do."

Astonishment deepened on Hector's face. "There's no 'of course' about it, for I do not."

"How do you keep your accounts, then?"

Now Hector looked as if Alex had just lapsed into speaking Chinese. "Accounts? I know what is owed to me and what I owe to others. A man doesn't need to read for that."

"I see."

Hector sat up in his chair. "You read? Latin?"

"English."

"How could you read and not have Latin?"

Good question. Alex summoned a lie. "My foster father had very odd ideas about what would be useful to me in my life here, and only had me learn English." And he'd learned it poorly, by the standard of everyone he'd met here.

Hector made a disparaging noise at the absurdity of learning to read English.

That day the MacNeil laird sent for his family, tacksmen, and additional servants to join him and attend him at the wedding celebration. In a few days his boat came with his wife and children, and the sons of Alasdair Og as well as the MacNeil sisters who were not yet married. Mama MacNeil stayed home, and for that Alex was grateful.

While the castle staff made the MacNeil laird's family comfortable in the lord's chambers and his armed retinue in the barracks, Hector came to Alex in the outer meeting room beneath the Great Hall, where he sat with Sir Henry discussing watch rotation. Hector had the eldest son of Alasdair Og in tow. "Brother, I've made a decision."

"Regarding what?" Alex dismissed Henry and gestured for Hector to sit at the end of the table with him by the small hearth, while the boy stood by at attention. Gregor was seven, and since Alex had seen him last he'd grown what appeared to be a foot in height. His father's death seemed to have sobered the boy, and when Alex looked at him he gazed back with a sharp, steady eye.

"Young Gregor is now old enough to enter service as a page. I wish to let you take him."

At first Alex didn't understand. Take him where? But then it clicked that Hector wanted Alex to be the boy's foster father and master. And it was plain Hector considered it an honor he was bestowing. Flabbergasted, he somehow managed a smile. "You honor me." He wished he hadn't sounded so hesitant. But if Hector noticed, he gave no indication.

"You will teach him to fight well, and to use his mind against his enemies. And if he were to learn something of letters along the way, so much the better."

Alex nodded. Declining wasn't an option. To refuse this offer would damage forever his standing with Hector, and he was in need of allies these days. Besides, as he considered it, he realized it truly was an honor. "Aye. Thank you. He'll be taught well, and he'll grow to be a fine squire and knight."

Deal closed. Alex felt a surge of pride as he looked at his new ruddy-cheeked foster son, who smiled in return at the prospect of learning from Sir Alasdair an Dubhar how to become a man.

ALEX and Lindsay were married two days before Martinmas, joined in matrimony in an interminable, tedious wedding Mass at the hands of Father Patrick, in the castle chapel. The wedding feast, on the other hand, was an enormous, festive affair for the small island, held in the pasture outside the gatehouse. The high revelry surged into the bailey and even into the Great Hall where music played and guests danced. Nobody wanted to miss the celebration of the laird's wedding; free food was rare in these times, and reasons for joy nearly as scarce. But Alex barely noticed the other people; he only had eyes for his bride.

Lindsay seemed happy, her cheeks pink and her wide smile bright. It was a sweet moment of his life, when it seemed he might never have been or done anything but this. He was Sir Alasdair an Dubhar MacNeil of Eilean Aonarach, and that was a very good thing. And finally Lindsay was his wife. In this time and place marriage was forever, and he was entirely cool with that.

Attempting together the intricate moves of a local dance by the hearth in the Great Hall, Lindsay's eyes sparkled and her cheeks flushed with the same excitement Alex felt skittering all through his body. He wanted to laugh aloud with joy, but instead he leaned in to kiss her.

"It will be a fiery ending."

The hair stood up on Alex's neck at the weirdly familiar voice, and he spun to find that elf from the knoll. The creature called Nemed, who had whispered in the ear of the Dowager

Lady MacNeil. The music was loud and the nearby voices numerous, but Alex could hear the elf clearly. He said, "All hope is lost, and all recourse closed to you. You doubt all that is certain, and are certain only of doubt."

Without a moment of hesitation Alex drew his dagger and stabbed, but the lithe creature was too quick. He laughed as he danced backward, barely missing the dancers behind him. "Take care. Never assume what others perceive."

Another swipe with the dagger, but the elf evaded. People around gasped and surged back to get away from him. A buzz of alarm swept the hall.

"Get out!"

The elf laughed. "You sow the seeds of your own end."

Without thought of anything other than banishing the intruder from this special day, Alex dove for him, but the elf disappeared before his eyes. Once again the dagger sliced only thin air, as if there had never been anything there. Alex turned and looked for the red tunic, but it was gone. The figure had fled.

Or had simply gone invisible. Could he still be there somewhere? Had he ever been there at all?

"Alex, what is the matter with you?" Lindsay grasped a handful of his tunic sleeve and hissed through her teeth near his ear. The rest of the partiers returned to their eating, drinking, and dancing, not to be cheated of the celebration by a small outburst from the groom.

"You didn't see him?"

She shook her head. "Who?"

"That blasted elf. He was here." Alex glanced around, still searching.

Lindsay looked around. "I don't see him. Didn't see him."

"He threatened us. Said something about a fiery ending."

"The fire that brought us here? Perhaps he meant that."

He looked into her face, searching for clues again. That hadn't been the ending for him. Only death was ever the end, and coming here had been a beginning for him. But she apparently felt otherwise. He said, "I doubt it. It sounded like he meant the future."

"What could he know about the future?"

"As much as we do. Maybe more. He knew who we were. He knows about Hershey bars. Him, or those folks in the knoll."

She thought about that for a moment, then said, "Perhaps he won't be back."

"He probably will."

"Perhaps he can send us home."

Again he searched her eyes, but couldn't tell what he saw there. Then he said, "Maybe." Maybe not. All he knew anymore was that he was certain of nothing.

CHAPTER 18

Cold weather swept in. The harvest had been adequate, and
the vassals' tribute given. Alex heard no complaint from
the farmers, but also knew he wouldn't hear it even if there had
been any. Nobody ever liked the taxman, and he was certain
that had been as true for the feudal middle managers called
tacksmen. Grain was stored and animals penned, and the island
settled in for the winter as the days grew shorter and the
weather sharper. The predicted attack had not come by
Samhain, nor by Martinmas, and the constant anticipation was
relieved by the bad weather. The colder it became, the less
likely the MacLeods would attack. Alex spent long, tedious
hours with Sir Henry, improving his Gaelic.

As the days marched on, Alex hated the inactivity and he disliked it for his men, stifled by the lack of exercise and the annoying stale air of the closed castle. They would all be on each other's
last nerve by Christmas, and he dreaded it. Rather than look forward to rampant gossip and bloody duels, he decided he would do
something about it while he still could. This year he was the master. He donned a few extra layers of linen and wool, then went to
the Great Hall where the boys were hanging out, sitting at tables
around the fire the way he once had in a ship's wardroom.

"Come run with me. All of you."

His knights, lounging in chairs by the hearth, gave him blank looks as if he'd just suggested they strip to their linens and dance atop the tables, singing, "I Feel Pretty."

"Come on. Let's go." Alex began to jog in place, then stopped to stretch a little.

Nobody moved.

He turned to his second in command. "Henry?"

Sir Henry blanched. "Run? For no reason?"

"No. Run for pleasure."

They laughed, and the knights all relaxed into their chairs again because they'd decided he was joking.

"It's not a jest. Come. Now."

Silence fell and glances darted around the room.

Alex stretched in the other direction, then stood straight and said, "Okay, here's the deal. We run because it makes us stronger. Just like drilling. When we drill with our weapons we become better at using them. When we practice running we become better at—"

"Fleeing?" Orrin was asking for it again.

"Chasing. We run toward the enemy and are never winded. Our hearts become stronger. We can fight longer. We outlast the enemy. In short, we stand a better chance of surviving a fight. Come. Now." He waved them up out of their chairs, and finally they stood. The twenty-six of them looked doubtful, but Alex was making it plain he was serious and wouldn't back down. "Remove your spurs, and any chain mail you've got on. Maybe later we'll try it in full armor, but for now let's take it easy." He was drifting further into modern American English again, and the blank looks returned. He said, "We'll not exhaust ourselves."

Doubtful faces, but at least they comprehended his English.

Running in single file, Alex took them out the castle gate and down a track that cut across the pasture and into a patch of forest. It felt good to stretch his legs, breathing fresh air again. Cold air. In fact, it was extremely cold air. His breath came in thick clouds that trailed past him as he ran. A glance back at his troops, and he found them strung out along the trail. So he slowed to jogging in place and called out, "Rig it in, men! Close it up!" Many evil looks came his way, and it amused him. It was tempting to give them a hard time and razz them like a drill sergeant as they passed, but instinct told him that would be going too far. He could end up dead, no matter how tight he might be with the king. So he called to them, telling the slowpokes to step more lively and not hold up the real runners.

When they came to the faerie ring and Alex saw his men were trampling the toadstools, he murmured softly to the air around him, "Sorry, faerie person, whoever you are."

In the corner of his eye he thought he saw someone in pale blue, but when he looked there was nobody near. For a moment he lagged behind, looking around, but found nobody and no sign of anyone. He might have thought he'd imagined it, except he knew how his eyes could deceive him with these folks. He hopped over the toadstools at the opposite side and continued on with his men.

The run was only half an hour today. Tomorrow they would go again, and every day until the weather no longer permitted it.

"They'll hate you." Lindsay kneaded his shoulders as he soaked in the iron bathtub he'd commissioned from Alasdair Ruadh. Hammered in the same way plate armor was made, the tub was similar to ones from the nineteenth century where one sat rather than lay. Somewhat top-heavy, it also rocked a bit with its uneven bottom, and sloshing was a danger. The thing was heavy as hell, a bitch to fill, not entirely watertight, and not much fun to empty, but Alex never had to deal with any of that so he didn't mind much. And the garderobes needed water tossed down them every so often in any case, so it wasn't as if the water had to be carried outside. Sometimes the maids used the wash water for cleaning other things afterward.

"They'll stop hating me once they realize they're better able to fight because of it. If there's one thing those guys care about, it's being able to fight better than the enemy."

Lindsay said only "Hmm," then took a shallow wooden cup to pour water over his head and wet his hair. A winter storm howled outside, rattling the window and whistling through gaps here and there throughout the castle. Rainwater trickled from the ceiling and down a rivulet along the section of bare cliff in their bedchamber, making the striations in the granite glitter in bright colors. Another small gap at the floor allowed the water egress below and out of the castle to the barbican, and the effect might have been somewhat pleasant, like a small indoor fountain, but for the chill and dampness it brought to the room.

"Your hair is awfully long now," she said.

He ran fingers through it, and realized it could cover his face. Then he leaned against the back of the tub to gaze at her upside down, and smiled. "Yours is getting longer, too." She'd stopped cutting it last summer after Bannockburn, and now it was past her shoulders, long enough to let herself be seen in public without her headdress. Usually it was kept in a loose braid woven and tied with colored ribbon to match her clothing, and he liked that for it meant she let it down only for him. In the sanctum of their chambers, he loved to untie the ribbon himself and free the dark locks to run his fingers through them.

Now he reached up with a wet hand to touch it. "So pretty. Wavy." God, she was beautiful! And when she smiled at him, as she was doing now, his heart melted until he would swear he could feel it go soft in his chest. She was as naked as he, and now he wished there were enough room in the tub for them both. He slipped his hand behind her neck, and she leaned down to kiss him.

"She loves you not."

Alex opened his eyes to find Nemed standing over them with his fists on his hips, all evil red eyes and pointed ears, and neatly trimmed beard coming to a long, sharp point. The furred cape hung open on his shoulders, and the tunic beneath was black today. Alex jerked away from Lindsay. Nemed receded and faded into the shadows of the room. Whether he was gone or just not seen, Alex couldn't tell.

"What's wrong?" She ran a thumb over his eyebrow to smooth it.

He was about to tell her, but hesitated and decided against it. Nothing could be wrong. Frightening her would accomplish nothing, and there was nothing he could do about the elf. Best to ignore him.

So he smiled and touched a finger to her lower lip. "Let people talk; I don't care what they say. I love my wife."

She chuckled and slipped into a bad approximation of an American accent. "Right. Even if she is a trews-wearing, mace-wielding, scarred-up, no-dowry-having skank."

He touched a gentle finger to the still-reddish scar across her ribs, and chuckled. "Even then." He glanced at the shadow into which the elf had disappeared, and hoped he was listening.

The cloth in her hand sloshed over his chest as he gazed at her, and she smiled back. Against his better judgment, he wondered what Nemed had meant. *She loves you not.* Why would anyone, even that creature, say that?

Christmas passed, and no attack from the MacLeods. Alex began to wonder if Ross had been scamming him. The informant was no longer in the running for the position of tacksman. Nevertheless, he frequently went to the roof of the keep to survey his defenses and contemplate his vulnerabilities. He disliked the open quay, but the sluices for hot oil at the top of the keep made the barbican a nice killing ground. It would be better, though, if he could keep attackers from even landing.

According to his best guess, gunpowder wouldn't come to Europe till later in the century and the metallurgy required to make even the crudest cannon was even further in the future. Artillery wasn't possible, let alone practical here.

A catapult, though, might do some good. Usually they were used as siege engines against stone walls, but looking out across to the water made Alex realize a small catapult could deliver a good-sized rock to an approaching ship if lobbed properly. One thing this island had plenty of, it was chunks of rock. His mind began to turn with building the weapon, and he ticked off his sources for materials. Wooden beams and dowels. Human hair. Leather. Oil. He put Alasdair Ruadh to work with another diagram.

Winter snows blew through during January and February, and everyone relaxed for an attack in winter this deep was unlikely. Short, cold days came one after another, and the sense of time passing dulled to a standstill. To Alex it seemed spring—and the attack—would never come, and an antsy sense of eagerness crept in, which he struggled to hide from Lindsay.

It was March, before the weather had broken, when a farmer came running to the castle, across the meadow and from the west. The gate watch shouted the alarm, and Alex went out to the bailey to hear. The voice was muffled by thick fog, and it was impossible to see even the inner curtain from there.

"Ships! Ships from the west! Ships!"

Knights scrambled from the Great Hall and from the barracks, headed for the stable and their horses. Without thinking, Alex turned to order Lindsay to bring his weapons. "Lin—"

She stood in the doorway, eyebrows up and head tilted as if deeply curious what he would say next.

He blinked, stunned he'd forgotten for a moment she was no longer his squire. And even more stunned that she'd been the first person he'd turned to in this emergency. Then he turned again and shouted for his page. "Gregor!"

"Aye, sir!" The boy was right there at his elbow, his eyes bright with excitement, and he danced on his toes in his eagerness to serve.

"Bring my armor from below. And tell Colin to ready my horse." More than likely Colin was already in the stable, but Gregor would make sure.

Alex called to the watch. "Who is coming?"

A shout replied, "MacLeod, by the sails!"

The farmer who'd given the alarm, one of the MacConnells, came out of the fog and hurried up the slope to where Alex stood. Alex had seen little of the island population since December, and now the farmer's excitement was made that much more alarming for his very presence. "My liege. 'Tis the MacLeods, and they've three hundred men! They thought to come by stealth, and have brought their boats to the west shore where the beach is flat."

"Did they see you?"

The man shook his head. "Nae. They yet believe themselves to be undiscovered. They follow the burn to the forest."

"They're on foot?" The farmer nodded. "What are their arms?"

"Pikes and axes. Some swords."

"No bows?"

The farmer shook his head.

Good. "Go to the village and raise the alarm there. Have Donnchadh lead to the west as many as will fight, and meet us at the edge of the forest."

"What have you got planned?"

A bit impatiently, Alex said, "You'll find out when we get there. Just do what I've told you, and quickly." He whapped the man on the shoulder to get him going.

The farmer nodded. "Aye, sir." Then he ran to follow the orders.

Alex returned to the Great Hall, running numbers in his head. He had about fifty men at arms, fewer than thirty of them knights. The village men would make a complement to match the number of MacLeods given by the MacConnell farmer, but Alex couldn't be certain that number was accurate. There was also that he needed to leave a contingent to guard the castle barbican from a rear assault.

In the keep, he found Lindsay calmly instructing Gregor, who had forgotten to bring Alex's spurs. The boy ran off to obey, and when she turned to Alex as if waiting to receive orders, he suddenly thought of his mother. He blinked, speechless, for a moment. Lindsay wasn't anything like Mom, but at this moment was exactly what his mother had been to his father: competent, unafraid, and ready to handle whatever needed to be done while he was away and in danger.

"Alex?" Lindsay peered at him, puzzled, and snapped her fingers to catch his attention.

He coughed and returned to himself. "Right. You get on the roof and watch to the south. You know how to mix the greek fire." He began to don his chain mail.

She nodded. "Oil, sulfur, pitch. We've oil in the kitchen, sulfur in the stores, and the pitch is in use so I'll have to gather the buckets."

"Hurry, then. Get a pot of it going now, and if there's a breach of the barbican give the order to retreat to the keep. Then let them have it. Dump everything you can set on fire onto the steps below. Have Henry get someone to man the catapult."

"Alex . . . Molotov cocktails."

He blinked, and knew what she meant. "Yes. Rags."

"Jugs from the kitchen."

"No, archers. Set archers with fire arrows on the barbican wall."

"Hunters from the village."

"Right. I'll send them to you." Too bad there wasn't any quicklime to set the water afire, but it was dangerous stuff and he wasn't yet equipped to store it, let alone use it.

Gregor appeared with the spurs, and Alex strapped them on. His blood sang with anticipation of the fight. He called out, "Henry! *Henry!*"

Sir Henry came down the steps from the roof, also donning his armor in a hurry. "Aye, sir?"

"You, Orrin, and your squires defend the barbican. Use the hunters I will send you as sharp-shooters and set them up with fire. My wife will relay my orders to you. You'll obey her as you would me."

A shadow crossed Henry's face. "Lady Marilyn?"

An edge came to Alex's voice. "Aye. As you would me, Henry. Remember that. And keep Orrin under control. I'm counting on you to trust me on this. Don't let me down."

The knight glanced at Lindsay. "Aye, sir."

Alex slipped his coif over his head, shook his head to settle the chains, then turned to Lindsay. "Whatever happens, I love you."

Her eyes glistened as she looked into his. "You will return."

"I can't guarantee that." *Just tell me you love me.* The elf's red eyes swam before his, and he shook his head to rid himself of the image. *No. He's a liar. An energy beast who will suck the life from you.*

She opened her mouth, then hesitated and closed it again. Then she said, "I know you must go. Remember I love you and I'll be waiting for you."

Relieved and bolstered at once, he pressed a hand to the back of her neck and kissed her, hard. Then he lifted his shield and sword from the wall and left the Great Hall. As he hurried toward his horse waiting by the stable, he cleared his mind and focused on the job at hand.

The knights of Eilean Aonarach rode from the castle at a gallop, toward their rendezvous with the village men, with Alex at their head.

What was she about to say before she changed her mind and said she loved you?

Alex shook his head to rid himself of the voice. *Concentrate. Focus on the real. The elf is a liar. He's a liar.* Alex shook his head again and took a deep breath as he and his men approached the rendezvous.

Gathered at the edge of the forest, the villagers presented a pitiful force and it took no more than a glance to know why. Only the MacConnells had come. The Bretons, long allied with and more often than not related to the MacLeods, had stayed away. Alex muttered a curse as his heart sank, and he immediately assigned the nearest squire to look out to the rear. The hunters he sent to the castle went at a run and carrying a warning. If the Bretons should decide to participate on behalf of the MacLeods, the day could be lost.

Alex then quickly turned his full attention to the threat before him, and as the battle plan formed he realized his runs throughout the island gave him an unanticipated benefit. Intimate knowledge of the lay of the land resided in his head, and he was no longer dependent on the natives for it. The island was now his as much as theirs. He figured he knew how the MacLeods would approach from the west beach. Believing themselves to be undiscovered, they would take the shortest route to the castle and that would mean negotiating the steep, narrow path along the burn that cut through the forest and between two low hills. Without delay he ordered his men forward through the forest, in hopes of catching the invaders before they would reach it. They rode hard in single file along the path, through dim, misty woods choked with moss.

Ahead, as they approached the narrow pass, there was a glimpse of pikes and shadows and Alex's blood surged as he signaled a stop. The MacLeods were still climbing beside the burn, but would begin topping the summit any second. And they were hurrying so as not to be caught in the pass.

"Dismount and follow me," Alex ordered quietly as he threw his leg over, and the command was passed along. The knights and squires dismounted, junior squires holding the horses by fours, and Alex ordered his men to fan out in the forest, with the village infantry bearing farm tools behind. The MacNeil force gained their position barely in time, and as soon as the first MacLeod came into sight on the path ahead, Alex shouted the order to charge. A great shout went up, metal on metal sang among the trees as swords were drawn, and the MacNeils surged forward. MacLeods roared their reply, met them, and the combatants clashed at the top of the path. Most of the invading force were still bunched up behind the leaders. Alex had their route to the castle blocked, and his men picked off the attackers as they came, professional knights at the fore, wielding swords against disorganized pikes and axes.

But the MacLeods were tough and enthusiastic fighters. The clan was fierce, and had a history of growth by conquest. They were accustomed to winning. They fought hard and long, and bloodied the MacNeils terribly before they finally broke and retreated down the pass.

Alex's men followed to the beach below, where the fleeing

MacLeods rushed into the water to get away. Alex shouted to his men to not follow, to let the remaining enemy flee, and so they stood on the beach and watched the boats disappear into the mist offshore. Darkness was approaching by the time the MacNeils returned to the pass, where bodies lay scattered among the rocks. They began stripping the dead, finding little more of value than dirks of varying sizes and an occasional sword. No ransom caches out here where cash was scarce.

A challenging shout went up somewhere near the top of the trail, and there was a scuffle in the undergrowth. Alex drew his sword to run toward it, but the cry was cut short so he stood down. Then one of his men nearby among the rocks in the rushing burn raised his sword to whack the head from a MacLeod body. When the body jerked and thrashed as the MacNeil took a second swing, then finally lay still in the water, Alex realized the MacLeod had been still alive. Alex looked upward, toward the spot where the shout had come from, and figured that had also been a wounded MacLeod dispatched by his men. He opened his mouth to order them to stop killing wounded, but then shut it. Perhaps it was a mercy to the dying, who otherwise might linger for days or weeks. And on another level—one Alex was forced to admit to himself— he was in no mood to coddle and nurse wounded men who had tried to take his island from him, even if they might have lived. He was disinclined to even feed such prisoners. He returned to the business of collecting weapons and let the two extra deaths slip into a small, dark compartment of his mind.

Most of Alex's force were wounded, but it appeared they all would live. Only one knight and two villagers had been lost in the battle, and Alex ordered their bodies loaded onto the horses for return to the castle. Eight MacLeod heads were taken, and slung from saddles by their hair. The headless bodies were thrown onto the beach to await the tide, and the MacNeil soldiers made their way back to the castle.

As they approached, Alex was stunned to see bodies scattered before the landside gatehouse. The portcullis was closed and secure, but it was plain there had been a skirmish just outside the gate. He rode among the dead, and when he recognized their faces he knew what had happened. "Bretons." His heart clutched for Lindsay's safety, for the attack had been bloody.

The watch on the gate let his men through, and he rode

quickly, up the winding path through the bailey, to the Great Hall. There he dismounted and hurried inside to be greeted by his wife.

Lindsay leapt upon him and held him tight in spite of the heavy mail, sweat, and blood covering him. "Thank God you're alive." There were no tears, but Alex thought she might never let him go.

"Tell me what happened here."

When she finished hugging him and stood back, she said, "The Breton women came to the castle, pretending to ask for sanctuary. But when the gate opened, men ran from the forest and tried to get through with their weapons. The men-at-arms you left here fought them off well enough to close the gate." Her voice lowered and she added with a note of surprise in her voice, "That priest—Father Patrick—he's very good with a sword. You wouldn't believe how he was right in the thick of things, slashing away like Errol Flynn, or somebody."

"No kidding?"

She shook her head. "Not kidding in the least." Then she continued with her report. "We lost three men. The remaining Bretons fled and scattered to their homes."

"What about the barbican?"

"We spotted a single boat waiting just within sight off the quay, but it never approached and finally went away as the sun began to set. I'm guessing they were waiting for a signal that never came, and gave up."

"That's a good guess; you're probably right."

"How many did you lose?"

"One knight. Two villagers." In the bailey the dead were being claimed by wailing kinswomen, who would clean and cover them for burial in the morning. The victorious MacConnell men had three graves to dig, but first there was something Alex needed to take care of. He turned and called for his horse again, and ordered all his remaining knights to accompany him, five with torches.

"Where are you going?"

"We're going to get rid of those Bretons."

"What, kill them?"

Alex looked at her and wondered why she had to ask. "Of course, I'm going to kill them. They've established themselves as enemy combatants. Every last Breton in that village is going to die tonight." Those people had threatened his wife. No way could he let them live. Any of them.

Her eyes were wide with horror. "You can't! There are children there!"

"That didn't seem to concern their parents—their *mothers*— when they decided to attack this castle. I don't think I need to be any more bothered about those children than their parents were. They are forfeit." Not to mention that children had a tendency to grow into vengeful adults.

"Alex, that's—"

"It's self-defense. What do you figure would have happened if we hadn't caught the MacLeods at the pass? What would have happened if those murdering, treacherous Bretons had managed to take the castle? They would have killed you, Lin. Without the slightest thought. They would have chopped off your head with an ax and stuck it on a pike outside the gate." The image shook him to his core, and he fought tears that rose. "And that's what I'm going to do to them."

"Give them a chance. Give them a warning, that—"

"Six men dead, Lindsay. I can't lose any more. If I give them another chance, next time they might win."

"Then send them away. Tell them to get off the island. If they're so close to the MacLeods, then they must have places to go. Relatives who will take them. Don't go into that village and commit murder."

"Lin, I can't."

"You must. Find a way. Make it work. Just, please, don't do this."

"But—"

"I couldn't stand to be married to a murderer."

His first thought was to inform her that she would be married to him till death and there was nothing she could do about it, but he held his tongue. There was no forcing her to love him, and he knew he had always been on shaky ground for that. He drew a long, deep breath and let it out slowly. Just as slowly, he realized that though he knew the action wouldn't have been murder, her words nevertheless touched him in a small, dim place where he knew it would be wrong. Then he said, "All right. I'll banish them."

"Good. Banish them. Don't kill them."

With a sigh, he kissed her and wondered how he would ever get her to accept the realities of this world.

The sky was still purple in the southwest as he rode to the village with his knights, banner flapping and torches flaring in the wind. As they cantered down the path between the low peat houses, he shouted out in Gaelic to the residents there. "Attend to me, all of you! Attend!" He pulled up his horse, and his torch-carrying knights surrounded him to shed light so the villagers could see his angry face. "All you Bretons, hear me!"

A few women came from houses, cautiously. There were no men visible. Contempt rose in Alex for the chickenshit Breton men. He continued. "The attack on the castle this afternoon was a treasonous act. All the Bretons on this island are in violation of their pledge to me." One of the women began to plead, and he cut her off with a bellow. "Silence!" She subsided to whimpering and weeping, holding her plaid to her face, and he shouted over her. "The penalty for this offense is death. The life of every Breton man, woman, and child on this island is forfeit."

All the women began to wail, and some fell to their knees.

"Silence!" He gazed around him, rage welling in him, and he relished their terror as compensation for the threat they'd presented and the men he'd lost that day.

The wailing subsided instantly to soft weeping.

"However, I am a merciful landlord. I don't kill children if I can avoid it." The women he would gladly have executed with his own hands, for they had quite willingly participated in the attack. He looked on the weeping, sniveling creatures before him and was disgusted. "You will all leave this island. By sunset tomorrow. I will return with my men tomorrow night, to put to the torch every Breton house, and to put to the sword any Breton who remains. Go to your MacLeod relatives you love so much. Let them support you. I no longer want you here." He raised his voice even louder, for the benefit of any MacConnells listening. "And mark this! I will not tolerate insurrection from anyone! Should the MacDonalds come, I will expect the pledges of the MacConnells to hold true to me. The Bretons have shown their lack of honor; if I find such a lack in the Mac-Connells, I will treat them as harshly!"

With that, he wheeled his horse and spurred the mount to a gallop away from the village, his men following.

That night Alex washed MacLeod blood from himself, then slipped into his warm bed with his warm wife. She clung to him, soft and welcoming, and held him close.

"I was terribly afraid for you today," she whispered into his ear so quietly he could hear her tongue on her teeth.

"Have faith." He kissed her neck, then loosed himself from her grasp to move lower. "Everyone else around here has faith oozing out their ears; you should try it."

"Everyone here has faith they'll go to heaven. Very different from being certain of not dying. In fact—" there was a sharp breath as he took her breast into his mouth. "In fact, the one thing everyone here is certain of is that they will die, and they don't seem to care how soon."

Alex only made a *hmm* noise, for his mouth was full. Happy for now, he settled into her arms to suck on his very favorite part of her. She fell silent, and pressed her face to his head as she ran her fingers through his hair. So peaceful, and so gentle. His soul quieted, for the time being not shouting anger. For the moment, he wanted nothing more than this.

After a while—he had no idea how long a while, for time had lost meaning—a shudder overcame Lindsay. She shook in his arms and made a small, surprised noise in her throat. He looked up at her and smiled, holding her nipple between his teeth. She sighed. "Well. That was . . . interesting."

He made another *hmm* noise, let go of the breast, and rose up to push between her thighs. More soft than she'd ever been, more pliable, she surrounded him with the warmth and softness that didn't exist in other parts of his life. This was the only peace there could ever be for him, and he was grateful for it.

In the morning, the sun rose to reveal the heads of dead Bretons and MacLeods stuck on pikes along the top of the outer curtain wall that faced the village. A signal to the MacConnells that Sir Alasdair an Dubhar MacNeil was here to stay.

That evening at sunset, Alex donned his armor, mounted his horse, and led his men into the village with swords and torches. There were no longer any Bretons to be found, for they'd all left in fishing boats. The houses had already been looted of everything left behind, and it was a simple matter to torch the empty houses. Alex, his men, and the remaining villagers watched them burn and throw sparks and smoke to a purpling sky.

CHAPTER 19

Misgivings arose at having to burn houses in his own village, but Alex refused to think of that and instead concentrated on how this would simplify conflicts. The MacLeods
no longer had allies here, and so might think twice about attacking again. Alex would send to Barra and invite some of the
poorer MacNeils to come fill his vacant tenancies, and that
would make his alliance with Hector even more secure. With
MacNeils living on Eilean Aonarach, and with a powerful laird
such as Hector backing him up, Alex thought, the MacDonalds
also might think twice about attacking. Alex knew this was the
first step toward making his island a relatively secure place to
live.

Alex dispatched a message to Hector, and in April boatloads
of MacNeils landed to occupy the forfeited Breton farms. They
brought with them their goods and skills, and also they brought
something Alex could only describe to himself as "MacNeil-
ness." Proud descendants of Niall of the Nine Hostages, they
considered themselves his people and their presence was a
foundation on which he felt he could build. Once again he was
surrounded by people with whom he had a blood kinship, and
he liked it.

Over the weeks more soldiers came, from the mainland and

Skye as well as from Barra. Landless knights wished to serve
under the man who had defeated the MacLeods by his wits. As
spring approached, the island came alive with new people and
fresh hope for prosperity as the specter of war with England
moved away to the south.

Aspects of Patrick's response during the raid made Alex
look to him now with a fresh and questioning eye. The priest
was a quiet man, though plain spoken and as straightforward as
any of the belligerent knights in Alex's service. Never having
been Catholic, or even particularly religious, Alex wasn't sure
how to act around him. Alex had been part of this century long
enough to know priests weren't much like the ministers he'd
met in his other life. Personal safety was such a pipe dream
here, he'd never been surprised to see religious leaders go
armed.

But if reports were true, Patrick was far more skilled with
his sword than even a well-trained knight. Alex couldn't help
wondering who Patrick was, and how the man could straddle
such wildly disparate disciplines so neatly. And if he could
wrap his mind around those, what of the magical creatures Alex
knew to exist who were entirely denied by Christians in his own
time? Alex decided to visit the chapel and have a chat.

"Yo! Tuck!" Alex stood in the middle of the reed-strewn
sanctuary, where stools and wooden chairs stood in rough approximation of rows, and the carved altar was stacked with can-
dlesticks, censer, and chalice, tools of Patrick's trade. By all
accounts this place was a wreck most of the time, but it always
somehow shaped up just before Sunday morning.

Patrick emerged from behind the heavy rectory door and
greeted him with a warm smile and a relaxed demeanor. "My
liege. What brings you to visit me on this ordinary day?"
Alex's attendance at Sunday service was punctual and unvary-
ing for the sake of appearances, but a slightly pointed note in
Patrick's voice made him wonder if the priest had picked up on
his religious ambivalence.

"Tell me, Father, do you believe in magic?" Alex knew it
was a dumb question, but there was no other way to approach
his concern. "In faeries and elves?"

The priest gestured to Alex he should take a chair. Alex
pulled up a stool, and Patrick sat also. His warm smile suggested

he had nothing to do with his time other than chat with Alex about the wee folk. Neither did he seem particularly distressed by the question. "Of course, there is magic," he said with a smile in his voice as well as his face. "God has created the world to be unknowable; there are many great mysteries around us." The priest gestured to the thin air, and Alex briefly wondered if Nemed could be standing right there at that moment, listening. It would probably suit the creature's sick outlook.

"Faeries? Wee folk?"

"Aye. Creatures of this world and of netherworlds, worlds we cannot know, and of darkness. Tenebrae, as we call the darkness of death. Many different folk."

"Are they evil? Can they hurt us?"

Patrick smiled, and peered at Alex as if wondering whether his liege was having him on. Slowly he said, "Aye. There is good and evil in everyone, and each man must purge himself of that which is evil to save the good." He held up both hands as illustration for each. "God separated the darkness from the light, and it is we who must choose. They must choose also."

"How can you believe in wee folk *and* in God?"

The answer seemed patently obvious to the priest, and he shrugged like a teenager. "God made us all. The faeries, elves, demons, everything. That much is no mystery. I believe in faeries for the same reason I believe in the king."

"Have you ever seen a faerie?"

"No. Neither have I seen the king. Have you?" The question was quite serious, as straightforward as anything Patrick ever said.

For a moment Alex considered lying, but then he nodded. "I've seen a faerie and an elf." A pause. "And the king."

Patrick's eyebrows went up. "Indeed? And you're afraid of the wee folk?"

"Well . . . not afraid." Afraid enough. Of one of them, in any case. "They don't seem all alike." Nor all that wee, some of them.

"No. And I pray none of the creatures you saw might be demons. Never let a demon talk to you, for they lie and cannot be trusted."

"How do I tell which are demons?" Alex had never before believed in such things, but any more he wished the pointy-eared folk would wear badges, or something. Faerie? Elf?

Demon? Gremlin? He was sure Nemed never used any of those terms to describe himself, and like anyone else would only be described as evil by those he'd harmed.

"You'll know in your heart what is evil and what is not. Look into your heart." Patrick caught himself short a moment, then looked around at the empty chapel and leaned close to say, "That is, when the pope isn't around to *tell* you what should be in your heart." A glint in his eye and a slight curling of his lips made Alex grin. He felt he could trust this man to tell the truth.

Alex asked, "How do you make certain a creature of darkness will do no harm? How do you protect yourself?"

Patrick peered at him. "You are afraid."

"Not afraid." Alex sat up and shook his head. "Cautious. If there are magical beings who would do harm, I want to know how to fight them."

Patrick laid a palm against his wool-robed chest. "Hold Christ in your heart."

Alex knew that wouldn't be enough. "Is there a prayer?"

"Any prayer will do. Simply ask."

For a moment Alex thought to reword his question to receive a more definitive answer, but changed his mind and rose from his stool. "Thank you, Father."

The priest rose also, and bowed. "I hope my answers will help you find the peace you seek."

Alex bade the priest good day, and knew peace would always be a dim, misty dream.

RED eyes. All was darkness except for red eyes and a smile that was human but not. Nemed ran his tongue over his teeth, all normal, except for unnatural whiteness. So white, they shone with a light of their own. "What does she do all day?"

Alex tried not to look at him, but the darkness all around was too deep. Too complete. There wasn't any telling where he was. He closed his eyes, and there the face still glowed with unearthly light. Panic rose as he opened them again and was unable to see anything but that blasted face. The only light he could see emanated from the elfin face. "What do you want?"

"Nothing. You have nothing I want. And don't you wish you did?"

Cold sweat broke out. Alex did wish it, mightily. Whatever it took to get this guy out of his life, he would do it or give it. Anything but Lindsay. "You don't talk about her, and what she does all day is none of your business."

"I'll talk about what and whom I like. And it's plain your most interesting conversation will be about her. So, answer my question. What does she do all day? Surely it's *your* business, at least."

"Don't know, don't care. She runs the household. Tells the staff what to do."

"I'm sure she's very hands-on with the staff."

Alex's jaw clenched. "What's that supposed to mean?" He knew he was taking bait, but couldn't help himself.

"And your knights. Why do you suppose she insisted on sleeping in the barracks before you were married?"

"You know why. You were on Barra and saw the whole thing." More than likely caused the whole thing. "Stop this."

"I'm only asking questions. What do *you* think is the truth?"

"I have faith in her."

"Do you? Really?"

"Get away from me." Alex tried to turn away, but couldn't face the darkness. It was too deep. Too complete. He turned back.

"You can't get away, Alexander. You can't flee yourself. No man can run away from that which he owns."

"No more lies. Keep your lies." Alex tried to make a fist and fight, but found there was no hand to clench. No body with which to fight. "She's my wife. I have faith in her." He needed faith in her, for where would he be without that?

"You need it, but do you have it?"

Alex looked around, stunned and frightened. The elf had read his mind. His pulse thudded in his ears.

"Where do you think I am, Alexander? Where do you think we both are? Your soul. I have found your soul. Now we can have some real fun." The light blinked out.

In the darkness, Alex screamed.

Then he awoke, trembling and sweating. The fire in the hearth of his bedchamber was falling to embers, and he sat up to gain his bearings in the dimness. Lindsay put out a hand to stroke his clammy back.

"What's the matter?" Her voice was calm and sleepy; he must not have screamed aloud.

"Nothing." He ran his fingers through his hair and struggled to calm his breathing. "Just an ugly nightmare."

She made a hum of sympathy, and sat up to press her face against his back. "You're shaking. It must have been a terrible dream. What was it?"

"I don't remember." That was a lie. He remembered every minute detail. Every line of that face and every inflection of his voice. Every blackened word.

"Come. It's cold out there. Come under the covers." Lindsay drew him back to lie on the bed, pulled the silk and fur up over them, and snuggled in beside him.

He held her close, but as he lay awake in the darkness he couldn't help wondering what it was she did do all day.

SPRING was well under way. By now the men were keeping up with him in their running, and nobody complained anymore about the mandatory exercise. Several times a week Alex took them through the forest, and now they added armor, bits at a time. Once they became accustomed to chain mail and plate, then he would add weapons.

One chilly morning in early April, as they passed the faerie ring, Alex had a thought and slowed to a stop. His knights ran on, knowing better than to stop for any reason, and he stayed behind to gaze at the ring. A faerie lived here. Someone who might know more than he did about magical beings. He stepped into the ring and looked around. Bright green moss grew everywhere, covering living trees and fallen ones in a thick, soft blanket that took the edges from sight. Grass grew underfoot, brindled with black fungus and dotted with small, white flowers. The toadstools of the ring were enormous, velvety brown shapes that tilted this way and that according to their whim. Surrounding him, they appeared nearly as a line of curious onlookers, staring at him and conferring with each other about who he might be.

"Hello?" He looked around. There had once been a woman here, dressed in blue. He was certain of it. "Miss?" How was one supposed to address a faerie? So far the wee folk he'd been exposed to had been fairly rude, and he wondered whether politeness would be lost on the lady in blue. "Ma'am?"

He turned, and there she was, sitting on a fallen tree gone plush with the moss. Glorious and golden, she appeared to give off a light of her own that radiated from her heart. She wore a long cloak over her shoulders, but didn't seem to need it, for she was a warmth herself. Her pale, long-sleeved blue dress shimmered as she moved, and when she smiled at Alex, he could feel it deep inside. It fought the cold day.

"Hello, young man."

Alex blinked. It had been an awfully long time since he'd thought of himself as young. "Hello." Now his mind blanked, and he couldn't remember why he'd stopped to look for her. "Are you a faerie?"

Her golden hair curled softly around the tips of delicately curved and pointed ears, and the corners of her eyes turned up ever so slightly. They reminded him of Lindsay's eyes, but a more pale blue. The woman laughed, the sound like a brook falling over many stones. "That is what you call us now, I think."

"What did they call you before?"

"Myself? I am called Danu. My people are the *Tuatha Dé Danann*, which means the People of the Goddess Danu."

His jaw dropped open as he recognized the name of the faerie Lindsay had said gave her a book of psalms. Quickly he recovered himself, closed his mouth, and said, "Pleased to meet you, Danu." Then what she'd said registered. "You're a goddess?"

She laughed again. "Well, you know what they say. Technology sufficiently advanced is indistinguishable from magic. In the sense that I appear to be a goddess, I may as well be one."

Now Alex knew the meaning of the term *cognitive dissonance*. He raised his palms and waved away the sensation of disrupted awareness. "Uh . . . well, they will say that. In about seven centuries."

"Yes."

"Where did you hear it?"

Her thin, graceful shoulders shrugged. "Around. I cannae say as I remember when or where. It's part of being who I am. Even I sometimes don't understand it." It seemed to amuse her in a mild, don't-give-a-damn sort of way.

"How can you not?"

"Do you understand the workings of your own mind? Are you able to say why you remember some things and don't remember others? Why you sometimes know things without knowing where you learned them? We . . . faeries, as you say, are different from humans, but not so very different at the end of the day."

"So, if you're a goddess, why are you here?"

"Here?"

"On my island."

Her laughter was light and pleasant to hear. "Oh, well, why not? Why not your island? It's a beautiful place, aye? Why should I not want to spend my days in such a place?"

Though he didn't entirely trust her explanation, particularly in the light of her previous contact with Lindsay, she did have an excellent point. He knew he could be a happy man to never leave.

"So." Her voice took on a note of getting down to business. "What moves you to call for me?" Her tone suggested she thought it was about time he did.

"Curiosity."

"But not idle curiosity."

How much did she really know? "Do you know a guy named Nemed?"

Her face paled to nearly dead white. Apparently she could be surprised. "You've crossed Nemed? In what way? How badly?"

Her fear alarmed him and his skin went cold so he shivered in the damp day. This woman was a goddess, and she was afraid of this guy. "Who is he? Is he one of the *too-ha* whoever?"

"Tuatha Dé Danann. And, no. Not in the least, and he would harm ye for saying such a thing. He and his people are much older. He struggled against the old gods, the Fomors."

"Older than you guys?"

Impatience tinged her voice. "The world is far older than anyone dreams, Alexander." It shouldn't have surprised him for her to know his name, but it did nevertheless. She continued. "The Fomors were terrible creatures, the offspring of Chaos and Night. The most gruesome of them was Balor—"

"Was. This Balor guy isn't around anymore?"

For a moment she thought that over, then said, "Not in the

sense that you can see him and do battle with him, but I think if you ever were caught out at sea, at night, with a storm lashing your boat with wind and rain and sea, you might ken something of him."

Alex recalled a particularly bad storm his carrier had weathered on his first cruise, and knew she told the truth. He nodded. He knew old Balor after all.

She continued. "Balor always kept one eye shut, for it was so venomous it would kill anyone it looked upon."

"And Nemed fought that guy?"

"Wouldn't you have done? Those dreaded, animal-faced Fomors in their glass tower levied a tax upon his people. Two-thirds of the children born to the people of Nemed were to be sacrificed to them, each year on Samhain. *Two-thirds.* And when the people of Nemed fought, they gained the glass tower of the Fomors, only to be slaughtered in the end and wiped from the face of the earth."

"Except Nemed himself."

"Including Nemed."

"But I've seen him walking around."

"I'm coming to that part of the story. Do ye believe in magic, Alexander?"

"Yes, I do." That he was living in this century at all was a compelling case for it.

"Then believe that Nemed once lived in the place from which he came, and no longer does. Something has brought him back from that nether-realm of creation."

"He was dead? A ghost? And now he isn't?"

She shook her head, frustrated she wasn't getting through, then thought a moment and said, "Ghost . . . in a way. But not dead. Many people of the old races have returned to our maker where they are truly what you would call dead, but not all. Nemed and the remnant of his race—"

"Elves."

Her mouth opened to continue, then closed for her to think a moment. "Another word given by mortals. As good as any, I suppose." Then she went on with her story. "Nemed and his . . . *elf* race fought Balor, and in losing went to a different existence, the nether-realm, waiting for their time to move on. And it made him a very bitter creature."

"Why?"

"Would you not be bitter if your entire race of people were destroyed by terrible, animal-like gods who wanted to kill your children? Sixteen thousand people returned to their maker in that final battle, leaving him with but a handful, living without life. An unhappy existence for anyone, and he was a king, responsible for the souls of his people."

"Why does he have a chip on his shoulder about me?"

"Have you asked him?"

"Yes. He's not forthcoming with information."

Her eyes went distant as she thought for a moment, then focused on him again. "What were you doing when you first encountered him?"

He thought about the knoll, but then thought further back. To the hooded figure in camp. Then to the red eyes in the burning sky. "I was flying a friend home from my ship."

"Flying?" This excited her very much. "Humans flying? Truly?"

"Yeah. You know about flying." She appeared to know about everything else.

"No, I don't. Tell me about it. Have you wings, then?" She leaned as if to see behind him where his wings might be.

"Well, no. I . . . it's a machine. I ride in it and it goes up in the air. At least, I did . . . I will. In about seven hundred years."

"Ah." She sat back and nodded, understanding. "Technology. Of course, you will fly. And that might explain why Nemed is so put out with you."

"Why, then?"

"Recently, I'm told, a large, fire-breathing bird flew into the midst of a spell Nemed was crafting for the sake of regaining the earth for his handful of people. With all the power he had at his disposal, he'd formed a rift between the worlds for his followers to pass through. He chose a time when thirty strange— and strange-looking—people would not be so easily noticed and feared, and they could live out their days as mortals where life would be easier and longevity more likely than here."

"I was several thousand feet off the ground."

"What better place to be certain of not sending them to become part of a structure that will one day be built?"

"What, like a transporter beam putting people inside walls?"

Danu frowned for a moment, puzzled, then her expression cleared as she worked it out and she nodded. "I suppose. He'd thought he could be certain of their safety on the other side."

"I hope they had parachutes."

That made her laugh. "I should think if he is capable of sending them through time he would have been able to make certain they did not fall to the earth afterward and die. It would have been part of the spell to give them all a soft landing after traveling the breach."

"I see."

"But the large bird—"

"My plane."

"Aye. You and your friend and your fiery machine flew into the midst of the spell and destroyed his effort. And his people."

Now Alex was struck silent, stunned. He gazed at Danu for a long moment, then finally found his voice. "Destroyed his people? All of them?"

She nodded.

"I killed thirty innocent people when I flew through that fireball?"

"You sent thirty innocent people to their maker, aye, leaving Nemed on the other side but once more on earth. He walks amongst us once again, alone. You took those people away from him. Even worse, that spell consumed nearly all his power. He'd given his all to send his people to the world, and he has nothing left to speak of as far as power or support. He's alone and broken."

Nothing left? After having been blown through the side of a knoll, Alex thought Nemed was pretty powerful. "Nemed hasn't lost his magic."

She shook her head. "Nae. He's lost most, but not all, and that makes him still a formidable creature to face. Be thankful he cannot kill by magic anymore."

"He can't kill?"

"With a sword, aye, but not with magic. Were he still able to kill by magic, I'm certain you'd have been sent directly on to the next world by now and we'd not be here speaking of him."

Alex shuddered. "He claims to have found my soul. He comes to my dreams."

"As open a book as you are, it's no surprise he's found your soul. And you're certainly not the first human he's terrorized in this way. You call him 'elf,' and some call him 'Legion.'"

That struck Alex sideways, and he shook his head. "I don't believe in Satan." Whatever he might believe in, it was not a guy with a pointy tail and carrying a pitchfork. "I think people are responsible for the evil they cause, not some mustache-twirling villain."

Danu nodded. "Nevertheless, your soul has been compromised. I assure you what he tells you is true. Has he shown it to you?"

"Shown what?"

"Your soul."

Alex remembered the dream. The bottomless black that had terrified him so horribly. "No," he lied. He pressed palms against his chest. "How do I get him out of there?"

"What does he desire?"

"I don't know. He keeps telling me he wants me to suffer. He keeps . . ." A flush of embarrassment colored his cheeks as he realized he was about to blurt his deepest shame to a stranger. But he needed her help and forced himself to continue. "He keeps asking me about my wife. It's like he's hinting . . . things. Infidelity."

"And you're certain he's not trying to warn you of—" Alex threw her a sharp glance and she sighed. "No, I suppose not."

"Listen, if you know this guy, do you think maybe you could talk him into leaving me alone?"

She smiled and waved away the silly thought. "I told you, the creature is bereft and without ties. Those few people were his entire world. Almost literally. He barely knows I exist, and would never listen to me if he heard me."

"How do I get him to back off?"

"What is it he finds so interesting about your soul?"

"Search me." A puzzled look crossed her face, and he clarified. "I mean, I don't know."

"Perhaps searching you is what you need to do yourself. Are you a good man, Alexander?"

"Yes." *No.* The voice echoed in his bones, and it was his own.

She threw her head back and laughed out loud, and anger rose in him. "So certain! I only wish I could be so sure of being good."

"I do my duty."

"And that is . . . ?"

"I defend my land. And my wife."

"You keep others away from what is yours."

"I fight for my country."

"Your land, as you said."

"My people. The Scottish people. The MacNeils."

"You have prospered well by your fighting."

"That's not why I do it, though. I do it to protect people."

"It's not? If Scotland and the MacNeils are protected and kept safe, do you not prosper then? How do you separate the protecting from the prospering?"

Alex fell silent. Anger roared in his head, and he stared at the ground to keep control over himself. He'd never hit a woman, but just then he was horribly tempted. While he gazed at the ground, she sighed again and when she spoke her voice was very, very soft.

"Alexander, *mo caraid*, tell me. Have you ever done anything—anything at all—only because 'twas the right thing to do? And no other reason?"

Moving only his eyes, he looked over at her. The expression on her face was of sadness. Nearly pity, and he couldn't stand that. Without another word, he backed out of the faerie ring, stepped onto the track, and resumed his run.

CHAPTER 20

Not long after Alex's visit with Danu, a messenger from the king came to Eilean Aonarach. Alex and his men were to meet Sir James Douglas in Lochmaben and support his efforts at expanding Robert's influence in the Lowlands. Both the Bruces were in Ireland, attempting to rid that island of English influence and so protect Scotland on that side. The fight in Scotland was left to Robert's staunchest supporters.

Alex felt a thrill of pleasure to be called upon, that overrode his dislike of Douglas. More than the prospect of having something interesting to do, this meant the king had faith in him, and since Alex had been well rewarded in the past he anticipated similar compensation. Or better. Perhaps somewhere down the road, if luck went his way and he found opportunities to demonstrate his worth and loyalty to Robert, he might one day even be elevated to the peerage. Ruling class. The prospect was heady.

He gave orders to prepare to leave Eilean Aonarach. Men loaded boats with supplies and new equipment. They checked and repaired armor and weapons, and stepped up training. Alex's knights were sharp. Not letting them turn lazy during the winter had given them an edge he knew would help them keep up with Douglas's experienced crew. Sir James had spent the winter harrying the Borderlands. They were, and always had been, the crack troops of the Scottish army, and Alex's contingent would need to step lively.

During these days Lindsay grew very quiet. In daytime she moved about the castle discreetly, keeping to the shadows and finding things to do away from Alex. Easy enough to accomplish, for women's concerns hardly ever brought her into his sphere. But he knew she was unhappy. At night she lay beside him, unmoving and silent. He said nothing either, for he didn't want to start an argument.

Vain hope. When he declined to address her issues, she pressed them on him.

"Why must you go?" She approached him in the anteroom of their chambers, and blocked his exit from the bedchamber. The maid had gone, and they were alone. Alex looked toward the door, but knew the maid wouldn't return until the argument was finished. He wished she would.

"It's my job."

"It is not. It's not even your duty. You know very well you could send your men and not go yourself."

He heaved an impatient sigh and wished this stuff weren't so hard to explain. "I certainly cannot. Maybe if I were an elderly English peer I could stay, but for me to do that right now would be to risk pissing off the king and eventually losing the island if he thought my sympathies might stray. At the very least it would damage my reputation among the vassals."

"Your reputation as a fighter?" Her tone suggested his reputation wasn't very important.

"Well, yeah." His tone suggested she should already know this and having to tell her was a waste of his time. "That's what I do. It's how I got here in the first place."

"Is this what I gave up my independence for? For you to go off and leave me?" Tears glistened in her eyes, and there was so much tension in her she was nearly as still as a mannequin.

The same tension filled him, and he also was quite still as he asked, "You're sorry you married me?"

"I wish there were some way to be with you more. I never see you in the daytime, and now I won't even see you at night."

Realization dawned. "You want to come with me."

"If you must go. I miss sharing the days with you. Take me with you on the campaign."

"I won't put you in that sort of danger."

"Alex—"

"No." His ears and cheeks warmed with anger. "The whole time you were my squire, I white-knuckled every day in fear for your safety. It was a nightmare. Now that you're safe, I want you to stay that way. I'm not going to let you within reach of the murdering Eng . . . of those who would hurt you in unthinkable ways."

"Alex—"

"You remember how frightened you were to be an unattached woman? Do you remember why you bound your breasts and picked up a mace to fight like a man? Well, now that I know what you knew then, I'm exactly as afraid as you were. I couldn't live with what might happen to you out there. So forget it. There's no way I'm taking you with me."

Lindsay turned and fled the room. Alex went after her and shouted from the door, "Lindsay!"

They both froze. Lindsay at the bottom of the stairs turned to glance around the room, her face gone pale. But nobody seemed to have heard. She frowned at him, then continued up the stairs.

But as Alex began to withdraw into the anteroom again, he saw a shadow move in the far corner of the meeting room. Sir Orrin stepped from the corner behind the hearth and watched her ascend, then immediately followed her. Alex hurried after with rising apprehension.

From the top of the stairs Orrin shouted to all who happened to be in the Great Hall, "Oh, ho! So the knight banneret has found a way to slip his member to his squire after all!" Alex broke to a run and arrived at the top of the stairs just as Orrin yanked hard on Lindsay's dress to rip away the fabric and reveal her breasts.

She screamed, and staggered backward. No bra, of course, so she was laid bare for all to see. Orrin's face betrayed a shock equal to hers. He'd obviously expected to find a man's chest and a false bosom.

"Orrin!" Alex bellowed. Rage blinded him and the room became a swarm of reddish shapes. Voices faded into the distance under the roar of blood slamming through him. He drew his dagger and strode toward the knight. Without the slightest hesitation, he plunged it into Orrin's gut.

The knight doubled over with a loud, outraged cry. Alex wrenched the dagger out sideways, to make certain Orrin would die. Eventually. Then he gave a shove with his boot and the offender toppled, wailing his pain and surprise.

"I thought . . ." Tears came to his eyes as he realized his foolishness and his approaching end. "You called her Lindsay."

Alex's chest heaved and he struggled to focus on the dying knight. "A mistake, Orrin. But only a slip of the tongue, and a far less serious error than yours." He looked around the room at faces gone white with shock. "Someone take this corpse to the barracks, where I won't have to listen to him anymore." He raised his dagger to gesture with its point at the onlookers. "And the next man to lay hand on my wife will suffer the same. I swear it."

Then he turned to Lindsay, who held her dress to her chest, gaping in shock at the man in agony on the floor. "Get downstairs."

She went without argument. He followed her, and her maid came behind. By the time they reached the bedchamber, she was weeping, sobbing uncontrollably. "How could you do it?"

The maid hurried to provide another outfit for Lindsay, and began undressing her.

Alex went to the wash bowl to clean his hand and dagger of Orrin's blood. "He had it coming. He's had it coming for a long time."

"You killed him. You know he's going to die of that wound."

He shrugged. "He might not. You never know."

The maid lifted a fresh shift over her head, then Lindsay said, "I do know. There was bile, I could smell it. He might not die till next week, but you know he won't survive the wound."

"I said, he deserved it. He's been begging for it for months. I had to do something; that was just going too far. The men wouldn't respect me if I let Orrin live after pulling a stunt like that."

"It's all about your pride, isn't it?" She waved off the maid offering a fresh dress, and stood there in her torn shift.

He turned to peer at her. "My pride? How about keeping this household together? Keeping the *island* in one piece? How about making sure I don't appear weak enough that someone might decide I'm an easy target for military attack, or even assassination? You just don't get it, do you?"

"I get that you've become something you never were before."

"You never knew me before."

"I knew you weren't like this."

"Like what?"

"Like . . . a tyrant. Alex, you just killed a man in cold blood. Necessary or not, before we came here you never would have shrugged it off like this."

"Like I said, he deserved it."

"You could have sent him away. Should have, long ago."

"What's that supposed to mean?"

"It means I think you've decided this little fiefdom is more like a kingdom and you're the sovereign. You've decided you own everything and everyone in it, and so it never occurred to you to send Orrin away. You simply tried to control him, and when he overstepped you put him down like an animal. As if he were a possession to keep or destroy at your whim."

"That's bullshit."

"It's what I see, Alex. I've seen it coming for a long time, and it's killing me to watch. You've become someone I no longer know."

"If you think that, then you've never really known me."

Eyes wide with grief, she fell silent. They stared at each other, and Alex wished there were something more to say. Something that would make it all go away. She didn't know him, and had never known him. And she apparently didn't like what she now saw. Nor did she love.

Without another word, he left the room.

For the rest of the day he kept busy with preparations to leave. He ate alone, taking his meat to the hoist platform outside the keep, where he looked out across the barbican to where his ships lay, waiting to take himself and his men and horses across to the mainland for the fight. He'd had the sails painted with his stylized bald eagle, wings spread and head facing dexter. It was a pleasure to see, for now folks on the water would know who he was. The bald eagle was unique, and becoming known. Alasdair an Dubhar MacNeil was a force to be reckoned with.

Tomorrow he would be away. After that, there was no telling what might happen to him. Whether he came back or not would be left up to fate. For a brief moment he was tempted to give in and bring Lindsay along, but now he wasn't sure she would go.

Damned if he was going to cave on that point and have it thrown back at him. Besides, he still wanted her away from danger. Even more, he wanted her away from Sir James.

No, she was staying here, and that was the end of it.

She was nowhere to be seen that night when he went to the bedchamber to sleep. Alex thought briefly of looking for her, but didn't care to be seen prowling the castle in search of his stray wife. So he undressed and slipped into bed. His heart was a knot in his chest as he dropped into an uneasy sleep.

The fire was still flickering on the other side of the room when he was awakened by a warm presence in the bed next to him. He knew the scent of his wife, and reached for her. She slipped into his arms, and everything that had been said that day melted away from his mind.

"I'm sorry," she murmured.

"Hmm," he replied, and when he kissed her it was a relief to let go of the anger and grief that had choked him so.

"I thought I would stay away until you'd left, but then I realized how long you would be gone, and how horribly I would regret not saying good-bye if you didn't come back."

He didn't care. All he cared was that she was there, and she was apologizing. Once again he could believe she loved him, and that brightened the dark world. He kissed her again, then bent to take a breast into his mouth and slip a hand between her thighs. But she eased his hand away, then kissed his chest in preparation to scoot down and take him into her mouth.

"No." He stopped her.

She kissed his chest again. "I thought you liked it."

"I do. I like it a lot. But not tonight."

"Especially tonight."

"I want you." He reached behind her and pressed her hips against him. Her cycle was well known to him. He didn't want her mouth at all tonight. "I want to make love to you."

"Alex—" Already she was breathless and ready for him. He could hear in her voice her resolve was weak. She wanted it, too.

He kissed her ear and murmured softly into it, "Please. I might not come back. Let me at least hope for a chance of leaving something behind." He kissed her neck, then her breast again, and nudged a knee between hers. His palm pressed the damp part of her. "Do you love me?" He wouldn't take it further if she resisted, but he held his breath that she would let him.

"You know I do." Her knee fell back to let him in, and she pressed herself to his hand. Hands clutched his shoulders as he settled between her thighs and buried his face in her neck. The feel of her and the scent of her filled him to his skin, and for now he thought she might truly love him after all.

AFTER journeying by boat to Ayre on the mainland, then making their way south and east through the mountains of Galloway, Alex and his men rode into Lochmaben Castle to find the contingent of Scottish knights belonging to Sir James Douglas fairly depleted. No wonder he'd requested reinforcements. Only a few squires went about their duties, and there were no knights to be seen. No horses in sight at all. Women and children far outnumbered the men here, quite a change from when Alex had seen the place last. While the MacNeil knights dismounted and went to find food and shelter for themselves and their mounts, Alex looked around at the small numbers of men about.

"You!" he called to one nearby, whose head had been shaved for nits. "Where's Douglas?"

The young man turned and pointed. "Through that portal and up. Knock on the door at the top."

Alex thanked him, then dismounted and handed his horse over to Colin. Then he gave some general orders for the night to Sir Henry before heading inside in search of Douglas.

The stairs inside were steep and narrow and led in odd directions to the top of the tower. They came to a dead-end at the door without any landing, and Alex reached up from the third step down to knock. The deep, muttery voice of Sir James ordered him to enter. Alex shoved open the heavy door and climbed the remaining stairs to find the large room nearly empty. A narrow bed stood against one wall, and a table strewn with papers and piled with weaponry stood beside one of the arrow loops.

Long, lanky Douglas sat on the bed, running his hands through his shaggy, black hair and coughing himself awake. He looked up at Alex, blinked at him in the waning firelight, and sighed. "Good. You're here. We'll waste no time, then." He reached over to a bell pull and yanked it. "They're lazy devils in this place. If someone deigns to respond before sunset, we'll have meat and wine."

Alex pointed with his chin toward a darkening arrow loop and said, "They'll need to hurry; the sun is nearly down."

Douglas blinked at the loop, then rose from his cot and went to peer out it, leaning heavily on the table. He grunted, then coughed up a wad of phlegm and spat it through the opening. "Damn. I slept longer than I'd intended." Then he stood and turned to face Alex. "Well, the men need a rest, I suppose. And your men will be fresh in the morning. We'll go then."

Alex wondered if this guy ever stopped fighting.

"Come," said Douglas. "Sit with me and we'll decide where to strike next." He went through a door to an adjoining room and brought back a chair for Alex to sit. Waving a thumb toward that room, he said, "That's where you'll sleep while we're here. Bare bones for comfort, but with any luck we'll not be here much at all." He sat back down on his bunk, and Alex straddled the chair backwards. Douglas opened his mouth to speak again, but there was a knock on the door and a serving man entered.

"Sir?" The servant hurried to light the candles in sconces about the room.

"Food," ordered Douglas. "The lamb, all of it, cold and in a hurry. MacNeil here is without doubt a hungry man. And wine." He held up two fingers, and Alex knew he meant two jugs. That would be a lot of wine. "Bread. There'd better be some."

"Aye, sir. There's bread."

"Not burnt, like this morning."

"Not burnt, sir."

"Very well, then." He waved the man off. "Hurry. We've a hungry and dangerous MacNeil to feed." He clapped twice, and shooed the servant out the door. Then he returned his attention to Alex and began briefing him on the tactical situation in the area.

Literacy rates and travel technology being what they were, most others in these times never expended much energy on the gathering of intelligence, but this guy was busy enough and determined enough to have constructed a network of communication throughout the Lowlands. The papers littering the table were missives from spies and patrols he'd deployed, and the two pored over them. Alex noted they were all written in plain language, and he considered introducing to Douglas the concept of encoding. Even a simple letter-substitution code would be better than this.

As they talked, Alex watched the man's face. His dislike of James Douglas simmered in his gut as he remembered how Lindsay had liked to hang out with him and his men.

"She wanted him to see her as a woman."

That damned elf. Alex shuddered and shut his eyes to wait for the revulsion to pass. Then he glanced at Douglas to be sure he hadn't heard the comment, but Douglas was oblivious as the voice continued.

"She asked to come with you so her dear friend might know he could have her. At long last. You know she's been longing for him since those weeks in Torwood."

Alex struggled to keep his face a mask and his voice even, but felt a chill crawl across his skin. He stared hard at Douglas's face, handsome in a way that even Alex had to recognize as attractive, and hated him. Then he took a deep breath and reminded himself who his real enemy was. He hated Nemed more.

The food came, and Alex ate little. Douglas ate even less. His enthusiasm for the fight seemed to leave little room for other considerations, and he kept Alex for hours, talking about terrain, English garrisons, territories and landholders loyal to each king, and the personalities of each man involved.

Lochmaben was their base, where they would retreat for rest and provisioning. The castle was supplied and manned by clans of the Highlands and upper Lowlands. Mountains rose to the north, where local clans supported King Robert and the Scottish army could disappear if they'd a need. The Scots would sweep over the border at will, like avengers, onto the English farmers.

By the time they were interrupted again, Alex had a detailed concept in his head of the situation in the Lowlands and understood Douglas's plan of harassment. A young woman entered the room without knocking. "Oh. Pardon me, James, I thought you were alone." She was about to withdraw, but Douglas waved her in.

"Come. Stay. MacNeil was just leaving." She hurried across the room to him, and he addressed Alex as he drew the girl onto the bunk. "Your room is in there, Alasdair. All made up for you.

Good night. We'll be off in the morning at first light." Then he turned to kiss the girl and Alex was forgotten.

Alex took the hint and rose to retreat to his new quarters; the only entrance was through Douglas's room. Alex grunted with disgust at the scant furnishings, and he returned to retrieve the chair he'd been sitting on all evening, ignoring the half-naked, writhing pair on Douglas's bunk. He also appropriated one of James's candles for the sake of lighting his own. Other than that chair, Alex's room contained only a cot and a pile of peats for the fire. Nothing else. Douglas hadn't lied, for the cot was made up for him with heavy blankets and rough linens. The small hearth held a failing fire, and Alex went to revive it.

The cot next door began to smack against the wall, a distant tap through the stone which must have resounded heavily within the room, and Alex felt so deeply homesick for Lindsay and Eilean Aonarach it stuck in his throat. Disgusted, tired, and lonely, he divested himself of his armor and spurs, dumped them on the floor, and crawled under the woolen blankets of the cot to drop into heavy, exhausted insensibility.

Early the next morning the Scots sallied out of the castle and across the countryside. All day long in the saddle, all night long alone in a tent, Alex, Douglas, and their men rode through the Lowlands in search of English holdings to plunder. Most days did not bring an objective, and they all considered themselves lucky to find a rich target. They worked their way south and into England, for Scottish farmers had little to take no matter what their allegiance.

And very often nobody knew where a man's loyalties lay. Alex often found himself following Douglas against farmers unlucky enough to be in disputed territory, and after a while it became too difficult to determine true allegiances. Worrying about the niceties of protecting noncombatants became next to pointless, and so Alex stopped worrying. Any farmer caught paying anything to Edward II, or caught not paying tribute to Robert, was fair game.

The Scottish raiders evicted, raided, and laid siege as before, torching houses and making off with livestock, and now it was with the surety of established territory to which to retreat.

Nights Alex spent alone in his tent, picking lice from his clothing and wishing Lindsay were there so he could run his hands through her hair again. At home, he'd grown so accustomed to her presence in bed he could hardly sleep through the short nights without her now. And when he did sleep it was fitful, filled with dreams. Often when he awoke, just as he reached consciousness he heard the voice of Nemed saying, "I wonder what she does all day."

He hated that voice. It shook him to his core to wonder about Lindsay. What she was feeling, what she was doing. How she was coping with those living on the island. Whether she would ever betray him. If that elf would show himself, Alex would lay him out and make sure he didn't get up. Terrible thoughts ate at him each day, and when time came to ride into a fray against other knights it was all he could do to put Lindsay aside in his mind and concentrate only on his job. Struggling against the weakness hardened him until his body ached from it. The longing to send for her nearly destroyed his resolve to keep her safe. And away from Douglas.

Douglas, riding on Alex's left, reined his horse over to be close enough to speak quietly. "There's a determined look. I would fear to be the man in your thoughts just now, Alasdair."

Douglas didn't know Alex hated him. Alex wiped the deep frown from his face and shrugged. "I long for news from home."

Douglas grunted. "Don't wish for news, for nobody ever receives good news on campaign. Only the bad. Pray you hear nothing."

Alex also grunted.

A grin crossed Douglas's face. "You aren't losing your heart for the battle, are you, Alasdair?"

Now Alex had to force a smile and hoped it was insouciant enough. "Never. Show me some Englishmen, and I'll show you how much heart I have for the fight."

Douglas laughed, and began to chat companionably about the campaign immediately previous to Alex's arrival. Much had happened during the winter, and Douglas told of funny things as well as exciting ones.

Much to Alex's surprise, the guy seemed to like him and wanted to hang out. One evening, after a particularly lucrative raid, Alex was in his tent, sewing up a nasty stab wound in his calf, when Douglas walked in with a ceramic jug dangling from one finger.

Not expecting company, Alex had his trews down around his ankles and his ruined boots tossed to the side. Without looking up at his visitor he adjusted his linens with a quick tug to be certain he wasn't poking out of them, then gestured to a spot on the ground nearby. "Have a seat. I'm afraid you've caught me with my trews down." He continued with his work, sticking his needle into the edges of his wound. As Lindsay had said, sewing while it still hurt at least kept it from hurting twice.

Douglas sat. "Is it a bad wound?" Meaning, was it still bleeding?

"No. I lost little blood and can ride tomorrow." Walking would be an entirely different prospect, but he'd be damned if he was going to hang back for a wound that had broken no bones.

"Good." Douglas lifted the jug to his mouth and tilted his head back for a healthy swig. Then he belched and said, "Ah. Good English wine."

Alex gave a dry chuckle. "Too bad it's not whiskey." He could do with a shot of something to clean his wound, and wished he knew more about distilling than he did.

Douglas peered at him as he handed over the jug and Alex took a drink. "You're a strange man, an Dubhar."

"Yes, I am." Alex handed back the jug and stuck himself with the needle again.

Douglas chuckled, and Alex looked at him slantways. Couldn't this guy tell Alex hated him? He was grinning and drinking his wine like a gomer, oblivious to the fact that his second-in-command wished him to drop dead. Or at least get the hell out of his tent, whichever might be most easily accomplished.

"That was a great excitement today, Alasdair."

Alex had to smile, for it was true. The foray had been to a small town to the east of Carlisle, and though the locals had put up a fight, they had been no match for the Scots. Douglas, Alex, and their men had chased off the defenders, who disappeared into the woods, then carried off hundreds of head of cattle, sheep, and horses. Alex that day had acquired, besides his wound, a courser with feathered fetlocks he liked very much.

"Excellent haul."

Douglas chuckled again at Alex's odd way of speaking, and offered the jug again. Alex tied off his last stitch, cut the thread with his dagger, then took another slug of the wine before standing to pull his trews back up around his hips. The wound in his leg burned like fire, and there was no telling whether he'd ever walk without a limp again, but he would never let on to Douglas any of that. He restored his belt over his tunic, then sat again to listen some more to Douglas reliving the day's raid.

The wine was not strong, but it was making pleasant inroads on Alex's sobriety. The praise from Sir James for his bravery and ingenuity during the fight washed over Alex, and a warmth kicked in. He looked over at the king's favorite and once again saw the angry young man who had accompanied his mentor to the coronation. The years had taken the chip from his shoulder, but not the edge from his desire for revenge against Edward. The English king had ruined and eventually killed Douglas's father, and Alex thought of how he'd be if that had happened to his own father. He might be just as ruthless and driven.

In spite of himself, Alex found himself thinking he should be glad to be riding with the guy. As clueless about strategy as most knights were these days, he was lucky to be taking orders from someone who gave a damn about something besides tilting willy-nilly against English lances. James Douglas may have been a danger to the ladies, but he was also an hellacious fighter. He led his men, and Alex, with an energy Alex envied. And he couldn't help admiring. It was no wonder Robert was so taken with the guy. His hatred of the English was evident in every gesture, and every syllable of his speech.

Further, as Alex realized this he also realized Lindsay could never be attracted to such a man. In that instant, the knot in Alex's gut loosened. He no longer hated James Douglas, and it was a relief.

He said, "Hey, James. You know those communiqués you send back and forth to your scouts and spies? How come they're never encoded?"

Douglas held up a palm. "No need. The messengers can't read, and never know what they carry."

"But if the messages were to fall into the wrong hands, the very people you wish most not to read them will still be able to."

Douglas shrugged to acknowledge the point. "What do you suggest?"

Alex lowered his voice and began to explain the letter-replacement code. It was the simplest of all codes and the easiest to break, but in these days of creative spelling and multilingual populace Alex figured he could throw in a few new slants on the idea. Douglas listened raptly, nodding and smiling.

Retreat to Lochmaben was in late May, and there was revelry all through the castle newly alive with victorious men. The Great Hall echoed with music and voices, and was stacked with foods hard to find north of the border, or even north of the English Channel. French wine flowed freely, and late in the evening Alex found himself parked at a table near a corner, sitting on a crooked stool. It had three legs, and he wasn't entirely certain whether they were horribly uneven or he was simply too drunk to sit up straight. In any case, he was too wasted to stay on by himself, and so leaned heavily on the table while idly sucking the marrow from a broken beef rib.

An extremely cheerful James Douglas heaved himself, laughing, onto the bench opposite, pulled his mistress down next to him, and began making out with her. She made it plain to the entire room exactly how pleased she was to see her lover again. One tit was hanging out the drawstring neck of her shift, which was all she wore, and Douglas was pawing it while sticking his tongue as far down her throat as he could get it. Alex was himself too drunk to care, or even realize, he was staring at Douglas's hard, dark fingers kneading deeply soft, white flesh.

Douglas took his mouth from the girl, turned to Alex, gazed stupidly for a moment, then said, "MacNeil! My friend! Would you care for a bit of this?" He jiggled the woman's breast.

Alex gaped, equally stupid for the moment. He would, indeed, care for some of that, but was taken aback at the generosity. He stammered, "Uh, your mistress . . ."

"She's nobody."

"I like that!" The girl had some cheek, at least, if not much intelligence.

Douglas shrugged. "Very well, you're somebody, but I don't own your bastards is my meaning."

"You could."

"I would if you had your way, but I'll have none of it. You're comely and I love you, but I've no illusions about how you spend your time while I'm away." He slapped her hip. "Now,

get over there and give the Hungarian a warm welcome. He's
handsome enough for you, and I happen to know his purse is a
heavy one."

The girl eyed Alex and shifted in her seat as if pleasuring
herself against the bench. "And what of his other purse?"

"Now, that I couldn't say. You'll have to find out for yourself."

She grinned and began to climb over the table, but Alex held
up his palms.

"No. No, thank you." Suddenly he was flashing on the look
on Lindsay's face the morning after he'd banged that whore at
Linlithgow. What she would say about this now as his wife was
ringing in his ears and echoing in his skull, though she was hundreds of miles away.

"No?" Douglas seemed genuinely shocked. "You insult me,
MacNeil!" It was said with a grin, but also an edge to his voice.

Alex shrugged. "Well, she's pretty and all. And I do appreciate the gesture. I think I'd rather wait till I get home to my
wife."

Nemed's voice in his head said, "And do you think your wife
is waiting? All alone in that castle, unhappy with you, surrounded by guardsmen. She'd be glad to know you were sticking yourself into a cunny that wasn't hers."

Alex looked around for the source of the voice, but of course
found nobody. He thought as loudly as possible, *Don't you ever
sleep you freak?*

Nemed's reply was nothing but a laugh.

Douglas laughed. "Saving yourself for your wife? I daresay
my wife would as soon see me worry the livestock as to bother
her." An enormous, small-toothed grin spread across his face.
"The poor woman cannot keep up with me, you see. I come
home and she barricades herself in her bedchamber for fear of
my enormous member." He reached under the table. "Would
you like to see?"

Before Alex could demur, Sir James had his tunic up, his trews
down around his knees, and was standing with his semi-erect penis lying on the table. "See? It's huge!" The girl squealed and
reached out to pet it. Alex, gawking with a head full of wine and
mead, couldn't help a mild relief the thing didn't seem all that
large and was in fact noticeably smaller than his own.

Then Douglas said, his voice overflowing with drunken glee, "So, MacNeil! Show us—"

He was stopped dead in mid-sentence as the girl bent down to take the organ into her mouth. Douglas emitted a loud moan that reverberated across the room over voices of other revelers, and sank back onto the bench behind him. The girl's mouth kept with him and she disappeared behind the table as Douglas threw his head back to enjoy, his Adam's apple poking from his long neck. Wanting to compare tools with Alex was entirely forgotten. Alex took the opportune moment to slip quickly and quietly away, still limping from his leg wound, giggling helplessly.

Drunk as he was, he made his way carefully up the winding stairs to his bedchamber and shed all his clothes to crawl into the narrow bunk. Delicious, wild images tumbled in his brain, of the girl sucking on Douglas. Then he imagined himself with her. That was nice. He rolled over to press himself against the mattress as that image danced pleasantly in his head and the room spun around him.

Then, unbidden and unwelcome, came a picture of Lindsay doing the same to Orrin . . . No, Orrin was dead. To Cullan, then. No, Cullan was dead. The image shifted to her bending over to receive . . .

Nemed. She was doing it with Nemed.

Heart thudding wildly in his throat, Alex sat up in his bunk and nearly fell out of it. He couldn't see past the image. It was clear. Perfect. Every detail, every hair on the elfin ass, every nuance of the pleasure in her voice. Not rape. She wanted it. God help him, she wanted it.

"Stop this." Pain filled him. He needed this to end or he would go crazy. *"Stop this now!"*

His sight cleared, but the memory lingered. Lindsay and Nemed. As if it had actually happened, and he had been there to see it. He shook, trembled with the terrible uncertainty, and as the sweat cooled on his body he shivered with the cold. He lay back down under the blankets and shut his eyes tight to sleep, knowing that even in sleep, deep within the castle keep, he wouldn't be safe.

CHAPTER 21

In early August, having served the number of days due his liege and bolstered by commendations from Sir James and hints of a peerage title in his future, Alex was released from service for the year and made his way back to Eilean Aonarach with his men. This year, in spite of losses sustained in battle, Alex headed home with more men than when he'd left. In addition, he brought back an entire boatload of goods and gold. Mostly goods, but he was now far wealthier than he'd been in April. The influx of livestock and materials would be a huge benefit to all the MacNeils and MacConnells on the island. He sailed from the mainland with light heart, eager to see home again, and Lindsay.

Eager to tell of his prospects for elevation, Alex could hardly contain himself as he leapt from the ship to his quay and strode through the barbican gate. Gaze flitting here and there in search of his wife, his heart fluttered against the fear of being greeted with bad news. There had been no communication between them for the entire four months, for sending messages and letters was an expensive and undependable proposition easily accomplished only by the very rich and powerful.

In the barbican, his breath was taken away by the sight of Lindsay hurrying down the steps along the cliff, her skirts in her fists and a huge, white smile on her face. Her eyes were wide and bright as they searched his face. He hurried to her, and at the bottom step she leapt into his arms.

His heart soared that she was still alive and happy to see him, and as she hugged his neck he nuzzled hers. The scent of her hair was home to him, and his soul calmed. Others moved around them, knights making their way through the barbican toward the keep, then beyond that the bailey and barracks, and they went ignored. Alex had regained his other half, and now he felt whole for the first time in months. He set her down gently and went to kiss her, but she stopped him.

"Alex, guess what." Her voice was so soft in his ear, he could barely hear beneath the din of arriving men. There was news, but he was reluctant to hear it. He went ahead and kissed her so she wouldn't spoil this perfect moment. Her lips were warm and welcoming. Her body felt wonderful in his arms. He held her to him and felt of the smooth, silken dress, her back and hips. He held her waist, and that was when he realized. Their lips parted, and he looked into her face, stunned. Her stomach was no longer flat. She'd gained weight, and he could only hope . . .

"Alex, I'm pregnant." The whisper was feather soft.

All he could do was gape at her. Anything he could possibly say now would sound shallow and unimportant. *Pregnant.* The image of her with Nemed rose, but he blinked it from his mind. That had been a trick. He needed more than anything to believe that, and it became true in his mind.

A worried look crossed her face. "This is what you wanted, yes?"

Finally, he smiled and sighed. "It's wonderful." Beyond wonderful. So far beyond wonderful that his vocabulary failed him. He held both her hands in his and kissed them, then knelt and pressed his face to the slight bulge of her belly, his hands splayed against her sides. He didn't care who might be watching, or making comment on his weakness. "On my soul, Lin, it's the most wonderful thing that could ever happen."

"If the little parasite lives."

Alex's gut clenched and he looked up. *Nemed.* A shiver took him as he realized how vulnerable he'd just become, and he looked around. No elf. Alex stood.

"He's here." His voice shook with rage and he stood.

"Who is?"

"That Nemed."

Lindsay looked around. "You see him? Why won't he show himself to me?"

Alex glanced at her, and for a moment wondered why she wanted that. "I heard him." He looked around. "I swear, I'm going to kill that sonofabitch." His fingers touched the hilt of his sword, and he held her hand to take her into the keep.

"You can't kill him." She held her belly as she climbed, and he put an arm around her waist for support.

"Sure, I can. I get my hands on him, he's one dead elf."

"He's the only one who can send us home."

Stillness overcame Alex. He stared at her, unbelieving. Incredulous. "We can't go home."

"We must." She continued to climb, and he followed her into the stairwell.

"We'd lose everything."

"Lose what? What everything?"

"Our home. Our life here. Lin, there's talk of making me an earl."

But she ignored that. "You wanted a baby, now we're going to have a baby, and now we have to go home to save its life."

"Lin—"

"*Alex.*" Now it was her turn to stare, uncomprehending. Inside the Great Hall, she let go of her skirts and gaped at him. Her wide eyes glittered with tears, and her voice shook. It appeared she'd been thinking about this for a long time. "Do you know what the infant mortality rate is here? Have you even noticed the death rate in general? Even among those who aren't soldiers? People don't live very long. The life expectancy here doesn't even come close to retirement age for us. Most babies don't live past the first year. After that, children can't be counted on to live to adulthood unless they've reached the age of ten or so. We must go home, for the sake of our child!"

As she spoke, his head moved slowly, side to side in denial. "No. Are you nuts? I can't go to Nemed and ask him for this. I can't ask him for anything, let alone this. He's dangerous and he hates us. He'd do something terrible. I won't put us in that position."

"Alex—"

"No." He turned to walk away, headed for the stairs down to the living quarters. He didn't want to talk about this. This life they'd happened upon was a done deal, and there was no changing their circumstance.

Lindsay followed. "You can, and you will. Or I will. Danu says—"

"No." At the top of the stairs he turned. "Danu knows nothing. You'll ask that elf nothing. Not that you need to; now that you've said it aloud he probably knows what's on your mind." Alex glanced around, half expecting to see those red eyes floating among the shadows, and shuddered. Quickly, he descended the steps to get out of the hall. Lindsay followed.

"Alex, listen to me." At the bottom of the stairs she stopped, but he kept walking. "Alex." He headed for the door to the living quarters anteroom. But at her next, strident, words, he stopped short. *"Bubonic plague, Alex."*

He turned toward her. "What?"

"In about thirty years. Plague will wipe out more than half the population of Europe. Whole towns will be emptied of people. Religious fanaticism will run rampant."

Alex snorted. "Worse than now?"

"Far worse. Unimaginably worse. There will be economic chaos. Widespread and chronic emotional depression. It will be a horror most modern novelists would find impossible to write, because nobody would believe it. And it will only be the first of several pandemics. Only the first, Alex."

"You and I are descended from people who survived the plague."

"And who survived smallpox, but we're not immune to it without vaccination. I wouldn't care to be exposed to plague. I certainly don't want my child . . ." Tears choked her and she blinked them back and forced the rest through her throat, ". . . my child to contract it. *Our* child, Alexander."

He had no reply to that, but only stared at her. They couldn't go home. Nemed would never send them, he knew it. And he would rather cut off an arm than to ask anything of that creature in any case. "We've built a life here."

"We had lives before we came here."

But not together. She was thinking of that Derek guy, he was

sure of it. Flatly, he said, "It isn't an option." Then he turned to
enter the apartments, and strode on into the bedchamber.

She followed him, "Alex, you must—"

"I don't want to talk about this. I said, it's not an option. We
can't do it. Nemed would never cooperate."

"We can try. Try to contact him."

"No."

"Alex—"

"I said, no!" He began to strip, first wriggling from his
hauberk and flinging it across the room to slide up against the
far wall in a jingling mound of tiny iron links. "Now, send in
Mary to fill the bath. I'm tired, I'm hungry, and I've got something insectile crawling around in my hair I want gone." He
poked his fingers into his hair in search of a bug that had been
driving him nuts all day.

She stared at him, unmoving.

He stopped to turn and address her. "Now."

Then she turned on her heel and left, presumably to find
Mary.

Alex collapsed into a chair by the hearth, propped his elbows on his knees, and laid his face in his hands until his anger
passed. Then he sat back and stared into the flames, his mind
turning fitfully with everything he'd just learned, and one thing
rose to the surface to fill his consciousness. If he could only get
his hands on that elf, he'd fix it so Lindsay would stop thinking
they could ever go home. And while he was at it, he might have
a turn at Danu as well.

Once he was in the bath he felt better, though Lindsay was
silent, staring out the window and declining to help him scrub.
He'd be damned if he would ask her. So he washed his own hair
and picked out the flea by himself. Then he stepped from the
tub to stand by the high fire and toweled off with a large piece
of linen. The towel was a little stiff with a grease residue,
though it had been laundered; he would need to have a talk with
Mary about letting the kitchen use the towels meant for his bath.
As he reached for another towel, he glanced over at Lindsay.
Tears glistened on her face.

"I really am happy about the baby." The towel went around
his waist.

"I expect you are." Her voice sounded bitter.

"But you're not?"

"I'm terrified."

"It'll be all right."

She turned to him, and her face crumpled to weeping. "No, it won't. It's already not all right, for I'm married to a man who won't even try to do what's best for his child."

"There's nothing to be done."

"Says you."

Anger rose again. "Yes, says me. Nemed is dangerous. He has powers I don't understand and can't counter. Going to him with my hand out is too big a risk. Going anywhere near him is dangerous. I won't take the chance." He went to her and took her hand, half-expecting her to dodge him but she didn't. She only stared into his eyes, her jaw set firmly. He forced his voice into a softness he didn't feel. "We'll be careful about the baby. We'll make sure you eat right, that you stay away from sick people, that your food isn't contaminated. I'll see to it."

"That's not enough."

"It's all we can do."

She looked away, defeated. He kissed her cheek, and a hic-cupping sob shook her, then he took her in his arms and held her. The slight thickening of her belly pressed against him, and he put his hand against her side. *A baby. Holy crap.*

ALEX held his son, so proud he nearly burst out laughing. The boy was perfect, pink and healthy, and everyone agreed he was the image of his father. Life was perfect. The world was perfect.

"My lord," said the soft-voiced maid, "'tis your wife." Fear tinged Mary's words. Alex frowned. "She . . . seems to have taken ill."

Alex handed the baby off to someone, and hurried to Lind-say's side. She lay on the bed piled high with blankets, pale and sweating. Her lips were white and dry, a terrible change from the health she'd displayed only moments before. "Lindsay, what's wrong?"

"I'm dying, Alex. I'm bleeding out." At that moment a rose of blood blossomed on the covers, and spread so fast he knew she was telling the truth. Wailing of the servants echoed in the room, and Alex then realized his voice had joined them.

Then Lindsay was dead, as white as the linen beneath her head. Her cheeks sank into her face, and in moments she'd withered to a tight, dry husk that darkened and crumbled onto the pillow.

The baby began to cry, a high, piercing scream of terrible pain that cut Alex to his soul. He turned to see what was wrong, and found his child covered in sores. The servant holding him had a face covered with black scabs, and now the baby was screaming from the pain of huge, white pustules that grew until they burst, then turned red and continued to cover him. Alex took him into his arms and the screaming continued. The infant writhed in agony as the sores ate into him, leaving only blood-covered bone, tiny, grasping fingers with no flesh on them. Then a final shudder as he, too, died.

Alex threw back his head, sank to his knees, and cried out his heartbreak.

"ALEX!"

He jerked awake to find Lindsay leaning over him and himself covered in sweat. Tears surged in the overwhelming relief it hadn't been real, and he sucked deep breaths to keep them down. He reached up to pull Lindsay down to him, and held her close.

"Another nightmare?"

He nodded, and continued to hold her. Slowly his heart calmed, and he felt of her to make certain she was truly there and alive.

"You were screaming. It must have been a terrible dream."

"I'm okay now."

"Are you certain?"

He nodded. But when she tried to free herself from his grasp, he held onto her. So instead she settled in next to him with her head on his chest. All he wanted was to listen to her breathe, to feel her chest rise and fall against his side and her breath in small puffs against the hairs on his chest. Sleep would be impossible for a long time.

A voice whispered in his ear. "They will both die."

Stupidly Alex looked beyond the bed curtains for the voice, and found the red eyes of Nemed floating in the darkness. He squeezed his own eyes shut, and his heart raced.

"Disease holds sway here, MacNeil. Death is voracious and the woman is naught but fodder. Particularly now. You've murdered your love by what you've done. Silly man."

Alex struggled to not listen, but in the silence of the night the voice was too loud to ignore. It went on.

"The only question now is whether to take them both before childbirth, or to wait and take them one by one after she's endured the pain. Then for her to see the child go before her." A short pause, then, "What do you think, MacNeil? Fast or slow?"

Alex pretended to be asleep, but knew Nemed couldn't be fooled.

The elf continued, forcing Alex to listen and not respond in front of Lindsay. "Scrofula, perhaps? Or leprosy? Or, perhaps, she'll simply never be the same afterward. Sickly and weak. Too weak to risk another pregnancy, and won't that leave you out in the cold? But, no, your comfort is too important to you. You're far too interested in what goes on inside your own skin to worry enough about whether she lives or dies."

That did it. Alex slipped from Lindsay's arms and from the bed, murmured to her he would return shortly, and threw on his shirt and plaid before leaving the room. He retreated to the Great Hall, where only a small pilot fire was falling to embers in the enormous hearth. Alex brought a stool to sit by it, and stared into the red heart that throbbed with heat.

Nemed's voice came from across the hearth, and Alex looked up to find the elf standing with his cape hung from his shoulders and his face bright with sweat and anger. "You can't hide from me."

"What do you want?"

"Nothing. You have nothing I want."

"I know. I can't give you back your people. I wish I could."

Surprise made the elfin face go slack for a moment, but then he recovered and sat in a chair opposite. Slowly, with infinite dignity, he arranged himself and his clothing so he lounged comfortably. Then he addressed Alex without looking at him. "Who have you spoken to?"

"Nobody."

"You lie."

"All right, none of your business. Why do you care who I talk to?" His teeth clenched. *"What do you want from me?"*

"To suffer as I do."

"Unlikely. I'll never have what you lost."

Once again the elf appeared taken aback and glanced over at Alex, but then the persistent rage returned. "Oh, but you do, MacNeil. Look around you." His lips pressed together in a white line and his eyes glowed as red and hot as the embers at Alex's feet. "You are as much lord of your people as I was of mine. And when they die, they will curse your name as mine did me." A painful memory crossed his eyes, then he nodded in the direction of the stairs to the living quarters. "I know she wants me to send her home."

"Us. She wants you to send both of us."

"Both of you? Are you certain? I'll wager she'd be equally happy if I sent only her. You know the only reason she acquiesced to your urging for conception was that she hoped you would see the danger to your progeny and come to me for a way back to your own century. She thought you would have more feeling for the child than you have for her."

"I love her." As he said it, he knew it was a mistake to admit anything personal to this monster, but he continued anyway because he couldn't bear the accusation. "I'd do anything for her."

"Anything except ask me to send her home."

"You wouldn't do it if I did."

The elf's eyebrows went up, and he nodded. "Well, there is that. But you wouldn't ask in any case. You like it here and don't want to go home. Because you know you'll lose her. You know the instant she returns home she'll go running to her Derek. More than likely she'll do away with the child as well. After all, you're the one who wants it, not her. Once she's home, you'll never see her again and you'll have given up everything to be returned to your lowly position, taking abuse from your superiors and from your father." Alex threw him a sharp look of alarm that Nemed could know so much about him. The elf continued, oblivious. "Nobody there will know what you've done here, nobody will ever hear of your accomplishments, your victories. Nobody, Alexander MacNeil, will know who you truly are."

A shiver skittered up Alex's spine at that last, for he knew he was hearing the truth. For better or worse, he was no longer the same man who had taken off from his ship with a civilian passenger that day so many centuries away. Were he to go home, he never would he be able to talk—or even hint—about what he'd done these past two years. A chunk of his life would be gone, and he knew they would become the most important years for him. He'd never again come close to achieving what he'd done here, and would never have the prospects he now saw for himself. His life as it had become would be over, and the man he now was would fade and wither.

He was glad Nemed would never consent to sending Lindsay and himself home.

"I'm going back to bed. Leave me alone, and leave my wife alone." Alex rose and tugged his plaid around himself as he headed back to the stairs down to the family quarters.

"Or what, Alexander? What will you do? Don't forget, I've nothing left to lose. I have naught, and I want naught but to see you suffer. Long and well."

Alex paused at the top of the stairs and gazed blandly at Nemed, then continued on his way.

"I will, Alexander. Mark me, I will."

CHAPTER 22

Out the next morning to survey his holding, counting cattle, observing the progress of the oat crop, and generally making his presence known to his vassals, Alex found himself on the track that took him straight to the ring of Danu. He'd avoided the place since that day he'd spoken to her, and wondered how he'd ended up here now. With a grunt he reined his horse back the way he'd come.

But soon up ahead, he saw the ring again. He turned in his saddle, confused now as to which way he was going. Once again he turned his horse, but farther on yet again found himself approaching the ring of toadstools. He sighed at sight of the lithe woman in the blue dress ahead, waiting for him. It was clear he was being summoned and wouldn't be allowed to avoid it. He succumbed and proceeded onward, reining in his horse just beyond the edge of the ring.

"You want to talk to me, ma'am?"

"Why do you dawdle?" Her chin raised and arms crossed, her eyes flashed with anger.

He frowned. "Excuse me?"

"For what do you stay here? She's with child, and now you should return to your home." Her words were short and crisp with her impatience at his negligence.

"Right, like there's a choice."

"There's always a choice. The only reason you think there is none is that you don't value the lives of your wife and son."

It irritated him she knew about the baby, though by now he should be accustomed to the intrusions of the wee folk. His breath hitched as he made another realization. "You know what it is?" *A boy.*

"Of course, I do."

"How do I know you're not just telling me what I want to hear?"

"Why should I have a care what you wish to hear? And how would I even know? Would you not be as happy with a daughter as with a son?"

The question caught him off guard, for he'd never pondered the issue. With two younger brothers in his family the babies had always been boys. He replied, "I suppose."

"Then quit your nonsense about what you wish to hear or dinnae wish to hear. 'Tis true what I'm telling you; you're to have a son. And soon. So do not change the subject, please. Why have you not asked Himself to return you to your home?"

"You mean, Nemed."

"Who else would be sending you anywhere? Certainly not me, or you'd be there already and never mind the asking. It's a terrible, cowardly thing you're doing."

Now his jaw dropped with the surprise. "Cowardly? Excuse me?" Nobody had ever dared call him that. *"Cowardly?"*

"Aye. As yellow as yon wildflowers. You're so intent on your own welfare, and on what pleases you, that you cannot even see that you jeopardize the lives of those you claim to care about most."

"I'm not the one putting them in jeopardy. I can't control—"

"You have not even tried. You have decided to take the easy way, the way that will lead you to wealth and power."

"And they will both benefit from that."

"You will benefit. They might be dead."

A cold lump landed in Alex's gut. "But they might not."

Danu nodded, and allowed as that could be true. But then she said, "Think on it, Alexander. Honestly, and without your prejudices in the way. Ask yourself whether at any time in your life you've done aught for the sake of someone else only. Have you ever made a true sacrifice?"

He opened his mouth to reply, but she cut him off. "That is, *only* for the sake of another. Have you ever accomplished a deed that did not at least bring you improved status in the eyes of someone, Alexander? A true sacrifice? Have you ever given up something important to you for the sake of someone else, and then not expected the reward of glory?"

That silenced him as he thought back over his life. Surely there was a time he'd done just that. But he couldn't think of one. There were several times he could point out when he'd made sacrifices, but in honesty couldn't say he'd not expected credit for them. He'd always thought that was the whole idea: to put one's self on the line so the world would think highly of one. To be known for bravery. To be a protector of people who couldn't protect themselves from the evils of the world.

"I fought for my country before I came here."

"And were you not paid?"

She had him there. He wouldn't have stayed very long with the Navy if they hadn't paid him.

Digging further into his past, he tried for something smaller but less lucrative. "One time in school I gave my little brother the cupcake out of my lunch."

Danu's reply was immediate. "And did you not expect him to look up to his big brother for it? To admire you as his benefactor?"

Alex was forced to admit he had. His horse took a step backward, and he realized tension was making him draw the reins. He flexed his fingers, but it didn't help.

"So you see, you wish to believe there is no recourse. The reason you think you have no way of doing right by your wife and son is that you are certain you'll lose them both by taking them home to the future."

Alex frowned. "What is that supposed to mean?"

"You think she'll leave you for that other once she's away from here."

"Is there anything you don't know?"

"Few things are as plain to read as the light in your eyes, Alexander Joseph MacNeil. You're afraid she doesnae love you."

The edges of his soul began to curl and pain crept in on him.

"So, if you know so much, can you tell me whether she loves me or not?"

Danu shook her head. "I cannae say, for I do not know, but if I did know I think I should not tell you. I think you should think on it yourself. Think of what it truly means when you say you are faithful. Consider the things you promised when you married her. And especially consider what could happen to her if she stays."

He tried to backpedal away from the question, to flee the pain, and said, "But it doesn't matter what I ask of Nemed. He won't do it."

"And were you to ask, what might happen then? Could you not find a way to convince him to do as you ask?"

"I've tried to fight him. He disappears on me."

A puzzled frown furrowed her brow. "He's either there or not there. If he's not, then he cannae hurt you, nor even touch you. If he is, then he cannae simply not be. Not so quickly as that, in any case. You could fight him. What ye cannae fight is the illusion."

Alex thought hard on that. He would love to kill that elf.

"Ye cannae kill him, Alexander, for you need his help."

He shot her a glance. *Get out of my mind.*

"Your intent is written on your face, *mo caraid.*"

He shut his eyes against her.

The mere thought of asking Nemed for anything gave him the creeps. He would surely use it against him. Perhaps the filthy elf would grant his request just for the sake of breaking his heart if Lindsay should leave him for Derek, and Alex realized that would be the best-case scenario.

He bit his lip and looked at her. "I don't trust him, even to ask. If he can send us back to the twenty-first century, then what's to keep him from sending us anywhere else into the past or future?"

"Och, if he sends you anywhere in time he'll send you to the moment from which you left, the moment of the spell where the breach was created, for he can do naught else without hurting himself. I cannot send you there, for 'tis not in my power. 'Twas not my spell. 'Twas his, and only he can send you there. The spell he cast on that day happened on that day and that power remains there. It is to the power he must send you, if he sends you at all. Since you cannot exist twice on this side of the breach, you must therefore find yourselves on the other side of it. 'Tis the way of things, and even Nemed cannae change it."

"His people were all killed there."

"Aye, and they cannot be saved. And you cannot be sent to that very time and place. 'Twas but an instant it took for them to die, but the portal was open for some moments longer; you would arrive before, as I said, for he cannot send you to the same time and place as they."

"Crowded sky."

Danu nodded.

"And if he lets us drop to the ground?"

"The spell has been cast. He cannae change it from what he'd intended for his people, whom he was trying to save. So you see, you must ask Nemed to send you back. For the sake of your family. So they will be well and happy."

Alex's skin went cold. His mind cast about for a reason it couldn't be done, but there was nothing. He knew Nemed would do this to make him suffer. Lindsay would want to return to her fiancé, and she could excise himself from her life once she was there. Danu knew it, and Nemed knew it. There was nothing in this for him, anywhere.

Except the lives of the people he loved most in the world.

After that, he found he couldn't sleep. He ate little, and dropped some pounds he could ill afford to lose. At night, lying next to him in bed, Lindsay laid her head on his shoulder and felt of his ribs.

"Are you not feeling well?"

"I'm fine."

"You're too thin. You haven't recovered from the campaign yet. This is the first I've ever seen you not eat like a horse when you could."

His response was a grunt, then he said, "I've only been home three weeks."

"You've lost weight just since you came back. You seem ill." She ran her hand over his hip as if to show where his bones stuck out too much to suit her.

"I'm *fine*. Now hush, and go to sleep."

"You worry me."

"You worry too much."

"I love you too much to not."

The comment washed over him like a wave, disorienting, making him at once giddy and confused. He wanted her so much, and wanted to do whatever it took to keep her, but he didn't know what that might be. Moments like this made him think she loved him and would stick by him, but his better sense told him he just wasn't that lucky. His real-world sense told him she only cared for him because of circumstance. As much as he wanted to believe she loved him more than Derek, that much faith eluded him.

He pressed his lips to her forehead and held her close as his heart swelled until it ached. He figured he would do anything for her. Anything. Then he said, "Go to sleep. Everything will be all right. I promise." In that moment he understood what he had to do to keep that promise, and his heart broke.

"ALL right, Nemed." Alex was alone in his bedchamber. It was mid-morning and the knights were all at their training, Lindsay was supervising in the kitchen, the staff had cleaned up breakfast, and Alex had requested solitude from the chambermaids. He stood in the middle of the room and looked around. "Nemed, I want to talk." He hoped the elf would want to take the opportunity to give him some more grief, and then Alex would make his request. "Come on, you elfin bastard. Show yourself."

That did it. The red eyes appeared near the hearth, then the rest of him followed like the Cheshire cat. "What is it?" He sounded bored, completely uninterested in whatever Alex might have to say. But the fact that he was there at all said something.

"I have a request. I think you'll want to hear it."

Nemed said nothing, but only stared at Alex.

"I want you to send Lindsay and me back to the future. We want to return to our previous lives."

"Well, MacNeil, you have me confused. How am I supposed to be pleased with this request?"

"You want to see me suffer. You also know she'll probably dump me when we get home. If you send us back to the moment we left, she'll still be engaged to Derek. She would probably even pass the baby off as his." Alex couldn't bring himself to consider she would abort the pregnancy, and shook the thought from his mind even as it began to form. This was Lindsay. She just didn't have it in her to do that.

"Tempting offer, MacNeil, except for one problem. I want to *see* you suffer. If I send you away, you won't be here for me to see it."

"You don't think you'll live long enough to catch up with me in the future?"

Nemed's eyes narrowed and his lips pressed together. After a long silence he said, "No. I don't think I will." His voice held a certainty that sent shivers up Alex's spine. Then he said, "In short, Alexander MacNeil, you have nothing I want. You'll never have anything I want. There's naught left but . . ."

A light appeared in the elf's eyes, and his head tilted as he peered closely at Alex's face. Alex hooded his own eyes, wary of what Nemed could be seeing, and shivered as the elfin mouth formed a huge, humorless grin.

"Wait. There might be something. There is one thing you could do that I want enough to grant your request." Alex waited for it, unmoving. Finally, the elf said, "Suicide."

Alex blinked. "Huh?"

"It would please me to watch you commit suicide." He glanced into the middle distance as if looking for an idea, then shrugged and said, "Fire. Immolate yourself as my people were burned. It's only fair."

"You're nuts."

"Aye, and I'm the one who can save the lives of your wife and child."

"You want me to set myself on fire? No way."

"Very well, then." The elf raised his hand. "I've but one recourse. Have a care for your wife." A snap of long fingers, and he disappeared.

Alex turned, but the elf was gone. *His wife.* "Lindsay?" Where was she? *"Lin!"* She was supposed to be in the kitchen. Alex hurried from the room and from the keep, to the bailey where he crossed to the outbuilding that contained the kitchen and bake house.

Workers looked up when he entered, quite surprised to see him there, for he'd never once set foot in the place before now. "My wife. Is my wife around?"

Those who dared to move shook their heads. The head cook said, "She was here, but some time ago left of a sudden."

"Where did she go?"

Unsure, the cook looked off toward the portcullis. "I believe she went down the hill. I had a thought she might be off to the village."

"By herself?" Distress rose, and panic strained his voice.

The man flushed. "I couldnae stop her, sir." Not that Alex believed he'd tried, but the cook would be afraid of being blamed for Lindsay's absence. "She simply walked away, appearing as if she'd heard someone beckon."

Without another word, Alex left the building and headed to the outer curtain. The sentry there told him he'd seen her hurrying across the pasture toward the forest. Alex blurted the most vile curse he knew, and mounted a horse being readied by one of the squires for another knight. Quickly he spurred the mount out of the castle and off across the pasture. Heart pounding, Alex prayed he would find her in time.

But it was in vain. Just within the forest he heard screaming that froze his spine. Lindsay. She was terrified. He kicked the horse to a gallop and followed the sound.

It was a clearing in the dark heart of the forest where he pulled up his mount, and the sight turned his guts to water.

Deep in the shadows, an iron-barred cage held Lindsay, naked. She whimpered and backed against the rear bars, attempting to cover herself with her hands. Nemed stood by, waiting for Alex, a bucket in one hand and a fire brand in the other.

"Alex!" Lindsay had been weeping for some time. Her eyes were red and her face streaked with tears that ran down her neck.

"Let her go!" He leapt from the horse and made a grab for the elf, but dodged the torch and had to back off.

"You shouldn't have asked, Alexander. It's your fault now she's going to die. Isn't it lovely how that worked out?" He picked up the bucket to toss its contents at Lindsay, and Alex could smell the pitch: Greek fire.

The oily liquid splashed over her skin, and Lindsay screamed again as Nemed waved his fire. She pressed herself hard against the bars, trying and failing to slip between them. "What did you do, Alex? What did you say to him? Take it back!" She began to weep as Nemed waved the fire at her, and held the bulge of her belly as if to protect it. "For God's sake, take it back!"

If only he could. "Nemed! Let her go!"

The elf held the lit wood through the bars of the cage and poked at Lindsay with it. She screamed and cried in terror as the flame came within inches of her, and pressed herself hard to the bars. Alex reached for Nemed, but each time he came near the elf poked closer to Lindsay. Alex backed off again. His heart choked him and his eyes were wide with terror.

"Let her go, Nemed! I'll do it! I'll do what you say! Now, let her go! Send her back now!"

"No. Not until you've done it. Not until it's accomplished."

"Send her back!"

Nemed's eyebrows lifted in mock surprise. "Who, then, Alexander, is the one who has nothing to lose? Certainly not yourself, for she and the brat are still alive. And the only way they will stay alive is if you do as you're told."

Alex gasped, panicky and desperate. "Let her *go*."

"No." Nemed poked the fire through the bars again. Lindsay screamed and cringed, weeping. The sound cut Alex's heart.

"All right!" The world slanted and his head buzzed. "All right, I'll do it." His pulse pounded in his ears. The only thought that came clear just then was that he would do whatever it took to keep from having to watch Lindsay die. "I'll do it."

"Good. Then go to the castle at Edinburgh. There you will douse yourself with the Greek fire and set yourself aflame for all to see."

"Edinburgh?" For one insane moment Alex was angry the elf wouldn't let him just do it now and get it over with.

"Aye. Start now, or she dies." To illustrate, Nemed poked the fire through the bars once more.

Alex held up both palms. "Fine."

"Alex!"

He ignored her. "I'll do it."

"Alex, no!" Tears ran down her cheeks and she came forward to reach through the bars for him and wailed, "No!"

His voice deserted him as he whispered, "Lindsay . . ."

Nemed crowed in victory. "Very well. We'll meet you there." With that, he waved a hand in the direction of the cage. Slowly, like a fading photograph, he, the cage, and Lindsay grew less distinct until finally they were gone.

Alex stood alone in the forest, aghast at what he'd set in motion, and slowly he sank to his knees. Nemed had found a way to kill him, more horribly than he'd ever imagined. His crazed and panicked mind cast about for a way out of this, but nothing came clear. The world was a spinning, buzzing nightmare from which he couldn't awaken. It was a long time before he found his legs again and could stand up to return to the castle and do the thing he must.

As quickly as he could, horrified by what might be happening to Lindsay during the time it would take to get to Edinburgh, Alex ordered a boat to be prepared and a small crew to take him to the mainland.

Then he sat down at the table in his meeting room outside his quarters. The trumpet of the watch announced an approaching boat, but he ignored it. There was nobody on earth he wanted to see right now. Quill and parchment before him, he began a letter to be delivered to Hector by fishing boat after he was gone. Hector was his next of kin after Lindsay, who would also be gone, and needed to know what to do with Alex's holdings. His last will and testament.

It was a difficult task, for his mind kept drifting to Lindsay, wondering where she could be. Where that creature was holding her. Was she cold? Certainly she was frightened. The quill trembled in Alex's hand and he forced himself to focus on the job. He'd be gone in the morning. Dead by next week.

Footsteps and Hector's voice came from the Great Hall above. "Alasdair an Dubhar! Ye summon me, then you forsake me! Where have you got off to, lad?"

Alex looked up as Hector hurried down the steps to the meeting room. The MacNeil laird stopped cold at the bottom when he saw Alex's face.

"You're a man with much on your mind, brother. Ye look defeated, and that's not something I'm accustomed to saying about a MacNeil." His voice had gone soft, unsure of what he was seeing before him.

"Hector—"

"I received your message. Urgent, she said, and I came as quickly as I could."

"Message?"

"The woman ye sent. She insisted I set sail immediately, for you had need of me." A sly smile touched his mouth. "Such a beautiful woman, I couldnae refuse her, even had you not been my brother and in need."

Finally Alex's mind was able to focus on something. "A woman. Blond."

"Aye."

"Yes. She . . ." Alex took a deep breath and looked at the letter before him. "She is a visiting friend from the mainland."

"Was she wrong in thinking you had need?"

"No, not wrong." Alex gestured to the chair next to him. "Hector, sit down."

The laird sat and leaned toward Alex to hear carefully. "What is the crisis, brother?"

"Hector, I need to leave."

There was a pause. Alex waited for a response. Finally Hector said, "You're free to come and go, Alasdair."

"I mean, forever."

Another pause. Then Hector said, "Why?"

"I can't tell you."

"Has it to do with your special friend the blond woman whose boat seemed to appear from nowhere and then return to it suddenly after delivering her message?"

"No. My wife is in trouble. I have to find her, then take her somewhere where she will be safe forever."

"She's nae safe here?"

"No."

"Will ye nae be returning, then?"

"No."

"You're going to take her to the eastern mountains on the continent?"

"Farther than that."

Hector gazed at him for a very long moment, then said softly, "Are ye my brother?"

"I'm your kinsman." A question rose to Hector's eyes, and Alex added, "A descendant."

There was a silence, then Hector said, "I'm not so old—"

"Centuries from now."

Again Hector's face gave away nothing as he searched

Alex's face. Finally he cleared his throat and said, "The blond woman was a most special friend, I could see that."

"I'm in trouble, Hector. Lindsay is in worse trouble. I can't say any more than that, except that I love you as my brother. I'm sorry, but I must do this. It's Lindsay's life. And our child's life."

Hector's eyes lit with brief joy over the news of the baby, that turned to confusion and sorrow as he realized the implications. "Aye. For your child ye must do what you must."

Alex sat back in his chair, looked at the half-finished letter he knew Hector couldn't read, and began telling in detail what to do with his property once he'd been gone a year and could be declared dead.

The next morning Alex boarded his boat and set out for Edinburgh.

As the vessel made its way across the water, Alex gazed at his island slowly growing smaller and smaller in the distance. He knew whatever happened, whether or not Nemed succeeded in killing him, he would never see his island again. The sorrow for leaving the only place he'd ever called home was nearly as great as his fear of what was to come, but far down inside was a core of calm. No longer did he worry about what to do—what would be best. He knew what needed to be done, and he knew it was the only right thing. All else receded to background noise.

Finally he turned toward the bow and put Eilean Aonarach, and all it meant to him, behind.

The journey was long and hard, the hardest thing he'd ever done, for it went against his every instinct. On the mainland, he traveled alone and as quickly as he could push his horse without killing it, his mind turning all the while with how he would rescue Lindsay from that elf. The water skin he carried slung over his back grew heavier as he went.

He knew Nemed wouldn't send her home, or even release her. Alex figured the creature would kill her, or keep her for a plaything. And what would be done with the baby? Would Nemed kill it? Raise it as his own? Neither was acceptable. No, Alex needed to find a way to take back his wife and make her safe. Entirely.

The castle at Edinburgh was a ruin. Robert had razed it, lest it be retaken by the English king in their ongoing struggle, so it was a pile of blackened rubble perched on a high, rocky hill that

Alex approached on foot with his bucket. He crossed from the town and climbed to the peak of the castle hill, where huge chunks of stone and remnants of wall lay about like a child's abandoned toy blocks. The wind buffeted his face and tossed his hair, and he looked out across the flatland toward the firth. Green pasture dotted with thick forest and an occasional thatched roof. The quiet was astonishing. The water was graced by only a few sails, and the rolling countryside beyond disappeared into a thick mist of rain.

Onward and around he went, picking his way among the ruins, to the top of a broken wall where he found the cage containing Lindsay, slumped against the bars. Nemed stood to the side, a lit firebrand rested against a thigh, uncaring about what he might do with it. Lindsay was silent until she saw Alex, then she gasped and rose to her knees, weeping, and clutched the bars. "Alex, no, get away from here."

"All right, Nemed. I'm here." Alex called to Lindsay, "Are you okay?"

Her hair was matted with the vile mixture poured over her, and her voice was clotted with tears. "Don't do it, Alex! Oh, God, don't do it!" Her weeping renewed, and she covered her mouth with her hands.

"Let her go!" Alex bellowed at the elf.

"Do what you came for." He waved the stick. "And get rid of the mail. I want you to burn completely."

Lindsay began to murmur beneath her weeping, sobbing, "Oh God, oh God, oh God . . ."

"How do I know you'll send her home?"

"You don't. Isn't it interesting how that works? You've but one choice. Do it. Now, before I decide to touch her off in order to liven things up."

Alex wiggled from his coif and hauberk, and tossed them on the ground. Then he picked up the bucket, and without hesitation, in one smooth motion, threw the contents at Nemed's torch. Not fast enough to douse the fire before the elf could touch it to Lindsay's shoulder. The Greek fire flared, but then was doused by the bucketful of urine Alex had been collecting since he'd left the island. It splashed over Lindsay and the oil covering her.

Alex drew his sword and attacked the elf. Nemed, taken by

surprise, retreated a few steps and parried with the stick in his hand, and the burnt end flew away. Then the elf drew his sword and came back with a hard riposte that jolted Alex's arm clear to his shoulder. He circled, and found the disarray of stone rubble made maneuvering difficult. He leapt onto a stack of loose pieces that tottered and shifted under his weight. Nemed attacked; Alex parried and leapt down the other side. He was trying to get the elf as far away from Lindsay as he could, so she'd be out of reach.

Once away from the cage, Alex came back with a quick, hard series of attacks. Their swords clanged, the sound carried off by the wind. There was nobody around, and the town seemed far away, perched on a distant rock. Nemed's eyes glowed bright red.

"You can't win, MacNeil."

Alex declined to reply, saving his breath for the fight. He parried Nemed's attack, then feinted, stepped in close, and clobbered the elf's mouth with his hilt. Nemed staggered backward, then with a roar of rage came at Alex with full-on berserker abandon. Alex was surprised at his opponent's strength, and in his retreat nearly tripped over a scattering of rocks. The elfin sword sliced his back as he staggered away, and hot pain ran through his entire left side. Alex swallowed a yell as he turned to assault Nemed once again. His left arm wasn't useless, but the flaming pain colored his vision so he had trouble keeping track of his opponent. He needed to finish this quick, before he passed out.

He hauled back and made a foray of quick, strong overhead hits, beating Nemed into the ground. Speed was his only hope, and he kept at it until the elf was backed against the wall remnant on which Lindsay was perched.

Panting, exhausted, Nemed stumbled and fell against the stone. Alex took the opportunity to lay his sword against the graceful neck of the ancient king, and landed his entire weight with his knee in Nemed's gut. A great cry of pain came with all the air in him. The elfin sword clattered to the cobbles beneath them. With his sword laid against Nemed's throat, quite ready to cut his head clean off, it was all Alex could do to not kill. It would be so sweet to settle all the questions once and for all in one instant, but Danu's words kept him from it. Lindsay's life and the baby were what mattered, and nothing else.

"Let her go. Now. I want her out of that cage and where she belongs."

For a long moment, Nemed couldn't speak. His mouth gaped as he struggled for breath, then finally his vision cleared and he looked at Alex to croak, "You'll take her back to your island?"

"No. I want you to send us home. Send us back to the twenty-first century, where we came from." He drew his dagger and set the point just below the navel. "Do it or I'll rip you from stem to stern and flay you alive. Then I'll watch you die, and enjoy every moment." His teeth clenched. "I've learned a lot since coming here." Alex looked at Lindsay, who was sobbing and clutching the bars that separated them. "Send us home. They need to be there. Safe."

Nemed was regaining his breath, and the fire of rage returned to his eyes. "And if I were to send only you?"

Alex leaned down to be face to face with the elf. "I'll find you. Wherever you are, dead or not, I'll find you and I'll make you sorry you ever walked this earth. Trust me, you freak, you don't want to make me a man with nothing to lose."

The elf's eyes narrowed to slits, and he raised one hand. Pain wrenched Alex's body. The world began to fade, like a photograph, dissolving to nothing but sky blue, and as the world resolved the pain left. Alex found himself tumbling through a bright, sunny sky as a jet engine blew past overhead. Suddenly it was gone in a flash of fire, then nothing, and he was still tumbling. Falling. Tumbling. Somewhere he heard Lindsay scream, and he looked down. The ground was like an expanse of crumpled green paper, dotted with shiny blue lakes. He was falling without a parachute. Danu had been wrong; there was no rescue spell on this side.

As he tumbled, he found Lindsay flailing beside him, screaming as she realized she was about to die. He grabbed her and pulled her to him. They clutched each other, and all Alex could think of just then was that they would be together at the end. She sobbed in his arms. He held her close and said over and over, "I'm sorry, I'm sorry . . ." The ground rushed up at them. The wind tore at them. Alex began to wonder how long and how much it would hurt.

Then, only a few yards from the ground, they slowed. Gently, without muss or fuss, a force above them let them down softly onto a chalk-lined football field. It was midday, and people watching applauded as they landed, then went along their way. Alex lay with Lindsay on the grass, both of them gasping, then laughing and crying at once.

Quickly, before anyone would come close, Alex stripped his plaid and tunic from himself so Lindsay could pull them on. Covered in oil and pitch, giggling and weeping, they sat on the empty field and held each other for a very long time.

Finally Lindsay said amid the tears, "We're home, Alex. We made it."

He looked around, at the planes overhead, the cars motoring past, children in the distance on a playground. He thought of what he'd returned to, and wasn't certain how to feel about it. "Aye. And debriefing on this trip is going to be a bitch."

CHAPTER 23

It was a week since their return, and that week had been a nightmare of debriefing—obfuscation and lies to his superiors and the British authorities about what had happened to his jet, how he'd received the wound on his back, and how he and Lindsay had ended up in medieval clothing covered in pitch and oil. Ultimately, the Navy concluded the F-18 had sunk in the Firth of Clyde. None of the bureau numbers from the plane recovered from the archaeological dig had been found, so only Alex and Lindsay knew of the connection. It would be a while before the governments involved would give up the search. The wound, clothing, and oil were explained by vague references to an explosion, loss of consciousness, and denial that the clothing—ostensibly borrowed to replace destroyed flight suits—was as medieval as it might look to some.

There was no telling what the witnesses on that football field had thought they were seeing when the two landed without parachutes, but Alex knew the human mind was a funny thing and would deny whatever it couldn't grasp. Alex remembered how long it had taken him to accept he'd traveled seven centuries to the past, and so wasn't surprised no witnesses to the miraculous landing ever came forward to accuse them of witchcraft. Perhaps the thing Danu had said about magic and technology also worked in reverse: magic being indistinguishable from sufficiently advanced technology. He could only guess the assumption had been miniaturized jet packs. In any case, the lack of parachutes never became known to Alex's superiors. The report and debriefing weren't questioned closely.

The first couple of days Alex had spent in a civilian hospital, for the wound he'd received from Nemed was deep and long. Surgery repaired the muscle, and his skin took dozens of stitches. Then he was transferred to the American military authority in London to be examined by U.S. Navy physicians. Just yesterday he'd been released on a month's medical leave before he would return to his ship.

And flying. It had been two years since he'd piloted an airplane. He was no longer qualified to fly, but the Navy didn't know it and couldn't be told. Yesterday he'd obtained a manual for the F-18 and would study it until he was cleared medically and returned to his ship. A couple of day hops, and he figured he'd be back up to speed enough to not kill himself.

But when he considered his long-term future in the Navy, all he saw now was darkness and doubt. Over the past couple of years, expectation and possibility had shifted so far for him that he no longer knew what he wanted, or whether anything he could ever want was possible for him. He'd been knighted—an honor impossible for any American—and by Scotland's greatest king. He'd distinguished himself in battle of a sort that none of his peers, nor even his superiors, would ever experience. He'd ruled an island and the people living on it, and had led men who followed him for his skill and strength. But he would never be able to tell anyone of these things. His future would proceed as if none of that had ever happened. All he knew for certain was that now he needed to rethink everything about the life to which he'd returned.

And now he looked to Lindsay as the only thing left to him he gave a damn about.

Today at breakfast in Lindsay's London flat, his heart thudded uncomfortably in his chest. He took deep breaths, annoyed with himself for feeling this way. He tried to let it go, as he had always divested himself before battle, but this time it was hopeless. Lindsay was going to meet Derek today, to talk. Alex wanted desperately to ask what she was going to tell him—to ascertain if she still thought of herself as his wife, but he didn't know how to even approach that question, and she'd made it clear the details of her chat with Derek would be none of his business. In fact, she'd been quiet since awakening that morning. Lips pressed together and cheeks pale, she wasn't giving up any of what she was thinking today beyond telling him in a flat, no-nonsense voice she wanted him to stay in the flat while she met with Derek.

Alex stopped chewing his sausage and glanced up at her as a great wad of doubt settled in his gut. She continued poking at her grapefruit, playing with the segments without actually eating any of them, seeming oblivious to Alex's reaction. She said, "This is going to be difficult for both of us, and I think it will go much more smoothly if you're not there to upset him."

Slowly, Alex began chewing again, then swallowed. "No. We wouldn't want old Derek upset."

Now she glanced up at him, and her voice developed an edge. "He was my fiancé. He thinks he's still my fiancé, and has no idea how much time has passed for me. This is going to be extremely difficult; he already is curious why I asked him not to come directly to the flat when he flew in last night. It isn't as if I could let him down slowly; you'd never stand for that."

"No, you're right, I would not."

There was a silence, and neither of them moved. She said, "You're not being very understanding."

"Are you asking me to let you string him along for a while? You think he should continue expecting you to marry him?"

"No."

"Then we're in agreement."

She returned her attention to her mangled grapefruit, and this time ate a piece. Carefully she sucked the juice out of it before swallowing. Then she ate another. Alex watched her, and ignored the rest of his breakfast.

The remainder of the morning passed in silence. Lindsay read a book and Alex watched the fish in her aquarium as he prepared for the worst, trying to figure out what he would do with his life if he lost her.

Finally she said, "I just don't think it's a good idea for you to be there. Your presence would only antagonize him."

"My presence would also discourage him from giving you any guff."

"He won't."

"If I go with you, he won't even be tempted."

"Alex, stop it."

He fell silent and turned on the television, and the subject was dropped. They spun out the rest of the morning watching a string of the most incredibly boring home decorating shows he'd ever seen, Alex counting down in his mind the minutes before Lindsay would leave.

Far earlier than he thought necessary, she looked at her watch and made a humming noise. "I've got to go."

"Don't keep Derek waiting. Wouldn't want him . . . upset."

She only sighed as she pulled on an oversized sweatshirt and raincoat over her five-month belly. "Good thing it's wet out," she murmured half to herself. "I couldn't bear to have to tell him this isn't his."

Though he understood what she meant, the comment stung anyway. As if she were ashamed the baby wasn't Derek's. Alex watched her gather her purse and gloves, then she kissed him quickly before walking out the door.

He gave her only a few moments before following her out and down the street to the train station. She fiddled with her purse as she went.

She didn't go far. The meeting was in Chinatown, in a close, busy restaurant with dim sum carts wending back and forth, where Alex watched from a lobby through a glass door as Lindsay greeted a young man he assumed was Derek. The fiancé's face lit up with recognition and familiarity, and Alex's gut clenched. She greeted him with a kiss remarkably similar to the peck she'd given Alex half an hour before, and now Alex's mind was turning, tumbling, with what that could mean. He couldn't hear what they were saying, and couldn't even see Lindsay's face because her back was to him. Restaurant hostesses and waiters brushed past him in the narrow space, but his eyes were glued to what was going on inside the glass door as he sidestepped to let them by.

Derek's face was quite visible. He was tall and thin, his dark hair neat and everything about him tidy. The impression he gave was of a nice guy with his wits about him, intelligent and handsome. Alex wanted to hate him, but had to admit he could see what Lindsay might have seen in him. Somehow that made it all infinitely worse.

He saw what she might still see in him. What if this meeting rekindled that flame? Even worse, what if that flame had never been out? What if Lindsay decided to pass the baby off as Derek's? Alex wished he could see Lindsay's face to know what she might be thinking just then. A young waitress in black skirt and white blouse pushed a cart to the table and after a short discussion served a small bamboo steam basket, marked Derek's ticket, then moved on. Lindsay apparently was talking while Derek's attention was on the food, and he picked up a dumpling with his chopsticks.

Whatever she was telling him didn't seem to bother his appetite much. His face was impassive. Not a flicker touched his eyes as Lindsay spoke, and the smile with which he'd greeted her—a slight curling of the corners of his mouth—was still there. Alex didn't like it. Derek spoke, not loud enough for Alex to hear. Alex shifted his feet, wishing Derek would raise his voice. He wanted the guy to turn red in the face and begin shouting. At least a frown would have been good. But the bloody Englishman was giving nothing away. Alex had no clue what Lindsay might be saying to him.

Finally Lindsay rose. A few more words passed between them, then she leaned down to kiss him again. She turned toward the door, and Alex spun quickly away and set his foot on a nearby bench as if he were tying his shoe. Lindsay passed behind him and down the stairs toward the restrooms.

Huh. Not leaving, just going to the bathroom. Once she was past, Alex then straightened and returned his attention to Derek. The guy was examining the contents of another steam basket, debating whether to accept, looking as if there were nothing amiss in his world. More doubt sunk into Alex's gut. Lindsay couldn't have told him yet. She must be stalling, undecided. Or maybe she didn't intend to tell him at all. Cold sweat broke out. Maybe she would return from the ladies' room to sit with him again, and then leave with him once he'd—

Someone slapped his arm from behind and his wound roared pain. "Hey!" He turned to find Lindsay there, anger dancing in her eyes.

"What are you doing here?"

Alex opened his mouth to make an excuse, but at that moment he caught a look through the glass door at Derek, who was watching him with Lindsay. The look of desolation in the man's eyes told Alex all he needed to know, and he suddenly felt sorry for him. He knew what Derek had lost, even better than Derek himself did. Then the Englishman's mouth became a hard line and he averted his attention.

Alex's sore shoulder was whacked again, and the pain brought him back to Lindsay's anger. "Not very sporting of you to come gloat, is it?" She went past him, out the door and down the stairs to the street, pulling her coat around her as she went.

Shoulder throbbing, he hurried after her. The alleyway was nearly deserted, for a cold drizzle had been going on all morning. He caught up to her and took her hand to make her stop and look at him. "You told him good-bye."

"Of course, I did. And it was one of the hardest things I've ever done, to break his heart like that."

"I know. It must have been tempting to not do it."

For a long, puzzled moment, she blinked at him. "What, and then tell you good-bye?"

To hear her say it aloud made his heart clench, and he had to look away for a moment to let the rain cool his face. Then he nodded.

"That's absurd. I'm your wife. Never mind we were married seven centuries ago; neither of us is dead yet so I expect our vows are still in force." There was a pause, then, "Don't you think so?"

"Of course. But—"

"Alex," she put a finger to his lips and he went quiet. "You need to understand. What I feel for you is so terribly deep I almost can't bear it."

Curious, he kept silent and let her talk. She continued. "Alex, you've been my protector for two years. If it weren't for you, I wouldn't be alive. And now, you've given up everything for me. You achieved so much, and now it's gone. I owe you more than I can possibly repay, and I love you more than I can possibly express." Tears began to rise, and she blinked them back. "Alex . . . Alasdair, I am so frightened. To be this vulnerable, and to just lay out my heart, to be that dependent on anyone . . ."

"I know. Scary, isn't it?"

She nodded. "Back then, it was all so very clear. The marriage was a deal and I didn't have to admit how I felt."

"I wish you had."

A deep sigh, and she looked at him with soft, blurred eyes. "I am now. Please don't hurt me; tell me it will all turn out okay."

He smiled and kissed her. "I swear it." And he knew he would do whatever it took to keep that promise.

AUTHOR'S NOTE

Though the traditional homelands of the MacNeil clan were on Barra, the MacNeil characters depicted here are entirely fictional. The laird at the time was Neil Og MacNeil, sixth of Barra, who is rumored to have fought alongside Robert Bruce at Bannockburn. Sir Hector and his kin, and of course the rest of the nonhistorical folk, are all fictional. And, as one can plainly tell by photographs of Kisimul Castle on Barra, it bears no resemblance to the MacNeil castle described in this book.

THE ULTIMATE IN SCIENCE FICTION AND FANTASY!

From magical tales of distant worlds to stories of technological advances beyond the grasp of man, Penguin has everything you need to stretch your imagination to its limits.

penguin.com

ACE
Get the latest information on favorites like William Gibson, T.A. Barron, Brian Jacques, Ursula Le Guin, Sharon Shinn, and Charlaine Harris, as well as updates on the best new authors.

ROC
Escape with Harry Turtledove, Anne Bishop, S.M. Stirling, Simon Green, Chris Bunch, Jim Butcher, E.E. Knight, and many others—plus news on the latest and hottest in science fiction and fantasy.

DAW
Mercedes Lackey, Kristen Britain, Tanya Huff, Tad Williams, C.J. Cherryh, and many more— DAW has something to satisfy the cravings of any science fiction and fantasy lover. Also visit dawbooks.com.

Get the best of science fiction and fantasy at your fingertips!